Books by Patricia Falvey

THE YELLOW HOUSE

THE LINEN QUEEN

THE GIRLS OF ENNISMORE*

THE TITANIC SISTERS*

*Published by Kensington Publishing Corp.

THE
TITANIC
SISTERS

PATRICIA
FALVEY

KENSINGTON
PUBLISHING CORP.

www.kensingtonbooks.com

KENSINGTON BOOKS are published by

Kensington Publishing Corp.
119 West 40th Street
New York, NY 10018

All Kensington titles, imprints, and distributed lines are available at special quantity discounts for bulk purchases for sales promotion, premiums, fund-raising, educational, or institutional use.

Special book excerpts or customized printings can also be created to fit specific needs. For details, write or phone the office of the Kensington Sales Manager: Kensington Publishing Corp., 119 West 40th Street, New York, NY 10018. Attn. Sales Department. Phone: 1-800-221-2647.

The K logo is a trademark of Kensington Publishing Corp.

ISBN-13: 978-1-4967-3257-6 (ebook)
ISBN-10: 1-4967-3257-X (ebook)

ISBN-13: 978-1-4967-3256-9
ISBN-10: 1-4967-3256-1
First Kensington Trade Paperback Printing: February 2021

10 9 8 7 6 5 4 3 2 1

Printed in the United States of America

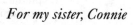

For my sister, Connie

Donegal, Ireland

1911

Delia

❧

The letter from America changed all our lives. The postman presented it to me with great ritual, as if it were a fine jewel. In his memory, he said, no one in my small village of Kilcross, in County Donegal, at the northwest tip of Ireland, had ever received such a thing, nor had he himself ever delivered anything so rare. After he pedaled away from our cottage whistling, I stood at the door holding the envelope, with its bright ribbon of stamps, in my hands like a colorful bird.

"'Tis addressed to me," Ma said, looking at me accusingly. "You should have brought it to me at once instead of standing there like a statue. You're useless, so you are!"

I watched her walk back down the hall and wondered, as I often did, how such a small woman could command such a large presence. She was no taller than myself, but in my mind she still towered over me the same way she had when I was a small child. After she disappeared into the kitchen, I fled outside. I ran around the back of the cottage and up the fields to my favorite place—a group of rocks, bleached white and smooth, which formed a circle beneath an ancient oak tree and from which I could look out across the vast Atlantic sea. I sat down on one of the rocks, panting, struggling to catch my breath. I shivered, suddenly aware of the winter cold settling around me. I had been coming up here since childhood to escape Ma's wrath. When I was young, I often cried out of self-pity, and I was convinced it was my tears that had washed the rocks so clean. Now, at eighteen, I no longer cried, but the hurt in my heart remained.

I was born a twin. My brother, born first, only lived two minutes. My ma took it into her head I was a "changeling" who had been left by the fairies in place of my brother, whom they had stolen away. Such stories about fairy children are common in our part of Ireland. The villagers thought it was the stress of childbirth that had put such a notion in my mother's mind, and that she'd get over it in time. But Ma couldn't be talked out of her belief and had always treated me with suspicion and, sometimes, disgust. I knew her reason, but it did not ease the pain of her rejection.

Had my brother lived, he would have worked with Da on the farm. It was the way of things. Fathers teach their sons how to run a farm so that they, at least the eldest of them, could manage the farm when the father died. Mothers, in turn, train their daughters to run the house—to cook, clean, do laundry and rear children so that they, at least the younger ones, would be well prepared for marriage. Sadly, it fell to the eldest daughter to stay and look after her father and brothers after the mother died and the rest of the family left.

As the elder daughter, my sister, Nora, born two years before me, should be the one to stay after Ma died, but Ma would never allow that. Her dream for Nora was that she become a wealthy man's wife, and thus have no need to learn to run a house. I took on a son's role on the farm; Da needed the help and Ma refused to have me in the kitchen.

Spending time alone with Da was the only good thing in my life. We set out together each morning before the sun was up. As if by unspoken agreement, no words were exchanged between us as we went about our labors. Farming on the rocky soil of County Donegal required a persistence often born out of desperation. Like his da before him, Da had learned how to eke out a subsistence on this unforgiving land. We had six dairy cows, which was rare around Kilcross, chickens and a few hardy sheep.

We harvested potatoes and grain, and carved turf out of a nearby bog to heat the house. My job was to milk the cows, collect the eggs and rescue the sheep that occasionally wandered too far up the hills. Had it not been for school, I would have stayed outdoors all day and night, enjoying Da's peaceful companionship.

Even on rainy days, I loved being outdoors. It rained often in Donegal, washing the hills green and slaking the thirsty soil. Sometimes it fell in a fine mist that caressed my face, other times in pellets sharp as glass, and every now and then in unrelenting waves propelled by fierce winds. I welcomed it in all its forms, turning my face skyward to greet its baptism. And when it was over, I waited in anticipation of a beautiful rainbow arcing across the sky.

When I turned seven, Da walked with me into Kilcross village to make my holy communion. Kilcross could hardly be called a village. It sat at a crossroads, with the local pub on one corner and the small grocery shop on the other, flanked by a row of a dozen houses in which lived a doctor, a veterinarian and a handful of elderly spinsters. Most Kilcross villagers lived in farmhouses or cottages like ours, scattered about the local countryside.

Kilcross church, on the outskirts of the village, was the largest building, and its spire was visible for miles. Next to it was the school, and the priest's house. Father McGinty, the parish priest, was a short, hunchbacked man who ruled as judge and jury over the morals of his flock. He had a voice like thunder and put the fear of God in every man, woman and child in the village. When I arrived in my secondhand communion dress, he wagged his finger at me.

"I see the changeling has come to ask for grace," he shouted, "but our Lord will only grant it if you convince Him that you are worthy of his mercy. You have reached the age of reason now, my girl, and your sins will be on your own head. 'Twill be your own fault if you fall from grace. And you know what happens then?"

"You go to Hell, Father," I whispered.

Da said nothing, but put his arm around me as if trying to protect me from the priest's wrath. After that, I went to Mass every Sunday and day of holy obligation, and confession every week, hoping to convince God and Father McGinty of my inherent goodness.

But there were also times when I was a child that a rebellious spirit took hold of me and I was tempted to do the "bad" things that a changeling might do. I dreamed of taking Ma's favorite plates from the dresser and smashing them; dousing the turf fire with water when no one was looking; pouring paraffin into the churn, turning the milk sour; and, when Ma confronted me, shrugging my shoulders and asking what else did she expect from a changeling? Such fantasies made my helplessness bearable for the moment, but I knew I wouldn't dare to make them reality. Ma was hard enough on me as it was, and doing such things might cause her to throw me out of the house altogether. So they remained in my head.

There were times, though, when I wondered if Ma wasn't right about me being a bad fairy. From the time I was quite young, I was often able to predict things before they happened. Sometimes I was wrong, but as time went on, I was right often enough that I realized it was not chance. I was nothing like the old biddies in the village who Ma often visited to get her fortune read from the tea leaves. This was something much more subtle and happened only once in a while. I knew when misfortune was going to befall a villager, or when good fortune would come someone's way. I never mentioned this ability to anyone; it would only have brought me ridicule.

Although he never said as much, I knew my da loved me. By contrast, I knew Ma did not. She doted on my sister, Nora, while she treated me as an afterthought at best and a burden at worst.

"By the sacred heart of Mary," she often said, "sure, I don't know what sin from the past has brought the scourge of yourself into my life."

My stutter did not help my situation. It developed soon after I began to speak and persisted over the years. It was worse when I was nervous, and particularly pronounced when Ma was shouting at me. I tried everything I could to suppress it, with no success. After a while I realized all I could do was limit the amount of talking I did.

As the years passed, I took refuge in books. The local school-mistress, Miss Fagan, a young woman from Belfast, took a liking to me and brought books to me from the library in Donegal Town. "You're a clever girl, Delia," she said, "you deserve more of an education than this wee school can give you." I was delighted with the books. They became my friends and my comfort on long winter evenings when the wind whistled through the window and rain pounded the roof. I would sit on my small bed in the stark attic holding a candle and devouring the pages one by one.

Over time, my dreams of outward rebellion were replaced with something more subtle. I came to find joy in the new words I was learning from my books—not just the joy of new knowledge gained, but joy in the notion that it was setting me apart from the rest of my family. Slowly, the word "imposter" began to take on a new and positive meaning. The books I loved best were the ones in which the people in them sailed away to foreign places in search of adventure, discovery and, sometimes, love. On fine days, I used to sit amid my rocks and stare out over the distant Atlantic, lost in visions of lush jungles, hot deserts, sea-swept islands and teeming cities that surely lay beyond it. Such places were a far cry from my little Donegal village, and even farther from my miserable home, and I longed to see them.

As I sat now on a rock looking out at the sea, its rough waves roiling with gray and white foam, I heard a noise behind me. I turned around and saw Da in the distance, his tall, gaunt frame bent against the wind. He trudged toward the cottage carrying a bucket in each hand, each containing sods of turf for the fire. As a child, I used to run to greet him, and he would nod as I ran along beside him, holding on to the handle of a bucket and trying to keep up with his long strides. I was used to his silence. I sometimes wondered if it was because he had grown up speaking Irish and was still uncomfortable with English words. I asked him once to teach me Irish, but he shook his head. "'Twould be of no use to ye," he said, "'tis the English that rule this country, and 'tis the English tongue ye'll be needing."

I went up to him now, took one of the buckets and fell into step beside him, lost in my own thoughts. Then I remembered the letter from America, and my steps quickened. What surprises might it hold? Had it brought fortune? But by the time I pushed in through the cottage door, I knew. No matter what fortune the letter held, it would not be for me.

Nora

ᦠᦞᦞ

The letter lay like a tasty, forbidden morsel on the kitchen table. Ma refused to open it until Da came home for his tea.

"Ah, Ma, would you not let me look inside? 'Twill only be a quick peek. I'll just tear off the corner. I won't even open it all the way," I pleaded.

But Ma wouldn't budge. She just sat, looking at me like a cat teasing a mouse. "We'll wait until your da comes in. Such an important thing as a letter from America should be opened by the man of the house."

I inwardly rolled my eyes. *Man of the house, my arse,* I thought. *When had she ever given the poor man say over anything in the house?* No, Ma liked things her way and Da never got a look in.

But why she was torturing me now, and seeming to enjoy it, I didn't understand at all. Usually I had only to hint that I wanted this or that thing and she fell over herself rushing to give it to me. After all, I was the favorite daughter. Ma made no secret of the fact that my sister, Delia, needed to fend for herself.

When Delia and I were younger, we played happily together. She was a delicate wee thing, fair-haired and gray-eyed, and at times I thought Ma must be right, she *did* look like a wee fairy. I was only two years older, but I was taller and stronger than she was, with hair as dark as a sod of turf. I was delighted to have a sister for company. But when we got a bit older, things changed. Ma did her best to divide us, pulling me into the house and shooing Delia outside like an unwelcome neighbor. I never really understood why Ma disliked Delia, but I never stood up for her. I was afraid that if I did, Ma would turn on me as well, and I liked being spoiled. Besides, I was jealous of Delia because of Da. She spent all hours of the day traipsing around with him on the farm, and just by the way they looked at each other I could see how close they were. Da was always kind to me, but I knew he was closer to Delia.

I often wished things were different, though. There were times when I would see other girls laughing with their sisters and sharing secrets, and I wished myself and Delia were more like them. It would have been great *craic* to giggle together over the boys in the village. But our Delia wasn't interested in things like that. She was always away up the fields, daydreaming about God knows what or sitting with her head stuck in a book. Slowly, I began to agree with Ma that she was a useless chit who'd never amount to much.

At last, Da was home. He came into the kitchen, ducking his head under the low doorframe. He went to the fireplace and dropped two buckets of turf on the hearth, looked around at Ma and myself and then at the table.

"Where's me tea?" he asked.

Ma sighed. I could see from the way she slumped her shoulders that some of the excitement over the letter had gone out of her. I wondered if she was thinking again of her mistake in marrying Da. She'd told me about it often enough, particularly when she was drilling it into me that I had to set my sights high when choosing a husband.

"Don't make the same mistake I did," she would say, "marrying for love! What good did it do *me*? Stuck out in the middle of nowhere with only the cows and sheep for company, no running water, not even an outhouse. I'd be disgraced if my old school friends knew how I was living. I was the best-looking girl there, and they all said I'd marry a toff. Don't end up like me, my girl."

She looked up at Da. "Hold your horses, Peadar, sure the tea'll be ready in a minute. Now, sit you down," she said, smiling, "we've had a great surprise arrive: a letter all the way from America. And we've been waiting all day for you to come home and open it."

Da looked suspiciously at the envelope and then at Ma. "'Tis addressed to yourself. Could you not have just opened it without all this oul' palaver," he said. "Or have ye forgot how to read?"

It was seldom Da spoke to Ma this way. In fact, it was seldom he spoke at all. The smile left Ma's face. She snatched the envelope and ripped it open, muttering under her breath. I felt a bit sorry for her. She'd wanted to make a big ceremony out of this thing that was so out of the ordinary in our everyday lives, and now Da had thrown cold water all over it.

She took the flimsy letter out of the envelope and unfolded it, holding it in her rough, red fingers and mouthing the words to herself. When she was finished, she looked up at us with glassy eyes, as if she'd just witnessed a miracle.

"You'll never believe this . . ." she began, and then stopped as she rummaged inside the envelope. She turned it upside down, and some foreign-looking bank notes tumbled out.

"Mother of God," she breathed, "will you look at that!"

I wanted to shake her. "Will you ever put us out of our misery, Ma?" I shouted.

Even Da peered at her with sudden interest.

Ma took her time. She smiled at Da and then at me before she took a deep breath and began to speak.

"'Tis a letter from my niece's husband. He says the poor girl died of the fever. Ah, may God rest her soul. She'd have been older than yourself, but too young to die. She was the only child of my oldest sister and that blackguard she married named Sullivan. I didn't know her that well, because Sullivan moved the family to America when Mary was young. . . ."

I thought I would burst with curiosity. "For the love of God, will you get on with it, Ma?"

Ma straightened up. "The letter is from a Mr. Aidan O'Hanlon in New York City. It seems he was married, as I told you, to my niece, Mary. . . ."

I was close to screaming. Seeing my face, she hurried up the story. "Well, he says Mary left him with a young girl by the name of Lily. He says before she died, Mary begged him to send for one of her Irish cousins to come over and help take care of the child, and asked him to write to me. He wants the girl to be a governess, he says. What do you think that means?"

"It means a t-teacher."

Delia must have come into the kitchen without us noticing. She often seemed to float here and there like a ghost. We looked up at her and then back at the letter. Ma cleared her throat and went on. "And here's the good part. He asks if I have any daughters who would be suitable."

I felt my heart flip inside my chest. Could this be my chance to get away to America? I'd secretly hoped for such a chance for years. There was nothing for me in Kilcross and, truthfully, Ma was beginning to suffocate me. I wasn't a good scholar and I didn't have many choices. But surely I could teach a young girl something useful.

"Wait now 'til you hear this." Ma pointed to the money. "He's enclosed the money to buy a first-class ticket on the *Titanic*, which he says is being built in Belfast. It's due to sail next April."

Ma was breathless now as she picked up the strange-looking bills and threw them down on the table again in triumph. "He says 'twas Mary insisted ye travel first class because ye'd be doing her the biggest favor in the world, coming to look after her child." Ma pursed her lips. "He must be swimming in money, so." She turned to me. "What do you think of that now?"

For once I was as speechless as Da. Surely Ma would pick me to go. But for the first time in memory, my confidence deserted me. What if she didn't? What if she picked Delia instead? After all, she'd made no secret of wanting to be rid of her. Maybe she wouldn't want me going so far away because she was so dependent on me for company. I held my breath and waited for what seemed like an eternity.

Finally, Ma grinned. "Ah, you should see the look on your face, darlin'," she said. "And who do you think I'd be sending? Not that sister of yours!"

As I was letting Ma's words sink in, I noticed Da looking off toward the door. I turned just in time to see Delia's back as she slipped out into the hallway.

Delia

I slid down on the floor in the corner of the attic, closed my eyes and rested my head on my knees. I wanted to cry, but no tears would come. It was no surprise, I thought, that Ma would pick Nora. Nora was bright-eyed and cheerful, dark-haired and buxom and sure of her place in the world. In contrast, I was of slight build, with fair hair and gray eyes. I always shrank away when I was beside Nora, believing no one would ever look at me twice while she was there. Of course, Nora was the better choice to take on the challenge of America.

What hurt was that I had finally held the possibility of escape in my very hands, only to have it snatched away. It caught me by surprise that I should be so disappointed when there had never really been any hope that one day I would see those faraway places I read about in my books. Maybe the arrival of the letter had made me face up to how much I really wanted to get away and live my own life. But how? I took in sewing from time to time, but given the little money I made from that, it would be a hundred years before I could afford to move to Dublin, let alone New York.

I ran away once when I was fifteen. I got a lift with a local farmer as far as Donegal Town and was lingering at the station, wondering how I would get money for the train to Dublin, when Da appeared. He said nothing, just lifted my suitcase and walked away. We drove home in the pony cart in silence. Ma said he should have let me go.

There were few jobs to be had in Kilcross for which I was qualified. I couldn't even get a job serving in a shop because of my stutter. That was why, after I left school, I went back to the farm. As I was free all day, Da gave me more jobs than before. Soon I was helping him sow and harvest the crops and cutting turf beside him on the bog with a two-sided spade, called a slane. But much as I loved the outdoors and Da's company, I had begun to realize it was time to leave.

My thoughts were interrupted by the sound of footsteps on the stairs. I stiffened. No one ever came up here. It was my bedroom—my safe place. The door creaked open, and there stood Da. He hesitated for a second, but then bent over to enter through the small opening. When he straightened up in the tiny room, he looked like a giant in a fairy tale.

I waited, saying nothing. He stood in the middle of the room, shuffling uncomfortably. Then he cleared his throat.

" 'Tis sorry I am," he said at last.

I pretended I didn't know what he was talking about.

"For what?"

"For your sadness. I could see it on your face when your ma told Nora she'd be the one to go."

These were the most words he had said to me in a long time. I wanted to ignore him, but I could see the effort it was taking for him to talk, and my heart softened.

"It doesn't matter, Da," I whispered, even though everything in me wanted to shout that it *did* matter, that I wanted this more than anything in my whole life.

He moved a little closer. I noticed, for the first time, that his boots were cracked and caked with dirt. His trousers were rolled up at the ankles and tied with string. As my eyes traveled up, I saw the stained old jacket he seemed to have worn for as long as I could remember. My gaze lingered on his face. His eyes were sad and watery and the same gray as my own. I realized then that I had never really seen my da, and my heart lurched. I rose to my feet and hugged him, something I hadn't done since I was a child.

"Do you want to go?"

I nodded my head.

"Aye, Da, I do. More than anything else in the world." I paused, and all my repressed anger finally erupted. "I *do* want to go! I want to get away from the misery I've suffered here. I want to be free to live my life without being criticized at every turn. I want adventures and, yes, maybe even love. Why can't I be loved, Da? Don't I deserve it like anybody else?"

"*I* love you, daughter," he whispered.

I looked at him in astonishment. I'd always known that he loved me, but to hear him say it . . . I wanted to throw my arms around him again, but my despair returned.

"What's the use in talking about it, Da? This will be like everything else. Nora will get what she wants and, as usual, I'll get nothing!"

He dug his hands into his jacket pockets and nodded his head.

"Maybe so," he said. "But what if I found a way for you to go, daughter. Would you want it?"

"Yes," I cried. "Yes!"

"That's the answer then, so," he said, and turned toward the door.

I wanted to cry out after him, *Why are you doing this, Da? Why are you torturing me with the hope of it?* but I kept silent.

I thought nothing more of it. For the next week I went about my business on the farm and Da went back to his usual silence. Then, one day, he came over to where I sat in the circle of rocks and thrust an envelope into my hands.

"There's an address in there of a house in New York needs a maid," he said. "Father McGinty gave it to me when I asked did he know of anybody. He said 'tis a good Catholic family and he'd pray they'd be a good influence on your soul."

Da's face didn't betray what he thought of Father McGinty's motives, and I decided it didn't matter whose idea it was.

"Their name is Boyle, and the housekeeper will meet you when the boat docks. Your man O'Hanlon in America sent enough money will buy you and Nora a berth in steerage on that new boat."

"B-but what . . ."

I looked up at him in astonishment. I waited for him to explain more. What would Ma say? Why was he letting me go?

I would get no answers. Da turned around and continued his way down to the cottage, leaning on a blackthorn stick, our old sheepdog lumbering behind him. As I watched him go, a thought, fragile and elusive as a tiny bird, began to form. Could it be that fortune had finally smiled on me?

Nora

❧

I was fit to be tied when I found out what Da had done. I screamed aloud at Ma, tears stinging my eyes.

"But it was *my* money, Ma. You promised I'd be the one to go."

Ma looked up at me from where she sat at the kitchen table. Then she looked away, staring out the window. She couldn't even face me.

"You're still going," she said quietly, "'tis only that your sister's going too."

"Aye, traveling down in steerage with the rabble. It might suit Delia, but it doesn't suit me."

I'd been looking forward to the journey in first class; I'd pictured myself strolling around the deck in the company of all the toffs. I even let myself imagine one of the rich young fellers would take a notion for me. And now Ma, by not standing up to Da, had ruined all of it. Who was I going to meet down in steerage? Second sons of farmers forced out because they wouldn't inherit the farm; scrawny shop boys who had a bob on themselves because their boots weren't caked in mud like the farm boys; chancers of every kind. I could stay home and meet the likes of them!

While the shame of having to travel in steerage fueled my temper, I realized there was something more to it. Da had proved, once and for all, that Delia was his favorite daughter. I'd always suspected it, but now I knew for sure; I meant little to him. I used to put my feelings down to jealousy of Delia, but I realized now it was not jealousy, but hurt. I'd wanted Da to love me. I suppose you always yearn for what you know you can never have.

After a while, my fury quieted down. "But why, Ma? Why did you let him do it? You never listened to him before."

Ma looked me straight in the eye. "Oh I fought him on it all right! We went at it hammer and tongs. But he wouldn't give an inch. I've never seen your da so stubborn." She paused, as if making up her mind what else to say. When she spoke again, her words were angry. "I should never have shown him that ticket. He took it down from the dresser and got the priest to help him exchange it for the two steerage berths. Went behind my back, so he did, the sly oul' fox."

She shrugged. "Besides, I'm not sorry to see her go. How could I have stood it with you away and herself left here to taunt me from morning 'til night?" She stood up and smiled. "At least she'll get her comeuppance in that house. If Father McGinty recommended them, they must be tyrants altogether."

She stood up, all business now, and came over to stand close to me. She wasn't a tall woman, but when she was right next to you, which she was now, you'd swear she was as big as Da. I leaned away from her, the way I always did when I felt her smothering me.

"I know what you've been thinking, my girl," she began. "You've been imagining that you'd have met a rich young feller in first class. Well, so you might have, but that's not what I have in mind for you. You'll go to work for Mr. O'Hanlon in New York, and you'll coax him into marrying you. On my oath, I'd bet that feller has more money than any of the young idlers you'd be meeting in first class, who would promise you anything to get their way with you and then throw you over for some girl more equal to their station." She paused. "On the other hand, Mr. O'Hanlon is a settled man who is most likely looking for a wife, and you'll be the one to fill the bill."

I could see the wisdom of her words, but a small part of me wanted to rebel at being told what to do. I should have been used to it by now; she'd been telling me what to do all my life, and I had given in because I was rewarded with praise and finery. I liked being told that I was beautiful and too good for the local boys. I liked wearing the latest fashions and making all my friends jealous. Some of them, like Delia, had to be satisfied with hand-me-downs, and others had to wear clothes their ma sewed out of dyed, rough flour sacks. I was far and away the best dressed of any of them, and I strutted into Mass on a Sunday morning knowing that everybody was looking at me. I told myself 'twas a small price to pay to let Ma have her say.

I did the same thing now. I nodded. "You're right, Ma. You always are."

She gave a satisfied nod.

From then on up to the time the *Titanic* was ready to sail, Ma took down from the dresser the wee box where she kept the money she'd saved from selling eggs. She took me to Donegal Town and spoiled me with new dresses and hats, ribbons and new boots, and even a small bottle of perfume I'd begged for. She even took me to get my hair styled. I was going to be the belle of the ball, she said.

It was a pity all that effort was going to be wasted in steerage.

The Titanic

1912

Delia

❧

I was trembling with nerves and excitement when the big day arrived; the day we were to travel to Queenstown in County Cork to board the *Titanic*, which would sail the next day. Queenstown Harbor was at the far end of the country and it would be a long journey. First, we'd have to go by pony cart to the station in Donegal Town and then on by train, making several stops to change lines along the way. It would take us a full day. I'd never traveled that far in my life, nor had Nora. I couldn't wait to see the rest of Ireland.

I'd scarcely slept the night before, my mind jumping between excitement and anxiety. As we left the cottage, the morning was still dark. Ma stood at the door, her arms folded, as Da readied the pony and cart. When he had hauled our luggage up into the bed of the cart, Nora ran over to Ma and threw her arms around her. Ma hugged Nora back. I knew by her loud sniffs she was crying, even though I couldn't see her plainly.

"God bless, darlin'," she said, "and remember everything I told you. You'll no doubt have boys traipsing around after you on the boat, but you're to set your sights higher."

"Yes, Ma. I will," Nora said fervently as she turned away, although I knew she was only humoring her. When it came to boys, Nora always did exactly what she wanted, no matter what she promised Ma.

I waited for Ma to say something to me. We stood looking at

each other for what seemed a long time. At last she said, "Safe journey," and turned and went back into the cottage. I fought back tears. I'd hoped against hope for some kind words. After all, this might well be the last time we would ever lay eyes on each other. I suppose I should have known better.

Just as we were ready to board the cart, our house cat raced out of the cottage door and jumped up into Nora's arms, purring. Nora let out a squeal of delight.

"Poor puss," she said as she stroked it. "Will you miss me? I'm sorry I can't take you with me. Be a good girl now and go and keep Ma company."

She gently set the cat back down on the ground. Nora was very fond of animals, a trait I always found curious in her. It seemed to me they were the only creatures she loved more than herself.

As we traveled away from the cottage, pale red streaks spanned the sky ahead of us. Dawn was coming, the last dawn I would see in Ireland, for I believed in my heart that I would never return. My sadness came as a surprise. I'd imagined I would feel only joy at finally being able to escape the cottage and Kilcross. But I hadn't realized I would miss Donegal itself. Its green hills rose on either side of us like hazy, dark shadows in the dim light. In the distance, I could hear the splashing of the Atlantic against the cliffs. A squealing sheep ran across the road in front of us. I thought back to my favorite place, the circle of rocks beneath the oak tree where I had spent so many afternoons, lost in my imagination. I took a deep breath. I would miss all of it.

Da said nothing to either me or Nora as the cart rattled along the rutted road. He sat upright, holding the reins loosely in his hands and looking straight ahead. Every now and then, he urged the pony on in the lovely, soft Gaelic of his childhood. I sat beside him while Nora sat up on the wooden seat behind us. She moved about restlessly, her dress rustling in the silence. She wore one of her fancy new dresses—hardly the thing for a long journey. But then, Nora never set foot outside the door without looking her best. I smiled to myself. She would hardly be caught dead in the likes of the plain cotton blouse and skirt I wore.

When we finally arrived at the station, I was surprised there were only a few stragglers on the platform. I had expected hordes of people, all making for the *Titanic*. I realized then the coming adventure loomed much larger in my life than in that of my neighbors.

Da lifted the suitcases out of the cart and brought them over to the platform. The two largest ones belonged to Nora. She had fussed and fumed the night before, refusing even Ma's advice to leave some of her clothes behind. I, on the other hand, had no such problems. My scant belongings fitted easily into a small suitcase. I also carried a leather bag containing our identity papers, tickets and the money left over from what Mr. O'Hanlon had sent, which I was to divide between Nora and me when we docked in New York. Nora had said she couldn't be bothered with all that carry-on, which was hardly surprising because Nora was used to having everything done for her. I did say she ought to take her share of the money, but she waved me away with a sigh. For all her confidence, our Nora could be very naïve at times.

When he had set down the luggage, Da straightened up and looked at us. We both waited to see if he was going to speak. At last he stepped closer, his arms held out stiffly, as if ready to hug us, but Nora stepped back and looked away.

"Goodbye, Da," I said quickly to cover the awkwardness, "wish us luck."

He nodded and let his arms drop. I could see the sadness in his eyes. Even though I knew he had no need to hug me to show his love, I realized I needed to hug him. I stepped forward and put my arms around him.

The moment was interrupted by the arrival of the train, the cloud of steam from its engine enveloping the platform in a momentary fog. We climbed up the metal steps to a third-class carriage, and Da handed our suitcases to the conductor. We found seats in an empty compartment. Nora rushed to the window and lifted it open. As the train began to move, she stuck out her head and waved in Da's direction. "Bye!" she called, "goodbye, Da." I wondered if she was doing it all for the benefit of the people left on the platform. Our Nora loved a bit of drama.

She sat down, sniffed and glared at me. "First-class compartments wouldn't have wooden seats."

I said nothing. As the train picked up steam, two young people came into the compartment. Nora jumped up and greeted them. They were a sister and brother named Maeve and Dom Donnelly, whom Nora and I had known from school. They too, they said, would be traveling on the *Titanic*. The girl's face was as white as a ghost, and she clung to her brother for dear life. Nora seemed to ignore the girl's fear as she attached herself to them, prattling away about the upcoming journey, leaving me to myself, as if I were a stranger. No matter, I thought. I reached into my bag and pulled out a book. A book was a better companion than my sister any day of the week. Eventually, I put down the book and sat looking out the window at the lush scenery. When I got tired of it, I went back to reading, dozing off now and then.

The other girl fell asleep almost immediately. The boy ran out of conversation, leaned back his head against the wooden seat and began to snore softly. Nora closed her eyes. Soon she was asleep too, her head lolling on my shoulder. I glanced down at her. In sleep she looked very young, and I had a brief memory of when we were both young children and had played happily together. I sighed. How different life would have been had our relationship stayed that way.

Nora

When we arrived at the Queenstown dock, I stopped in my tracks and looked up in awe. The *Titanic* loomed above me, like a massive, rocking beast.

"A hundred feet tall and almost nine hundred feet long," said Dom, who stood behind me. I looked around at him. His ruddy face glowed and his eyes were wide. His sister, Maeve, clung to him, still looking terrified.

I strained my neck to look up at the top deck. There were people looking down at us. Although they were only small specks, I could see the outline of fancy, feathered hats on the women and black bowler hats on the men. They would be the first-class passengers who had boarded at Southampton and Cherbourg the day before. My annoyance with Delia returned. If it wasn't for her, I'd be up there among them, looking down on the ragged crowd below; men in shabby clothes and women carrying babies wrapped in shawls.

We went through the health examination, where we were poked and prodded like cattle. I suppose they were afraid we'd bring our germs on board and infect the toffs up on the first deck.

"Come on, Nora, hurry up." Delia took me by the arm and steered me toward the gangplank. "Here's your ticket!" I shook off her arm and took the ticket. She'd become bossy all of a sudden. She wouldn't have dared speak to me that way at home. I followed her up the gangplank, struggling a little with the weight of my suitcases.

As I walked up the gangplank, I caught sight of the dark water lapping below. I swallowed hard. I was deathly afraid of water, ever since the time Delia tried to drown me in the river near our cottage. She always denied it, saying she was only trying to hold me up when I started to struggle. But I didn't believe her. Ma didn't either. I looked away quickly and let my eyes bore into the porter's back instead.

The porter led us down several sets of stairs. The suitcases grew heavier in my grip and my breathing labored from exhaustion. With every new flight of stairs, I groaned. Mother of God, was he leading us down into Hell itself? At last we came to a long, narrow corridor with doors lined on either side. The porter stopped at number 23 and unlocked the door. He smiled at Delia and me.

"Here's your cabin, girls," he said, as if it was the Taj Mahal. "You should find everything you need. Ye are lucky, ye have this cabin all to yourselves; the other two passengers canceled. The toilets are around the corner there." He pointed to his right. "They're flushing toilets," he went on. "I bet ye have never seen the likes of them in your life."

I glared at him. "That'll be all, thank you," I said in my most polite voice. "We'll let you know if we need anything."

His mouth dropped open. Then he let out a loud guffaw. "Ah sure, you're a great teaser, love," he said. "A great teaser altogether." With that, he moved on to the next cabin.

The space was tiny, with four berths and a washbasin. The pine walls were painted white and the floor was linoleum. I suppose it wasn't as bad as I'd feared, but I wouldn't give Delia the satisfaction of telling her so. I heaved my suitcases onto the nearest bed and sat down. I watched Delia, who was humming to herself as she opened her suitcase to unpack.

"We'll only be needing two changes of clothes, and we can

rinse them in between," she said. "No need to take everything out of the cases."

I glared at her. Rinse them out my arse! We were to be on the ship for five days, and I for one was going to be wearing clean knickers every day. I watched her take out two blouses and skirts and two pairs of knickers. I supposed it was all the clothes she had. I shrugged and turned away to avoid feeling sorry for her. Then she pulled out her books and set them on the bed. Her and her books—you'd think they were her children. On account of all that reading, she used words so long they would choke you. I always believed she did it on purpose to make me look ignorant; school hadn't been my strong point.

She turned around, smiling. "Do you need help unpacking, Nora?"

As I watched her, my irritation grew, and when she spoke to me, I blew up.

"No!" I shouted. "I'll be needing no help from you. If it wasn't for you, I'd be enjoying the luxury up in first class instead of being down here in this dungeon."

Delia stood there, her mouth a perfect O, waiting for me to finish shouting. But I wasn't finished.

"You're a devious little devil. How you got around Da to arrange a passage for you, I'll never know." Tears stung my eyes and I balled up my fists. "You've been jealous of me since the day you were born. You'd do anything to spite me, wouldn't you?" I paused to catch my breath. "Well, just you wait, you'll get your just dues. A week from now you'll be down on your knees scrubbing floors for strangers, while I'll be at ease in Mr. O'Hanlon's posh home with nothing to do but amuse his young daughter!"

I turned my back on Delia so she would not see the fear on my face. The truth was, I was nervous as a cat at the thought of going to some posh house and pretending to be a governess. What if the seven-year-old daughter was already able to read and write better than me? I shook off the doubts as best I could and turned back to Delia. She was quiet for a moment before she spoke.

"I'm sorry you feel that way, Nora. But it comes as no surprise. You've always been a selfish girl. And to tell you the truth, I'll be happy to scrub floors day and night as long as I'm away from you and Ma. All you two have ever done is torment me. The only one who ever showed me any kindness was Da."

I stared at her in shock. Where had she found the nerve to speak to me like that? And she'd said it all without the hint of a stutter. I was going to say more, but I was already sick of fighting with her. I opened the cabin door and looked out. Young people with accents from all over Ireland were milling in the corridor, talking and laughing. There might be some good *craic* to be had down here after all. I smoothed out one of my new dresses, a lovely blue one with a low-cut neckline. I put it on, along with a matching hat, and stepped out, closing the door behind me.

Delia

When Nora had gone, I heaved a sigh of relief. How was I going to put up with her for the entire journey? I could understand why she was upset—she'd been used to having her own way—but I didn't want to keep fighting with her. I liked peace and quiet. I decided to ignore her as best I could.

The little cabin was quite cozy. The walls smelled of fresh paint and the linoleum floor was bright and clean. The washbasin gleamed. I supposed the newness wouldn't last long after a string of passengers came and went in this cabin. It was thrilling to be the first people to sail on the *Titanic*.

I must have been asleep when Nora returned. I had heard some traditional music coming from the other end of the ship. Many of the lads would have brought along fiddles and accordions. I'd no doubt my sister was out dancing in the middle of the floor. She was a big, curvy girl, but she was light on her feet, and the boys were drawn to her like bees to honey. She'd never be short of a partner at a dance. It was always that way. I hated going to dances in the village. If a boy I didn't know approached me, I'd stutter, and he would back away, muttering excuses. After a while I refused to go. And while it made me a little sad that I wasn't out enjoying the music in steerage, I believed my experience would be no different than at the dances in Kilcross. So, as usual, I took refuge in a book before I fell asleep.

In the morning we were awakened by a bell announcing

breakfast. Nora and I walked in silence down the corridor to the large room that had been set aside for dining. We sat down at a table, but Nora got up immediately when she spied some of her new friends from the night before. She ran over to them, full of smiles and greetings, and they made room for her to sit down among them. I was left to myself.

I was astonished when I saw the breakfast menu. I had expected just porridge, bread and tea, but this was like a banquet. Besides the porridge, we had a choice of smoked herring, potatoes and ham and eggs. There was even butter and marmalade for the bread. My mood brightened. Even Nora couldn't complain about this feast.

We took our breakfast, dinner and tea in the same room, and the food was equally plentiful. The rest of the time we were free to go back to our cabins, out onto F deck, or, if we wanted company, we could socialize in what they called the General Room. From the morning until night Nora and I spent no time in each other's company.

I didn't mind being alone. I was content to sit and watch people coming and going. They were mostly young like us, faces shining with the excitement of this new adventure. There was talk of what they would do when they arrived in America. For them, the *Titanic* was the ship of hope. I was sure most of it was fantasy, but they were having fun and would face reality soon enough. There were some older people as well: mothers with young children, prim older spinsters and a few clerks in cheap suits. From conversations I overheard, most of them were going out to meet some relative who had already established him or herself in the New World. I felt a jolt of homesickness. I would know no one except Nora and, I realized, once we landed, I might never see her again.

The next morning, Dom, the lad from Kilcross, came over to where I was sitting. As usual, his sister, Maeve, trailed along behind him. He took off his cap and put it in his pocket.

"Are you by yourself?" he asked.

I nodded.

"Mind if we sit down and keep you company?"

My insides started to spasm with sudden panic. I looked around for Nora, but she was busy laughing with her friends. I turned back to Dom, and his earnest face calmed me a little.

"O-of course you can," I said, putting on what I hoped was a smile.

He pulled out a chair for Maeve and dragged another one over for himself. He sat down, smiling pleasantly.

"So what are ye making of it so far?"

My heart lifted at hearing his soft, lilting Donegal accent, and I relaxed.

"'Tis grand." I smiled. "A great adventure."

He looked over at the table where Nora was telling a story while her new friends drank in her every word. "I see your Nora wasted no time making friends," he said.

I said nothing and changed the subject. I looked at Maeve.

"How are you feeling, Maeve? You looked very pale on the train."

She flinched, startled, as I spoke to her. "I'm all right," she said, her head bowed.

"Ah, she'll be grand after we get there," said Dom. "She's taken an awful case of seasickness, but I've walked her outside on the deck as much as I can. The fresh air does her good."

I smiled at Dom. He was a thoughtful lad. I wondered why I hadn't known him better in school. But then, I hadn't been interested in any of the boys. I don't know if it was because I was afraid of them or they were afraid of me. I suppose I wasn't too popular. I used to blush with shame when the teachers singled me out, telling the class I was the scholar they should all look up to. I wanted to crawl into a hole every time the teachers praised me.

"'Tis a pity we weren't friends in school," Dom said, as if reading my thoughts. "Maybe 'twas because you were cleverer than the rest of us. I was afraid to talk to you."

I blushed. "Ah, sure that wasn't true, I was just the one the teachers picked out as an example. I wanted to disappear into the ground every time they did it. Anyway, you're talking to me now."

"Aye. Being on this boat and on our way to America changes everything, doesn't it? It's as if Kilcross never existed. Maybe we'll be friends in New York." He hesitated, and a faint flush covered his cheeks. "I'll give you the address where we'll be staying, so. Maybe we can meet some day for a cup of tea."

Later, as I walked back to my cabin, my heart fluttered. Dom was the first boy to ever take an interest in me. I could hardly believe it. Suddenly, the promise of the New World took on a shine I had never thought to see.

Nora

❧✦☙

I was enjoying myself. I'd made a lot of new friends, girls and lads, and was having the time of my life. I giggled with the girls and gossiped about other passengers. It was like being back in school again. As usual, just like at home, the boys were tripping over themselves to dance with me. I had no intention of being friends with them once the journey was over, even though they all wanted my address in New York. It wasn't just Ma's advice echoing in my ears; I realized that I'd have no future with any of these lads. Mr. O'Hanlon was the better prospect; Ma was always right.

One particular lad set his cap for me, though, and I almost forgot myself. His name was Robert and he was tall, handsome and English. He was a steward who worked up in first class but had been drawn down to the third-class deck by the sound of the music and the carry-on that was drifting up to the upper decks. I bombarded him with questions about first class, and he was happy to tell me all about it. I think it made him feel important and sure, what was the harm in that? When he promised to sneak me up to the first-class dining room the next morning at breakfast, I was over the moon with excitement.

I went over to Delia to tell her the good news. I was, of course, hoping to make her jealous. But when I got closer, I saw her talking to Dom. I was shocked. Delia always ran like a scared rabbit any time a boy came within a mile of her. And here she was now, laughing and carrying on with Dom. I shrugged. *Let her have him*, I thought. *I have better fish to fry.*

The next morning, good to his word, Robert came and fetched me. He knocked on the cabin door, and I opened it at once. He put his finger to his lips to be quiet; then he smiled. Ah, he had lovely dimples, so he did. He led me up to the steps to the second deck, then up a series of gleaming mahogany curved staircases. I noticed the difference at once. The air smelled fresher than down below, and the light was better. Instead of the noise and chaos downstairs, with people knocking each other over to get into breakfast, up here passengers sauntered about as if they had all the time in the world, murmuring quietly while soft music played in the background.

Robert led me across a carpeted floor and into a huge, formal dining room, where tables were decked out with white linen cloths, glistening drinking glasses and polished silver cutlery. Even the butter was carved in wee curls and arranged on a silver plate. There were flowers on each table and in big brass urns around the room. I'd never seen the likes of it. My eyes opened wide and I fought not to open my mouth as well. Then I caught a couple of older men staring at me and I straightened my shoulders, held up my head and tried to act as if I belonged there.

Robert led me to a table and gave a small bow as he seated me. I felt like the Queen of Sheba. If only Ma could see me now. Robert left me alone and I read the menu. Mother of God, you should have seen the lovely sounding dishes on offer. The variety available in third class had surprised me, but this was the last word. A waiter startled me.

"Has madam made her choice?"

As he waited, he gave me a wink, and I knew then that Robert had set up the whole thing with him. I smiled back.

"I believe I will start with the baked apples, and then the

smoked Finnan haddock with eggs and potatoes, and a pot of tea," I said, doing my best to imitate how I thought toffs would talk. "Oh, and perhaps a scone with blackcurrant jam."

"Very well, madam," he said, and left.

While I waited, I looked around the room. Passengers were beginning to drift in. I admired the women's finery: silk dresses, silk stockings and fine leather boots. And some wore hats, even at this time of the morning! The men were just as smartly dressed, with gleaming white shirts and collars, and tailored jackets. I was glad I had worn my best dress. But as a few of the women looked my way, I stuck my feet under my chair so they wouldn't see the plain, cheap boots I was wearing. When I bought them in Donegal Town, I'd been told by the saleswoman they were the last word in fashion. A lot she knew! Stubbornly, I stuck my little finger out as I picked up my teacup and raised my chin as the women moved past me. But even though I tried to act as if I hadn't a care in the world, deep down the fear of whether I'd ever fit in with this new world roiled in my stomach.

The feeling passed, and Robert came to escort me from the table. I wanted so much to stay in this lovely place, surrounded by beautiful people. But I knew if we lingered it wouldn't be long before we were found out. I didn't want him getting in trouble, so I stood up as gracefully as I could, took his arm and walked with him to the door, my head held high.

When we got back down to the third-class deck, the two of us collapsed laughing. It had been great *craic* altogether. Robert said he'd be back for the dancing tonight. It would be the last night of the journey; we were to dock in New York the next day. The *craic* tonight would be even better, with all the young ones determined to make the most of their last night together.

I told Robert goodbye and sauntered back to the cabin, humming softly to myself. A mild sadness suddenly came over me, and I stopped humming. I stood at the cabin door without opening it; I wanted to be alone with my thoughts for a moment. Part of me wanted to curse Robert for bringing me up there—even though, to be fair, I was the one who'd egged him on. Because now that I'd got a taste of the grand life the toffs had, the more I wanted that for myself. After all, Ma had always said that's where I belonged. I said a prayer that Mr. O'Hanlon would give me a crack at a life like that.

Delia

⟨❀⟩

It was the last full day of our voyage. Tomorrow we would dock in New York and our lives would change, maybe forever. Our days on the *Titanic* had been like floating in limbo, suspended between the old world and the new. The joyous excitement in steerage had been infectious. Promises to meet up in New York had been made, handshakes sealing vows of new friendships; secret kisses stolen in the hidden nooks of F deck; small mementos exchanged between new lovers; and, tonight, music and dancing would raise the rafters in final celebration. Tomorrow, cries of "Good luck, now!" would echo across the docks as the young pilgrims strode down the gangplanks and into a new world.

Up until now, I had not let myself think about the future. I'd been afraid my dream would evaporate. Now, I allowed myself to finally believe that fortune had indeed smiled on me. Here I was, almost in New York, and my dreams were about to become a reality, though along with my new optimism came fear. The frightening prospect of landing in the middle of a world of strangers filled my mind. What would the "good Catholic family," as Da had called them, really be like? How would I find my way around the streets? Would I get lost? Would people be kind to me? With every new question I felt myself growing more and more anxious. Gone now were the fantasies I had made up about stepping out bravely to embrace faraway adventures. This was no fantasy; this was real.

The cabin walls began to close in around me. I had to get out. I shut the door behind me and hurried up to F deck, my breathing ragged. As I stood leaning over the railing, looking out at the horizon, my trembling eased, and I took several deep breaths. Then I looked up at the sky and made a vow to God. *Whatever awaits me,* I whispered, *I will face it with courage. I will not squander this chance you have given me at happiness.*

That evening, as I had expected, the sounds of music and singing outside the cabin soared. I closed my book and ventured out into the corridor and down toward the General Room, where the noise was loudest. This was the first night I had done so, but the music enticed me. The pulsing rhythms of accordions and fiddles filled me with sweet memories of Ireland, and when I drew closer and heard a lad singing a sad, familiar air, tears stung my eyes. The reality was that my life in Kilcross had been an unhappy one, but, at this moment, homesickness overcame me like a crashing wave. Instead of fighting it, I let it seep through me and allowed my tears to flow.

Nora, of course, was having the time of her life, dancing and carrying on in the middle of the crowd in the General Room. She raised her dress up to her knees and spun around, her feet beating out the rhythm of the music on the floor. I couldn't help but smile along with everyone else. Her good humor was infectious. I knew she would probably stay there until the dancing was over. I went back to the cabin, packed my suitcase and then lay down on my bed with a favorite book.

I must have dozed off, for I was awakened by a strange noise. I sat up and looked toward the door. Maybe it was Nora returning. But her bed was empty. I came fully awake and realized that it was not really a sound I had heard, but a sensation, like a bump. At first, I thought it was the music that had awoken me, but it had already stopped, and there were no sounds out in the corridor. I was about to dismiss it as my imagination and go back to sleep when I felt another bump, followed this time by a loud grinding, scraping sound, as if the ship had grazed against something.

I sat straight up in bed and held my breath. I knew now it had not been my imagination. My ability to predict events, which had started in my childhood, had never left me. It always started with the same signs: a quivering deep in my stomach, sudden chills and a sense of elation or, more often, foreboding. It was foreboding I felt now. Something was not right with the ship. I went to the door and opened it to look up and down the corridor. All was quiet. I went back inside and stood as if at attention, listening and waiting.

Eventually, I heard Nora giggling outside the door. I presumed she was with her new conquest, the young English steward, Robert. Maybe she was angling for another visit to first class. She came in humming to herself, sloughed off her dress and boots onto the floor and, ignoring me, fell into bed. In seconds she was sound asleep. If she'd heard the noise, she paid no attention to it.

Nora

❧✦☙

The bed was moving. Blearily, I wondered if a storm was tossing the ship about. That was enough to make me finally open my eyes. I hated water. It was then I realized it was Delia shaking me.

"In the name of God!" I shouted. "Can you not just leave me the feck alone! 'Twas bad enough you spent your days following me around the ship. Every time I turned around, I'd see you watching me. For God's sake, could you not at least leave me to sleep?" Groggily, I turned over, pulled the bedclothes up over my face and tried to go back to sleep.

"There's something wrong with the ship!" she yelled. "We have to get out!"

Just then, there came a loud banging on the cabin door. Groaning, I sat up. Robert burst into the cabin carrying life belts. One look at his face and I could tell something was wrong. Before I could open my mouth to speak, he began giving out orders.

"You have to get out, now!" he said, his voice louder and more demanding than I had heard it before. "Put this on," he said, shoving the bulky life belt at me.

"I could suffocate in that thing, 'tis so hot," I protested.

"Now, Nora!" he shouted.

I looked at Delia. She was busy throwing my clothes into my suitcase. My temper flared. "Stop that!"

She stopped in her tracks and gave me a strange look.

Robert looked at Delia, then back at me. "You don't understand, Nora," he said, speaking slowly, as if he was talking to a child. "The ship is going to sink. You have to get out of here now!"

I didn't like him talking to me that way. "And how would *you* know?" I demanded.

He sighed and kept talking in the same tone as before. "I was just up on the bridge," he said, "and I heard the captain and the first mate arguing. The first mate said an iceberg was about to hit the ship, and he had to slow down or we would sink. The captain wouldn't believe him at first, said it was too early to change speed, but the first mate insisted. He wanted the captain to give the order to prepare the lifeboats and start alerting the passengers."

Robert paused, sweat running down his face. "You can't wait. You have to go now! There aren't enough lifeboats, Nora. If you don't go now, there'll be no room left."

"He's right," said Delia. "I felt just now that we hit something, or something hit us."

It was then I came to my senses. I looked at Delia, and her face was white as a sheet. I jumped out of bed, not caring that Robert would see me in my underthings. I picked up the dress I had dropped on the floor earlier and shoved my feet into my unlaced boots. Robert helped me fasten the life belt. I reached for his hand, and together we ran out into the corridor toward the stairs to the upper decks.

As we ran, I heard Delia's voice behind us. She was yelling about identity papers, but I paid no attention. I couldn't care less about identity papers. I'd even left my suitcase behind. All my fine new clothes. *But I'll go back for them later*, I thought. As we ran, a few passengers poked their heads around the cabin doors and then closed them again when a porter told them to get back in. Fear clutched at me. My throat turned dry and pounding filled my ears. I could hardly breathe. I clung desperately to Robert's arm for fear he would let go. I tripped going up the stairs and kicked off my unlaced boots, which were holding me back from running. Through the drumming in my ears, I could hear the crew shouting to one another. I wanted to be sick.

For the entire voyage I'd tried not to think that I was on a floating pile of wood and iron out in the middle of the Atlantic Ocean. I'd distracted myself from my fears by dancing and flirting and carrying on. And I'd succeeded, almost to the point where my fear had gone. But now it all came roaring back.

Robert was almost dragging me now, for I wasn't fit to keep up with him. As we rushed across the second-class deck, I fancied I heard Delia calling my name. I pried myself free of Robert and turned around, but I couldn't see her. I yelled out her name, but my voice was drowned in the clamor of sounds around me. I tried to run back the way I had come, but Robert caught me and forced me forward. "Keep going," he shouted. "She's right behind us."

We reached the first-class deck, and Robert pulled me through the crowd to where a line of women stood.

"Get into the lifeboat!" he said before disappearing into the crowd.

"Robert!" I cried.

But he was gone. I looked around frantically for Delia, hoping against hope that she would appear, but there was no sign of her in the crowd that was surging up the stairs toward me. I was well and truly alone.

"Mother of God, save me," I whispered.

Delia

᷾᷾

I wanted to shake Nora. At last the penny dropped and she jumped out of bed, dressed and ran out with Robert. I glanced at the suitcases, but instead reached for the leather satchel containing our identity papers and money. I could hardly lift the cases by myself, let alone run with them. As an afterthought, I lifted my books and stuffed them into the satchel. When I left the cabin, Nora and Robert were halfway down the corridor, running toward the second-class stairway.

"Nora! Wait!"

As I ran, passengers opened their cabin doors and peered out, looking confused. A porter, the one who had escorted us onto the ship, was urging them back inside. Most nodded and did as he said. I wanted to scream at them to run, but I was almost out of breath, and Nora and Robert were getting far ahead of me. I pounded up the stairs after them as they raced across the second-class deck. I shouted again, but by then I had lost sight of them. I stopped and bent over to catch my breath. Anxious passengers milled around me. The sounds of children wailing, and the shouts of crewmen filled my ears. I looked around, trying to get my bearings. I had lost track of Nora; there was nothing I could do for her, but it occurred to me then that I *could* at least do something for Dom and Maeve.

I retraced my steps back down to steerage, pushing through

hordes of people coming toward me. Icy water swirled around my ankles as I ran along the corridor and pounded on Dom's door.

"Delia?" Dom's earnest, open face peered out at me, his sister Maeve behind him. I reached into a pile of life belts on the floor, thrust two at them and told them to follow me. They did what I said without a word.

When we reached the second deck, an older woman came toward us. "Get into the boat, my pets," she said, indicating myself and Maeve.

She led us across the second-class deck, where women were being eased down into a lifeboat. "Get in there, dears," she said, "before it's full up."

"B-but what about you?"

She shook her head. "Don't worry about me, my dear," she said. "They're not letting men into the boats—women and children only." She gestured to a man with a gray beard. "I won't leave my husband. We've been married forty years, and whatever happens we'll face it together. Go on, now!"

When we reached the lifeboat, I breathed a sigh of relief that it had not yet been loosed from its mooring. Dom and I tried to lift Maeve into it, but she struggled so violently against us, we had to let go of her.

"No, please," she cried. "I want to stay with Dom."

Dom took her in his arms and looked at me over her head. "'Tis all right, Maeve," he said. "We'll wait together for the next boat. They're bound to be letting men into them by then. Isn't that right, Delia?"

I nodded. But as I did, I had the awful feeling I would never see either of them again. Reluctantly, I eased myself down into the lifeboat and turned my face toward the sea.

Nora

I sank down on the nearest seat, then sat bent over, clutching my ankles, my teeth chattering, and my eyes closed shut. The boat rocked each time a new passenger was helped in, and my stomach did a cartwheel.

I kept my head down at first, but soon my curiosity got the better of me and my fear eased a bit. I looked up at the women who sat on the rough seats, prim and proper as if in a church pew. You'd have thought some of the passengers were off to a garden party with their silk dresses, big hats and fur stoles. Some wore fur coats over their nightgowns. Fecking fur coats, if you please. I nearly choked on their strong perfume. Their faces showed no signs of fear as they sniffed through long noses at the conditions around them. Must be a great thing to be brought up that way, I thought, expecting that trouble will never touch you.

I looked up at the deck, doing my best to keep myself distracted. I wondered was Delia up there, but there was no sign of her. I knew I had no right to expect it after the way I had treated her, but I wished fervently that she was here beside me; she would have known what to do. She would have eased my panic.

A mob of people, mostly men, pressed forward, even as the crewmen were trying to hold them back. They barked orders at the crew, like men used to having their own way. But the crew held their ground.

"Women and children only," they repeated over and over.

One ignorant lout pushed a crewman aside and jumped into the boat. The women squealed like schoolgirls. You'd think they'd never seen a man before. I smiled in spite of myself. The feller was thrown out in short order, and he disappeared into the crowd, cursing mightily. He'd no sooner gone than a tall, thin woman smothered in lace, rapped her walking stick on the floor of the boat and called up to an old man with white whiskers.

"Charles, go and find the maid and have her bring a pot of hot tea. It's freezing in here. Go along now, there's a good chap. No sense standing about. It will be a while before they begin letting men into the lifeboats."

I was dumbfounded. Who did she think she was, Queen Victoria? Surely, I thought, they can't all be like her. There were a couple of young ones who looked as if they were holding back tears. I knew if it was my husband being left to fend for himself on a sinking ship, I'd have been beyond comfort. As it was, I wanted to cry for Robert. I supposed he'd be expected to go down with the ship. Such a lovely lad he was, and if it wasn't for him, I might be drowning down in steerage at that minute.

I wasn't one for prayers, but I bowed my head and said one for Delia, one for Robert and one for myself.

After a while, the stream of women being eased down into the boat stopped. It was only half full. I thought the crewmen would go and look for more women who might have been too frightened to come out to the deck, or maybe even maids who thought it wasn't their place to step into the boat with their mistresses. But I hadn't counted on the selfishness of the women around me.

"What are we waiting for?" called one. "There are no more women in line. We need to lower the boat now!"

I could hardly believe my ears. Without thinking, I turned toward them. "But we're only half full!" I shouted. "We have room for two dozen more women."

My words were met with silence and more than a few dirty looks. It was obvious to them, and to me, that I didn't belong to their class. One woman spread out her gown, taking up two seats, and sighed.

"I would so hate to have this crushed. It's brand new from Harrods."

I bit my lip. If I said any more, they might insist that I leave the boat because I clearly didn't belong with them. But inside I was seething. How could I ever have admired these stuck-up bitches? I thought, remembering how impressed I had been with them in the first-class dining room. God, was that only this morning?

No more women arrived, and soon the crewman in charge of our lifeboat jumped aboard and gave the signal to loosen the ropes that held the boat to the side of the ship. As he did, the deck turned into a madhouse, people shouting and crying and protesting that the boat wasn't full. A large man pushed his way through the crowd and tried to jump into the boat as it was lowered. As he did so, a ship's officer pulled out his pistol and shot him. He staggered backward and collapsed. The women in the boat let go of all pretense of civility and began to scream. Bile rose in my throat and I wanted to jump out and run to the safety of the deck. I closed my eyes and did my best to beat down panic.

As the boat was lowered, it swayed and bumped against every deck. The front of it rose up and the back went down so that we were at a slant. Then it slanted the other way as the seamen fought to control the ropes. My knuckles were white as I grasped the side of the boat. I began to sob, but the wind whipped away my tears as soon as they appeared. I cried out to God and all the saints I could name to take pity on me.

We landed on the surface of the water with a thud. Freezing cold waves splashed over us. I trembled like a wisp of straw in the wind, and my teeth chattered so hard I thought they would fall out.

"Mother of God," I cried, "don't let me die! I'm too young. I promise I'll go to Mass every week and light a candle every day, if only you'll save me. And I promise I'll be good to Delia, and I won't be selfish ever again, and . . ."

I carried on for a while, trying to bargain with the Blessed Virgin. When I ran out of promises, I quieted down. We had moved well away from the ship and our boat sat rocking in the water. The crewman told us we would have to wait there for rescue.

The *Titanic* was all lit up like something out of a fairy tale, and I could hear lovely music coming from the first-class deck. For a minute I thought I had already died and gone to Heaven. But a ferocious slap of water from a cold wave brought me back to reality. I looked back up at the ship, this time letting my eyes wander along its length and down to F deck. There were no lights down there and I couldn't see much in the darkness, but I could hear sounds that I couldn't make out at first. I strained my ears and realized I was hearing screams and splashes as people leaped off the deck and hit the water. It sounded as if the screams were coming from Hell itself.

It was then I lost all control, and panic took hold of me. I stood up and screamed, keening and wringing my hands like the old women at funerals in Donegal. The devil squeezed my chest until I could no longer breathe. I heard the banshee, the spirit of death, calling my name. I had no choice; it was time. I climbed up on the seat and waited for God or the devil to take me. A young woman, wearing a mauve shawl, threw her arms around me, trying to haul me back down into the boat. But as we struggled, a rogue wave washed over us, breaking her hold on me, and I fell into the freezing water. As I floated there, looking up at the stars, a violent pain in the back of my head blinded me, and the world turned black.

Delia

❦

The lifeboat shunted unsteadily, scraping the side of the ship as the seamen loosened the ropes. It rocked from side to side until we landed with a thud in the oil-black, freezing water. The women in the boat screamed and wailed. A lady next to me holding two infants fainted, her head lolling on my shoulder. I wedged my satchel between my knees and took the wailing children into my arms. Their little bodies were warm against mine, and I soothed them as best I could while they looked up at me with dark, luminous eyes. But as the seamen began rowing, the freezing air cut through us like a knife, and I began to shiver along with the babies. I thought of Nora. I fervently hoped she had made it into a lifeboat. Even if she had, she must be terrified. I bowed my head and said a prayer for her. Eventually, the babies stopped crying, and I handed them back to their mother, who had recovered from her faint.

I was suddenly aware of a sound so terrifying that I had to cover my ears. At first, I thought it was a fierce gale, like those that roared across Donegal in the winter. But this was different. I put my hands down and looked around me. The other passengers had stopped screaming and sat in mute fear. It was as if we were surrounded by a wall of sound. It was then I realized this was no gale, but the sound of wailing from the poor souls still left on the ship. We were a good distance away when the ship split in two. Slowly, the stern began to sink, and we watched as if hypnotized. Within minutes, the stern had disappeared beneath the waves, and the prow of the ship was thrust upward into the sky like a contorted cathedral spire. We watched in horror as it slipped plumb straight into the sea, leaving no trace that the great ship had ever existed.

Suddenly, through the wailing, I imagined I heard a piercing scream. It sounded like a banshee—the spirit of death in Ireland—and I knew in my heart it belonged to Nora. There was no rational reason I should have known that, but my premonitions were never rational. All the familiar sensations came over me, and I knew, deep in my bones, that Nora was about to drown. I had to save her. I shot up from my seat, ignoring the protests of the passengers and crew, and peered out through the murky light in the direction from which the cry had come. Eventually, I made out the outline of a lifeboat floating nearby. A girl with long, dark hair was standing up on a seat, while a woman tried to pull her back down. I heard the screams again as the girl tried to wrestle free before she fell. I squeezed my eyes shut in terror. When I opened them, she was floating faceup in the freezing water. If it had just been a vision, I didn't know, but I trembled with the possibility it might have been real.

"Row over there," I screamed at the crewman in charge, pointing in the direction of Nora's lifeboat. "Now!" I shouted. "We have to save her."

He hesitated, while a chorus of protest arose from the passengers. "Please," I begged. "She's my sister. I have to save her."

At last he gave the signal to the seamen to start rowing. He stepped up on the prow of the boat, waving his lantern as we moved slowly through the black water. The faint sound of whistles echoed in the gathering mist. I looked down at the whistle attached to my life belt and realized the sound was coming from passengers floating in the sea. Maybe one of them was coming from Nora.

"Nora!" I cried out. "Nora!"

The crewman looked at me. "She won't last long in these waters, miss," he said.

A violent headache struck me, and I felt dizzy. Despite the cold, I felt as if I was burning up. "Please . . ." I begged again, "please."

"Blow your whistles," the crewman called into the distance, "so we can find you."

I held my breath as we rowed closer to the floating bodies. As we approached, the whistling stopped, replaced by anguished cries. *Dear God*, I thought, *some of them are still alive.* One poor soul managed to clutch the side of the boat with gnarled fingers. A seaman leaned over to haul him in as the women in the boat screamed and shrank away. One terrified woman tried to pry the grasping fingers loose. I watched in horror as the poor wretch finally lost his grip and slid back into the sea. The whistle sounds had faded now, as had the wall of sound. The boat I had imagined was Nora's had disappeared, and I knew in my heart she was gone.

The crewman made the sign of the cross and bowed his head.

"May God have mercy on their souls," he whispered.

After the *Titanic* sank, we sat for what seemed like eternity in the lifeboat, waiting for rescue. In an eerie way, the silence was almost as deafening as the wailing had been. No one moved. The crewmen assured us that another ship would arrive soon to pick us up. I wondered if they were reassuring themselves as much as us. We waited, huddled together to stay warm, the smell of fear surrounding us. I think few us believed such a ship would ever come. I remember looking up at the empty space where the *Titanic* had been and wondered if it had all been a dream. How could such a colossal vessel have completely disappeared? Had it been a ghost ship, like the ones I had read about in stories of long ago? As I remembered the ghostly tales I had grown up listening to beside Irish firesides, I closed my eyes and began to weep. I wished fervently that I was back in my warm bed in the cottage attic, surrounded by my books.

I drifted into a state somewhere between sleep and wakefulness. I prayed the eternity of waiting would end, if not by rescue, by death. It was then that sudden shouts startled me, and I looked up. In the distance I saw lights. Was it a mirage or the rescue ship the crew had promised? I prayed to God it was. As it came closer, I knew my prayers had been answered. I learned later that the ship, the *Carpathia*, had arrived within two hours of the *Titanic* sinking—at four in the morning. The horizon was tinged with a faint orange halo as dawn started to break over us. If we'd had the strength, I suppose we would have cheered, but, as it was, we sat mute and shivering.

I only vaguely remember how I arrived on the deck of the *Carpathia*. I had a burning sensation as I clung to the rungs of a rope ladder with a rope curled around my waist. I felt the rough pressure of the seaman's hands as he pushed me upward, and the sharp pain in my knees as I fell on the rough, splintered wooden deck. One thing I do remember clearly was my fight to hold on to my satchel, even though the seaman shouted at me to let it go. Instead, I cradled it to my chest, my arms tight around it. I was never so determined about anything before. The satchel contained all that was left of my and Nora's old life. Without it, I would always be a stranger—even to myself. I now believe that I would have risked drowning rather than let go of it.

I must have passed out after the rescue. When I awoke, I didn't know where I was, but I fought off the panic that threatened to engulf me. I looked down at myself and saw I was wrapped in a blanket. I looked from side to side and saw other passengers—some sleeping, some wailing, some stunned into silence—some huddled together, others lying in lines across the deck as if in a dormitory. A young seaman was passing among them offering mugs of hot tea. I took a mug, grasping it with shaking hands, and gulped down the hot, sweet liquid. It did little to calm my shivering limbs. In a sudden panic, I looked around for the satchel

I had clung to throughout the disaster. I couldn't lose it now. When I felt it beside me, I picked it up and stroked it like a child. Inside this bag was my identity, my proof of who I was and where I had come from. But it was not just the papers themselves that I treasured, it was the memories they held, the comfort of knowing I *had* a past.

By the second day, thanks to the constant rounds of hot tea and soup brought by the crew and passengers, and the wool blanket I was wrapped in, warmth began to seep back into my body, and I was able to stand up and walk about. The fog cleared from my brain and I was bombarded with images of Nora. What if I'd been wrong? What if she was on the ship somewhere? I began running around the deck, examining the face of every woman. Below deck, knocking on cabin doors, I shoved Nora's identity photo at them. "Please tell me if you've seen her," I begged. "Her name is Nora Sweeney." No one had.

A ship's officer came to me with a logbook. He was collecting the names of all rescued passengers, he said. I almost tore the logbook out of his hands.

"Have you my sister's name down?" I said. "Nora Sweeney?"

He scanned the pages and shook his head. "I'll come back when I've finished my search," he said gently. "I still have to check the state rooms, but it is most unlikely there are any survivors there."

When he returned, I could tell by his face that he had not found Nora. "There are over seven hundred names," he said, indicating the logbook. "I'm sorry, but her name is not here."

"Were there any other rescue ships?"

"We were the first ship on the scene. I understand the SS *Californian* arrived long after us; I doubt there were any survivors left to rescue by then."

Later, when I had no more tears to shed, I found a deserted corner of the deck and leaned over the railing, looking out to sea. A shadow covered the moon, as if in mourning. I thought back over my life growing up with Nora. We had never been close, and I had resented her much of the time, but there were also times when I realized she never set out to deliberately hurt me. Who could blame her for adopting Ma's attitude toward me? After all, she was Ma's favorite, and it was in her best interests to agree with her. I doubted now that she had even given me much thought. She was too busy enjoying herself. And then another memory came to me. I recalled the way Nora sometimes looked intently at Da, as if willing him to acknowledge her. I realized that if Ma had hurt me by her rejection, Nora had felt a similar rejection from Da. In that moment I let go of every jealous thought I had ever harbored toward my sister.

"Goodbye, Nora," I whispered. "May you rest in peace."

New York

1912

Delia

❧

On Thursday, April 18, when the *Carpathia* finally arrived at Pier 54 at the New York docks, it was nine in the evening and the rain lashed down in buckets. I could see very little in the dusk except for a large archway. As we sailed beneath it, I had the impression I was approaching the altar in the chapel in Kilcross. I shook my head to clear it. After we tied up at the dock, I waited with the other passengers for instructions. At last, first- and second-class passengers were instructed to disembark, but third class were told to stay behind. I backed away from the ship's railing just as an officer, the one who had carried the logbook, came up and took my arm.

"Tell them you're from second class," he said, "otherwise you'll be here all night. The immigration officers will want to question the third-class passengers more thoroughly than the rest."

"But my papers say . . ." I began, but he cut me off.

"Pretend you have no papers," he said, smiling. "Tell them they went down with the ship."

He gave me a slight shove, and I climbed unsteadily down the gangplank, clutching my satchel. We must have looked like a procession of ghosts.

At the customs checkpoint, an officer stopped me. "Name?"

"Delia Sweeney," I said, "from Kilcross, County Donegal." I waited nervously as he consulted the manifest, and then blurted out, "I sailed in second class, but I've lost my papers."

He looked at me for a moment and then whispered, "It's all right, love, go on ahead."

He knew I was lying. He would have seen from the manifest that I was traveling third class. I thanked God that he had taken pity on me.

Thousands of people were waiting on the dock for the *Carpathia* to arrive. As I stepped down from the gangplank, I felt my legs go weak, and I had to stop and steady myself. I made the sign of the cross and thanked God that I was back on solid land. As I moved on into the midst of the crowd, a wall of noise enveloped me—wailing, screaming, shouting. Those who could squeezed in together in an enclosed waiting area, sheltering from the rain. From the level of noise, I could tell there were as many or more people waiting outside, all desperate for news of their loved ones. Many carried signs bearing the names of passengers in big letters.

As I pushed my way through the throng, I was surrounded by people calling out to me. Had I seen this one or that one? Some of their faces shone with anticipation, while others had the desperate look of someone still hoping for a miracle. Newspapermen demanded I tell them everything I remembered, while other bystanders shoved papers in my face for me to sign as a souvenir. I pushed forward, trying to ignore them.

Outside, the rain poured down, soaking the black streets and creating halos around the lamplights. I was wearing a pair of flimsy shoes a *Carpathia* passenger had given me, along with a thin coat. Within minutes I was soaked to the skin. I tried to look around, but my vision was blurred. Besides the noise, I was assaulted by smells. I was used to the odor of fish back in Donegal, but here it was overpowering. The stench mixed with the aromas of strange foods cooking in steel carts. One cart was filled with roasting nuts, another with what looked like small, pale sausages. A vendor called out to me, "Peanuts, miss. Hot roasted peanuts!" The other pointed to the sausages. "Hot dogs!" he called. "Get your hot dogs here." Their accents were as foreign to me as were the smells that began to turn my stomach. By rights, I should have been hungry. I had managed only tea and broth on the *Carpathia*, but at the minute food was the farthest thing from my mind.

I had been told the housekeeper from the house where I was to work would meet me at the dock. She would have seen my name on the manifest and would be waiting for me. Nora was to have been met by Mr. O'Hanlon's housekeeper. I decided to look for *her* first. Even though she surely knew by now that Nora's name was not on the survivor list, she, like the other people here, might still be hoping the information was wrong. I knew by now it was not wrong and thought the kindest thing to do was to let her hear it from me.

I picked my way through the bustling crowd, paying close attention to the signs. As I neared the fringes of it, I saw a small, thin woman with a hard face holding up a sign bearing my name. I halted. My stomach tightened, and I swallowed hard. I peered at the sign again, hoping I had been mistaken, and then at the woman's disagreeable expression.

"Would you be Delia Sweeney?" she rasped.

I took an instant dislike to her. She conjured up images of Ma. I backed away. I wasn't ready for this yet.

"The third-class passengers are still on the boat," I said. I turned and hurried on, sick at the thought that I would have to return to her once I had located Mr. O'Hanlon's housekeeper.

The crowd was finally beginning to thin out, and I was just starting to turn back when I saw a large-bosomed woman, her shoulders slouched with fatigue. As she turned to walk away, I glimpsed the sign she carried, with Nora's name on it. I squared my shoulders and walked toward her, preparing to give her the sad news.

As I walked, time began to slow, and the sounds around me became muffled. I was oblivious to the rain pouring down my face and flooding my shoes. As I drew close, the woman turned back, and her eyes settled on me. I smiled at her. She smiled back and, dropping the sign, held out her arms. I walked straight into them and let her wrap me in her embrace. I looked up at her and opened my mouth to speak.

"I am Nora Sweeney."

I was so shocked at the words that came out of my mouth that I was almost paralyzed. I stood stiffly as the woman let go of me and clasped her hands together.

"'Tis a miracle," she said in a thick Irish brogue. "Wait 'til I tell Mr. O'Hanlon. 'Twas himself insisted I come here to meet the rescue ship even though ye were not listed as a survivor. He was sure the reports were wrong!" She paused and beamed down at me. "And look at ye," she said, "like a wee angel. God has blessed ye, saving ye from a watery grave. He must have great plans for ye, darlin', great plans indeed!"

She grabbed me by the hand and bustled off, pulling me behind her. "'Tis not far to Mr. O'Hanlon's house. And then we'll put ye to bed with a hot whiskey and ye can have a grand sleep and be right as rain in the morning."

She prattled on as she walked, clearly not expecting me to answer. It was just as well, because I could not have forced any words out of my mouth. It was as if I had been struck mute as soon as I told the lie.

A large black car was waiting for us. I'd never been in a car before and I peered at it in wonder before climbing in and sinking down in a soft leather seat.

"Where's her luggage, Mrs. Donahue?"

She looked at the driver, then at me. Then she slapped her forehead with a big hand. "Ah sure, of course, the child has no luggage. She would have lost everything when the boat sank to the bottom of the sea." She pointed at my battered and scarred satchel, "except for this wee bag," she said. "'Tis a miracle you managed to hold on to it. It must be very important."

She clambered in beside me, looking at me with a satisfied smile, and patted my hand. I closed my eyes, wanting desperately to hold on to this dream. For I believed it *was* a dream, and that I would wake up and find myself back in my cabin on the *Titanic* in no danger at all.

After a while I opened my eyes and looked out of the car window, hoping to get my first glimpse of New York. But I could see nothing but sheets of rain, blurred lamplights and hulking, dark shadows. I closed my eyes again.

When the car came to a stop, Mrs. Donahue tapped me on the arm.

'Wake up, Nora, love. We're here.'

I was about to say, "No, I'm Delia," but I caught myself in time.

When I climbed out, I was facing a tall, narrow house with a black front door set back from the street. The rain had eased by now, and in the lamplight I was able to make out three tall windows marching across the front of each story, and a wrought-iron balcony on the second floor. Lamps burned in the ground-floor windows, the way they often did in Donegal to welcome travelers.

Mrs. Donahue was all business now. "Mr. O'Hanlon is away at the minute, but he's expected back tomorrow."

She ushered me inside and up a short flight of stairs into a front room. At her bidding, I sat down in a big, plush armchair beside a blazing fire, balancing myself gingerly on the edge of the cushion. She rang a bell and a young woman wearing a black dress and a white apron appeared. She stared at me with open curiosity.

"Is this herself?" she said in an Irish brogue.

Mrs. Donahue waved impatiently at her and told her to bring two hot whiskies and a towel. When the girl came back with them, Mrs. Donahue handed me the towel and a whiskey and took the other for herself. She sat down and sighed.

"Such a day!" she said.

She held her glass up to me. "Sláinte," she said, "and welcome ye are, Nora Sweeney."

I gave her a faint smile and sipped the whiskey, letting her talk away, hardly hearing what she was saying. Despite being soaked from the rain, I was covered in sweat. I didn't know if it was from the blazing fire, or the whiskey, or fear. I looked around the enormous room. The armchairs and sofa were slightly faded, as was the thick, patterned carpet. On the walls, paintings of what looked like Irish landscapes were lit from above by small lamps casting them in a golden glow. The room offered comfort rather than stiff formality. And when my eyes lit on the far wall, where floor-to-ceiling bookcases held volumes and volumes of books, tears pricked my eyes, as if I had just met some long-lost friends.

Mrs. Donahue saw the tears and stood up. "Come on now, child. Let's see ye up to bed. Ye've had a terrible experience." She made a sign of the cross. "How ye lived through it, I'll never know. But ye are here now, safe and sound."

I allowed her to escort me up a curved staircase and into a small room at the front of the landing.

"I'll have Kathleen bring up a hot-water bottle to warm the bed, and find one of the mistress's nightgowns, God rest her soul. Tomorrow I'll have her go out and buy some clothes for ye. I think I can guess your size. You'll be needing underwear and dresses and boots, and a warm coat. 'Tis been chilly for April."

Later, after the maid had returned with a nightgown and placed the hot-water bottle between the sheets, I crawled gratefully under the covers. The feeling of being in a dream returned. I closed my eyes tight and fell into it. The dream was gentle at first, but then images began to collide with one another: sitting in a boat, freezing waves splashing over me; Nora's panicked face when she realized the ship was going to sink; the image of her body falling into the water. I awoke in a sweat. I lay awake until dawn, terrified the dream would return. But as light broke through the bedroom window, I could stay awake no longer and let sleep wash over me.

I had no idea where I was when I awoke. I lay trying to remember how I had arrived here. Images began to slowly follow one on another, forming pictures in my mind. I remembered getting off the ship, the smells at the docks and the crowds. Then I remembered the hard-faced woman who held up the sign with my name on it. I shivered. Had she brought me here? As if in answer, a shaft of sunlight pierced the window, sending dust mites dancing and lighting up the cozy bedroom. No, I thought, she couldn't have. This room was far too nice for a servant girl. Surely that housekeeper would never have let me sleep here. Then new images followed quickly on: Mrs. Donahue and the car, the tall, stately house and the hot whiskey by the fire. At last I realized where I was and remembered what I had done.

I began to panic. How could I have done such a thing? How could I have pretended to be my dead sister? I had meant to say I was Nora Sweeney's sister, but the rest of the words had stuck in my throat. What had come over me? And how could I have just walked on past the first woman, ignoring the sign she carried? My da had arranged for me to go and work there and I had thrown it back in his face. What would he ever say if he knew? I had hardly ever told a lie in my life. Father McGinty used to bang his fist on the pulpit and say lying was the worst of all the mortal sins. There was no forgiveness for lying, he said, you went straight to Hell. I believed him then, and I believed him now.

A knock came on the door, and the maid, Kathleen, came in with a cup of tea and some sort of a bun on a plate. She set down the tray beside the bed.

"W-what time is it?" I whispered.

"Ah, 'tis past twelve," she said, "but no bother. I'll be back with some clothes for you, and when you're ready, you can come downstairs."

I finished the tea but couldn't look at the bun. My stomach was roiling with nerves. Kathleen came back with an armful of clothes, set them on a chair beside the bed and left again. I climbed out of bed, took a quick wash and prepared to get dressed. I found underwear and stockings, but there was no sign of a uniform. Instead, there were three cotton dresses: one a plain, dark blue with a small white collar, another gray with a delicate floral pattern running through it and a bright yellow with a matching belt and hat. The last one must be for Mass, I thought. I pulled on the blue one, assuming it must be my uniform, although I found no apron to go over it.

I dressed quickly and shoved my feet into a pair of black, low-heeled leather shoes, which fit perfectly. When I was ready, I slipped out of the bedroom and hovered for a minute on the landing. Then, taking a deep breath, I started down the stairs.

The hallway was quiet. I stood looking around me. I realized I knew nothing about the layout of the house, except that the library was just off the hall upstairs from the front door. I knew that in any house I'd ever been in the kitchen was always at the back, so I walked in that direction, hoping Mrs. Donahue was there and I could unburden myself of the lie I was after telling. But there was no sign of the kitchen. I looked around in confusion. Then I heard the clattering of dishes and smelled the aroma of vegetable soup drifting up from downstairs. The only downstairs kitchens I'd ever heard about were in Irish manor houses. I swallowed hard and hurried down the stairs. Tentatively, I pushed open the door. Kathleen stood at the stove, stirring a big pot of soup.

"Hello, Kathleen. Thank you for the clothes. Is-is Mrs. Donahue about?" I said.

If Kathleen noticed my stutter, she did not let on. Instead, she shook her head. "Ah no, miss, she has the day off. She'll be back tomorrow."

My heart sank. I had been so anxious to speak to her.

"Sit down and I'll make you a cup of tea," she said.

I hesitated, then did as she said. When she put the tea in front of me, I looked up at her. "You don't have to be treating me special," I said. "I'm a servant like yourself."

Kathleen gave me a confused look. "But you're not a servant, miss. You're here as a governess for young Miss Lily, not a maid like myself." There was a sharp, almost resentful edge to her tone.

I ignored it.

"B-but you left me a uniform," I said, looking down at the blue dress. "And I expect I'm to sleep in the servants' quarters, aren't I?"

"No, Miss Nora, you're to have your own room. You're to stay where you slept last night. And that dress is not meant to be your uniform. Mrs. Donahue has everything all arranged according to Mr. O'Hanlon's orders."

Kathleen seemed impatient. I blushed, my discomfort growing. Nora should have been sitting here now, not me. As I sat lost in thought, I had the sudden sensation of being watched. I turned to look, just in time to catch sight of a small girl before she darted away. Kathleen must have seen her too. She went out into the hallway.

"Lily," she said, "come in now and meet your new governess. Come on now, love, she won't bite you."

After some more coaxing, Kathleen returned, holding the little girl by the hand. The girl hid as best she could behind Kathleen's back, but the maid gently forced her out in front of her.

I leaned over toward her and said as gently as I could, "Hello, Lily. It's grand to meet you. My name is Miss Nora."

The child stared up at me, her blue eyes wary, but said nothing.

"Poor wee mite," said Kathleen, "she hasn't said a word since her ma died. Her da doesn't know what to do with her. He's tried coaxing her and saying how much he misses their conversations. He's taken her to all sorts of doctors as well." Kathleen shrugged. "Nothing has worked."

As I looked at the child, my heart swelled with pity for her. She reminded me of myself when I was young. As a young girl, I only spoke when I was forced to; I was ashamed of my stutter. I believed no one would want to hear what I had to say anyway. Any utterance was met with silence from Da and a harsh rebuke from Ma. So, in sadness, I had hidden myself in my books and shut out the world. I sensed this child's sadness was as acute as mine.

"That's all right, Lily," I said gently. "You don't have to talk if you don't want to. I didn't talk much either when I was your age."

Lily's eyes grew wider, but her solemn expression did not change. I realized, looking at her, that she resembled me. She was of slight build and had the same fair hair. We could have been sisters—we certainly looked more alike than Nora and I ever did.

"We will have some good times together, Lily. And I'll do the talking for both of us. Tell me, do you read?"

The child gave an imperceptible nod.

I smiled. "Me too," I said. "I have read lots of books. And I've seen your da's big library. I can read stories to you every night."

Lily stared at me intently but made no move.

Kathleen took her by the hand. "Come on now, it's time for your lunch. Go and wash your hands."

The girl disappeared, giving one last glance at me over her shoulder.

"Poor wee mite," said Kathleen again as she began to ladle soup.

I refused Kathleen's offer of lunch, saying I wasn't hungry, although my earlier nausea was gone and I was starved. But I had a greater need at that moment to be alone. I left the kitchen and climbed the stairs up to my room. I could not get Lily's face out of my head. She had touched me in a way I would never have expected. I understood her as if I had known her all her life. And I hadn't even stuttered in front of her. In that moment I knew, without a doubt, that God had sent me here to help her. Lily needed me and, deep down, I realized, I needed her.

Later that evening, I went down to the library and over to the bookshelves that had so fascinated me the night before. I began to look for stories that might please Lily—adventure stories or classics—just like those I had enjoyed at her age. As I drew my fingertips across the leather-bound volumes, lost in memories, I heard a noise behind me. I swung around. A man I judged to be in his thirties stood staring at me. I swallowed hard. Surely this could not be Mr. O'Hanlon? The Mr. O'Hanlon I had pictured in my mind was much older, with a fat belly and a walking stick. This man was too young and far too handsome. He was tall and broad-shouldered, and his black hair curled around his collar, giving him a boyish look. I concluded he must be a visitor.

"E-excuse me," I said, "Mr. O'Hanlon is not here just now. Please sit down, sir. I'll fetch the maid."

I hurried toward the library door. Behind me, the visitor let out a hearty laugh.

"Well, this is the first time I've been greeted as a visitor in my own house! You have it all wrong, miss. I would say it's you who are the visitor."

I turned back to look at him. He stood grinning, his dark, blue eyes fixed on me, his hand held out expectantly. I was overcome with embarrassment and fought the urge to race from the room. How could I have made such a fool of myself? I stood rooted to the floor, clutching a book, ignoring his outstretched hand. He walked closer, still smiling. I lowered my head so he wouldn't catch me staring at his even, white teeth. I'd never seen the likes of them at home.

"Too embarrassed to speak, eh? A guilty conscience, perhaps? Maybe you are a book burglar I have caught red-handed. Maybe . . ."

Even though I knew he was teasing me, my heart lurched at the words "guilty conscience." "Ah no, sir," I interrupted him, the words gushing out of me. "I-I'm no burglar. I was just looking for books to read to Lily." I gave a small curtsy. "I'm the new governess you sent for. My name is Nora Sweeney."

His smile disappeared, and he let his hand drop to his side. He studied me in silence for what seemed like an eternity.

When he spoke again, his voice was gentle. "It is good to meet you, Miss Sweeney. I cannot imagine the horror you have been through. Even though you were listed as missing, I had the strongest feeling that you had somehow survived. You are very welcome to my home."

His grin returned. "Oh, and just so we are straight on matters, I am Aidan O'Hanlon, Lily's father, and your new employer."

I muttered a quick thank-you. I couldn't wait to get out of the room and flee upstairs. As if reading my mind, he took my hand in both of his and smiled. "You should rest for a few days, Miss Sweeney. Take some time to recover and get settled before you take up your duties. There is no rush."

His hand had sent such a shock through mine I pulled it away immediately and moved to return the book to the shelf.

"Please take the book with you. As many as you like. In fact, I'm pleased to see you have such an interest in reading. It will be good for Lily." He paused, and a cloud passed over his face. "I try to read to her when I can. But I am not often home in time."

I nodded and waited. He straightened up, all business again. "You may go now, Miss Sweeney. Good night."

Released, I almost ran from the room, but managed to control myself and walk slowly. Once I reached the stairs, though, I raced up two at a time and into the safety of my room. Panting, I sank down on the bed, still clutching the book in my arms. My thoughts collided with one another; I'd lied again about being Nora. The words had rolled so easily off my tongue, I would surely go to Hell. This was the first time in my life I'd ever felt a physical attraction to a man—but there again, Aidan O'Hanlon was the most beautiful man I'd ever seen. Ah, sure what did it matter what he looked like? I would never deserve such a man. It was several minutes before I calmed down.

I stood up and went to the window. Evening shadows had dropped like ghosts onto the wide avenue below, softening the sharp edges of the houses opposite. A sudden bout of homesickness assaulted me. I wished I could run out the door and up the fields to my favorite place among the smooth white stones. But they were far away now, and I might never see them again.

For the next few days, I tried to rest as Mr. O'Hanlon had suggested. The truth was that I was exhausted. But every time I tried to sleep, a melancholy would creep over me, so heavy it threatened to drown me. Alone in this strange, new place, I longed for the familiarity of home. I realized now how sheltered a life I had led in Donegal, and even though I had yearned for adventure, there was a big difference between dreaming of such things and being dropped abruptly into the middle of them. How was I to cope in a huge, noisy city where accents and habits were foreign to me? Things I had taken for granted all my life—the predictable routines of the days on the farm or at school, Mass on Sundays and Holy Days, even Ma's sharp rebukes whenever I displeased her—had anchored me in a way I had not realized. Now I felt adrift in the world, the ground beneath me as unstable as the deck of the *Titanic*.

At last I realized there was nothing for it but to grit my teeth and throw myself headlong into this new life. Besides, I already believed God had sent me here to help Lily. I began by spending as much time as I could with her. Each day she stood still while I helped her dress and combed her hair. She paid attention to her lessons, and in the evenings listened patiently while I read to her, all the time staring at me with her large, blue eyes but never saying a word. I talked away to her, ignoring her silence. One day she nodded when I suggested we take a little walk. It would not only be good for her, I thought, but also for me. And somehow, venturing outdoors seemed less daunting if I had her with me.

Mrs. Donahue had said the street was called an "avenue," which made it sound very grand. Lily and I walked along together. The street was wide and clean and quiet. A row of trees stretched along a grassy strip that ran down the middle of it and houses lined both sides. Most of them were far larger than the O'Hanlon house. Some were so imposing they took my breath away. They looked like the palaces I had seen in picture books. They were built mostly of brick or stone, with turrets and spires rising from the roofs, while ornate carvings, some of them ugly gargoyles, lined the balustrades. Many of the houses were surrounded by wrought-iron fences with big gates in front for carriages or cars to enter. I shivered. There was nothing welcoming about them; in fact, they reminded me of fortresses. I was glad Mr. O'Hanlon's house was nothing like them.

Now and then a motorcar or horse-drawn carriage moved leisurely along the roadway, breaking the serenity of the silence. Nannies in black dresses and white frilly aprons passed us pushing huge prams, and young women in modest costumes and hats towed children along by the hand. I guessed these were governesses. Most of them had stern expressions, and I noticed Lily staring up at them.

"Let's go back," I said to her. "It's almost time for lunch."

Without looking up, she slipped her hand into mine as we walked. My heart skipped with delight. Her small gesture meant more to me than if she'd suddenly uttered a thousand words.

On Sunday, Mrs. Donahue insisted I must take the day off.

"But what will I do?" I said, suddenly nervous.

She looked at me in confusion, then nodded her head.

"Ah, sure, I wasn't thinking, Nora. You're a stranger to the city. Ye have been no farther than the end of the street and back." She reached for her coat. "No matter. I'm on me way to Mass at St Patrick's. I'll be taking ye with me. Then I can show ye a few places, and next time ye can go by yourself."

Before I knew it, Mrs. Donahue was marching me down the avenue, her arm linked in mine, prattling away in the early May sunshine. I was too busy looking all around to reply to her. I stared at the people on the street: families with children dressed up as adults and jaunty young men in a hurry. There were gentlewomen in coats with fur collars on the arm of men with top hats and walking sticks. They nodded at us without smiles. They reminded me of the first-class passengers on the *Titanic*, and I brushed the memory away. It was bad enough I had constant nightmares about the sinking. I didn't want such memories ruining my days as well.

When we arrived at St Patrick's Cathedral, a crowd of people were rushing up the steps as the bells pealed. I stopped and stared up at the enormous, beautiful stone building with its stained-glass windows. I had never seen the likes of it. Mrs. Donahue smiled at me. "Lovely, isn't it?" she said.

We followed the crowd in, blessed ourselves with holy water and knelt in a pew near the back of the church. I didn't know where to look first. The main altar was covered in red carpet and gold candlesticks gleamed among vases of beautiful white flowers. There were side altars too, each one honoring a saint with a statue and flickering candles. The smell of flowers and candle wax and polished wood filled my senses, along with the sounds of feet clattering on the stone floor. I said a quick prayer and stood up just as a blast of organ music filled the building.

As the Mass progressed, I held back tears. Amid everything that was new and strange to me, the familiar rituals gave me comfort, but they also stirred loneliness inside me that was never far away. I thought of the small village church at home, where I knelt surrounded by our neighbors, and listened to Father McGinty. This American priest, however, spoke with little of the fiery passion Father McGinty summoned up every Sunday to scare the devil out of us.

Mrs. Donahue nudged me, and I started. She nodded toward the altar, and I realized it was time for communion. A row of priests stood at the foot of the altar, chalices in hand and communion hosts held aloft. As it happened, I'd had nothing to eat since midnight, as was the rule, and so without thinking I stepped out of the pew and joined the line of people moving toward the altar. It was a practice I had followed since I was seven years old, and as natural as my own breathing. I was halfway up to the altar when I froze. What was I doing? I was in a state of mortal sin and I had not been to confession. How could I take communion? Sweat began to pour down the back of my neck. My panic rose as I looked around me, and then at Mrs. Donahue.

"I-I don't feel well," I whispered. "I think I'm going to faint."

She looked at me in alarm. "Go on outside, love," she said, "and get some fresh air."

I nodded and pushed my way through the crowd to the huge front doors of the cathedral. Once outside, I stood on the top step, my breathing ragged. I had not lied to Mrs. Donahue; I literally felt sick.

I walked to a corner of the steps and sat down. In all the years I had put up with Ma's abuse, I had never felt so empty and so worthless. *It was only a small lie*, I told myself. *After all, it didn't hurt Nora; she was already dead. And I'm doing it for Lily.*

But a lie is still a lie! roared Father McGinty, his image crowding close to my face.

Part of me wanted to roar back at him, *It's all your fault. If the likes of you hadn't filled my head since I was a child with threats of the fires of Hell for even the smallest sin, I wouldn't be suffering the way I am now!* But my courage failed me. Guilt, once it's imprinted deeply on your soul, is almost impossible to get rid of. It becomes as much a part of you as your heart or your reason, and you realize if you let go of it, you will lose a part of yourself along with it.

Nora

When I woke up and opened my eyes, I had no notion of where I was. I stared around me at the walls and ceilings. The glaring lights above nearly blinded me. Where was I at all? An awful fear came over me. I had a faraway memory of floating in water. Was I still there? I patted my body with my hands. No, I was dry enough. Mother of God, had I drowned, and was this what Heaven was like? Well, if it was, it had hardly been worth giving up sin so that we'd be let into it.

A woman in a nurse's uniform peered down at me. She put her nose so close to my face, I thought she was going to kiss me. Suddenly, she pulled back, as if she'd seen a ghost. The next thing, she went racing out the door screaming like a banshee.

"Dr. Taylor!" she called, "Dr. Taylor, she's awake! It's a miracle!"

I wondered, was she astray in the head?

I began to think I must be in a hospital. Nurses and doctors, walls the color of piss and bright, bare light bulbs—surely that was where I was. I sniffed. The smell of disinfectant nearly choked me. How had I landed here? I sat halfway up in bed and glanced down at myself in horror. I was half naked under a sheet. Where were my clothes? And my shoes? I had a sudden notion I might be in prison. But what had I done? My head began to throb, and I lay back down and closed my eyes.

"Can you hear me, miss?"

A man's voice roused me, although he was almost whispering.

I opened my eyes and looked at him. He was an older man with silver hair and wore a white coat. He smiled down at me.

"Just nod your head if you can hear me."

"Why are you talking to me as if I'm a fecking eejit?"

He stared at me. Then he began to laugh—a hearty, full-throated guffaw. I decided he must be the eejit, not me.

He looked over at the nurse, who stood on the other side of the bed. "Yes, I'd say she's definitely awake, Nurse Mason."

He turned serious as he took my hand. "Can you remember your name?"

I decided they were both eejits—himself *and* the nurse. I sighed and rolled my eyes. Of course I knew my name! I opened my mouth to tell him what it was, but stopped. Why could I not remember something as simple as that? In panic, I wracked my brain, but no answer came.

Dr. Taylor glanced over at the nurse, nodding his head. He turned back to me. "It's all right," he said gently. "You've been unconscious for a while, and you've suffered a terrible trauma. Your memory will come back in time."

The doctor took my hand in his. "Do you remember how you got here?" His voice was soft and patient. "Take your time, now."

My head began to throb. All the annoyance slipped away from me. I tried to squeeze a memory out of my brain, but it wouldn't come. Tears of frustration stung my eyes. I looked up at Dr. Taylor, all my earlier confidence gone.

"I-I remember being in the water," I said. " 'Twas freezing. People were crying. But it might have all been a dream."

A spike of fear cut through my body. Why couldn't I remember? Had I lost my mind? Oh, sweet Jesus, had something awful happened to me? Had my mind been destroyed entirely? I stared up at the doctor, pleading in silence for him to tell me everything was all right. He squeezed my hand gently.

"Rest now," he said. "The mind has a way of hiding bad memories away until you're ready to cope with them." He smiled, suddenly cheerful.

"The fact that you've woken up at all is a miracle. You've been unconscious ever since you arrived here, probably caused by the nasty blow on your head. You were also suffering from hypothermia. Don't worry about anything else just now. Just sleep."

After he left I lay thinking. The room was darkened, and I could see the nurse sitting in the shadows in the corner. Dr. Taylor had told me not to worry. But how could I not? I knew that what had happened had something to do with water—water had been filling my dreams. But what? And how had I arrived at this place? How long had I been here? How long had I been asleep? And who was I at all?

The questions swirled in my head. But no answers came. Would the answers ever come? My eyelids felt heavy, and a drowsy feeling came over me. There was not a sound to be heard except for Nurse Mason's quiet breathing. I wondered had she fallen asleep, and I envied her. I fought back the sleep that was claiming me. How could I sleep with so many questions still to be answered, and so many worries to be eased?

The image of a woman's face appeared in front of me. She knelt, crying, beside an empty bed, lit candles placed all around it. "Don't cry," I called out to her. "Don't be worrying your head about me. I'm still here. I didn't die."

Over the next week I began to get my strength back. Nurse Mason had me walking down the corridor and back several times a day. In the beginning I felt an awful weakness in my legs, and a dizziness would come over me. I'd limp back to bed, leaning on the nurse. But in time I was able to walk without her help. My new-found freedom, such as it was, raised my spirits. Surely everything would be sorted out soon.

I expected the answers would flow easily out of my memory. But I was wrong. The answers came one day from an older, well-dressed woman who came into my room and sat down beside my bed.

"Ah, there you are. Thank God for His miracle."

I stared at her. She was very tall—tall as a man. Even sitting down, she towered over me. Her hair was bright red, a color far too young for her age. Her eyes were clear blue and seemed to look straight through me. Her stare made me jittery.

"Who are *you?*" I blurted out.

She paid my question no heed. If I hadn't known better, I'd have thought she was smiling at me.

"My name is Felicity Barrett Shaw," she said, her accent an odd mixture of Irish brogue, marble-mouthed English toff and drawling American.

I stared at her. She patted my hand, and I noticed her long, slender fingers and a ring with a diamond the size of my fist. My mouth fell open.

"It's perfectly all right," she said. "I wouldn't expect you to remember me."

I swallowed hard. "What is my name?" I whispered.

"Oh, you poor dear. You must be so confused. Dr. Taylor told me you have no memory of who you are or what happened to you." She paused and took a deep breath. "None of us knows your name."

She must have seen the eyes popping out of my head, for she stopped talking for a minute. Then she went on. "I know this must all be such a shock to you, my dear, but you may as well hear the whole story now. No sense dragging things out, I always say."

I waited, holding my breath.

"Your name is undoubtedly on the list of the missing, but there are almost fifteen hundred names on it, and you could be any one of them."

"Missing?" I said. What in the name of God was this woman on about?

She seemed confused. "Missing as in drowned. The *Titanic!*" Her hand flew to her mouth. "Oh, what's wrong with me? You don't remember a thing about it, do you? The *Titanic* was a new ship that sailed from Southampton to Queenstown and then on to New York four weeks ago. It was said to be the greatest ship ever built." She paused and sighed. "There I go again, slipping away from the main subject. You were one of over two thousand passengers and crew. The night before it was due to arrive in New York, it was hit by an iceberg and sank. Some seven hundred souls were saved, but the rest drowned."

Mrs. Shaw took my hand in hers. "You were one of the lucky ones, my dear. A sailor carried you onboard the rescue ship, the *Carpathia*. Apparently, you had fallen out of the lifeboat, hitting your head on the way. You were in the water for some time, but eventually two seamen managed to pull you back into the boat. I was a passenger on the *Carpathia*, and when I first saw you, I thought you were dead. Then I looked closely at your face and realized you were still breathing. I ordered the sailor to bring you to my stateroom. A ship's officer came to my cabin, checking for survivors. I told him there was no identification on you. He marked you down as an unidentified survivor, and most likely because your name, whatever it is, was on the manifest, it is now on the list of the missing. I watched over you until we arrived in New York, and then I arranged for you to be brought here. Dr. Taylor is an old friend of mine. As soon as you are well enough, I intend to bring you home with me so that you can convalesce."

I let out a whimper. Nurse Mason, who I hadn't noticed in the room, came over to the bed. "I think that's enough for now, Mrs. Shaw," she said, her tone making clear she would stand for no argument. "This girl has been through a great deal. I don't think it's advisable to relate all these details in one fell swoop. Perhaps you can return later in the week?"

Mrs. Shaw nodded and stood up. "You are quite right, of course, Nurse Mason. I don't know what I was thinking. I shall give her a few days to absorb what I have told her." She turned to me and patted my arm. "Goodbye, my dear. I can't wait to take you home."

When she had gone, I lay back down on the pillow and closed my eyes. I felt sick. I wondered if I had dreamed the whole thing. My imagination had been running wild ever since I'd woken up, and so had my dreams. I wasn't sure what was real and what was not. Bits and pieces of her story flitted about in my mind. Who was that woman, and why did she want to take me home? Where *was* home? The only thing I believed was the story about the ship—the *Titanic*. It made sense of all the dreams I'd been having about drowning. But I hadn't drowned. I was here, lying in this bed in a hospital. Or was this just a dream too?

The thoughts exhausted me, and I longed for sleep. As I drifted off, the image of the crying woman kneeling beside the empty bed came back to me. She looked familiar, but I couldn't place her. I began to weep quietly. *What's happening to me?* I thought. *What have I done to deserve this?*

A week later, I was sitting in a red, open motorcar tearing along like the hammers of Hell away from New York City. The scenery rolled by faster than I could take it in. I didn't know how fast we were going, but it scared the wits out of me. At the wheel was Mrs. Shaw, a scarf tied around her brilliant red hair. I was grateful that the roar of the wind whistling by prevented any conversation. I had a thousand questions, but I wasn't sure I wanted to know the answers. Instead, I decided to let things stand for a while.

Every now and then, she would look over and smile at me and pat my arm. I smiled back and then looked away, as much to force her to keep her eyes on the road as anything else. She was driving like a bloody eejit. The car seemed to be flying half the time as it bounced over the rough surface of the roads. I'd never been in a car before that I knew of, and my knuckles were white from gripping the leather seat.

Eventually, we came to a small village and, mercifully, she slowed down. With its narrow streets and tidy shop windows, the village looked vaguely familiar, and my heart leaped at the thought I might be remembering something. But no memory came. Herself blew the car horn and waved to the shopkeepers out brushing the pavement and shoppers carrying loaded baskets.

"She's home," she yelled to whoever would listen, "the dear girl is home."

They nodded and smiled in reply. I slid as far as I could down in the seat, my cheeks burning. This woman, whoever she was, was astray in the head. No normal person acted like that.

We left the village behind us and she sped up again. I was beginning to feel sick. *Wherever we're going*, I prayed, *may we get there soon before she bloody kills both of us.* Just then, the car screeched as she swerved left onto a narrow lane. I closed my eyes as I was thrown forward and held on for dear life. Jesus, I was at the mercy of a madwoman.

Eventually, the car shuddered to a stop. I was afraid to open my eyes.

"Come on, dear," Mrs. Shaw said cheerfully, "come and see your new home."

Slowly, I opened my eyes. In front of me was a massive, three-story house made of red brick and covered with ivy. I sat looking up at it, unable to move.

"Do you like it?" Mrs. Shaw said as she climbed out of the car and adjusted her scarf. "My dear late husband had it built for me. It is identical to the house where I grew up in County Longford. He thought it would cure my homesickness, and it did." She looked down at me. "And when your memory returns, I hope it will do the same for you, because I can tell by your brogue that Ireland is where you grew up as well." She stretched out her hand. "Come along now, dear."

My legs trembled like jelly as I climbed out, and I put my hand on the car to steady myself. I thought I might faint. I must have turned pale because Mrs. Shaw put her arms around me. "Sit back down in the car, dear. I will have Beatrice bring you some water."

She disappeared into the house and I leaned back against the car seat, breathing heavily. A few minutes later, I squinted at a figure coming toward me. It was a woman carrying a tray with a glass of water with lemon in it. As she came closer, I saw she was wearing a black dress with a white apron and was flashing a big smile. I sat upright. I thought I must be seeing a ghost. The woman's skin was black as tar. I was sure I'd never seen the likes of it. If I had, it was buried with all my other memories. My mouth fell wide open and I gaped at her like an eejit. If she realized I was in shock, she never let on. She just kept smiling that big smile.

"Here you are, miss," she said, handing me the glass of water. "You like some more lemon?"

I shook my head no, unable to speak.

"Cat got your tongue, child?" she said, laughing. "Ain't no need to be afraid of old Miss Beatrice. I ain't never done nobody no harm." She slid the tray under her arm, all the while peering into my face. "I 'spect you never saw the likes of me where you come from, did you?"

Again, I shook my head no.

"Mrs. Shaw, she was the same way when she first laid eyes on me. Young bride she was, just over from Ireland, and when she caught sight of me, she let out a cry would scare the haints out of their graves. She tried to run away 'til Mr. Shaw grabbed hold of her. He was laughing up a storm. Been here forty years now, and she ain't never tried to run since."

I finished the water and handed her the empty glass. She waited while I got out of the car. My cheeks burned with shame. "I'm sorry," I said, "I just have never . . ."

She linked her free arm through mine as we walked toward the house. "Don't you worry none about it, child. You and me, we's gonna be the best of friends. Mm-hmm, yes we are."

The next morning, I was awakened by a girl drawing the curtains back on the windows. A bright shaft of sun shot over me and I squinted.

"What the feck are you doing?" I shouted. "Could you not see I was sleeping?"

"Aye, well, that's the point. I was sent to wake ye up, ye lazy lump."

I couldn't believe my ears. I opened my eyes wide and glared at her.

"You've no right to speak to me that way," I said. "Draw them back again and leave me alone."

"No hope of that. Breakfast is waiting for you downstairs, and Mrs. Shaw is like a spitting divil when people are late."

I recognized the Irish brogue at once. "You're from Ireland?"

"Well, I suppose it takes one to know one. I'd have said your accent is from Donegal. As for myself, I'm from Kerry, although here's me thinking that after two years in America I sound like a real Yank."

Donegal, I thought. *Is that where I'm from?* It was the first glimpse I'd had into my past, but the place meant nothing to me.

The girl turned away and pointed to a wardrobe. "There're clothes in there for you," she said, her tone still sharp. "Mrs. Shaw's after ordering them. She guessed your size. Must be well for ye to have all this finery bought for ye. I don't know who ye are, but don't go thinking you're better than the rest of us. Hurry up now, or she'll skin both of us. She has an awful temper when she's roused."

After she'd gone, I lay in bed for a few minutes. Why should I be taking orders from the likes of her? And why had she taken such a dislike to me? What harm had I ever done her? Despair threatened to take hold of me, but I brushed it away. My curiosity about what was in the wardrobe got the better of me, and I got up and pulled open the door. Inside were hangers full of dresses of all colors. Rows of shoes were lined up on the bottom shelf and, on the top shelf, a half dozen hats. I gasped. Whether I'd seen such finery before, I didn't know, but, regardless, I was delighted at the sight of it all.

My delight faded when I reached for one of the dresses and

held it up to inspect it. Sure, I'd never fit into the likes of that. I was a large girl, with curvy hips and a big bosom. I took off the nightgown that had been laid on the bed the night before and looked at myself in the wardrobe mirror. I let out a cry of surprise. I was thin as a rail. I slumped down on the bed and put my head in my hands. What was happening to me at all? Why had I thought I was supposed to be big? Had I lost the weight in the hospital, or was this the body I had all along? If I'd been this way in the hospital, why hadn't I noticed? I supposed I'd been so preoccupied with other things, I hadn't bothered to look at myself under the hospital shift.

A sharp knock on the door from the maid roused me into action. I pulled on a bright-red dress and matching low-heeled shoes, arranged my hair as best I could and rushed down the stairs.

After breakfast, Mrs. Shaw suggested to the maid, whose name was Teresa, that she show me around the house and grounds. I glared at Teresa behind Mrs. Shaw's back, and she glared back at me.

"I have to go into the village today. But you will be in good hands with Teresa."

Little do you *know*, I thought.

"Are you taking the car again?" I blurted out, afraid that she might do herself or someone else harm.

She laughed. "No, as a matter of fact I'm taking my horse. He hasn't had much exercise since I've been going in and out of the city to visit you. I will see you for supper."

With that, she strode out of the room. I watched her, open-mouthed.

"You'll get used to Mrs. Shaw's ways soon enough," laughed Beatrice. "You sure ain't ever seen the likes of her at home. Hmmm. No, ma'am."

The word "home" sent a cold chill through me. Where *was* my home? I was satisfied it was Ireland because I had an Irish brogue, but whereabouts? The Teresa one had said I was from Donegal. What was the truth?

For the rest of the day I distracted myself exploring the house and grounds. Teresa, a sour look on her face, took me to every room on every floor of the house, including the rooms on the third floor, where she and Beatrice slept. Those rooms were tiny and made me feel a bit suffocated. I wondered how they could stand them. But the other bedrooms, including the one I slept in, were big and bright and airy, with lovely, oak-carved furniture, velvet curtains and patterned rugs. I tried not to open my mouth too much or stare, but inside I was trembling. This place was like a palace. Was it possible I grew up like this? If I had, it was hard for me to believe it.

The house began to bear down on me like a heavy blanket, and I was glad when we went outside. It was a lovely day, with a light breeze and not too warm. Teresa didn't say much, but when she did, I paid more heed to her brogue than to her words. For some reason, I took great comfort in listening to her Irish accent.

I had seen the tall trees on either side of the lane when we drove in the day before, but I had not been ready for the view at the back of the house. I followed Teresa around the corner, and my heart leaped out of my chest. A great expanse of smooth, green lawn gave way to woods and, on the far horizon, to hills covered in a lilac haze. Daffodils and peonies and white snapdragons dotted the pathways that crisscrossed the lawn. I had seen these flowers before somewhere, and I knew their names. A small thrill of joy lightened my step.

Teresa pointed her finger into the distance.

"Over there's a lovely garden," she said, "like the ones you'd see at home. There's flowering bushes and benches and a swing. It's nice and quiet and a grand place to get away to and think."

A sudden image of a fair-haired girl sitting on the grass reading a book came into my mind. She was surrounded by a circle of white stones. She was lost in the book, as if nothing else around her mattered. I knew this girl, I was certain. But why couldn't I remember her name?

When we got back to the house, Beatrice said Mrs. Shaw hadn't returned yet. I took the chance to complain of a headache.

"I think I need to go and lie down," I said. "Would that be all right? Will Mrs. Shaw mind?"

Beatrice gave me a huge smile. She came over and put her arms around me. "You just get some sleep. Poor child, you done been through so much trouble already. You bound to be tired. I'll leave a tray of food outside your door later in case you hungry. Go on, now."

Gratefully, I pulled away from Beatrice and dragged myself up the stairs. I lay down to think. But I was too tired even to do that. I floated straight into my dreams.

After that first day, I slowly began to get my bearings. Mrs. Shaw was like a madwoman, rushing in and out of the house, giving out orders to Beatrice and Teresa. It wasn't so much that she was bossy, more that she was keen to get on about her business. She moved as if the divil was right behind her. I supposed it explained why she was so firm about everybody being to meals on time. One day I risked asking Teresa what business it was that took herself away all the time. Where was she going at all?

For once, Teresa laughed. "Ah, sure, you'd be hard-pressed to keep up with that one. She has a finger in everything—charity work, rescuing animals, not to mention the women's movement—'suffragettes,' they're called."

"What in the name of God are *they?*"

"They want the right to vote."

I shrugged. "What's so important about *that?*"

"You should ask herself. You'll get a lecture and a half."

I made up my mind to stay away from *that* subject altogether. Besides, I could never have pronounced the word.

Teresa turned to go but paused and looked back at me, a sly

expression on her face. "And taking in strays like yourself is another one of her hobbies."

I was dumbfounded. What did she mean, "strays"?

Teresa went on her way and I stared after her. Her words had struck me like a blow to my stomach. I almost bent over from the force of them. Stray? Wasn't that the word you used for lost dogs? Is that how Mrs. Shaw saw me—a lost dog?

I went up to my bedroom and lay down. I forced away tears with balled fists. At first, I was angry—how dare Mrs. Shaw think that way, and after all her palaver about wanting to take care of me until I got my memory back. I had a good mind to get up right now and leave. I heaved a sigh. But where was I to go? I had no money and no way of getting away from this godforsaken place by myself. No matter; I would wait for her to come home and demand she drive me back to New York City so I could sail for Ireland. The fact that I had no money for a ticket never occurred to me. And even though I had no idea where in Ireland I belonged, and even though the thought of going back on a ship terrified the life out of me, it was better than staying here, so it was.

Just before dinnertime that night, I heard the roar of the car coming up the driveway, and I stood up, smoothed out my dress and put on my shoes. My anger was still boiling when I went down the stairs and waited for her in the hall. She blew in, as always, like a gale-force wind, the front door slamming behind her. She stopped in her tracks when she saw me.

"Why, hello, my dear girl. Did you have a good day?"

She took my arm and started leading me toward the dining room. I supposed she couldn't see the anger on my face in the shadows. I shook her hand off my arm, turned around and lifted my face up to hers. She stared down at me.

"How dare you?" I shouted. "How dare you treat me like a stray animal? If that's how you think of me, you may take me back to New York this minute and I'll make me own way from there. And no worries, I'm sure you'll have no trouble finding another stray to take my place!"

The words took all the breath out of me and I stood there, trembling. I could have sworn she smiled at me. My anger exploded.

"How dare you laugh at me, you cruel oul' bitch!"

She grabbed both my arms in a strong grip so that I couldn't pull away from her.

"My dear girl, I am not laughing at you. I just find your outburst so preposterous. Who on earth put that idea in your head? Certainly, I take care of stray animals and those I cannot keep I take to a shelter. But never in a million years would I put you in that category. Where on earth did you get this notion?"

My lips curled up like a child ready to cry.

"Teresa's after telling me. She said one of your hobbies is taking in strays like myself."

She made a tutting sound and sighed.

"An unfortunate choice of words by Miss Teresa. She should know better because she was one of my so-called 'strays' herself. I will speak to her about it. But I know she did not mean it the way you took it. It is true that in the past I have taken young women, just like you, under my protection until they were strong enough to go back out into the world. It's part of my philosophy that women should help one another, that's all. I brought you here because we had no way of finding your family and you would have been all alone." She paused and smiled at me. "And something about you reminded me of myself at the same age." She straightened up, all business again. "When your memory returns, we shall sit down and decide what is best for you." She reached over and stroked my hair.

"I'm so sorry you misunderstood my motives," she said, her voice gentle. "I hope you will give me a chance to prove to you that I care about your welfare."

What was I to say to that? I still wasn't sure I believed her.

Words were cheap. I realized, though, that I had few choices but to stay. I nodded my head and pulled away from her.

"Good," she said. "Now, let's go in for dinner."

The stubborn child still ruled me. "I'm not hungry," I said, although I was famished. "I'll be away upstairs to bed."

She nodded. "As you wish, dear. A long sleep will do you good. Good night."

She moved on down the hall, and I stood at the foot of the stairs, watching her. Should I believe her? I wanted to, but I still had my doubts. If only my memory would come back to me, I could be free of all this nonsense. In the meantime, I had no choice but to wait.

"I swear to God that one doesn't know her arse from her elbow. The way she slurps down her tea and licks her knife are disgusting. I can't imagine the circumstances she was brought up in, but it wasn't a palace, I can tell ye that!"

I was passing by the kitchen when I heard Teresa's voice. She was talking to Beatrice, who seemed to be paying her no heed. Teresa's attitude toward me had worsened ever since she called me a stray. Now she was like a divil. I didn't know if it was because Mrs. Shaw had chastised her for what she'd said, or because I'd found out she'd been a "stray" herself, but something had happened for her to make her dislike me even more than before.

"And have ye heard the mouth on her? The vulgar language she comes out with. She belongs with the sailors beyond on the docks."

I tried to hide in a corner when Teresa came out of the kitchen, but it was too late.

"I should have known listening in at doors was not below you. Well, you know the old saying, 'eavesdroppers rarely hear well of themselves.'" She looked shamefaced all the same.

With that, she turned and strutted down the hall. I wanted to run after her and shake her bony shoulders. How dare she talk about me like that? But a small voice told me that what she said was right—my manners *were* awful compared to Mrs. Shaw's—although she'd exaggerated, particularly about me licking the knife. 'Twas true, though, that I had an awful mouth on me. I stuffed down the urge to hammer the living daylights out of her.

Instead, I walked out into the garden at the back of the house. It had become my favorite place to go in the long afternoons. I would sit on the swing and listen to the birds. One of the house cats had taken a liking to me and came most days to keep me company. I christened her Silver on account of the silver streak that ran through the fur on her head and down her back. She gave me comfort as she purred peacefully beside me. I supposed my time would have been better spent reading books, but I had no interest in them. Whenever I thought about books, though, the same image I'd had before of a fair-haired girl sitting on a white rock in a green field with her nose in a book came back to me. Again, I wondered who she was.

Teresa's words had slit through me like a knife. I had no notion my manners were *so* bad. And I didn't know where my swearing came from. It just seemed as natural as day for me to talk like that. It made me wonder about loss of memory. "Amnesia" they'd called it in the hospital. Why could I remember so many things—like the names of flowers and animals, or know what a car looked like—but not remember me own name? It struck me then that even so, my personality had not changed. I realized I was quick to anger and jealousy. I loved parading in front of the mirror wearing the nice clothes Mrs. Shaw had bought for me. Whoever I was, I'd had a bob on myself, that was clear.

A new thought came to me. I realized that if my memory never came back—or even if it did—I could make up my own story, maybe one where I would pass myself off as a lady. If so, I'd have to start with my manners. I decided that I'd watch and learn. I shot to my feet, causing Silver to jump off the bench with a loud meow, and made my way back toward the house.

From then on, Teresa and I kept our distance from each other. She passed no more remarks about me—at least none that I could hear. Calling me a stray still stung, no matter how Mrs. Shaw had tried to explain it away. But I tried hard to put it out of my head.

Instead, I put my mind to improving my manners. At meal-times I watched Mrs. Shaw like a hawk, copying how she held her teacup, what knife or fork she used for meat or for fish, and how she dabbed her mouth with a cloth called a serviette. She always swallowed her food down before she spoke and took wee sips of wine rather than great gulps. I copied how to pour various sauces onto the food, learned that the green stuff wiggling in a bowl was mint jelly for the lamb and the red stuff was cranberry dressing for turkey. Changing my brogue was harder—my words came out faster than I could catch them, but I was able to tame my bad language most of the time—except the times when my temper got the better of me.

I had a lot to learn and it was going to take a while, but I was convinced it would stand me well in the future.

Delia

❧

After my outing to Mass with Mrs. Donahue, I forced myself to venture farther away from the house. Sometimes I took Lily, other times I wandered by myself. One day I returned alone to St. Patrick's Cathedral. On this midweek afternoon, when the Sunday crowds were long gone, it was quiet and comforting. I sat in a rear pew, staring up at the main altar, letting my thoughts roam. The noises from outside—the deafening roar of motorcars, the rattle of horse-drawn carriages and the clamor of voices— faded away, leaving me wrapped in a peaceful cocoon. In the silence, my other senses were heightened. I smelled candle wax mingled with faint, sweet incense. I noticed people dotted about the pews, most of them alone, heads down, hands clasped, and I wondered what stories they had to tell. I became mesmerized by the flickering candles. I felt small in the cavernous space and my concerns shrank to insignificance.

I had intended to arrange for a "Month's Mind" Mass for Nora. Back in Ireland, relatives arranged for a Mass to be said for a loved one who had been dead a month. I stood up, preparing to go and find one of the priests, when a noise startled me. A priest in a black cassock was entering the confessional. The tall, wooden door shut with a click and an inner window slid open. I watched a handful of people go one by one into the confessional, then exit making the sign of the cross. I remembered the first Sunday I had come to Mass and panicked at the thought of taking communion. I knew I needed to confess my sin and seek for-giveness. As the waiting line dwindled to nothing, I steeled my-self and rose from the pew.

The door on the priest's side of the confessional opened just as I was entering the other door, and the priest stepped out. For a split second we locked eyes, then panic rose inside me and I turned to hurry away. He touched my arm gently to restrain me.

"Forgive me, miss," he said. "I thought the last of the peni-tents had gone. Please," he gestured toward the confessional, "please step in."

I was trembling as I lowered myself on to the hard, splintered kneeler. After some rustling, the window separating us slid back to reveal his shadow outlined behind a latticed, wooden rectan-gle. He could no longer see me, nor I him. *But he has seen me*, I thought. *He's not supposed to have seen me. He's not supposed to know who I am.* Reason told me it didn't matter—I was a stranger to him. But the thought did little to ease my panic.

He made the sign of the cross: "In the name of the Father, and of the Son, and of the Holy Ghost. Amen." The familiar ritual calmed me a little, but still I couldn't force any words out of me.

"Have you come to make your confession, my child?" he said gently. For a minute, something inexplicable made me smile. After all, by the look of him, he was no older than I was. I chased the errant thought away.

"Yes," I murmured. Then the ritual words I had recited since childhood took over. "Bless me, Father, for I have sinned. It has been several months since my last confession."

I waited for his response, but there was none. I had a sudden memory of my childhood confessions, when I could not remem-ber any specific transgressions, so I would make up sins just to satisfy the priest. They were always the same: I disobeyed my parents, I was uncharitable, I was lazy. I kept them vague on pur-pose, so the priest wouldn't give out to me or pronounce a heavy penance. But I was no longer a child, and I totally understood the sin I had committed.

"I have committed a mortal sin, Father."

I waited, but the priest was silent.

I took a deep breath then, and let it all out, beginning with the night the *Titanic* sank and up to the present day. When I had finished, I was drained. I waited for the rush of outrage that certainly would have come from Father McGinty. Instead, the priest's voice was gentle, his words kind.

"My child, in the circumstances you describe, this lie is one that God will understand."

"But it's still a mortal sin, Father," I protested.

I thought I detected the hint of a smile in his voice. "Yes, lying can be a mortal sin, but such definition is based on circumstances, including intention and whether or not someone was harmed by it. In your case, your intention was not immoral; you were simply seeking a way to survive, and your poor sister was already dead, so you could not have harmed her by your actions."

"But I told the same lie many times over! And each time it was an occasion of sin."

He sighed. "You have been well-schooled in sin. I see it in many immigrant girls like yourself. But you must stop believing that every move you make or every thought you have is a sin that will lead you to burn in Hell. God is not wrathful. He is compassionate and loving." He paused and cleared his throat. "I'm sorry that you have had to carry this burden for all this time—particularly given the pain and loss you have already suffered."

Tears stung my eyes as a wave of self-pity washed over me. Perhaps I had punished myself far too harshly. I wanted to believe this young priest's words

"For your penance say an Act of Contrition, and a decade of the rosary for each time you told this lie."

"Yes, Father."

"I absolve you from your sins in the name of the Father and of the Son and of the Holy Ghost. Amen. Go in peace, my child, and sin no more."

The window between us slammed shut. I waited until he had

left before I opened the door, stepped into the aisle and genu-
flected before the altar.

After confession, I found another priest and paid him to say
Nora's Mass. Back out in the May sunshine, I felt light and
cleansed for the first time since arriving in New York. A great
weight had been lifted from me. My guilt, if not entirely erased,
had been folded away like an out-of-style garment that had
served its purpose but was not quite ready to be thrown out.

After that day, my mood grew lighter, and I was suddenly
eager to explore more of New York; I wanted to swallow the city
whole. On my days off, I ventured farther and farther away from
the O'Hanlon house on swanky Fifth Avenue and into the areas
where the Chinese lived, and the Italians, and the Jews. I inhaled
the aroma of exotic foods and spices. I marveled at the black and
brown people I saw, some in foreign dress and speaking lan-
guages I had never heard. I thought about my village back in Ireland and realized, for the first time, that everyone there looked
alike. Not so here. At times I must have stared too much because
every now and then a stranger would wave a threatening hand at
me, and more than one spat at me. Still, my delight in such new
and heady moments knew no bounds.

But one day, when I wandered to the area known as Hell's
Kitchen, where many Irish immigrants lived, I no longer marveled. Instead, my heart sank at the sight of ragged children and
scarred, sooty buildings crammed together row after row. Children in tattered clothes ran after me, chanting insults while their
mothers looked on with faces of stone.

Where were the streets paved with gold that the Irish sang
about? The people in these tenements, as I learned they were
called, were under no such illusions. What a disappointment
America must have been for them after a long, arduous sea journey filled with hope.

That evening, Aidan O'Hanlon came into Lily's bedroom
where I sat reading to her. He stood for a moment watching us, a
faint smile on his face. Lily looked up from the book and put her

arms out to greet him. I got up from the bed, allowing him to sit in my place, and made for the door.

"I thought this was your day off, Miss Sweeney," he said.

I did my best to hide my nerves at finding Aidan O'Hanlon in such an intimate place. But my stutter betrayed me. "Y-yes, but I still like to read to Lily at bedtime, especially when y-you're not home."

He lowered his head. "And I am not often home. But tonight, I decided to escape from a business meeting early." He looked at Lily. "I miss you, Lily, when I'm not here."

Lily cuddled up to him.

"Perhaps it's impertinent of me to ask, Miss Sweeney, but I'm curious as to what you do on your days off. You don't have to tell me, of course."

His question prevented my quick escape, and his direct gaze increased my discomfort. I realized my hands were shaking and hid them behind my back as I leaned against the bedroom door.

"N-no, I don't mind. I walk around the city. I love seeing people from all over the world mixing together. You'd never see the likes of it in Donegal."

"I suppose not. I take it you find New York exciting?"

"Yes," I said, "but—"

"But what?"

"Today I went to Hell's Kitchen. I could hardly believe the conditions I saw. I'd heard of such slums in Dublin, but I never expected to see such a thing here."

After I spoke, I realized my nervousness had disappeared.

His face clouded. "So much for New York being paved with gold. I agree with you, Miss Sweeney, it is an awful thing to see, but I doubt that much will change. Even the prosperous Irishmen in this city turn a blind eye to their plight." His lips tightened in a thin line.

Lily watched him intently as he spoke. She put her small hand in his, as if to comfort him.

"I should go," I said. "Good night, Mr. O'Hanlon. Good night, Lily."

As I turned to leave, he rose and came toward me. He took my hands in his and looked into my eyes, his face inches from mine. For a wild moment I thought he was about to kiss me.

"Miss Sweeney, I am moved by your compassion for the suffering of your countrymen."

He backed away from me and turned toward Lily.

Unlike Aidan O'Hanlon, Mrs. Donahue was horrified when I told her where I had been and what I had seen.

"Ye've no business going all them places on your own," she said. "Who knows what kind of diseases ye could catch there? Ye need to stick with your own kind. There're plenty of respectable young Irish lads and lassies about, dying for one another's company. There's Irish priests do run dances for them on Friday or Saturday nights at some of the churches nearby, or over in Brooklyn. Kathleen does go to them. I'll tell her to take you with her next time she goes."

I wanted to say to Mrs. Donahue that if I wanted to mix with my own kind, I would have stayed in Donegal. But I knew she meant well, and I agreed to go with Kathleen next time she went.

The following Saturday evening we left the O'Hanlon house and boarded a subway train to Brooklyn. I had never seen the likes of a train like this, that ran above and below the ground. When we were in a tunnel, Kathleen said that we were under the East River. I nearly died of fright, remembering the frigid waters beneath the *Titanic*. I turned to Kathleen.

"Are you not destroyed with fear? What if the river swallows us up, the way the sea swallowed the *Titanic*?"

Kathleen shrugged. "Don't be talking so loud," she said. "People will think we're greenhorns."

I blushed to the tips of my ears.

My anxiety vanished as soon as we stepped off the train. The air was mild, and a cool breeze wafted in from the river. Kathleen led me down a street past row houses each three stories high and with a dozen or so steps leading up to the front door. They stood at attention, shoulder to shoulder, along the tree-lined street, their brick façades the deep hue of chocolate that glinted in the setting sun. I paused to admire them. They were nothing like the large, elegant houses on Aidan O'Hanlon's street, nor were they like the tenements of Hell's Kitchen. They exuded a quiet dignity I found calming.

St Anthony's church, where the dance was being held, lay at the end of the street. Kathleen stopped before we got there and took out a compact and lipstick from her bag. Grinning at me, she slicked on red lipstick and patted powder on her face. She wore a dress with a tight bodice and a flared skirt that showed off her trim figure. It was bright crimson, and the lipstick matched it perfectly. I smiled to myself, imagining Nora in the same dress and lipstick. She would have been delighted. I looked down at myself. Kathleen had suggested I wear the bright yellow dress that I wore for Mass. It was the fanciest of the three she had brought for me when I first arrived. Still, it paled in the face of the vibrant crimson.

Kathleen put the lipstick and compact back in her bag. "Mrs. Donahue doesn't approve of makeup," she said, "so don't you be telling her."

"I thought only rich people used that stuff," I said. I didn't add that prostitutes were known to use it as well.

Kathleen shrugged. "You have to catch up with the times, Nora."

Even though she could be sharp-tongued at times, I had to admire Kathleen. She was a farmer's daughter, the same as me, and grew up the oldest of six children in an Irish village not much bigger than Kilcross. She'd lived in New York for only two years, but she had embraced this new adventure with gusto. She seemed to enjoy taking me under her wing and teaching me all she had learned, and I appreciated it, even though there were times when I felt she was talking down to me.

As we approached the parish hall next to the church, I heard strains of Irish music. Someone was playing the accordion. I was transported back to the third-class deck on the *Titanic* and the crowd of young lads playing the familiar airs of home. I wondered how many of them had survived. For a moment, I was overcome with sadness and homesickness.

Inside, the hall was crowded with young people dancing and laughing. Warm, stale air and the smell of spilled beer wrapped around me, making me feel vaguely sick, and I longed to be back outside in the cool breeze. I tried to smile as Kathleen dragged me over to a group of girls she knew and introduced me.

"Girls, meet Nora Sweeney," she announced. "She's the new governess in the house. I was afraid she might be a pain in the arse and get above herself, but I've taken her down a peg or two. I've made sure she knows she's just a greenhorn like the rest of us are when we first arrive. Haven't I, Nora?"

The girls laughed, and I hid my sudden annoyance. They introduced themselves one by one. Some were very pretty, others plainer, some shy and others outgoing, but every one of them had an Irish brogue, which comforted me and made me homesick at the same time.

"I *love* your dress, Kathleen," a girl who bore a strong resemblance to Nora said.

Kathleen patted her skirt and beamed.

"Come on, then," she said, "let's get out on the dance floor so I can show it off. You too, Nora."

Images of the village dances back in Kilcross arose in my mind and I was overcome with shyness. "I-I'll just watch for now," I said to Kathleen. "You go on and dance. I'll be all right." I watched with relief as they all ran to join in the dancing, and I was left alone at the table.

"Can I get you a lemonade?"

I'd been sitting there for a few minutes when a familiar-sounding male voice startled me, and I looked up into Dom Donnelly's smiling face. I put my hand over my heart to calm the shock of seeing him.

"Dom! Sure, I thought you were dead!" I blurted out.

Dom grinned. "Now is that any way to greet an old friend?"

"And Maeve? Where is she?"

His grin faded, replaced by a haunted look.

"She drowned, Delia," he said, his voice shaking. "I held on to her as we jumped into the water, but I lost my hold. I heard her screaming and I tried to find her, but . . ." He roughly wiped away tears and took a deep breath. "White Star sent ships from Canada to collect what bodies they could find, and thank God they found hers. They identified her by the Saint Christopher medal Ma had given her. It had her name engraved on it." He blessed himself. "At least they had a name to give her, not like the other poor *craturs* with no names on them, or them that sank so far into the sea they'll never be found."

He stopped talking and I could say nothing to comfort him. A lump formed in my throat and I fought away tears. I leaned forward and put my hand on his. At length, I managed to speak.

"Where did the Canadians take her?" I said gently.

"To Halifax, up in Nova Scotia. There's a whole graveyard full of them there."

"I wonder if Nora is buried there as well?" I whispered, forgetting for a moment that Dom was there.

He squeezed my hand. "I saw her name on the list of missing," he said. "Maybe one day, please God, you'll find her."

He fetched two lemonades and we sat in silence at the table. The music that had so enchanted me earlier was now a din that drummed in my ears. The dancers had formed circles, arms aloft, locking hands, their feet moving with precision as they spun faster and faster. Soon they were a blur, and I closed my eyes to avoid getting dizzy.

I felt Dom's hand on my arm. "Are you all right, Delia?"

I started. "Yes. I'd like to leave, but I'll have to wait for Kathleen. I wouldn't know how to get back without her."

Dom smiled. "Aye, and you'll be waiting a long time for herself to be ready to go home. I've known Kathleen for a while, and she'd dance 'til the sun came up if she could. She's a *quare* one for the *craic*."

I nodded.

"I could see you home if you want," he said, suddenly shy. "I can go and tell Kathleen you're leaving with me. I've seen Kathleen home on occasion, so I won't get you lost."

"That would be grand, Dom," I said, and then, in a sudden panic, I added, "Dom, Kathleen keeps calling me Nora. She hasn't caught on yet that my name is Delia."

Dom gave me a curious look but said nothing. I held my breath and watched as he went on to the dance floor and took Kathleen aside. As he spoke to her, I noticed her face turning red. She glared over at me and then shoved Dom away and went back to the dancing. She seemed very annoyed with either Dom or me; I didn't know which. I passed no remarks to him.

When we arrived outside the O'Hanlon house, Dom shuffled his feet, as if weighing what he wanted to say. I waited.

"Will you come to the dance with me next week, Delia?" he said. "I promise we'll dance our feet off. We need to enjoy ourselves after what we've lived through."

"But what about Kathleen?" I blurted out.

"What about her?"

I shrugged. "I don't know, she just seemed very annoyed when you told her you were leaving with me."

"Ah, sure pay her no mind," he said. "Kathleen always wants everything her way."

I didn't press him further.

"So will you come with me next week?" he said again.

"I will," I said.

* * *

By July, the heat was beginning to take its toll on me. The pavement almost singed my feet, and by the time I got home, my damp clothes were stuck to me. I found myself longing for the green hills of Donegal, where the sun shone gently and rain showers refreshed the soul.

After three months in New York, I believed I should have got over my homesickness. But then an image would enter my mind, or a smell waft around me, and I would be back in Donegal, working on the farm with Da in companionable silence. What I missed most, though, was the sanctuary of the ring of white stones where I often went to find peace, sitting among them while a fresh breeze played with my hair.

When I thought of young Lily, though, my homesickness faded. She had become very attached to me. She followed me everywhere. If I disappeared up to my room for a few minutes, she would burst in, panic on her tiny face. I suppose she was afraid I had left her. In those moments, I would reach out to her and give her a hug. "I'm not going anywhere, love," I would say, and she would clutch me hard.

Often, she sat at the kitchen table drawing pictures. Over and over she would draw a log cabin, or a man with a hat riding a horse under a blazing sun, or odd-looking plants with pointy leaves. When I asked her about them, she would bow her head, put down her crayons and leave the table.

"I think she's pining for Texas, poor wee mite," Mrs. Donahue said. "It was where she was born, ye know."

She sighed. "Sure, we all feel a tug back to the place we were born. 'Tis our real home, after all."

Mrs. Donahue explained that Aidan O'Hanlon and his wife, Mary, had lived in Texas for a while, and that Lily had spent a few years there.

For the rest of that summer, Lily and I spent many happy days together—walking in the park under the shade of giant oak trees, sitting by the pond feeding the ducks or wandering through a museum admiring the paintings. Lily seemed to love the muse-

ums, often pulling me by the hand up the steps if we were passing one. Inside, she would sometimes linger in front of a picture,
her eyes wide and a hint of smile on her face.

"I'm very pleased to hear from Mrs. Donahue you've been
taking Lily to museums and galleries to look at paintings. I think
that art contributes greatly to a child's education."

I was in the library late one evening when I heard Aidan
O'Hanlon's voice behind me. I turned around, nervous but excited at the thought of seeing him again.

"S-she seems to enjoy it," I murmured.

As I looked at him, my face grew hot and I hoped he could not
see me blushing. I hadn't seen him in a while, and I was once
again aware of his good looks. He looked particularly well
tonight, dressed in evening clothes, with a dark jacket, a shim-
mering white shirt and a white bow tie. He wrestled the bow tie
from his collar and threw it on a nearby table.

"Gosh, awful things," he said. "They'd be after strangling the
life out of you."

This was the first time I had heard even a hint of an Irish accent from him. I knew he had been born in New York, but that
his late wife was from Ireland. Perhaps some of her brogue had
rubbed off on him. He took off his jacket, removed his cuff links
and rolled up his sleeves. I tried hard not to stare at the sprin-
kling of black hairs on his forearms.

"I-I'll be going now, sir. Can I have Kathleen bring you anything?"

While I hated to leave, I was anxious to get out of the room before I made a fool of myself.

"I'll ring for her," he said as he sat down on a chair beside the
empty fireplace and put up his feet on the fender.

"Very well," I said. "I-I'll be away, then."

"No, stay." It was not a command; more of a polite invitation.
I hesitated, not knowing what to do. Just then, Kathleen came in.

"Ah, Kathleen, bring me a whiskey." He paused. "And for
you, Miss Sweeney?"

Both he and Kathleen stared at me expectantly.

"I . . . er . . . just a soda water would be grand."

Kathleen glared at me as she disappeared out the door.

He gestured to a chair across from his. "Sit down, Miss Sweeney," he said. "I think it's time we got to know each other better."

He began by asking me questions about how Lily was getting on. It was easy for me to answer because I was so excited about what Lily was learning. I leaned forward, smiling. "Even though she doesn't speak, she devours every book I give her and writes lovely wee compositions about them," I said, "and she shows a flair for mathematics."

My mouth was dry after talking, and I took a gulp of soda water.

Then his questions turned to me. "I don't know much about *you*, Miss Sweeney," he said, his eyes fixed on my face. "Why don't you tell me about your family? Do you have brothers and sisters? Did you live on a farm or in the town? What were you like in school?' And why did you want to come to America?"

My mind raced. What was I to say? I didn't dare give away my secret.

"T-there's not much to tell," I said, trying not to look at him. "I had a twin brother who died, but no sisters."

I rushed on, anxious to be finished. "My da is a farmer, and my ma keeps the house. I-I was shy in school but had a nice teacher who brought me books. A-and I wanted to come to America for the adventure of it."

I stopped talking and tried to control the trembling in my hands. He looked at me for a long time, as if measuring what I had just said. I felt sure he knew that some of it was lies. I steeled myself, ready for the accusation. Instead, he laughed aloud.

"You are not one for long speeches, are you, Miss Sweeney? I wish some of the long-winded politicians I was in the company of

tonight could have heard you. They might have learned something."

I was nervous under his scrutiny. I smoothed out my dress and
tucked a lock of hair behind my ear. I wasn't used to people staring at me unless they were making fun of my stutter. Men like
him would never have given me a second look. But he seemed to
be appraising me, almost like a potential suitor. I chased the
thought away. *You're nothing but an eejit, Delia.*

At last he spoke again, his tone gentle.

"Forgive me, Miss Sweeney. It did not occur to me until just
now that you are sensitive about your stutter. I should not have
made fun of you." He leaned back in his chair, his fingers inter-
twined like a steeple. "I've noticed it does not affect you when
you speak about Lily."

I didn't reply.

"I also notice that you do not have a particularly Irish accent;
more English than Irish, I would say. My dear wife, Mary, had a
brogue you could cut with a knife, as she often said herself."

I allowed myself a smile. I was back on firmer ground. "I've
been told that often, sir," I said. "I put it down to my teacher—
the one who gave me the books. She was from the gentry and
had no trace of a brogue at all. I suppose some of it rubbed off on
me. A-and, besides, I lived in a very quiet house. Nobody in my
family spoke much."

I sat back in the chair. He looked away from me and stared
silently into the empty fireplace, lost in his own thoughts. I was
afraid to make a move in case I disturbed him. The voices of Mrs.
Donahue and Kathleen drifted up from the kitchen and the
grandfather clock in the hallway chimed eleven times. He broke
the silence by ringing again for Kathleen, signaling for more
drinks. It occurred to me that he'd probably been drinking earlier
that evening. If I didn't know better, I'd have said he was determined to get drunk. When Kathleen came in, as before, she gave
me a curious look, this time raising an eyebrow. I didn't blame

her; it must have been very odd to see the master of the house and myself sitting there like an old married couple. I had not finished my first soda water, and I tried to wave away the glass she held.

"If it 'twas myself, I'd be having a whiskey," she whispered as, ignoring my signal, she set down the glass.

Aidan O'Hanlon, however, had no such reluctance. He raised his glass with gusto and, with each swallow, his tongue loosened more. It was then he began talking again, this time about himself, and I breathed a sigh of relief. I judged that he would not expect any more talk out of me, and I was right.

Some of the things he told me I already knew about from Mrs. Donahue. He explained he'd been born in New York and that his father was a banker, that his mother had left the family when he was young, and his two brothers had followed their father into banking. So, he was the black sheep, I thought. I was dying to ask a million questions but didn't dare.

As he talked, I got the impression he had forgotten I was in the room. I fought back the drowsiness that had suddenly come over me. I wanted to hear every word he said. I was almost giddy that he was sharing so much with me, yet at the same time I felt like a guilty intruder, prying into his private thoughts.

"And then I met Mary. She was so beautiful. . . ."

My ears pricked up as he mentioned her name. I was very curious about her. From the photos I had seen of her on a side table in the library, she was indeed beautiful, and the way Mrs. Donahue spoke of her, she could have been a saint. The truth was that I was a bit jealous of her.

He looked up at me as if suddenly remembering I was in the room.

"She died because of me," he said, his speech slurring. "If I hadn't taken her to Texas, she would still be alive." He took another gulp of his whiskey. "She left me, Miss Sweeney, just like my mother left after she told me she never would. The ones you love will always leave you in the end, one way or another. It may have been my fault they left, but I will never let it happen again. Love is a curse, Miss Sweeney; don't ever let yourself fall in love."

He was rambling now, and making no sense. Surely he couldn't be equating Mary's death with deliberately leaving him? And quite likely there was more to the story of his mother's departure than he was saying. The events had evidently become all mixed up in his mind. What was clear to me was that his trust in those close to him had been destroyed, one way or the other, and the poor man was tortured by it.

His head drooped, and the sound of his deep breathing told me he had fallen asleep. I watched him for a while, then stood up and went over to him. Gently, I took the empty glass from his hand and set it on the table. He didn't stir. I draped a blanket over him and tiptoed out of the door and up the stairs.

I lay in bed recalling each word he'd said and how he had looked at me. At first, I'd been giddy that he'd finally noticed me and had taken me into his confidence. But then a small voice inside my head told me the encounter meant nothing at all. All he'd done was recite the bare outlines of his past. He might as well have been talking to a stranger on a train. The closest he came to betraying emotion was when he mentioned Mary.

"Don't ever let yourself fall in love, Miss Sweeney," he'd said.

I realized then that we were alike. I was afraid to fall in love as well. I still believed no man would ever have me. Ma had told me that often enough, drilled it in until I believed it. Whatever feelings I had for Aidan O'Hanlon were schoolgirl fantasies, and I needed to put them out of my head.

By the next day he had returned to the aloof and slightly distracted man I had come to expect. He nodded at me in the hallway, as if the evening before had never happened. I wondered if he even recalled it.

"So how was your evening with himself?" Kathleen's question sounded more like an accusation. "The two of yez looked very cozy, sitting talking as if ye'd known each other for years." She turned to Mrs. Donahue. "You should have seen them," she said. "If I didn't know better—"

"That's enough, Kathleen," said Mrs. Donahue. "We'll have no such gossip in this house." She turned to me. "Sit down, Nora, love. Have your breakfast and don't listen to this one."

Kathleen shrugged and laughed as she turned away toward the sink. "I wonder what Dom would think if he found out you were making eyes at the master of the house?"

"I want to hear no more about it." Mrs. Donahue's voice was sharp. "We're having society to dinner tomorrow night and we have to be getting on with it. Take off your apron now, miss, and go and buy everything I have on this shopping list."

Kathleen pulled a face and snatched the list from Mrs. Donahue. I stood up and excused myself, leaving my boiled egg and toast only half-eaten. Kathleen's attitude was beginning to wear me down. She seemed to take every opportunity to pass remarks on my behavior. I suppose I should have complained that, as Mrs. Donahue often said, she didn't know her rightful place. But who was I to complain—after all, this was not *my* rightful place either—I was still as much of an imposter as I'd been in Donegal.

After that night, Kathleen's attitude toward me seemed to shift. She was polite enough while Mrs. Donahue was present, but when we were alone, she snapped at me over the smallest things and ignored me when I asked her for something. I grew more and more frustrated.

"What's got into you, Kathleen?" I said.

"Nothing," she said, glaring at me. "I'm just the maid doing me job."

I made no reply, but you could have cut the air between us with a knife.

I discovered the cause of her anger when Dom arrived the following Saturday evening to take me to the dance. Kathleen banged the door in his face, leaving him standing on the front step.

"Your boyfriend is here to see you," she said as she made for the stairs back down toward the kitchen.

I caught her arm and turned her to face me. "What's wrong, Kathleen? What have I done to you?"

Her face was flushed and her eyes glinted with anger.

"Well, listen to Little Miss Innocent," she snapped. "Didn't take long for the greenhorn to steal Dom away from me, did it?"

My mouth dropped open. "What do you mean? Dom and I have known each other since our schooldays. Besides, I thought you and he were just friends."

"We were on our way to more than that 'til you interfered."

"I'm so sorry Kathleen. I'll tell him to leave right now."

She shrugged. "Don't bother your head. There's plenty more fish in the sea." She turned around and flounced down the stairs.

I sighed and went out to join Dom. I was about to tell him what Kathleen had said, but he spoke first. He obviously had other things on this mind.

"You've done well for yourself, Delia," he said, reaching out his arm toward me.

I didn't answer.

When we reached the footpath, he stopped and looked back up at the house. "This house is a far cry from the likes of the one you told me about on the ship. And you said you'd be down on your knees scrubbing."

He waited for me to answer. "You're right," I said at last. "I passed myself off to them as Nora."

"But you're not Nora," Dom said quietly. He reached for my hand. "And you're not one can live with lies."

I bowed my head. "I'm doing it for Lily," was all I said.

"'Tis your own business, Delia. I'll not say another word about it. Come on, we'll be late for the dance."

Nora

❧

It was pleasant enough living at Mrs. Shaw's house, and I wasn't unhappy, but after a while I started to get bored. The sameness of every day began to suffocate me. There were only so many times I could go for a walk or sit on the bench in the garden playing with Silver. I was desperate for something else to do, or other people to meet. One day, when Mrs. Shaw was on her way out for the day, I plucked up the courage to ask: Could I go with her? Even if it meant taking my life in my hands riding in that car of hers, it would be worth it to get away from here even if just for a day.

"I'd be delighted to have you join me, dear," she said. "I didn't invite you earlier because I thought you needed peace and quiet for a while. But I can see for a young girl like you, peace and quiet has its limits."

Gingerly, I climbed into the car and slid down in the front seat while she started up the engine. The car roared to life, and I gripped the seat as she took off down the drive and out on to the road. I said a prayer to the Virgin Mary to let me come back alive.

"You chose a marvelous time to come with me," she shouted over the engine noise. "I'm going to join the ladies marching to protest against poor working conditions for women. I imagine you won't have seen the likes of such a protest back in Ireland."

My mouth fell open. She must be talking about them women Teresa mentioned—the ones demanding that they be let vote. I couldn't remember what Teresa called them. It was a word I'd never heard before. *Feck!* I thought to myself. I'd been hoping for a day out shopping, where I could get a gander at the latest styles—and maybe Mrs. Shaw might even buy me something. Or maybe a nice lunch at a posh place where I could show off my new manners. But a fecking protest march? I groaned at the thought.

I paid her little heed as she prattled on about the protest and what fine women I was going to meet. Instead, I fixed my eyes on the open road. It was late June and the weather was warm. I leaned back and let the smell of fresh flowers and mowed grass surround me. I smiled to myself. Something about the weather and the smells felt familiar. Had I enjoyed days like this in the past? I shrugged. How would I know?

We left the countryside behind and tall buildings began to appear here and there. As we drove, they became more crowded together. I surmised we must be getting close to New York City and my excitement grew. Although I'd lain in hospital there for weeks, I'd never had a chance to see it. Even the day I left with Mrs. Shaw, nothing much had registered with me. Now I sat up straight and looked around me. I didn't expect what I saw. The streets were dirty and covered with rubbish. The smells that poured out of open doorways would make you boke.

The car stopped, stuck behind a crowd of cars, carts, carriages and bicycles, and people hurrying to and fro across the street. To my right, young women in drab clothes loitered outside a dismal-looking, soot-covered building with grimy windows. The women stared at us, a suspicious look in their eyes. One or two shouted something that I couldn't make out, but I was sure they were cursing us. I looked at Mrs. Shaw to see had she heard them.

"Poor creatures," she said, "locked up in that filthy building all day. You should see the conditions inside—dark and dusty and hot as Hell."

"You've been in there?"

"No, not in *this* building. But there are dozens of them all over the city, and all of them alike. You probably never heard of the Triangle Shirtwaist Factory. It burned down a year ago last March. One hundred and forty-six workers perished, most of them women—women just like these. The doors were all locked and they couldn't get out. Most died of smoke inhalation, the rest from jumping through windows. The youngest was a child of fourteen."

I stared up at the grimy windows, trying to imagine what it would have been like to be so desperate you'd have to jump from them. "God rest their souls," I whispered. I looked back at the women, and my heart filled with pity for them. I recognized somehow that pity wasn't something normal for me, and I wondered again about my past.

Not far past the factory, Mrs. Shaw pulled over the car in front of a small building and stopped.

"Come along, dear," she said as she jumped out.

I was struck again at what a strange woman Mrs. Shaw was. Any other woman her age would be bent over on a walking stick, but here she was with more vim than someone half her age. I knew fine well that she could leave me in the dust any day of the week.

Inside, in a small room, a group of women of all ages bustled about, organizing stacks of envelopes, writing on big pieces of cardboard in black ink and attaching them to wooden sticks, and gluing ribbons together to form rosettes. They talked away as they worked, joking and laughing. One of them stopped what she was doing and ran over and greeted Mrs. Shaw like a long-lost friend.

"Felicity!" she said. "How good to see you."

Mrs. Shaw smiled and pulled me forward. "This is the young lady I told you was staying with me. The girl from the *Titanic*."

The woman trained her clear blue eyes on me. Her face was kind and she took both of my hands in hers.

"Welcome," she said, "we're all delighted to meet you. Felicity has told us so much about you. What you must have been through—I cannot imagine. Come. Have a cup of tea."

She pulled me toward the back of the room, where a woman was pouring tea into mugs. I had a sudden urge to cry. It was as if this stranger had wrapped me in a warm shawl like an infant.

Before I could finish the tea, I found myself being pulled along by the group of women toward the door. Someone pinned a rosette on me and thrust a pile of printed leaflets into my hands. The others hoisted the cardboard signs with sayings like "Equal Pay for Equal Work" and "Strike for Better Working Conditions" on them. Outside, they fell into step, two by two, and began to march, Mrs. Shaw at the front. I walked beside a young, pleasant-faced girl about my own age. She nodded at me.

"First time?" she asked.

"Aye," I said, wishing I could disappear into the ground.

She nodded to the leaflets I carried. "You should start giving those out."

I pushed the leaflets at passersby. Men and some women shouted insults and dropped the leaflets on the ground. When we came to the factory where we had stopped earlier, the workers watched us in silence before disappearing inside. It was then that my anger flared. Those women deserved somebody to stand up for them. I began to thrust the leaflets at people with new energy. I picked up the ones they threw on the ground and shoved them back in their faces. I matched them insult for insult. I laughed to myself—my vulgar tongue had come in handy. Pleased with myself, I turned to the girl beside me, who was staring at me with her mouth open.

"That's the way you do it," I said. "You've got to give them as good as you get."

On the way home in the car with Mrs. Shaw, I leaned back in the seat and closed my eyes. I was wrecked from the long march, but a new feeling had crept into me. It was pride. Not the sort of pride you might get from being admired, but the feeling you'd get from doing something that mattered to somebody else. I knew I had never felt this before. I reached over and touched Mrs. Shaw's arm.

"Thank you," I said.

When we got back to the house, I was too tired to eat dinner and went straight up to bed.

That night I dreamed of girls jumping out of windows, a massive fire raging behind them. Their screams grew loud and I sat straight up in bed. It was then I realized the screams were coming from me. Mrs. Shaw rushed into my room, Beatrice right behind her, and turned up the lamp.

"Are you all right, my dear? Were you having a bad dream?"

I nodded my head.

"That's what happens when you don't eat your supper," scolded Beatrice. "I always done say an empty stomach bring on all sorts of trouble."

"I expect she's had a memory come back to her," said Mrs. Shaw. "Is that right, dear?"

It was then I realized she was right. "I was dreaming about the girls we saw today; they were jumping out of the factory windows and the fire was raging behind them. But then the fire turned into water and . . ."

"Go on, dear girl," Mrs. Shaw urged.

"And I saw people jumping into the water from a big ship. They were screaming too, just like the factory women."

Mrs. Shaw and Beatrice exchanged looks. Beatrice folded her hands on her breast. "Thank the Lord," she said. "The child's memory is come back."

"Not yet," Mrs. Shaw said, "but it's a good start."

After they left, I slid down under the bedcovers and tried to remember the details of the dream. The ship must have been the *Titanic*—Mrs. Shaw had told me about the sinking when I was still in the hospital—but this was the first time I'd had an actual image of it. It could have been something I'd made up, of course, but I knew in my heart the image had been real. It was my first memory of that night.

A cold fear came over me. What if I remembered who I was and it was someone awful? What if I was an escaped prisoner, a murderer, or worse, a prostitute? No, I couldn't bring myself to believe that. What if, on the other hand, I was married or had a child? What if I had left a poor, helpless infant somewhere? Was someone looking after it, or was it left defenseless. Was it even still alive? What if I had a husband desperately searching for me? What if my family was destroyed with grief, thinking I had died? What if they were poor and penniless and depending on me to help them? In my fear, I fervently prayed that my memory would come back soon.

For the next few days after my nightmare, I refused Mrs. Shaw's invitations to join her on one outing or another, afraid that something else would spark my memory. But my boredom grew, and I began to overcome my fear. I was delighted, then, when Mrs. Shaw announced that her nephew and his friend were coming to visit.

"Sinclair and his friend, Ben, are just a couple of years older than you, my dear," she said, "so you should all get along well. It will be nice for you to have young people around for a change."

My heart jumped when she told me the news. I was even more delighted that it was two fellers who were coming. Two girls would have been all right, but two boys would be much better *craic*. I was dying to ask Teresa what they were like, but she and I hardly said a word to each other now, ever since the "stray" comment.

I passed the time until they came making rosettes for Mrs. Shaw's group—I'd finally learned how to pronounce the word "suffragette." When I got bored, I began picking out what dress I would wear and fiddling with my hair so that I would look my best when they arrived. I also practiced extra hard on my table manners and my accent. I didn't want them thinking I was a poor Irish country girl just off the boat.

I heard a car tearing up the driveway faster than Mrs. Shaw ever had and swerve to a halt in front of the house. I ran to my bedroom window, anxious to get a gander. There was a hand-some, blond feller behind the wheel. He must be Sinclair. He leaped out of the car, and I saw he had long legs and a lean build. He took off his cap and gloves and ran his fingers through his hair. When Mrs. Shaw came out to greet him, he grinned, show-ing lovely white teeth. I was in love just at the sight of him. The other feller, Ben, was short and dark, with a pleasant face and a loud laugh. Mrs. Shaw hurried over and hugged Ben but gave her nephew only a stiff handshake.

Then Teresa ran out, all smiles. I was sure she had a notion for one or the other of them. Sinclair handed her his cap and gloves to carry, while Ben waved her away, stuffing his own into his pockets. They all disappeared into the house, and I had to hold myself back from racing down the stairs. The polite thing, I real-ized, was to wait to be called. I paced the room on pins and nee-dles until Mrs. Shaw knocked on the door. I took my time going to open it.

"They are here," she said with a bright smile, "and anxious to meet you. Come downstairs when you are ready, dear."

I counted to one hundred, smoothed out my dress, patted my hair, took my time going down the stairs and sauntered into the dining room. Sinclair Shaw, Ben and Mrs. Shaw stood in front of the fireplace, sipping sherry. Mrs. Shaw looked relieved when I appeared.

"Let's sit down, shall we?" she said, pointing to the huge din-ing table.

I could hardly take my eyes off Sinclair Shaw. He was even more handsome up close. Teresa served the others politely but glared at me as she slammed down the dishes in front of me. I supposed she was jealous, and I didn't blame her. I'd have felt the same way in her place. I ignored her slights. I was so wrapped up in watching Sinclair Shaw's every move that I almost forgot my new table manners. I had to remind myself to cut the cold roast beef into tiny slices before eating it, but when Sinclair turned to smile at me, I spluttered some sherry onto the tablecloth. He raised an eyebrow, and I must have turned the color of a turkey cock. I began coughing to cover my embarrassment. I set down the glass and dabbed my lips with my serviette, as I had often seen Mrs. Shaw do.

"Do excuse me," I said politely. "I'm not used to sherry. Normally, I never drink at all."

I gave Sinclair a shy smile and lowered my eyelids. Ah, but who could blame me for looking at him? He was gorgeous, so he was. His hair was the color of straw and his eyes as blue as cornflowers. When he smiled, two deep dimples creased his cheeks. I forced myself to look away from him and concentrate on Ben instead. He was a nice lad, with an easygoing manner. He was easy to talk to and, for a while, I almost forgot Sinclair was there. But then I felt his eyes on me, and while I tried to ignore him, I lost the thread of what Ben was saying altogether. He must have thought I was an eejit because he turned away from me and started talking to Mrs. Shaw.

When lunch was over, we all stood up. I wasn't certain what to do next, but suddenly, Sinclair was beside me, towering over me.

"Would you care to accompany me on a walk through the garden, Miss, er . . ."

My cheeks reddened. Fortunately, Mrs. Shaw came to my rescue. "I told you, Sinclair, that the dear girl still can't remember her name," she said. "The trauma of what she's been through has taken her memory. But we hope that it will all come back to her soon. Don't we, my dear?"

She looked down at me, and I nodded.

"Oh dear, I forgot you told me that, Aunt. Well, we must call you something," Sinclair said, laughing. "I shall invent a name for you. Let's see, now. You're Irish and you came out of the sea onto land, just like seals were said to do in Irish mythology. They shed their skins to sun themselves, but men often fell in love with them and hid their skins so they couldn't go back into the sea. What about Selkie? It means 'seal' in Irish."

Something in the word "selkie" struck a distant chord. Where had I heard it before? Or had I?

"But you cannot name her after a seal, Sinclair!" said Mrs. Shaw. She seemed very put out. "If you insist on being clever, at least call her Grace—after Grace O'Malley, the sea pirate."

Sinclair shook his head. "No, Aunt Felicity. I still think Selkie is much more apt."

At that moment I didn't care if he named me after the divil himself. He was paying attention to me, and that was all that mattered. He reached out his arm to me.

"Shall we take that walk, Selkie?"

I slipped my arm into his and began to walk as if my feet were not even touching the ground.

We sat down on the garden swing where I spent so many afternoons. Silver came running over and jumped up on my lap. I began to stroke her, but suddenly she stood up, the hair rising on her back. She bared her teeth and let out a hiss so loud it would have wakened the dead. Sinclair jumped to his feet.

"Get that thing away from me," he shouted. "I loathe cats."

I grabbed Silver and carried her out of the garden and set her down near the house. When I turned back, I saw Sinclair in the distance, brushing off his trousers, such a scowl on his face I was almost afraid to go near him. I crept over.

"I'm sorry," I said. "Silver never acted like that before. I had no notion . . ."

"Just keep her out of my sight," he said, interrupting me. "Or it will be the last time she'll hiss at anyone."

The brightness of the day seemed to dim a bit just then, and a wave of queasiness made my stomach clench. But Sinclair was smiling down at me now and, slowly, my bad feelings went away.

We left the swing and strolled on through the garden, my arm still tucked through his. He began telling me stories of his past adventures—the scrapes he and Ben often got themselves into. He was so charming, it was as if the Silver business had never happened.

"Mrs. Shaw's husband and my father were brothers," he said in answer to one of my questions. "Unfortunately, my father and mother are dead, and so is Mrs. Shaw's husband. So, you see, I am all alone in the world.

"Have you brothers and sisters?" he said.

"I can't remember," I said. "Right now, the only person I can almost call a relation is your aunt."

The words surprised me. At what point had I decided that?

"Not such a bad relation to have."

"I suppose not."

It was late afternoon when we got back to the house, and I followed Sinclair into the library. Ben looked up from a book.

"Well, you two seem to have had a fine walk," he said, winking at Sinclair. "Wasn't sure if you'd ever come back."

"I wasn't sure we would either, my friend," said Sinclair. "Selkie here is wonderful company."

I blushed to the tips of my ears. When I'd first gone downstairs to meet Sinclair, I'd thought I looked well in the pretty white dress with a pattern of red flowers all over it, and my hair nicely curled. I wasn't as buxom as I once was, although I didn't still look like a scarecrow. But the minute I saw him, I began to doubt myself. After all, he must have dozens of girls after him, and all of them pretty. Well, he'd said I was good company at least, so maybe there was hope.

I knew the polite thing would be to excuse myself and leave them alone. But I couldn't tear myself away, so I just stood there like a spare dinner, not knowing what to say or do. I was saved when Beatrice came in and said she'd laid out a light supper for the two of them.

"Mrs. Shaw said you'd be on your way soon. No sense going anywhere on an empty stomach," Beatrice said.

Ben got up from his chair. He turned to me and smiled. "It was a pleasure to meet you, Selkie," he said. "I hope to see you again soon," and went out to the dining room.

I nodded, disappointed at the news they were leaving so soon. Sinclair lingered after Ben left. "I'm sorry we have to leave," he said, "but we have an engagement in the city."

I realized then I'd been showing my feelings too much, so I gave him a wide smile. "It was lovely meeting you and Ben," I said. "I hope you will visit again soon." I reached out my hand to shake his, but he ignored it. I wondered if I'd made another mistake; did young ladies shake hands with gentlemen they'd only just met? I was busy scolding myself when he bent down and kissed me on the cheek.

"The pleasure was all mine," he said softly. "And I intend to visit you again very soon."

It was all I could do to hide the excitement that filled me. I managed a shaky "Goodbye, then," before I walked, weak-kneed, out of the library, defying every instinct in me to clutch him and kiss him back.

In the days after Sinclair left, I hardly knew what to do with myself. I spent long hours watching out the window, hoping for a glimpse of the blue roadster roaring up the driveway. I didn't want to ask Mrs. Shaw when he was expected back for fear she'd think me too forward. Besides, I didn't want to give away my feelings for him.

I went back to my usual habit of spending time in the garden every afternoon with Silver. At first, she wanted nothing to do with me, running away every time she saw me. But, after a while, she began to sidle up beside me as I walked, and then one day she jumped back on my lap, purring louder than ever. I knew she was afraid Sinclair would be with me, and even though I'd tried to put that memory out of my mind, deep down inside me, it still bothered me. What was it that made her hate Sinclair on sight? I shrugged. Sure, how would I ever know what was in a cat's mind?

One day not long after Sinclair left, Mrs. Shaw announced she was having a tea at the house for her friends from the suffragette movement. When she asked me to join them, I was pleased— anything to break the monotony. Besides, I had taken a liking to them.

They arrived in the afternoon, bustling into the hall chirping like birds and removing their hats and capes. It was still only late summer, but the day was chilly just the same.

"My dear, would you mind helping Teresa with the hats and capes?"

I'd made a point of avoiding Teresa as much as I could, so I wasn't too happy with Mrs. Shaw's request. But I could hardly refuse her. I stayed in the hall and took the ladies' capes, while Teresa took their hats. One lady gave me an old-fashioned shawl to hang up alongside the capes. It was a lovely mauve color, soft as a lamb's coat, and edged with fringe. I held it in my hands for a moment and looked at the woman who had given it to me. She was about Mrs. Shaw's age, but struck me as so delicate she might crumble at any minute.

"I know it's not fashionable, but it's lovely, isn't it?" she said. "My daughter made it for me because I so admired one she made for herself." Her pale eyes misted over. "She died not long after she finished it."

I stared at her with my mouth open. My feet were suddenly rooted to the ground. Teresa was nudging me to get on with it, but I ignored her. My head throbbed and I was afraid I might faint. I shoved the shawl at Teresa. "I'm so sorry, I think I'm going to be sick. Tell Mrs. Shaw I'm sorry."

Teresa rolled her eyes at me and started to say something, but I turned away from her and fled up the stairs.

In the safety of my room, I lay down on the bed and stared at the ceiling. As soon as I saw that shawl, I remembered. There was a young woman who had tried to help me in the lifeboat. . . . She'd been wearing a mauve shawl. I could see her clearly. Her hands gripped my arms and her voice was gentle as she tried to coax me down off the seat where I stood. I remembered her scream as I fell backward into the water. The images were sharp and clear in my mind. I wondered if she'd been this woman's daughter, but surely she would have said if the girl had drowned. Besides, there must be a lot of women with mauve shawls. I shivered. It was eerie just the same.

As I lay there, more images came—the posh women in the lifeboat refusing to let more women in even though there was still room; the boat tilting and scraping the side of the ship as the seamen lowered it into the water; the ice-cold wind as we floated on the black sea. I shivered, remembering how desperately cold I'd been. The images were as clear as if they'd happened yesterday, and a terrible fear came over me. It was as if the ice had broken on a river and I had fallen through, water crashing over me in all directions. My throat tightened and my breath came in short spurts. My heart hammered in my chest and I felt panic rising in me—the same panic I had felt that night. Then everything went black.

It was dark when I awoke. Mrs. Shaw hovered over me.

"How are you feeling, dear? We've all been worried about you."

I tried to smile. "I'm all right. I had a dizzy spell and felt faint. I'm sorry I missed the tea."

She patted my hand. "You mustn't be sorry. It could not be helped. And besides, I believe we missed you more than you missed us. Young Martha—remember, you marched with her in the protest—is especially fond of you. She sends her regards."

I tried to raise myself up from the pillow, but I hadn't the strength. My head sank back down, and I let out a groan. Mrs. Shaw looked at me in alarm.

"Oh my dear, I think you had more than just a dizzy spell. I fear you might be coming down with something. You must rest. I will ask Beatrice to bring you up some soup."

After she left, I closed my eyes and tried to sleep. But more images kept coming. I was running, holding on to a young man's hand as we raced up one staircase after another. Someone behind us was calling after me. It was a girl, but I couldn't turn around because the people behind were pushing me forward. When we got to the top deck there was a crowd of people. They were going mad, shouting and screaming, while seamen were lifting women into a lifeboat. The young man pushed me toward the boat and disappeared. I remembered hanging back, calling for the young woman who had followed us. "Delia!" I called, "Delia!" Then a seaman pushed me into the lifeboat.

I tossed from side to side in the bed like someone in a fever. I wanted the images to go away and give me some peace. But they wouldn't. They kept playing over and over. I took deep breaths and tried to calm down. Mercifully, sleep began to take over. As I drifted off, I whispered the name Delia. Who was she?

After that first night, a flood of memories came thick and fast. I took advantage of Mrs. Shaw's insistence that I stay in bed. I wanted to be alone while all this was happening. Mrs. Shaw and Beatrice came in and out to make sure I was all right. Teresa, though, was spitting nails. She accused me of playacting.

"I'm on to you, miss," she said. "Sick indeed. 'Tis lovesick ye are, over that feller Sinclair." She laughed. "As if he'd give you the time of day!"

I ignored her. The truth was I hadn't given Sinclair a second thought since these visions had started. I slid down under the covers and went over the new memories in my head. I had remembered who Delia was. She was the fair-haired girl I had seen in my dreams, and I wondered how I knew her. I had visions of my journey to the *Titanic*; they came like jagged pieces of glass that didn't fit together now but I knew were part of a whole picture. I saw myself in a horse and cart driving down a rutted lane with green hills on either side, and in a train compartment, where I was talking to a lad and a young girl. The fair-haired girl called Delia was there as well. Was she a friend, I wondered, or a stranger? Then I felt crowds of young people pushing in on me on a dock where an enormous ship loomed above us.

I wondered at times, was I making these images up? Was I

going mad? Or was I about to die? They say your life passes in front of you when you're ready to die. Sweat ran down my neck and chest and I wanted to cry out.

On the third day, Mrs. Shaw came into my room carrying Silver. The cat jumped from her arms and landed beside me on the bed. I was delighted to see her. I looked up at Mrs. Shaw, who was smiling down at me.

"Thank you for bringing her, Mrs. Shaw."

"You are welcome, dear. I could see how agitated you were becoming. I thought she might help calm you down."

She was right. Silver snuggled next to me, and the steady rise and fall of her small body as she breathed soothed me. That night I slept for the first time without waking up terrified.

By the fourth day I was anxious for all my memories to come back. I forced myself to lose my fear of them. I wanted them out in the open. No matter who I turned out to be, I was ready to face it. It was then the miracle happened. My entire life came back to me, not in fragments, but in one whole piece. I remembered the farm in Donegal where I grew up. I saw my da sitting in silence by the fire, and my ma talking away to me about my future. And I saw Delia sitting on a white rock in the field, nose in a book, just as I had seen her in an earlier image. Tears welled in my eyes as I realized she was my sister. I had been feeling so alone these last months that the fact I had a sister overwhelmed me. I saw my bedroom in the cottage and realized that the woman kneeling beside the bed with the candles all around it was my ma.

I sat straight up in bed. Dear God, my parents must think I was dead. The thought sent shivers through me. I wondered if Delia was dead too. I'd not seen her since she ran after me on the boat, calling out my name. And I remembered Robert, the sweet lad who had taken me to breakfast in the first-class dining room. Was he dead as well?

The next morning I got out of bed and went over to the window. I drew back the curtains and looked out on the front garden. It was a beautiful day, and the sunlight flitted through the tree branches, playing peekaboo. I felt light, as if a great burden had lifted from me, the same feeling I always had after I'd been to confession. I had finally remembered where I came from, and my family, and the journey to the *Titanic*. I even remembered the name of the man I was to work for: Aidan O'Hanlon.

I had remembered my sister, Delia, but along with the memory came the fact that Ma and I had treated her like a servant. I could hardly believe I had acted like that, and I was ashamed. I wondered again: Was she dead or alive? I decided I would look on the survivor list. But there was likely to be more than one Delia; it was then I had to face the fact that, while I had remembered everything else, I still hadn't remembered my own name. And without knowing our last name, how would I find out about Delia?

As I stared out the window, I saw Mrs. Shaw's car coming noisily up the driveway. She jumped out and, as usual, rushed toward the house. I realized then how fond I was of this woman. She'd been so good to me; what would have happened if she hadn't taken pity on me?

I closed the curtains and went and lay back down. I was suddenly exhausted, my earlier happiness gone. A terrible thought came into my mind. How could I let on that my memory had come back and I knew the truth about my family and where I came from? If I told her, she would arrange to send me back home. And I realized I didn't want that. I wanted to stay here.

Delia

❧

Two nights after Aidan and I sat together in the library while he drank whiskey and told me never to fall in love, the doorbell rang several times and excited voices rose in the hall. It was the company Mrs. Donahue said would be arriving. I had meant to be upstairs and out of sight when the visitors arrived, but Mrs. Donahue said Mr. O'Hanlon wanted Lily kept up past her bedtime so he could introduce her to his guests. I suggested the child wear her favorite blue dress and tied a matching ribbon in her long, fair hair. She looked like a wee angel. When she was ready, I brought her down to the kitchen to wait.

Mrs. Donahue had been in a fine tizzy most of the day, ordering Kathleen to scrub the dining-room floor, dust the furniture, polish the silver and set the table for six. A young girl had been hired to help in the kitchen. By the time the visitors arrived, however, the house was a calm, cool oasis from the outside heat. Kathleen brought them drinks in the library.

"You should see the style of them," she said when she came back into the kitchen. "There're six of them, including himself. I counted one older married couple, a single gentleman and two single women with enough rouge and lipstick on them they could be floozies."

Mrs. Donahue banged down a pot on the counter. "Mind your tongue, Kathleen, 'tis not your place to be judging Mr. O'Hanlon's company. Now, get these serving dishes filled and ready to bring into the dining room when they sit down."

I sat on a kitchen chair in the corner, Lily standing stiffly beside me. "You must do your best, Lily," I said. "Your father will be expecting you to be on your best behavior. Try to smile, if you can, and maybe give a little curtsy. And I'll be right there."

I was so concerned that Lily do well, I forgot to be anxious about myself. It was only when Kathleen told me Lily and I were wanted in the dining room that shyness threatened to paralyze me. Taking a deep breath, I stood up and took Lily by the hand.

The guests fell quiet as we entered, and all eyes turned on Lily. I squeezed her hand to reassure her. Aidan came over to where we stood. I fancied his gaze lingered on me longer than was proper. *You're imagining things*, I told myself as I nervously smoothed down my navy-blue dress, the one with the white lace collar. I nudged Lily toward him.

He took her by the hand and led her to the nearest guest. I backed away into a dim corner of the room. As the guests gushed over Lily, I took my chance to look at the two women Kathleen had described. My first thought was that they could have stepped right off the first-class deck of the *Titanic*. Their satin dresses rustled as they moved, and fine necklaces glittered in the light of the crystal chandelier that hung above the table. Their pale, white hands were adorned with diamond rings, and their hair was coiffed in the latest style; a chignon, Kathleen would have called it. They were not much older than myself, I thought, although their sophisticated bearing made them seem older.

As I watched them smile brightly at their host, one of them letting her hand linger on his wrist, I was overcome with the sense of being invisible. Invisibility was not a new state for me—back home, it had often spared me from my mother's wrath—but this was different. I felt like a nobody—a plain little bird among the colorful peacocks—and my heart shrank inside me.

I tore my glance away from the women to see how Lily was

doing. Her father was making a circle of the table, still holding her by the hand. She nodded solemnly to each guest and stood stoically as the sallow-faced, single gentleman tickled her under the chin. And when one of the coiffed women pulled her to her bosom in an awkward hug, Lily wrinkled her nose—probably at the woman's perfume.

When he was finished with the introductions, her father brought her back to me. "You may take her up to bed now, Miss Sweeney," he said. And, turning away from me, he went back to his guests.

I was about to leave when the older gentleman turned to look directly at me. "Sweeney?" he said. "You wouldn't be Delia Sweeney, by any chance?"

I felt dizzy and clutched Lily's hand so hard she wrenched it away from me. The next minute seemed like an hour. My heart thumped in my chest and I was unable to utter a word.

Aidan O'Hanlon broke the silence. "Answer Mr. Boyle's question, Miss Sweeney."

The minute he said Boyle, I knew exactly who the man was, for Boyle was the name of the master of the house where I was supposed to go to work. I looked anxiously toward the door, praying for a chance to escape. But there was to be no reprieve. By now the other guests had stopped eating and were staring at me with great curiosity. I began to sweat.

Mr. Boyle addressed me again. "Come, don't be shy, Miss Sweeney; it's a simple enough question."

I was trapped. Taking a deep breath, I muttered an answer. "N-no, my name is Nora, sir. Nora Sweeney."

"Perhaps you have a sister, then."

"Ah no, sir, I-I have no sisters."

Mrs. Boyle broke in. "There was a Nora Sweeney listed among the missing from the *Titanic*."

"I know, ma'am, but some of those on the missing list turned out to be survivors, l-like myself."

My heart pounded as I said the words, and the two young

women gasped. They gaped at me with open mouths, but Mrs. Boyle kept talking.

"It had been arranged for a Delia Sweeney to join our household staff, but the chit never arrived. She survived the voyage on the *Titanic*; that much we know because her name was on the survivors' list. Therefore, we believe she is somewhere in New York, ungrateful hussy."

Mr. Boyle patted his wife's arm. "That's enough, dear. This girl sounds English, and Sweeney is a common enough name."

"Still," said Aidan O'Hanlon, "it exhibits poor character in this Delia Sweeney not to fulfil her obligation to you."

Then he shrugged his shoulders. "You may go now, Miss Sweeney."

After I put Lily to bed and read her a story, I returned to my own room and sat down in a chair, my spirits low and on the verge of tears. I thought I'd left the imposter role behind me when I left Ireland. But it had followed me to New York—and this time it was my own doing. Tonight, I'd almost been caught out. I had hoped to disappear in New York, but the appearance of the Boyles in this very house told me that would be impossible. New York, even though it was home to millions of people, was as small as Kilcross when it came to the gentry. Was my past to follow me wherever I went?

I recalled the look on Aidan O'Hanlon's face after the Boyles had finished quizzing me. His eyes had bored through me. I cringed at the thought that he might be suspicious. And from what he'd said about how he disapproved of those who didn't fulfill their obligations, if he found out the truth, he would more than disapprove of me—he would dismiss me.

I got up to wash my face. *Pull yourself together,* I said to the face in the mirror. *You made your bed and you must lie in it.*

For the next few weeks after meeting the Boyles, I was skittish as a cat. Every time the doorbell rang, I raced upstairs in case it was the Boyles returning to challenge me on my story. I refused to go outside, blaming a summer cold, in case I should encounter them on the street. But as the days passed, the memory of that evening began to fade and, eventually, I was able to push it to the back of my mind.

I had also made excuses to Dom, even though I was afraid my actions would drive him away. I needn't have worried. He called for me every Saturday night until I finally agreed to step out again. The truth was I had begun to look forward to his visits. We had fallen into an easy friendship, enjoying our time together. We had both survived a terrible ordeal, and that had forged a stronger bond than almost anything else could.

"Kathleen's been spitting mad at me ever since that first night you took me home," I said as we began to walk.

He shrugged. "Ah, sure Kathleen's a lot like your Nora. She thinks every man should be in love with her."

"And are you?" I teased.

He turned to face me. "Are you fecking joking me? Sure what would I ever see in Kathleen? She's got a bob on herself, and for no good reason. You're a good-looking girl, Delia. No wonder she's jealous of you."

I stopped in my tracks. Had Dom just said I was good-looking? Never in my lifetime had such a thought ever crossed my mind. I had always lived in Nora's shadow.

"Ah now, who's joking who?"

"'Tis true, Delia. I suppose you never thought you'd be able to compete with Nora. But she's gone now. 'Tis time you saw yourself for what you're worth."

He had turned to face me, and I could see by his earnest gaze that he meant every word he said. Suddenly uncomfortable, I hurried to change the subject. I linked my arm through his.

"Come on now," I laughed, "or you'll have to fight off the crowd of lads lined up to dance with me."

One Saturday night I came into the house humming Irish tunes. The dancing had been especially lively, and the melodies still lingered in my head. As I closed the front door, Mrs. Donahue came hurrying down the front hall, her finger to her lips.

"Be quiet now, Nora," she whispered, nodding toward the library. "Mr. O'Hanlon has company."

The memories of the dinner party and the Boyles came flooding back and panic engulfed me. I stopped humming and made for the stairs. But Mrs. Donahue grabbed my elbow. "Come with me," she said as she led me to the kitchen. She bustled about, taking two glasses down from a cupboard and pouring whiskey into a decanter. She put everything on a tray and thrust it at me.

"Here, take these into them."

I stared at her.

"Well, go on," she said.

"But who's in there?"

Mrs. Donahue rolled her eyes. "'Tis Mr. O'Hanlon's father-in-law," she said, "poor Mary's da. He's the high and mighty James Sullivan." She sniffed as she pronounced the name. "There's always ructions when the two of them get together. Now go on in. They'll stop the shouting when they see ye—they pay no heed to me at all. And besides, I've to be getting on with the dishes."

"Where's Kathleen?" I said, hoping for a reprieve.

"Still out gallivanting with some boyo. Now, go!"

She shoved me out of the kitchen. In the hallway I could hear the raised voices from the library. I wished Kathleen was here. She would have thought Aidan O'Hanlon and his father-in-law fighting was great *craic* and would have jumped at the chance to witness it. As for me, I hated confrontation, but I had no choice but to go in. I tapped on the library door, but the men kept shouting.

"You're a fool and you always were!" It was the father-in-law's voice, revealing a faint Irish brogue. "I knew you'd come crawling back to New York when you'd had enough of Texas. Damn ridiculous idea, going to look for oil! And dragging my poor Mary with you. Texas is what killed her, and you know that."

A fist thumped on a table and Aidan's voice rose. "Leave Mary out of this, you bastard, or—"

James Sullivan laughed. "Or what? There's nothing you can do to me, my boy! I own this house. I bought it for Mary, and I can throw you out any time I please. And I'd do so if it wasn't for the child."

"And I'd be happy to go!"

"Go on then, you ungrateful spalpeen. Back to the Texas dirt where you belong. But you'll not be taking Lily with you. I'll fight you tooth and nail to keep her, mark my words."

"Lily is my daughter, and as soon as she is ready, I'm taking her back to Texas and you'll never set eyes on either of us again." Aidan's voice was so cold it sent chills through me.

Silence fell. I knocked on the door again, this time more loudly.

"What is it?" Aidan snapped.

I opened the door and went in. He stood in front of the fireplace, his face red. I hesitated. "M-Mrs. Donahue asked me to bring in your drinks. W-where shall I put them?"

"Anywhere. Just pour them and leave!"

I could see his temples pulsating with anger. Quickly, I set down the tray on the nearest table and poured the drinks, my shaking hands causing some of the whiskey to spill.

"Another servant?" James Sullivan's voice boomed from behind me. "I would have thought you had enough staff. And this one doesn't seem very bright!"

I stiffened. All I wanted to do was escape. I picked up the first drink and brought it over to him. He took it without comment, but held me with such a piercing stare that, instead of feeling invisible, I felt exposed and naked. He had a big, powerful frame, and his face had the florid look of a man who drank too much, but his blue eyes were keen. The odor of power radiated from him.

"I must admit she's good-looking, though!"

Aidan's eyes blazed. "Miss Sweeney is none of your business!"

At last I was able to back away from Sullivan's scrutiny. Red-faced, I picked up the second glass and handed it to Aidan. My hand grazed his, and I felt as if I'd had an electric shock. Whether he felt it or not, I didn't know. Then again, I thought, it might just have been my ragged nerves. The room had grown silent except for the heavy breathing of both men. A sudden storm had come up, and fierce wind and rain rattled the windows. I took the opportunity to back out of the room.

"Them two will be the death of me." Mrs. Donahue sat at the kitchen table. "When they're together there's not a civil word spoken."

I lifted the teapot and poured us both a cup. As I sipped, I looked around the kitchen, with its gleaming pots and spotless white counters. It was much larger and grander than our kitchen in Donegal, and it might have been a bit sterile had it not been for Mrs. Donahue's warm spirit, which seemed to fill the place. I looked back at her and thought how fond I had become of this woman. Over the past months she had been a kind, reassuring presence in my life, and I was suddenly very grateful to her. I reached over and patted her arm.

"Thank you," I whispered.

If she heard me, she didn't let on. She was obviously still upset with the men arguing in the library.

"It goes back a long time," she said, as if I had not spoken. "James Sullivan never wanted Mary to marry Mr. Aidan. He had in mind for her a banker or solicitor, not some restless feller with big dreams but not a penny to his name."

"But he's always at business meetings," I said. "He must have *some* money."

"His da cut him off, but I'd say his ma left him some. He invested it all in the oil. I think now he's out trying to raise more money so he can go back to Texas."

I was intrigued. "And what did Mary think of all that?"

Mrs. Donahue smiled, a faraway look in her eyes.

"Mary could be as stubborn as her da when pressed. She told

him she loved Mr. Aidan and would go with him to the ends of the earth."

She stirred the tea absently, then made the sign of the cross. "God rest her soul, when he asked her to go clear across the country with him, she went despite her da's threats to disown her. Ah, she was a great girl, so she was."

She swallowed the rest of her tea and banged down the cup on the saucer.

"To Texas of all places! May as well have been to the moon. He was going to drill for oil, he said, and it turned out he made a fortune. But poor Mary took sick with the fever. While he was caring for her, he took his eye off the business and lost a lot of his money. When she seemed on the mend, Mr. Aidan brought her and Lily back from Texas and they moved into this house. But she had a relapse. . . ."

She sighed and looked toward the ceiling. "And now that poor Mary's gone, I know Mr. Aidan is itching to go back to Texas to build things back up. Sullivan is dead set against it. He blames Mr. Aidan for Mary's death and he doesn't want the same thing to happen to Lily. Mr. Aidan doesn't want to uproot Lily either, given the state she's in. He's torn."

She stood up and brought the cups over to the sink. "That's what they argue about all the time," she said over her shoulder.

That night I lay sleepless. I had never seen Aidan so angry, although I had long suspected he had a temper. It had alarmed me, but not as much as his father-in-law's behavior. I cringed when I thought about how he had stared at me. When he said I was good-looking he leered like a hungry wolf. Still, his words had shocked me. No one back home had ever suggested such a thing—quite the opposite, in fact. Then I remembered Dom's words a few weeks ago—"You're a good-looking girl, Delia. 'Tis time you saw yourself for what you're worth." *They're seeing things, the two of them,* I said to myself. *I'm plain and I'll always be plain, and that's the size of it!*

I turned my mind to what was really bothering me: the news

that Aidan had plans to move away to Texas. Texas? I had barely even heard of it. All I knew was that it was far in the southwest of America, with expansive, flat lands, and cowboys. How I longed to see it. What a wonderful new adventure that would be. But then, fear set in. What if Aidan didn't take me with him and Lily? What if he found out I was a liar and left me behind? What if I never saw either one of them again?

Everyone predicted that the storm that came up the night before would turn into a full-blown hurricane. It had all the signs, they said. I had read about such storms in books like *Wuthering Heights* and *Typhoon*, and even in *The Tempest*, but I had never experienced one. While Ireland had its share of fierce gales and rain, we had never seen a hurricane.

Now I felt an odd excitement born of curiosity. The window shutters were secured, and sandbags placed in front of the outside doors in case of flooding. The car was locked in an adjacent shed. Mrs. Donahue and Kathleen bustled about, finding candles in case all the lights went out, and putting up sandwiches in case they were not back to cook for a day or two. Aidan had insisted that Mrs. Donahue go to stay with her sister, who lived nearby, and Kathleen with her aunt and uncle, who lived farther inland. I chose to stay. I wanted to be with Lily in case she became frightened. And, anyway, where had I to go? Besides, there was something about the prospect of this coming storm that excited my thirst for adventure.

As the afternoon wore on, the wind died down, although the rain kept up at a good pace. Disappointed, I began to wonder what all the fuss was about. Aidan was in the library, and I kept Lily occupied drawing pictures on the kitchen table and waited for something to happen. Eventually, Aidan emerged and came into the kitchen. I jumped up to get him some food, but he waved me away.

"Don't bother, Miss Sweeney. I'll just get myself a sandwich. Have you and Lily eaten?"

"We have, sir. Let me make you some tea."

He sat down next to Lily. The child smiled up at him and thrust her drawings toward him. He examined them, then looked at her in surprise. "These are very good, Lily." She beamed and ran out of the room. Aidan turned to me, frowning.

"Are you sure she did these?"

I nodded. "I watched her draw them. Mrs. Donahue said she thought they were her memories of Texas, even though Lily was quite young when she left there."

Aidan laid the drawings down on the table and gazed toward the window, where the rain beat against the shutters. The quiet of the kitchen was broken by the murmur of distant thunder. Aidan appeared to have forgotten where he was, his thoughts obviously far away. I risked a glance at his profile. A lock of black hair had strayed over his forehead and curling black eyelashes shielded his eyes. I wanted to reach out and stroke his hair, but I shrugged off the temptation. Instead, I stood up and cleared the cups from the table. When I went to lift Lily's drawings, he put his hand on my wrist.

"Please leave them, Miss Sweeney."

"Of course, sir," I said.

He rose and, gathering the drawings in his hands, went back to the library, passing Lily in the hallway. Her face clouded as she watched him go, then, with a sigh, she sat down and began drawing a new picture.

I was beginning to think the hurricane had been just a mild storm after all, and was about to swallow my disappointment, when a sudden blast of lightning lit up the kitchen. Startled, I jumped up from my chair and threw my arms around Lily. The child tried to fight me off, and I realized I was more scared than she was.

"She was used to worse than this in Texas," Aidan's voice rose from behind me. "A tornado will beat a hurricane any day."

Lily broke free of me and ran to the window.

"I-I thought it was over," I said.

He chuckled. "Hardly. Haven't you heard of the calm before the storm? Hurricanes fool a lot of people, Miss Sweeney. When the eye of the storm is overhead, all appears as peaceful as a summer's day. But then the back end hits with a fury you cannot imagine."

"What shall we do?"

Aidan was about to speak when a tree outside the window began to groan and creak. Its branches clawed against the glass panes where a shutter had dislodged. I had a sudden vision of shattered glass and Lily's bloodied face. Without thinking, I dived for the child and pulled her away from the window just as the shutters gave way and the tree branches broke through, causing glass to shatter all around us. Rain poured in relentlessly, soaking us both as I lay over Lily on the floor, shielding her with my body. Aidan's agonized voice rose behind me.

"Lily!"

He knelt beside us and I rolled away from the child and stood up. Sobbing, she threw her arms around her father's neck. He soothed her as best he could and then looked up at me.

"Thank you," he whispered. "Thank you."

I moved slowly toward the window. Rain continued to pour in. Outside in the garden, bushes were flattened against the ground and debris of all kinds rolled across the lawn. The roar of the wind was deafening, and I imagined the house was about to break free of its foundations. A knot formed in my throat as I recalled the last few minutes. I dreaded to think what might have happened to Lily had my intuition not arisen just in time.

As I stood, the rain soaking me to my skin, I was suddenly back on the *Titanic*, clinging to a deck railing as the water swirled about my ankles. The cries of drowning passengers echoed around me and I covered my eyes and ears to block the sights and the sounds. I screamed as my legs gave way and I began to sink. Darkness engulfed me, black and cold as the sea that had swallowed the great ship.

* * *

I opened my eyes to see Aidan crouching over me.

"W-what happened?" I whispered.

"You fainted."

"I thought I was back on the *Titanic*."

He nodded. "I guessed as much."

I realized I was lying on a sofa in the library. I wondered if he had carried me there, and my face flushed at the thought. "How's Lily? Did she get hurt?"

He stared at me. "Don't you remember?"

I struggled to sit up. "No," I said.

"You saved her from terrible danger, Miss Sweeney. But for you, she would have been badly hurt." He paused, then went on, a slight choke in his voice. "How do I thank you?"

Tears filled his eyes, and we stared at each other. My head began to throb, and I lay back down. Aidan sat down on the edge of the sofa and took my hands in his.

"When you fainted, I thought at first it was from the effort of saving Lily, but then I realized you might be remembering the *Titanic*," he said, his tone gentle. "How awful it must have been for you. And you're such a brave girl not to ever have talked about it. And it was thoughtless of us—er, me—not to mention it."

I gave him a weak smile. "I don't usually think about it during the day. It's at night the memories come to me. They've begun to fade, though, and I really thought I was over it u-until now."

Aidan laid a finger on my lips. "Ssh," he whispered, "just rest. I must go and see what damage there is to the rest of the house."

He leaned over and kissed me lightly on the forehead, then tiptoed out of the darkened library. I lay in a daze. Had I been dreaming? Surely so. The thought of Aidan O'Hanlon picking me up and carrying me from the kitchen to the library was clearly absurd, but even more so was the notion of him holding my hand and kissing me on the forehead. What a fool I was. The shock of my memory of that awful night must have affected my reason. Still, I thought, it had been a lovely dream.

I must have dozed off. When I awoke it was dark. The rain

and wind had stopped, and the silence was almost more unnerv-
ing than the storm had been. I got up and went into the hallway.
At the top of the stairs, I met Aidan coming out of Lily's room.

"Is she all right?" I whispered.

"She is safe, thanks to you. The question is, are *you* all right,
Nora? You gave me quite a scare earlier."

"I-I'm fine now, sir," I whispered.

He turned on the light and grinned at me—the mischievous
grin of a young boy.

"I think it's time you let go of this 'sir' business," he said.
"Please call me Aidan. And, besides, when we get to Texas you
will find that people are much more informal there. My friends
would laugh their heads off if they heard you referring to me
as 'sir.' "

I swallowed hard. This could not be real. Heat flooded my
cheeks. Surely this was a joke. Sensing my distress, he came
close and took me by the shoulders.

"I know Texas is very far away, but think of it as an adventure,
Nora. No need to cry about it."

I looked straight into his eyes. "I-I thought you were joking
with me," I began. And then the words tumbled out. "I would
like nothing more than to go to Texas with you and Lily, sir. Er,
Aidan. Ever since Mr. Sullivan mentioned it, I have been reading
about it, but I never thought I'd have the chance to see it. I-I assumed you would go alone with Lily, and . . ."

He smiled. "And why would I do that, silly girl? I can see how
much Lily likes you, and you have been good for her. Before you
arrived, she seldom seemed happy. Now she is a different child
altogether. And," his voice fell to a whisper, "I can see how much
you care for her."

I nodded. "Oh, I do. I would miss her something awful if I was
separated from her."

"Well, now you know that won't happen. I intend for us to
leave New York in early spring. There is much I must attend to
first; then we'll be on our way. Spring is a lovely time of year

there." He paused, and a faraway look came into his eyes. Then he turned back to me and took my hands in his. "Oh, Nora, you are going to love Texas."

That night, visions of Texas, or at least the Texas of my imagination, marched through my mind in an unending stream. I was so excited. I was setting out on another great adventure. I recalled how Aidan looked when he told me the news. His face was shining with pleasure, and when he gazed at me his eyes were gentle. I admitted to myself now that I had been attracted to him for a long time, but never did I think he might return those feelings.

In the morning I woke in a cold sweat. Instead of the happy dreams I had expected, my night had been filled with nightmares. Nora's ghost had risen from the dark sea, her eyes hollow, a grotesque grin on her face. She gripped my arm.

"You're a selfish bitch!" she croaked. *"You stole everything from me: my life, my future, everything! How can you live with yourself? Wait 'til Ma and Da find out what you did."*

No sooner had Nora gone than Father McGinty appeared. His face was florid with righteousness, and he poked his finger at me.

"You lied about who you are," he shouted, *"and you've taken no action to renounce it."*

"But I confessed it," I cried. "The priest absolved me."

Father McGinty shook his head. *"You've told the same lie over and over. You've committed a mortal sin. And if you die in a state of mortal sin, you'll go straight to Hell!"*

Dom's face appeared over Father McGinty's shoulder. *"He's right, Delia,"* he said. *"You've told a string of lies to cover up the first one."*

I realized then that, regardless of the absolution I had received, my guilt for my actions had never left me—and never would—for as long as I continued this deception. It would follow me to Texas and cast a long shadow over my happiness. I had to admit to myself that all the adventures in the world would not cure what really ailed me. I still felt unworthy and unlovable.

Aidan was getting too close to me and me to him, and that frightened me. I had to push him away before one of us got hurt. There was nothing left for me to do but confess to Aidan what I had done and then leave his house.

The next morning, I went into the library. He sat at his desk, his head down. When he looked up, I saw immediately that something was wrong. After last night, I expected a smile and a greeting. But his face was pale and his lips tight. He pointed to a chair.

"Sit down." It was a command.

He waved an envelope at me. "Please explain this."

My stomach pitched. The envelope bore a row of colorful stamps, and deep down I knew it was from Ireland. I swallowed hard and said nothing.

"It's a letter from Mrs. Sweeney from Donegal. In it she begs me to let her know if her daughter, Nora, ever arrived. She wants to believe that Nora did not drown, although she was listed as missing. She enclosed a photograph of her daughter. I must say, she bears little resemblance to you, Miss Sweeney."

He held the photograph up for me to see, but I had no need to look at it. Stowed away in the back of my mind had been the fear that one day Ma might write to him, but as time went on and I heard nothing, I'd dismissed the thought.

"When . . ." I began.

"It appears to have been sent several months ago, not long after the *Titanic* sank, but Kathleen only gave it to me this morning. She said she must have misplaced it and only just now found it."

I knew immediately what Kathleen had done. She'd had the letter all along. She'd probably steamed it open and read it, then bided her time until just the right moment to expose me. When she heard I was going with Aidan to Texas, that was her moment to get revenge. And all this because of her jealousy over Dom? How could she?

"You owe me an explanation, Nora, or whatever your name is."

I stood up and approached the desk. Close up, I saw another emotion on Aidan's face: pain. I took a deep breath.

"I have lied to you, Aidan, and I need to make it right. I am not Nora Sweeney," I hurried on. "My name is Delia. Nora is— er, was—my sister."

Aidan's brow furrowed as he waited for me to say more. I took another deep breath and I let it all come out in one fell swoop.

"You see, it was my sister who was supposed to come and be Lily's governess, and I was to be a domestic servant in a house here in New York. But Nora drowned when the *Titanic* went down. When I arrived at the docks and saw Mrs. Donahue with Nora's name on a sign, I went to tell her what had happened to Nora, but she jumped to conclusions and thought I was Nora. And she was so nice and welcoming that I let her think I was."

I paused. Tears stung my eyes, and my cheeks grew hot. "I . . ." I said, about to continue. But Aidan put up his hand to stop me.

"And what about the house where you were expected? I assume you went to explain why you had not arrived?"

"No," I said miserably, "I didn't go." And then I blurted out the rest. "T-they were Mr. and Mrs. Boyle, your guests here some months ago, and—"

He stared at me. "And you stood here in this room and told them a bald-faced lie?"

"Yes, but I was afraid if I told the truth you'd dismiss me and make me go there . . . a-and by that time I had grown so fond of Lily I couldn't bear to leave her."

I didn't add that I could not bear the thought of leaving him as well.

"And I presume you never wrote to your mother and told her where you were?"

I bowed my head. "No," I whispered.

Aidan sighed and looked away from me toward the fireplace. I stopped talking and waited for him to tell me to pack my bags and leave. But it was not to be that easy.

When he looked back his face was pale, and there was a hint of sadness in his eyes.

The tears I had been holding back threatened to erupt. I had nothing left to say in my own defense. I stood, waiting for my sentence. Aidan tore his gaze away from me and stared past me toward the front window.

"All that time you were telling me about your family, you were lying to me," he said, his voice hoarse. "How could you?"

I realized then how much I had hurt him. I began to cry.

His voice was almost a whisper. "If you'd told me right away, we might have worked things out. After all, your sister was dead and you were not harming her. But you continued to lie to me, you never wrote to your mother and said where you were and you lied to Mr. and Mrs. Boyle. Just when did you propose to tell me the truth?"

"I know you won't believe me, but I was going to tell you today," I sobbed, "but the letter got here first. I'm sorry. I'm so sorry."

I turned to leave, but he got up and caught me by the arm. "As I expect you realize by now, I can't take you to Texas."

I nodded. "I know that, sir."

"Where will you go?"

I shrugged my shoulders in defeat. "Back to Donegal, sir. 'Tis where I belong. I never belonged here in the first place. I always dreamed adventure would make me happy, would change me, but I realize now I'm still the same Delia—the same worthless chit that Ma always said I was. She always said I didn't deserve happiness, and she was right."

I looked up at him, trying not to notice the hurt in his eyes. "I'll leave as soon as I can make arrangements."

I could feel his eyes on me as I left the room. Out in the hallway, I caught sight of Kathleen hurrying down to the kitchen. She had been eavesdropping. I wanted to confront her, but what was the point?

For weeks after I confessed to Aidan, he hardly looked at me, and when he did, his mouth was drawn into a grim line. Kathleen grinned in my face, as if enjoying my discomfort. Mrs. Donahue looked at me with pity and sighed but said little. Her rejection of me hurt my heart. But what hurt most was the sad look on Lily's face, and the tears that floated in her eyes each time she saw me. Aidan had most likely told her I would be leaving. It was Lily I had hurt most of all, and I would never forgive myself.

I decided to write to Da and tell him where I was. Aidan had been right; it was unforgivable of me not to have let Da and Ma know I was alive and well. Not that Ma would have cared that much, but Da had gone out of his way to arrange for me to come to New York along with Nora, and I owed him. He probably knew by now that I never arrived at the Boyles' house. They'd have written to Father McGinty, who would have wasted no time in tormenting Da with the fact that I was the sinful girl he always knew I was.

I told Da that I had lied and said I was Nora, and that I had seen Nora drown. I did not explain why I was leaving the O'Hanlon house—only that I would be coming back to Donegal in a few weeks, and that I would wire him when I knew the exact date. It was only after I got no reply that a thought struck me. Maybe Ma had got her hands on it first and never given it to Da. I would have put nothing past her. I shrugged. It didn't matter much; as soon as I landed in Donegal, she'd pry the truth out of me.

While I had told Aidan that I was going back to Donegal, when it came down to doing it, something in me rebelled. I had escaped that life once. How could I possibly go back there again? Maybe I could find another job and stay in New York. But God was having none of it. He blocked me at every turn—doors closed in my face when people heard my brogue; other, more kindly people said the position was already filled. It turned out that girls were arriving from Ireland every day looking for work, and the competition even for lowly servant jobs was fierce. It was as if God was saying, *you had your chance, girl, and you destroyed it. Now you must step aside and give some other girl the chance.*

At last, defeated, I went to the White Star Line offices and booked third-class passage back to Donegal.

Nora

❦

After a while, my thoughts turned to Sinclair. What would he think when he found out I was just a farmer's daughter from Donegal without a penny to my name? He wouldn't want anything to do with me. As I turned this over in my mind, a plan came to me. What if I told him and Mrs. Shaw some of my memories had returned, but I made up some of the details? I would say that I remembered my journey on the *Titanic*. I would mention I was from Donegal, but instead of the farm, I would make up something grander, like a manor house. I had a good imagination; I was sure it could all be sorted out.

Satisfied that I had solved my problem, I settled in for the first good night's sleep I'd had in a while.

The weather turned colder, and time seemed to stand still. Autumn came, or "fall," as they called it here, and a rainbow of orange, brown, red and yellow leaves covered the trees. I wrapped up warm for my walks. Silver followed me faithfully wherever I went and, as usual, jumped up on the garden bench beside me. Ever since Mrs. Shaw brought her to my bedroom when I was sick, we'd been inseparable. I was grateful for her company; she eased the loneliness.

I still hadn't remembered my name. I told Mrs. Shaw that I had finally remembered all the details of my voyage on the *Titanic*, and the night the ship sank. I told her it was her friend's mauve shawl that set off the memories, and I recounted how a young woman wearing a shawl just like it had tried to stop me from falling overboard.

"Do you think it could have been that lady's daughter?"

'No, dear, it couldn't have been. Mrs. Henry's daughter died from the flu over two years ago—long before the *Titanic* ever sailed."

I shrugged. "I thought myself it was probably too much of a coincidence."

"Unless it was that young lady's ghost," put in Beatrice, who had been listening. "Mm-hmm, sent by the Lord to save you!"

I smiled. "'Tis a lovely idea, Beatrice, but I don't think I was ever that special to the Lord."

"You might be surprised, child."

Every now and then Mrs. Shaw asked me if anything else had come back to me, but I said no. I was afraid of letting too much slip. I shooed away the thought that my parents still thought I was dead.

Sinclair Shaw finally showed his face at the end of November. Mrs. Shaw was hosting a dinner to celebrate Thanksgiving, an American holiday I had never heard tell of. He came on his own this time, without Ben. I must say Mrs. Shaw didn't look too delighted to see him, but he paid little mind to her. He just sat down at the extra place Teresa had quickly set for him at the table and began to charm everyone. Some of Mrs. Shaw's friends were there, including the young Martha, who I had marched with in New York, and they all seemed delighted with him. Not as delighted as I was, though I tried hard not to show it too much.

"I've come to ask you something, Selkie," he said, turning to me just as dinner was coming to an end. "Would you do me the honor of accompanying me to a Christmas Eve ball being thrown by the Van Clines?"

I must have looked at him like an eejit. My mouth fell open and I turned red in the face. "Who?" I choked.

He took my hand. "The Van Clines, my dear Selkie. I don't suppose you've heard of them, but they are among the richest families in New York. Their house is obscenely opulent, and they are famous for their parties." He looked at Mrs. Shaw. "You know them, don't you, Aunt Felicity?"

Mrs. Shaw nodded, while the other guests whispered to one another.

"I know the granddaughter," Sinclair went on, turning back to me. "It should be capital fun, Selkie. And they'll be fascinated to hear that you fell off the *Titanic*."

After Sinclair and the guests had left, I was giddy with excitement. "Oh, what'll I wear, Mrs. Shaw? I've never been to the likes of anything such as that in my life! What do they do at those things? Can you believe Sinclair has asked me, when he could have picked from a million other girls?"

Mrs. Shaw stood up from the table, took me by the arm and led me into the library. We sat down on either side of the fireplace. She looked at me for a while, as if making up her mind what to say.

"I know you are thrilled, my dear," she began. "*I* certainly would be in your shoes. But . . ." She hesitated, and I sensed caution in her voice. "But I feel I must warn you about something. As you know, Sinclair is my husband's nephew, and I have known him since he was born. He is a high-spirited young man, and charming. You saw it yourself this evening. But he has a streak in him that I find—"

"What is it, Mrs. Shaw?"

"I find him somewhat insincere. In short, he uses people for his own amusement, and when they no longer please him, he abandons them. I've seen him do it time and time again." She leaned toward me. "I don't want to see you hurt, my dear. Go with him to the party and enjoy yourself. But don't misread his intentions."

I knew she meant no harm, but I felt my anger rising. She'd assumed I was just like other girls, but she didn't know me. She didn't know that I was always the belle of the ball, and that men fell over themselves to be with me. I wouldn't have known this either had my memory not come back. I remembered how Ma had filled my head with such notions from when I was a child, and every time she was proved right, my confidence grew.

I shrugged my shoulders and stood up. Sinclair Shaw wouldn't be abandoning *me* anytime soon, I was sure of that.

Christmas Eve night arrived, and I felt like a queen. Mrs. Shaw, who confessed she was not up on the latest fashions, had asked young Martha to help. Now I was rigged out in the most beautiful dress I'd ever seen. The bodice was pale blue, with a low neck and wee shiny beads all over it. A broad silver ribbon was wrapped high around my waist. The skirt was the same blue as the bodice and fell to my ankles. It hugged my hips and had a slit up the front that, I was told, was so your legs would be free to dance. I had matching silver shoes with shiny silver buckles. And, to top it all off, Martha suggested a silver headband. She said headbands were becoming all the rage, and I would look very up-to-date.

As I paced back and forth, admiring myself in the mirror, I was glad I hadn't put much weight back on. I remembered that I'd always been big and curvy, but when I came out of the hospital I was like a skeleton. I'd filled out since then, but only enough so I no longer looked like a stick. I tossed my long, black hair, running my hand through the waves. Martha had insisted that all the modern young women had short hair, but I refused to let go of mine. Anyway, I'd rather be different.

Finally, Martha arranged tall, blue feathers into the back of the headband. She stepped away, admiring her handiwork, and said I would be the belle of the ball. I laughed. Mrs. Shaw sighed and told me I looked beautiful. I saw tears in her eyes, and I went over and hugged her.

"Thank you, Mrs. Shaw," I whispered. "For everything."

She nodded just as the blare of a horn sounded outside.

I heard the noise long before we even arrived at the Van Clines' house. Orchestral music filled the night air, along with blaring car horns, shouts and cries of laughter. As we drew closer, I saw tiny lights strung between all the trees across a huge front lawn. There were Christmas lights too, all around the roof and windows of the house, making it look like a fairy castle. When I looked up at the house itself, it took my breath away. Sinclair had said it was "obscenely opulent"—words I'd never heard before in my life—but now I saw what he meant. It was as big as a castle, and the roof rose and fell in peaks of different heights and shapes. There were windows everywhere, some floor-to-ceiling, some tiny ones beneath the roofline. A man with the same color of skin as Beatrice, dressed in a white shirt and gray vest, helped us out of the car and then drove it away.

I put up my hand to make sure my feathers were still in place, slipped my arm through Sinclair's and let him lead me to the front door. At the entrance, a waiter in a black vest stood with glasses of champagne on a tray. Sinclair took two and offered one to me. I was relieved that I had come to learn what champagne was. I sipped it gingerly and felt the bubbles on my tongue. I had never been so happy.

The door led into a wide hall with white marble floors. We had no sooner set foot in there when a tall girl, about my age, came rushing toward us.

"Ace, darling," she said, throwing her slender, white arms around Sinclair's shoulders. "So wonderful to see you."

Who the feck is Ace? I wondered.

She turned to me. "Ah, is this the *Titanic* girl you told us about? She's charming. Come on now, everyone's here!"

Without waiting for us to say anything, she turned around and hurried back up the hallway.

"That was Caroline," said Sinclair, "the Van Clines' granddaughter. Come on, the ballroom's this way."

"Ace?" I said.

"Oh, just a nickname," he said, smiling.

As we stood in the doorway to the ballroom, people turned to stare. I knew then that we were the most handsome couple there. Sinclair was gorgeous in his black tailcoat, white waistcoat and white bow tie. And my dress was as fine as any in the room. I said a silent prayer thanking Martha. As we stood, Ben, Sinclair's friend, hurried up to us.

He took my hand and kissed it. I blushed. No man had ever done that before. "You look beautiful, Selkie," he said, nodding toward Sinclair. "I do hope you'll save a dance for me."

He disappeared into the crowd. I thought again what a nice feller he was—nowhere near as handsome as Sinclair, of course— but lovely all the same. After that, so many people pressed in on us that I was beginning to get dizzy. I noticed, though, that many more women were greeting Sinclair than men. I supposed it was to be expected; after all, he was the handsomest man there. I tightened my grip on him and smiled at everybody.

Martha had taught me all the modern dances: the one-step, the two-step, the fox-trot, the Argentine tango and the one with the silly name, the Castle Walk. When the band started up, I was anxious to show off. Sinclair danced the first few numbers with me, but then excused himself to go and get a drink.

"I'm not a great one for dancing," he said as he released me. "I'll find Ben and send him over."

I wasn't happy to be left standing in the middle of the floor, but I fixed a smile on my face as some of the women stared. Thank God Ben showed up quickly and swept me up in the tango.

After a while I excused myself from Ben to go and get a glass of water. I looked around for Sinclair and finally saw him in an al-cove off the ballroom. He sat playing cards with some other men, a pile of money on the table, and a couple of women draped over him. When I approached, he looked up. "Oh, hello, Selkie. Hav-ing a good time?"

"Marvelous," I said, imitating the other women I'd heard. "What are you up to?"

"Oh, just a little game of poker."

"That's why we call him 'Ace,' honey," said one of the women in a throaty drawl. "He loves his card games."

I sipped my water. Up close, the two women were much older than I'd first thought. Their heavy powder had begun to crack, showing fine lines around their eyes and lips. The one who'd spoken to me held a cigarette in a long, thin holder, gripping it with fiery, red nails that reminded me of lobster claws.

"Say, are you the girl who fell off the *Titanic*?" said the second woman, her voice as deep as a man's. She looked me up and down. "Ace has told us all about you. He said you were Irish, and you were probably traveling in steerage when you almost drowned. And he said that when you woke up, you'd forgotten who you were, so his aunt took you in. What a story!"

I winced. I'd never told anyone about traveling in steerage. Sinclair couldn't have known, which meant he'd made it up. He'd belittled me in front of these disgusting people. Is this what he really thought of me?

"Yes, that's right," I said. "I almost drowned and then I lost my memory." I tried my best to sound polite, even though these two were starting to annoy me and I was furious with Sinclair. I felt like an act in a carnival. I shrugged and went back to the ballroom.

The band had taken a break, and a man at a piano was playing Christmas carols along with some popular tunes, while the guests sang along. I sat in one of the chairs that lined the wall, watching the people come and go. As I sat, my annoyance grew. How could Sinclair bring me to such a grand event and then leave me sitting like a spare dinner? Mrs. Shaw's caution about how he often abandoned friends crept into my head, but I shook it away.

When the dancing began again, I was relieved when one young man after another came over and asked me up onto the floor. *To hell with Sinclair*, I thought, *I don't need him*. But as I was dancing with a tall, dark-haired feller, I felt a hand on my shoulder. Sinclair tugged me roughly away from my partner and tried to pull me off the dance floor. There was an ugly look on his face, and the smell of whiskey was all over him.

"Go back to your cards," I said angrily. "I'm having a fine time without you."

I looked around for my dance partner, but he had disappeared. People were beginning to stare. I took a deep breath, shrugged Sinclair off me and walked as steadily as I could to the edge of the ballroom. I asked for directions to the powder room and hurried down the hall. I could feel Sinclair close behind me.

"Don't run away from me, you slut!" he shouted.

The tips of my ears burned with embarrassment. He was closing in on me as I pushed open the powder room door and tried to close it behind me. But he wedged his foot in it to keep it open. He put his hands on my shoulders and forced me backward into the room, kicking the door closed behind him. He began pulling at my dress, forcing the bodice down off my shoulders. He grabbed at my breasts and forced his mouth down on mine. He was pawing at me the way young lads had done back home in Kilcross. I tried to knee him in the groin as I had learned to do with them, but it only made him angrier. He let go of my breasts and reached his hand up my dress, his rough fingers poking at me, trying to drill inside me. I tried to push him off, but my strength was no match for his. I raised my hand to his cheek and dug in my nails, drawing blood from his temple to his jaw. He pulled back from me, his hand on his face, a wild look in his eyes.

"You little bitch!" he cried. "You'll pay for that!"

I began to scream, and he lunged at me again. There was a sudden pounding on the door, and I screamed louder.

"Help me! Dear God, somebody help me!"

Sinclair growled like a rabid animal and started toward me again. "I know you want it. You've been making sheep's eyes at me ever since we met. Come on, Selkie, let me give you what you've been asking for, I—"

I don't know where I found the strength, but something in me snapped and I pushed him, hard, sending him reeling to the floor.

The door swung open and there stood Ben, a horrified look on his face. In one glance he took in my torn dress and Sinclair's bleeding face.

"Get away from her now, Sinclair!" he shouted.

I stepped over Sinclair and made for the door, but before leaving, I turned back.

"My name is not fecking Selkie!" I shouted. "My name is Nora Sweeney!"

I pushed Ben aside and ran out of the powder room, down the marble hallway and outside into the freezing night air. I bent over to catch my breath, which was coming in spasms. My head spun and I thought I might collapse. And when I looked down at my tattered dress—my lovely dress—I began to sob.

Panic set in. How was I going to get back to Mrs. Shaw's? I had no money, no transport. All I knew was that I had to get away from this place. In my dazed state, I kicked off my silver shoes with the shiny buckles and began to walk.

I hadn't gone very far when a car drew up beside me. "Selkie? I mean, Nora. Come on, get in or you'll freeze to death."

We drove in silence. Ben wrapped me in a blanket, and I slid down in the seat, trying to blot out the world.

Mrs. Shaw ran out of the door as soon as Ben stopped the car in front of the house. It was as if she knew something was wrong.

"Ben? What's happening? Where is Sinclair?" Then she turned to me. "Are you all right, child?"

I hadn't the strength to answer.

"Let's get her inside, Mrs. Shaw," said Ben. "I'll explain shortly."

I sank down in bed with Silver curled next to me and drifted off into an exhausted, thankfully dreamless, sleep.

* * *

The next morning I sat up in bed sipping a cup of tea while Mrs. Shaw sat in a chair beside me. Her expression was a mixture of sadness and anger.

"I'm so sorry about what happened."

"'Twasn't your fault, Mrs. Shaw. You tried to warn me."

She shook her head. "Not about that sort of behavior. I never thought he was capable of that."

I shrugged. "I didn't either."

A wave of self-pity came over me then, and I began to cry. I thought about how over the moon I'd been about the party; how much I'd loved showing off my new dress; how I secretly hoped Sinclair might be the man I'd been waiting for. But then he'd gone and ruined everything. I felt dirty, my body aching and bruised from the force of his fingers trying to invade me, full of shame at his accusations. I'd made a fool of myself and maybe I deserved what I got.

As if reading my mind, Mrs. Shaw left her chair and lay down on the bed beside me. She took me into her arms.

"It's not your fault, dear child; you did nothing to bring this on. It is Sinclair who should be ashamed." She paused and stroked my hair. "Ben told me what happened. He said Sinclair lost a great deal of money in that card game. Then he got very drunk and took his anger out on you."

"'Twas Ben who saved me," I whispered. "Who knows what might have happened if he hadn't interfered?"

Mrs. Shaw nodded. "Ben is a fine young man. His loyalty to my nephew has always puzzled me. But after last night, he has finally seen Sinclair for the monster he really is."

She went quiet but continued stroking my hair. I had a feeling of contentment I'd never known before—certainly not with my ma. I'd always thought my mother loved me, but I realized now that for all her sweet talk and compliments, what she was really after was control. Her own dreams had never come true, and she was hell-bent on realizing them through me. Real love, I knew now, was when somebody cares about you while expecting nothing back from you. What I felt now from Mrs. Shaw was real love. I looked up at her and smiled. How I wished this woman had been my mother. How different my life might have been and, more to the point, how different a girl I might have turned out to be.

"Ben told me you remembered your name."

"I have. I was as shocked as anybody when it came out of my mouth."

"Nora Sweeney. It's a lovely name. It suits you."

I smiled. But I knew then she deserved to know the rest of it. "I've been keeping some of it back, Mrs. Shaw. And I'm sorry. I was afraid you'd make me go back home if you knew and, well, I didn't want to go."

She said nothing as I told her the details of my story—how I was born on a farm in Kilcross, Donegal; how I had a sister named Delia; how I was supposed to go to work for a man named Aidan O'Hanlon; how my ma had told me to try to get him to marry me. Mrs. Shaw's eyebrows went up at this last bit, but she passed no remark on it.

"I'm sorry I didn't tell you sooner," I said, my voice trailing off to a whisper.

She patted my hand and got up from the bed. "Don't be sorry, Nora. You were right to wait until you felt ready to tell me. You just rest now, and we'll talk about what we should do next when you are feeling stronger."

A few days later, Mrs. Shaw came into the kitchen, all business, and sat down. Beatrice was humming away at the sink, and Teresa was away on an errand.

"I've been thinking, Nora," Mrs. Shaw began, "the first thing we should do is contact your parents to let them know you are alive. They deserve to know the truth."

I nodded. I knew she was right.

"I've looked up the list of the *Titanic* survivors I saved from the newspaper. There was a Delia Sweeney from Donegal listed."

I put my hand to my mouth. "Thank God," I whispered.

"We must find her. Do you have any idea where she would be?"

I shook my head. I was embarrassed to admit I had paid no attention to where Delia was going to work. "I'm sorry, I just don't remember. She was to go to work as a domestic in some house in New York that my da had arranged, but I never knew the name."

"But how would you have contacted her after you both arrived in New York?"

I blushed. "Delia and myself didn't get along so well."

Mrs. Shaw pursed her lips but said nothing, though Beatrice said an "mm-hmm" as if to herself. I knew she had been listening. Now I was doubly embarrassed.

"And this Mr. O'Hanlon. Do you have his address?" Mrs. Shaw's tone was brisk.

I shook my head no. "Delia carried all the papers," I said miserably. "She was to give them to me when we docked. I'm sure he has taken on another girl by now and, anyway, I'm not sure I want to go there," I finished stubbornly.

"Have you thought about what you *want* to do now, Nora?" Mrs. Shaw's voice was gentler now.

I wanted to tell her I didn't want to go home, and I didn't want to find Delia or Mr. O'Hanlon, that I wanted to stay with her, but I didn't have the courage, so I said nothing.

"It's all right, Nora, you don't have to rush your decision. Give it some thought, and when you're ready we can talk again." She stood up. "Now, come with me into the library, please."

Beatrice let out another "mm-hmm" as we left the kitchen.

When we were alone, Mrs. Shaw sat me down.

"I'm going to discuss something important with you, Nora. You know that I have become especially fond of you. In fact, I think of you as my daughter."

I drew a deep breath.

"I would like nothing more than to see your future secure—financially, I mean. But you should understand that Sinclair, after inheriting from his own father, also stands to inherit this house and all my other assets. You see, my late husband left everything to me as long as I was living, but upon my demise, his will states that what assets remain are to go to his only living relative, Sinclair."

I winced at the sound of his name.

"So, you see, Nora, I cannot change the terms of the will. However, what I *can* do is transfer a sum of cash into an account with your name on it." She paused and laughed. "It's good we finally know your name. That way I'll be satisfied you'll have the means to get on your feet and start on a new path if something were to happen to me."

I opened my mouth to protest, but she put up her hand.

"I have something else for you, Nora. Something more personal than money."

She put her hands up to her throat and unfastened the locket she wore. I had often silently admired it. It was solid gold, heart-shaped and engraved with what I recognized as a Celtic knot.

"Turn around," she said. "My dear husband gave this to me on my wedding day, and I want you to have it."

I held my breath while she fastened the delicate chain around my neck. I put my hand up to touch it and turned to look at her. "I . . ." I began, suddenly at a loss for words.

"Ssh, my dear," she said and enveloped me in her arms.

It was then that my tears began to flow, and I hugged her back fiercely. At last I drew away from her. "Nothing's going to happen to you, Mrs. Shaw," I whispered.

She threw back her head and gave a loud, husky laugh. "Dear girl, I have no intention of letting anything happen to me."

I suppose when God hears you declaring your own intentions, He sometimes lets you know it's His intentions that count.

A week later, Mrs. Shaw was dead.

She'd been on her way to the bank to make the money transfer she'd told me about when she skidded off the road in that curse of a car of hers. She was most likely driving like a madwoman as she always did, thinking no calamity could ever touch her. She had the rest of us believing that way too.

After Mrs. Shaw's death the household was gripped by paralysis. Beatrice wrung her hands and sang hymns, Teresa went silent and I hid in my room with Silver. A minister came to talk about funeral arrangements. None of us knew what to tell him, and he sighed and went away again. The only comfort we had was when the suffragette ladies came, including young Martha, who had helped me with my preparations for the Christmas Eve party. Mother of God, was that only a month ago? Martha said the ladies had talked among themselves, and they would take over Mrs. Shaw's arrangements.

It might have been better for the three of us—Beatrice, Teresa and me—to have busied ourselves with the wake and the funeral and the reception afterward. As it was, with nothing to do, we were left to our own thoughts. I couldn't bring myself to cry, although my heart was breaking. I thought of how the old Nora would have behaved. She would have worried about herself first. She'd have been spitting mad about the money she'd never get now, and the fact that she'd have to find another place to live and complain about how she didn't deserve this. Had I really changed so much in less than a year? I knew in my heart the change in me was in answer to what Mrs. Shaw gave me. When you're given love, it seemed, you respond with love. What would happen now that Mrs. Shaw was gone?

It took that bastard, Sinclair, only three days after Mrs. Shaw's funeral to show up at the house and hammer on the door.

I refused to be afraid of him. "What do you want?" I cried. "Sure, the poor woman's not even cold. Where's your respect?"

He sneered down at me and shoved me back inside the hallway. "I've come to collect my inheritance," he said. He waved his arm around. "All of this is now mine, Miss Nora Sweeney, and if you ever had any thoughts of getting your grasping little fingers on any of it, you can forget it."

I wanted to claw the eyes out of him. He pushed on past me

and went into the kitchen. Beatrice stood wide-eyed, while Teresa tried to fold herself into a corner. He banged his fist on the table.

"You two," he said, "you work for me now, and I will tolerate no slacking. I have also discovered from the financial records that your wages are excessive. You will take a cut in pay and improve your work habits, or you can leave. I will give you to the end of the week to decide."

He swung around to look at me. I stood glaring at him with my arms folded. I stood within easy reach of the kitchen knives. If this feller made a move toward me, I was ready to swing for him. He must have sensed the danger, for he backed up a couple of paces.

"You," he said, "you have no such options. You'll go and pack your things this minute and get out of my house."

I stood my ground, while Beatrice began praying aloud. As I stared at him, I believed I was looking at the Divil himself. How could I ever have thought I was in love with this man? A cold shiver ran through me, as if somebody was walking on my grave, and I knew I had to get away from him as quickly as I could.

I gave no thought as to where I would go. I just wanted to get out of this house. Silver sat meowing as I threw some clothes into a bag. Beatrice came into the room, tears rolling down her cheeks.

"Oh, Miss Nora, what's to become of you?"

I stopped what I was doing and hugged her. "Don't worry about me, Beatrice, I'll be grand."

I looked down at Silver, who was rubbing against my leg. "Beatrice," I said, "would you take care of Silver? Otherwise Sinclair will torture her."

"I sure will," said Beatrice, drying her eyes with a big handkerchief. "Now, you run over to next door to where Mr. Frankie works. You tell him Miss Beatrice sent you. Tell him she says he's to give you a ride in 'is cart into the village." She gave a quick smile. "Ole Mr. Frankie, he's got a soft spot for ole Beatrice. He do 'most anything I ask him."

As if the effort of speaking was too much for her, Beatrice sank down on the bed and began to weep again.

"Will you stay?" I said.

She stopped crying at once. "Stay?" she said. "I'd rather go and work for the Devil."

A half hour later, I left the Shaw house for the last time. I ignored Sinclair's taunts as I pushed past him. Good to Beatrice's word, Mr. Frankie hitched up his horse and wagon and helped me up into it. Tipping his old, crushed hat, he climbed up beside me and we began the slow drive toward the village. I never looked back.

As the old horse plodded along, I was reminded of the ride Delia and I had taken with Da from the cottage to the train station on our way to board the *Titanic*. What a lifetime ago that seemed.

We were just entering the village when we met a car coming at speed from the opposite direction. I recognized it at once, and asked Frankie to stop. The car came to a stop alongside us, and Ben jumped out.

"Nora!" he cried. "Where are you going? Have you seen Sinclair? He told me he was coming here, and I followed him to make sure he didn't cause any trouble."

"He tried to, Ben," I said. "But then he just sent me on my way. To tell you the truth, I was glad to go. I'm going to New York. I'm not quite sure how, but I'll find a way."

Ben looked from me to the cart. "Not in *that*, you're not," he said in astonishment. "Let me drive you."

I almost refused, but I stuffed down my stubbornness. How else was I to get to New York? I climbed down and thanked Frankie. "Make sure Beatrice is all right," I said.

He nodded, and drove away.

Ben threw my bag in the back seat and settled me into the front. We said nothing for a long time. As we drew close to the city, I began to worry. What was I going to do? My first instinct was to find Delia, but that would be impossible. Besides, at this point all I wanted to do was run away and lick my wounds. I wanted nothing more at that minute than to go back home to Donegal. But how was I to do that with hardly a penny to my name? My tears began to flow, even though I fought to hold them back.

"What's wrong, Nora?" Ben said.

I let the words pour out of me. "Oh Ben, I just want to go home, and I've no money. I don't know what I'm going to do."

Ben looked at me and said nothing. When we arrived in New York, he drove straight to the White Star offices to inquire as to when the next ship was sailing for Ireland. He talked to the clerks and came back smiling.

He handed me a ticket. "There's a ship sailing in two days," he said.

I looked at him in shock. "But . . ." I began, "I didn't mean for you to buy me a ticket. I've never begged in my life and I don't intend to start now."

"Do you have money for a hotel?" he asked, ignoring my protest.

I looked at his earnest face. I realized that in my hurry to get away from Sinclair I hadn't even thought about where I would sleep tonight. I lowered my head.

"No," I said.

He smiled. "I thought not. Here, take this."

I started to refuse, but he pushed some banknotes into my hand. I held back tears as I thanked him. He drove me to what he said was a respectable hotel. When I got out of the car, I stood on the sidewalk with my bag. He and I looked at each other. I don't think either of us knew what to say. Finally, he broke the silence.

"Good luck, Nora. Safe journey."

"Thank you for everything, Ben," I said, "You've been a good friend. I promise I will pay you back one day." Without thinking, I reached up and kissed him on the cheek.

When I reached the hotel entrance, I turned back and waved to him one last time.

Dallas, Texas

1913

Delia

❧

The transcontinental train rolled in a steady rhythm along the tracks, slow enough for me to take in the passing scenery. I put down my book and looked out the window. City landscapes gave way to wooded acreage and then to open flatlands. It was like watching a moving picture show. My imagination ran wild—making up stories of adventurers like those in my books, exploring new and unchartered territory. I was like a child, delighted with my own make-believe. I must have been smiling because, when I looked away from the window, Aidan was eyeing me with curiosity. I blushed and turned away to Lily, who sat beside me, drawing pictures in her notebook.

I was bursting with love for the child. It was she who had given me this second chance, and I would forever be grateful to her.

About a week before I was to sail for Donegal, I knelt in front of the child and took her stiff little body in my arms. "I'm so sorry, darling," I whispered. "I have to go away soon. Your daddy is taking you to Texas and I will not be going. You see, I did a bad thing. I told your daddy a lie—well, several lies—and he is very upset with me. I told him my name was Nora. But I'm not Nora. I'm Delia."

She stared at me solemnly. "And—and I have been s-staying away from you on purpose because . . ." My voice cracked. "Because you must get used to life without me."

I expected her to burst into tears. Instead, she pulled away from me and stuck out her chin. What I saw in her eyes was not sadness, but some other, stronger emotion. If I'd not known better, I would have said it was anger. My heart sank.

"I'm so sorry, Lily," I said. "I didn't mean to make you sad or angry. I love you very much and I never wanted to leave you. But your daddy . . ."

Without waiting for me to finish my sentence, Lily seized my hand and pulled me forward. I got to my feet. Still holding on to my hand, she pulled me out of the room and down the stairs. When we reached the door to the library, I froze. I knew Aidan was in there, and the last thing I wanted was to face him. I tried to wrench away my hand, but Lily was having none of it. She pushed open the door without knocking and, with me in tow, marched straight over to Aidan.

He looked from Lily to me.

"You may go now," he said.

I nodded and turned to go, but Lily's small hand was like a vise. She looked Aidan in the face and shook her head from side to side, as if to say she was not letting me go anywhere.

I could see Aidan was working hard to control his temper. "Now, now, Lily. You mustn't be impudent. I know you are fond of your governess, but you must get used to life without her."

I noticed he could not even refer to me by name. I wrested my hand from Lily's, nodded and turned toward the door.

"No! Stay!"

Her small voice echoed behind me. I thought I was hearing things. I swung around and stared at her. She stood facing her father, her arms akimbo, like a little warrior.

"No, Daddy," she said, 'I won't go to Texas unless Miss Delia comes too."

A heavy silence fell over the room. Aidan and I stared at Lily, openmouthed. Had she really spoken? Had she just uttered her first words in years? Tears welled in my eyes and I wanted to rush over and hug her. But I was rooted to the floor. Aidan jumped to his feet, his face pale. Lily did not move.

He knelt in front of her. "Lily," he whispered, as if afraid to break the spell, "Lily, did you just speak? Did I really hear you?"

"Yes, Daddy," she said. "I told you I won't go to Texas unless Miss Delia comes too."

Aidan looked from her to me, suspicion in his eyes. I guessed he thought I had hidden from him that she was speaking all along. As if reading his mind, she said, "I have never spoken in front of Miss Delia, Daddy. I have not spoken to anyone since Mommy died."

"Then why now?" whispered Aidan.

"Because this is important, Daddy. There was nothing before that was important. It was easier to be silent. But I love Miss Delia, and you can't leave her behind, so I had to start talking again."

I was shocked. Not only was Lily speaking, but she sounded more like an adult than a seven-year-old girl. I always knew she was intelligent, but this—this was beyond belief.

Suddenly, Aidan had tears in his eyes. He hugged Lily tight. She buried her head in his shoulder, whimpering. Poor wee thing. It was as if the effort of talking had been too much for her. Aidan looked at me over her head.

"Will you come with us, Miss Sweeney?"

All his anger was gone, replaced by uncertainty.

"Yes." I nodded.

As night fell, the train slowed down and heaved to a stop, and I became anxious. Where was I to sleep? Aidan had purchased Pullman tickets, which offered small sleeping compartments with pull-out beds. They were close together, but each was shrouded by a curtain for privacy.

We ate supper in the first-class dining car. Aidan and I said little to each other, and I was grateful for Lily's constant prattling. It seemed to me she was making up for all the words she hadn't spoken in the previous four years. When we finished eating, he rose and stretched.

"We may as well turn in for the night," he said.

I followed him and Lily back to the carriage, picked up my traveling bag and waited for the conductor to open the curtain that hid the sleeping compartment. I stepped inside and quickly pulled the curtain tightly across the opening. Inside, there was a small bed covered in silken sheets. I stood, my heart thumping. I was acutely aware that Aidan was in the compartment right next to mine, separated only by a curtain. The distance between us was so small I could have put out my hand and touched him. A sadness came over me as I imagined how different things might have been.

I was awakened with a start when I felt someone's presence beside the bed. I sat straight up and turned up the lamp. Lily stood looking down at me. She carried the small, well-worn plush rabbit she always slept with.

"What's wrong, Lily?" I whispered.

"I can't sleep. I'm frightened."

The poor wee thing, I thought. I'd probably have felt the same way at her age if I was lying in a strange bed by myself on a moving train. I pulled aside the bedcovers.

"It's all right, Lily. Climb in with me. I'll keep you safe."

The warmth of her small body was comforting. Soon her steady breathing told me she was asleep. I lay awake for a while, but soon the rocking rhythm of the train lulled me back to sleep.

I awoke with a start again, sensing someone was watching me. I hadn't drawn the window curtains aside, and the red rays of dawn filtered into the Pullman car, giving enough light that I could make out a shadow. I knew instinctively who it was.

"Aidan?" I whispered. "Is something wrong?"

He came closer. "Nothing," he whispered back. "I went to check on Lily and she wasn't in her bed. I guessed she might be with you."

I nodded. "She came in last night. She was afraid of being on her own."

I thought then he might be hurt that she didn't seek comfort with him. As if reading my thoughts, he said, "I am surprised she didn't come to me, but I suppose . . ."

He let the words trail off.

"She is missing her mother, I think."

The light in the small space grew brighter as the sun edged up from the horizon and I could see him clearly. He was fully dressed, although his shirt was unbuttoned from collar to waist. I stared at the black hair that spread across his bare chest, suppressing the urge to run my fingers through it. I forced myself to look at his face instead. He was staring at me as if seeing me for the first time. I flinched under his scrutiny, aware of my unbound hair spread across the pillow, and that I wore only my nightgown. In her sleep, Lily had drawn all the bedcovers around herself, leaving me fully exposed. I took in a deep breath and prayed he would look away. Instead, he drew closer, bent down and kissed Lily on the forehead.

"I expect you are correct," he said, "she *is* missing her mother."

He gathered the sleeping child in his arms and lifted her up. I thought he was taking her back to her berth. But instead he laid her down on his own bed. Then he turned and came toward me. I had hurriedly pulled the bedcovers back over me. He sat down on top of them and, taking my hand in his, fixed his eyes on me.

"I was wrong to be angry with you, Delia," he whispered. "I see the love you have for Lily and she has for you. I was being selfish."

He began to finger the strands of my hair. "I was very hurt when you told me you'd lied to me. I tried telling you that my anger was because you had violated my strong principle of truthfulness, but the irony is I was lying too. What really hurt was that I had become very fond of you, Delia. I'd dropped my guard for the first time since Mary died and let you get close. And when I found out you'd lied to me about who you really were, I felt like a fool."

I waited for him to finish; I could find no words to reply. All I could do was gaze at his face in the early morning light.

"Daddy? Miss Delia?" Lily's small voice broke the spell.

Aidan pulled away and spun around.

"It's all right, Lily, I'm here," he said, his voice husky.

"I want to get up now," she said. "It's morning."

"You're right. Let's go back to your berth and get you dressed."

He reached up and drew the curtain between our berths closed.

Later, I joined them at breakfast. If Lily had seen her father sitting on my bed, she passed no remark. Instead, she prattled on excitedly about the things she would do when she got to Texas. Aidan and I said little, focusing our full attention on Lily. When we finished breakfast, we went back to the carriage, where I found a corner seat and took refuge in my book.

The journey became monotonous. I was tired and stiff from sitting, even though the seats were plush velvet, not wooden, as they would have been on the trains at home. I was excited when we stopped in Chicago to change trains and climbed down on to the platform along with crowds of people. I was anxious to see Chicago, but we had to board another train without ever going outside.

At last, the train crossed the Texas border. I sat up straight and peered out the window, anxious to see the place that was to be my new home. For a while we passed through thick stands of pine trees. I hadn't expected to see them because all that I had read about Texas suggested it was flat and arid. I wanted to ask Aidan about it, but, although he was smiling as he looked out the window, an unexpected shyness had overcome me, and I thought better of it. In time the woods gave way to vast stretches of brown, parched acreage. Stunted trees grew at odd angles, and dried-up bushes rolled across the land, propelled by the wind. It was like nothing I had ever seen—more like the surface of the moon than anything on earth. In my astonishment, I looked over at Aidan and realized he had been watching me.

"What do you think, Delia?"

"It's different from Ireland."

He laughed. "That's what Mary said when she first saw it."

I turned back to the window. The flatness of the land was relieved now and then by small hills and crude, rustic cabins. Occasionally I saw men riding horses in the distance, kicking up clouds of dust behind them. My stomach sank. Texas looked lonely and desolate, and I suddenly wished I had never agreed to come. I looked over at Lily, who stood with her nose pressed to the window. She turned to me, smiling.

"You'll like Texas, Miss Delia."

I gave her a faint smile back and nodded.

If I'd been honest, I would have told her that as long as I was close to her and her father, I didn't much care where I was.

When I climbed down from the train at a depot called Fort Worth, I felt as if I had been traveling forever. My clothes were crumpled and dusty, and the heat inside the train carriage had made me drowsy. I set down my bag, then straightened up and stretched. Aidan walked up to me, holding Lily by the hand. The child was skipping with excitement.

"Come," Aidan said. "José should be waiting for us."

I was a little confused. "I thought we were going to Dallas," I said. "Didn't we pass that depot a little while ago?"

He grinned. "I wanted to come here first because there's something I'd like to show you."

I followed him out of the station. Outside, a scorching heat enveloped me, setting the back of my exposed neck on fire. I thought I might faint. I took a deep breath and tried to shake myself awake. The heat seemed to have no effect on Aidan or Lily. They both smiled broadly at a short, brown-skinned man walking toward us. He wore tall leather boots, narrow pants and a large black hat. He removed his hat and gave a small bow.

"Welcome, Señor O'Hanlon," he said.

"Hello, José," Aidan said, shaking the man's hand. "It's good to see you after all this time. You remember Lily, and this is Miss Sweeney, her governess."

José bowed to me, then looked down at Lily. "The *niñita*, she has grown."

He led us down the steps to a mud-splattered blue car. Its top had been rolled down, meaning the passengers would be exposed to the merciless sun. José held open the doors and Aidan climbed into the front seat, while Lily and I settled ourselves in the back. José went off to fetch our luggage. Aidan took off his jacket and tie and threw them in the back seat beside me, then he opened his shirt collar.

"Ah, it's so good to be back," he said, "where we can leave all of the stuffiness of New York behind us."

I wanted to ask how he could stand such heat, but I didn't want to complain. As if reading my mind, he said, "It's hot for early May, Miss Sweeney, but you'll have to get used to it. The next three months will be even hotter. It shocks Northerners when they first arrive, and those who cannot take it go home. It's a test of their resilience. Those who stay are the ones who truly belong here."

I wanted to point out that he was a Northerner himself, but I kept silent.

A rank, unfamiliar smell suddenly assaulted me, taking my mind off the heat. I looked up, and thudding toward the car was a herd of cows, but not like any cows I had ever seen. They were huge and had horns on them that spanned outward wider than the width of their bodies. I shrank back in fright. Lily looked up at me and laughed.

"Don't be scared, Miss Delia, they're only longhorns."

Aidan turned around, grinning. "I wanted to see the look on your face when you first saw them. I suppose they are frightening at first, but you'll get used to them. You see, Fort Worth is the place where ranchers bring their cattle to be shipped far and wide by railroad. People say this is where the West begins. Its nickname is "Cow Town.""

I was somewhat put out with Aidan. How dare he try to deliberately scare me this way? But then I looked at him, his eyes dancing with merriment, and my heart melted. For all his reassurance, though, I still shuddered as the herd thundered past. Men with weather-beaten faces sheltered by large white hats rode on either side of the animals, ropes in their hands.

José came back carrying our luggage and put it in the boot of the car. Smiling, he slid into the driver's seat and started the engine. I was thankful for the faintest of breezes that moved the hot air around. Maybe when we were out on the main road it would be better, I hoped. The streets bustled with traffic and pedestrians. I was shocked to see such activity in the middle of the brown flatlands; it was like a mirage in the middle of the desert. Women wearing lace-trimmed blouses and long skirts, some carrying parasols to keep off the sun, picked their way daintily along the pavements. Many of the men wore boots with spurs, their faces shaded by big hats like the one José wore. Some leaned against buildings, one foot raised behind them, watching the scene before them with keen eyes. Brown-skinned women with long, black braids, some carrying babies, wove in and out of the crowds. Cattle mingled with horse-drawn carriages, cars and trams, and manure dotted the streets. This place would never be mistaken for New York City, I thought.

José threaded the car through the traffic, and soon the town disappeared behind us, giving way to small, wooden cabins scattered haphazardly on either side of the road. As we drove on, even these disappeared and all that was left was a carpet of brown, sun-parched land spread out before us and to either side, dotted here and there with a few misshapen trees and low-lying bushes. Aidan and José talked easily to each other in front. I strained to hear them but could not make out the words over the noise of the engine. Lily had fallen asleep, her head leaning against my arm. I smiled down at her.

Eventually, the monotony of the landscape and the relentless heat overcame me, and I nodded off. I awoke with a start when the car stopped. For a minute I didn't know where I was. I rubbed my eyes and tried to shake myself awake. Lily sprang up and darted out of the car before I could stop her. I called after her, but she didn't turn around. It was then I saw the house. It was two stories high, with a low, flat roof of red tile and over-hanging eaves. A veranda spanned the width of it, held up by ta-pered pillars anchored in a foundation of stone. The exterior was of wood, painted the color of sand, with brown trim. A flight of stone steps led up to a wide brown door with glass panes. It faced a green lawn edged with a profusion of colorful flowers and was shaded by tall trees. *I must be dreaming*, I thought. How could such a beautiful house and verdant landscape have sprung up in the middle of this arid land?

I rubbed my eyes again to make sure I was awake. But the house and lawn and flowers were still there. My mouth must have dropped open because Aidan leaned close to me.

"Welcome to my Dallas home, Delia. Not what you expected, is it?"

"I-I never thought there'd be such beauty," I said.

"Not out in this wilderness?"

I nodded, worried that I might have offended him.

"N-no, I didn't mean . . ."

"It's all right, Delia. It's a natural reaction. José and the staff take great pride in the flowers and the bushes and the lawn. They baby them as if they were children. As you can imagine, it takes skill to grow something like this in this climate." He paused and sighed. "Before Mary came, there was nothing but gravel. She was the one who insisted on all this. She wanted to be reminded of Ireland. We all thought she was mad, but she per-sisted. I'm truly overcome that the workers have kept everything just the same as when she was here."

He looked away from me, but not before I saw the moistness in his eyes. I stepped out of the car and walked toward the house, leaving him to his memories.

Inside, the house was blessedly cool. A short hallway led into an open room dominated by a huge stone fireplace. Oak floors gave way to stained-wood walls and exposed beams. Built-in cabinets displayed decorated pottery, and side tables held lamps with hammered silver bases and stained-glass shades. The furniture was of brown leather, and patterned rugs in shades of green, red, yellow and orange covered the floors. A large dining table and chairs with simple, straight lines stood beneath a window at the far end of the room. This house had none of the formality of the house in New York and I felt like I could breathe here.

A short, stocky woman with a solemn expression appeared from another room and came toward me. But before she could get close, Lily rushed to her and threw her arms around her waist. The woman's brown face creased in smiles. She took Lily's face between her hands and beamed down at her.

"*Hola*, Miss Lily," she said, "*Bienvenido a casa*. Welcome home."

"*Hola*, Miss Rosa."

I fought back tears as I watched them. Joy glowed on both their faces. I could see now why Lily had been so sad in New York. This was her real home.

I was distracted by Aidan and José bringing in the luggage. Aidan went immediately to Rosa and kissed her on the cheek. She said something to him in Spanish, her eyes moist as she did so. Aidan stepped back and put his hand out toward me.

"This is Miss Sweeney, Rosa," he said. "She is Lily's governess. She is from Ireland."

Rosa nodded. "Like Señora Maria," she whispered.

"Yes, like Mary."

"Welcome, Miss Sweeney," she said.

Aidan turned to me. "Rosa is José's wife. They have been with me for many years."

I smiled and nodded.

Later, when Rosa had shown me to my room, upstairs under one of the eaves of the house, I sat down on the bed with its patterned quilt and took a deep breath. I was here. I was finally in Texas. I didn't know what to make of it yet; everything was so strange and different.

A sudden wave of melancholy swept over me. I thought at first it was homesickness for Ireland, but while that was part of it, the bigger part, I admitted to myself, was due to Mary. The ghost of Aidan's late wife was everywhere. She dwelled in the profusion of flowers in the garden, her touch evident in the welcoming warmth of the living room and her memory alive in Rosa and José. And what hurt most of all was that by coming to this place she had been newly resurrected in the minds and hearts of Lily and Aidan. This was their home, this was where the three of them had been happy, and it was I who was the imposter.

I stood up and tried to compose myself. How could I be so jealous of a dead woman who had never done me any harm? I made up my mind there and then to let all thoughts of Mary go, and to concentrate on my duty to Lily.

I opened my bag, took out the books I had brought with me from Ireland and hugged them like old friends. They were much the worse for wear after the journey on the *Titanic* and the long trip from New York to Texas, but they had survived intact, just as I had done. As I flipped through their pages, a small curl of excitement rose in my stomach. I was finally living the adventure promised by the stories they contained. Fate had handed me a wonderful and unexpected gift, and I was determined to make the most of it.

The evening after we arrived, two visitors burst into the house, disturbing the calm quiet of the place. Lily ran to the door to greet them.

"Uncle Hans, Aunt May!"

Laughing, the man reached down and picked up Lily, swinging her around in the air.

'You have grown, *mein kleine mädchen*. Soon you will have to pick *me* up instead."

"You're silly, Uncle Hans."

Aidan rushed toward them wearing a wide grin.

"What a surprise!" he said. "I wasn't expecting you until the end of the week. Come in. Come in."

"We couldn't wait," said the woman called May. "We were so excited to see Lily again."

Aidan led the visitors into the living room, where they sat down in the big leather chairs and beamed. Rosa scurried away to get drinks, while I stood to one side, not knowing what to do. Aidan had apparently forgotten I was there. It was Lily who rescued me, bounding from May's side over to take my hand and pull me back toward her.

"Aunt May, this is Miss Delia, my governess. She came with us all the way from New York."

Aidan coughed. "I'm sorry; I forgot my manners. Hans and May, this is Miss Sweeney. She's been Lily's governess for over a year. She's from Ireland." He turned to me. "This is Mr. and Mrs. Humboldt. They are my dearest friends. Hans is also my business partner."

Hans Humboldt stood and gave me a small bow. "I am delighted to meet you, Miss Sweeney. It seems we are both immigrants. I am from Germany. I hope you will come to love Texas as much as I have."

When he had given his formal little speech, he sat down. He was a short man with a round belly that strained the buttons of his jacket. He had a bald head and small, round spectacles. His blue eyes struck me as mischievous, at odds with his formal manner. He reminded me a bit of a leprechaun.

His wife, May, stood up and enveloped me in a hug that nearly knocked the breath out of me. She was at least a foot taller than her husband, and her voice was loud, deep and a little raspy.

"Well, darlin'," she began, "my name is Mayflower Humboldt. Welcome to the great Republic of Texas. This ain't like any place you've ever seen or are likely to see. Don't you mind my Hans; he thinks he needs to act as proper as if he was still in Germany. Now, sit down here beside me and tell me all about yourself."

Mayflower Humboldt was American, but she sounded nothing like anyone I'd met in New York. She drew out her words in a long drawl, often adding syllables where there was no need for them. She was what the Irish would have called a handsome woman. She was tall and lithe and had high cheekbones and wide-set, brown eyes. Her skin was tanned, and her black hair was coiled thickly beneath her extravagantly adorned hat. But for a few wispy lines at the corners of her eyes and mouth, I would have guessed she was years younger than her husband.

"I'm so glad you're here," she went on. "I was afraid Aidan would come by himself and he and Hans would be so preoccupied with their little ole business that I'd be left out entirely. Mary and I were the best of friends, and I surely miss her. But here you are, another Irish girl. I aim for us to be great friends too."

I nodded and smiled, although my heart sank at the mention of Mary's name yet again. I was relieved when Rosa brought in the drinks and Mayflower turned her attention back to Aidan and Lily. When Rosa announced dinner, I excused myself, intent on going to my room. I had never dined with Aidan or his guests in New York and did not expect to do so here.

"Where are you going, Delia?"

I turned around to see Aidan standing behind me.

"I am leaving you to your guests."

He smiled directly at me, and my heart missed a beat.

"We're not in New York now. In Texas we have no such stupid rules. Come!"

He took my elbow and guided me to the dining room. His closeness and the heat of his hand on my arm unsettled me to the point that I wanted to flee. Instead, I braced myself and took my seat without daring to look at him. When Mayflower led us in a prayer of thanksgiving for the meal, I bowed my head and thanked fate again for bringing me to Texas.

Early the next morning I ventured out of the house. Rosa had said the morning was the coolest time of the day and the best for walking. The street was lined with trees and fine houses set back from green, well-trimmed lawns. Each house was of a different style, large and elegant. Mayflower had told me that the street was named Swiss Avenue, after two Swiss brothers who had built the first house here. Many of the richest people in Dallas lived here. And it had the only paved street in the city, Mayflower said, and a private trolley to take residents into Dallas. It occurred to me that Aidan's house, while still beautiful, was modest in comparison to its neighbors. I smiled to myself. I was not surprised that Aidan's house would reflect his impatience with the showiness so prevalent in New York. It was one of the many things I liked about him.

I sighed, remembering how much more relaxed he had been at dinner last night. Perhaps the move to Texas had made him more at ease. I hoped that our newfound relationship would flourish. I knew that it would take time. I could hardly expect to pick up where we left off that morning on the train, when he had stroked my hair and confessed how close he'd grown to me. Who knows what would have happened if Lily had not interrupted us? I scolded myself for such a thought. *Don't be so greedy, Delia. Why isn't his friendship enough for you?* But I knew that it would not be enough. My soul yearned for an intimacy beyond mere friendship. *Why not?* I protested. *Surely anything is possible in this wild, unruly place—even love.*

At the end of the week, Aidan and Hans Humboldt left for the oil fields. Aidan was anxious to see his wells; Hans said a few had come in while Aidan was in New York, but none of them were "gushers." Aidan was planning to acquire some new leases in the hope of expanding production. The oil fields were located southeast of Dallas, near a town with the curious name of Shotgun City. I laughed when I heard it.

"Crazy, ain't it?" said Mayflower. "But it sure describes the place. I wouldn't even call it a town, just a bunch of ole tents and lean-tos. It used to only have about four hundred souls, but now it's closer to four thousand, and growing every day—folks of every cast and creed coming there hell-bent on making their fortunes in oil."

I was horrified. "Will Aidan and Hans be sleeping in a tent?"

She laughed. "Oh no, honey. They stay in rooms above the saloon. It ain't the Biltmore, but it sure beats the other places. Although I don't suppose they'll get much sleep. Any night some drunken cowboy is liable to ride his horse down the main street, shooting off his pistols. You can see how the town got its name."

I listened in amazement. I had never imagined such a place existed, and part of me was dying to see it. I was disappointed that Aidan had gone off without me. Suddenly, I realized Mayflower was talking to me.

"The men have left us girls by our lonesome. But never you mind, Delia. I intend to keep you entertained. I aim to show you everything Dallas has to offer. I can tell you it'll be much more fun than them ole oil fields. You and me's gonna have ourselves a ball."

Good to her word, she called for me the next morning, and together we boarded the trolley. I asked Lily to come with us, but she shook her head, hardly looking up from the flour dough she was rolling out under Rosa's watchful eye.

"I'm making tortillas with Rosa," she announced.

I had no idea what tortillas were, but she seemed very content, so I didn't press her.

The ride from Swiss Avenue to Dallas was short, and soon we were on the main street. As the trolley trundled down the middle of the street, I looked from right to left, trying to take in all the sights at once. Buildings two and three stories high lined the street, all of them displaying bold signs in large lettering indicating their wares. Furniture shops were crammed next to liquor stores and dry goods stores on one side of the street, leather goods, hat shops and saloons on the other. Horse-drawn carts were lined up along the street on both sides, men loading and unloading goods. The scene had the cheerful feeling of Donegal Town, but it had a throbbing energy beyond anything I could ever have imagined in Ireland.

"We'll get off at the next corner," said Mayflower.

I followed her down onto the pavement and looked around.

We had reached an area where the buildings were much taller and built mostly of stone and brick. Many of them appeared to be banks, but she led me to a building with red canopies overhanging large windows and an ornate front door.

"Neiman-Marcus," she announced proudly. "They carry the best merchandise in Dallas, shipped all the way from New York City. They put the other clothing stores to shame."

I had been in some of the clothing stores in New York, but this one was more than their equal. Artful window displays almost compelled you to come inside. And inside did not disappoint. Soft lighting and delicious aromas combined to seduce customers to stay and shop. Well-dressed women moved about, examining fashionable coats and dresses, trying on hats or stopping to examine jewelry displayed beneath glass-topped counters.

"All the new, oil-rich women shop here," Mayflower said, more loudly than was necessary, "and of course some from the old cotton and ranching families. Next time we come we'll buy ourselves something fine."

I gasped. "But I could never afford any of this," I said, gesturing around.

She winked at me. "Maybe not, honey, but Aidan sure can."

I was astonished and a little angry. Did Mayflower think I was the sort to take money from a man? I decided to leave it alone; there was no point arguing with her.

Our outing to Neiman-Marcus was followed by lunch in the nearby Adolphus Hotel.

"Best damn hotel in Texas," Mayflower declared. "Just look at these chandeliers, and you could sink up to your ankles in the carpeting."

The restaurant was formal, with white tablecloths and flowers. The first-class dining room on the *Titanic* had probably been just like this, I thought. But for all the formality, there was no hint of stuffiness. I found myself not even worrying if my table manners were up to snuff. I was beginning to like this aspect of Texas life.

"Can I ask you a question, Mayflower?"

"Shoot!"

"How did you get the name Mayflower? It's so unusual."

She gave a loud, husky laugh. "It was my momma's doing. She was from back East, and though she loved my daddy, she thought she was better than other folks 'round here. My momma held up her nose so high, she'd of near drowned in a rainstorm, and that's the truth. Her people had come from England on the ship the *Mayflower*, so she decided to name me after it so as folks would realize how important she was."

I smiled. "And did they?"

She laughed again. "Oh, honey, they wouldn't have cared if she'd been born in a barn. Nobody 'round here is impressed with things like that. I got stuck with this name for nothing."

"I rather like it."

"Most folks call me May, but there's them that still uses the full name."

"Well, I shall call you Mayflower."

Now I understood why Aidan had been so anxious to get out of New York and back here to the wide-open spaces, where he could breathe easily, and people took one another at face value. Thinking of him now made me blush. I looked up to see if Mayflower had noticed, but she was busy talking with a friend who had happened by, so I indulged myself in my secret longings. I had grasped at every bit of attention Aidan had sent my way in the last few days, and I was hungry for more.

But now he had gone off to the oil fields, to this Shotgun City, and who knew how long he would be away. My heart sank at the thought. Of course, I would have plenty to do with Lily's lessons, and Mayflower was determined to entertain me with more trips to Dallas. And while these pursuits would be rewarding and enjoyable, they would not make up for Aidan's absence. I knew I was being foolish, but my days would be empty without him. I was shocked at how much a part of my life I had let him become over the last year.

Suddenly, Ma's words came into my mind: *You'll never amount to anything, my girl, and you may as well chase away any dreams you have of things getting better for you in the future. They won't. You don't deserve it.* I bit my lip to keep from crying out, *You're wrong, Ma. I do deserve happiness. I do.*

"Is everything all right, darlin'?" said Mayflower.

I smiled back. "I'm grand, Mayflower."

She stood up from the table and walked toward the door. As I followed her outside, my smile disappeared. Indignation, anger and resolve took over. I was not the old Delia anymore. This new Delia was going to reach out and seize her chance at happiness.

No matter how often I broached the topic of going to visit Shotgun City with Lily, my pleas fell upon deaf ears. At first, Aidan just shook his head. Later he'd utter a curt "No!" Finally, in exasperation, he turned to me one day and put his face close to mine.

"I want to hear no more of it, Delia. I have said 'no' a dozen times. It is no place for a young woman, let alone a child. The place is filled with roughnecks and criminals. As your employer, I am responsible for your welfare, and as Lily's father, I am responsible for her life. Let this be an end to the matter."

With that, he turned on his heel and left the house, letting the front door bang shut behind him. I sat down on the nearest chair. All the air had gone out of me, like a pierced balloon. I realized I couldn't keep pushing Aidan on the matter or he would ask me to leave once and for all. I sighed. I should be grateful for this chance I'd been given in Dallas. From now on, I'd be satisfied with educating Lily as best I could and being satisfied with the scraps of time Aidan would see fit to give me.

He'd been growing more and more distant ever since we arrived in Dallas. The morning on the train had raised my hopes that romance could flourish. The truth was that the minute he'd set foot at the house in Dallas and seen Mary's flowers, Aidan had begun to pull away from me. Her ghost would never leave him alone.

There was a sudden rustle at the door and Mayflower strode in without knocking. She took one look at me and stopped.

"What's wrong, darlin'?"

"I'm all right, Mayflower. Just a bit disappointed."

She waited for me to continue.

"It's just that Aidan won't let Lily and me come to Shotgun City. I've tried telling him it would be good for Lily to see where he spends his days, and that I'd like to learn something about the oil business. But he keeps saying no. He says it's not safe."

"He's right, darlin'. The only women there are hussies. They sure ain't no ladies, and the men don't treat them as such."

I looked at her. "But I really want to see it, Mayflower. I expected Texas to be exciting, and Dallas—well, Dallas . . ."

"You think Dallas is the dullest place in the world." She laughed. "You've no idea how many girls your age growin' up on ranches and farms 'round here would give their eyeteeth to come to the big city. And here's you dying to go out to an ole oil patch. Seems to me your thinking is all upside down."

"I know. I must seem very ungrateful."

Mayflower gave me a shrewd look. "If I didn't know better, Delia, I'd say you're pining more for a certain man's company than for adventure."

"Is it that obvious?"

"Don't you be expectin' that Aidan knows your feelings. He's oblivious to these things, like all men. But I can see it in the way you look at him."

"Wouldn't matter if he *did* realize it. He's still in love with his wife."

Mayflower nodded. "I'd say there's truth to that. He and Mary were very much in love. It's been hard on him all these years since she died. But, honey," she rose and came over and patted my knee, "no good will come of moping over it. It's about time he started to think of his future—and Lily's. We've got to get us a plan, you and me. Faint heart never won fair lady—or, in this case, fair gentleman."

"But . . ."

"Now, no buts, darlin'. Ain't the first time I've played match-maker. I've coaxed the most stubborn of men into marriage in my time," she paused and giggled, "including my Hans." With that, she picked up her bag and made for the door without ever saying what she'd come for in the first place.

After she left I sat lost in thought. Part of me wanted to plead with her not to interfere, yet a small sensation deep down inside began to flutter. I recognized it as hope. I shoved it away. No. If Aidan O'Hanlon wanted me, it would have to be of his own free will and not because Mayflower Humboldt had played some trick on him.

Donegal

1913

Nora

❧❧❧

I stood outside the hotel watching Ben's car pull away, a sick feeling in the pit of my stomach. I'd never felt so lonely. All the glittering possibilities that New York once held for me were gone. No life of luxury, no admirers, no rich husband! My dreams were destroyed, and now I was going home to lick my wounds. I wondered what sort of greeting I'd get. Surely Ma and Da would be happy I was alive. I tried to picture the scene, but my memories of Donegal and the people in it were faded, like ghosts.

I fought back angry tears. The old Nora wouldn't have stood for this self-pity. She would have fought and spat and connived her way to a future that suited her. But the old, hard Nora had faded, replaced by the soft Nora Mrs. Shaw had brought out. I wanted to curse the woman for changing me the way she had, but I couldn't. I'd loved her and always would, and that was the size of it.

The next morning, after I wired Ma to say I was coming, I stood on the dock looking up at a gigantic ship called the *Olympic*, my heart beating a mile a minute. I was terrified at the thought of setting foot on it, let alone sailing out across the open Atlantic for days. I was a far cry from the girl I'd been the day I boarded the *Titanic* in Queenstown. Back then, I'd marched up the gangplank, full of myself and ready for anything. And I'd had the time of my life all right, right up until the ship sank.

I assumed the ticket Ben had given me was for steerage, so

when the porter started to lead me up the stairs to the first-class deck, I was irritated and asked him where he thought he was going

He grinned at me. "Ah now, girlie," he said in his Irish brogue, "either ye've a great sense of humor or you can't rightly read. Look at your ticket."

I peered down at the ticket. I read it twice and looked back up at him. He was grinning like a monkey.

"But how . . ." Ben? I didn't know whether to cry or squeal.

"Come on, now," said the porter, "let's get ye settled."

The *Olympic* was another ship owned by the White Star Line. Along with the *Titanic* and *Britannic*, the three were supposed to be the jewels of the White Star's fleet. So much for that, I thought, after what happened to the *Titanic*. I prayed *this* ship would not end up at the bottom of the ocean as well. The closer the porter and I came to the first-class section of the ship, the more anxious I became. I couldn't even look around and admire the plush carpets, brass fixtures and fine furniture, or the view over the sea. I wanted to push the porter to move faster so that I could get into my cabin and lock the door.

I was relieved to find I had a cabin all to myself. I bowed my head and silently thanked Ben again. I was in no mood to be talking to anybody, so the arrangement suited me. I set down the bag carrying what few clothes I'd salvaged from Mrs. Shaw's house and lay on the bed. I thought of the old Nora. She would have been over the moon in a cabin like this, filled with luxury beyond her wildest imagination. She would have flung her bag on the bed and rushed out to the deck to see what young men were out there. She'd have attached herself to one or more of them, sizing them up as prospects, if not for marriage then at least for a good time. But I wasn't the old Nora. I knew I wouldn't be able to look at any of them without seeing that bastard Sinclair. I'd had my fill of rich young men, and maybe even of men in general. I was sad to think that all the fire had gone out of me.

That night I fell into a deep sleep. My dreams were filled with gushing, freezing water and drowning people trying to pull me under. Their faces were skeletons and they moaned and clutched at me with bony fingers. I woke up terrified and drenched with sweat. It took me a while to realize where I was, and when I did my fear overwhelmed me. I prayed to God to spare me on this journey and let me arrive safely in Ireland.

I ate only lunch in the dining room, taking my breakfasts and dinners in my cabin. After lunch I took a walk around the deck for some air and a bit of exercise. When young men smiled at me, I looked away and pretended I hadn't seen them. They probably thought I was a stuck-up bitch, but I didn't care.

One afternoon I went down to the third-class deck. I couldn't tell you why I went, but something seemed to be pulling me down there. As I walked through the near-empty General Room, I fancied I heard the music and laughter of the young ones and saw myself in the middle of them, dancing and flirting. They were ghosts now. I heard their screams again as they jumped off the deck into the dark water. The Ship of Hope had turned into the Ship of Despair. I spun around and fled back up the stairs.

When we finally docked at Queenstown, I was first in line to get off the ship. I couldn't wait to set my feet on solid ground. When I did I made the sign of the cross and vowed there and then never to set foot on a ship again. I picked up my bag and made my way to the station to begin the train journey to Donegal. I settled on a bench to wait. As I sat shivering in the February cold, I was struck by how quiet the station was. The faint smell of manure and turf wafted around me, bringing old memories with it. Even the people looked different—Irish faces and Irish accents. I was home. The crowds grew as more passengers arrived. When the train steamed into the station there was a mad dash for the third-class compartments.

On the spur of the moment I bought a first-class ticket using some of the money Ben had given me. I knew rightly it was a rash thing to do, but I didn't do it to show off. Instead, I did it in honor of Mrs. Shaw, the woman who'd been so good to me. In a first-class carriage I'd have the peace to think back over all that she'd taught me and feel for one last time the comfort of her love.

As I sat in the empty carriage, steaming through the Irish countryside, I fingered her locket and let myself weep openly for her and for the future that might have been. By the time the train pulled into Donegal, my tears had dried. My mourning was over, and my memories were stowed away deep inside me. I squared my shoulders and stepped down off the train.

I saw Da before he saw me. His tall, gaunt figure looked out of place among the hordes of people streaming past him on the station platform. There was a stillness about him, like a man used to waiting, a patient man in an impatient world.

"Hello, Da," I said.

He looked down at me, his shaggy eyebrows knit together as if he wasn't sure who I was.

"It's me, Da, Nora."

He nodded then. "Aye, it is surely," he said.

Awkwardly, he reached over and took my bag. "Is this the lot of it?"

"Aye, Da. Not as much as when I left. 'Twill be easier to carry, so."

I was aware of my brogue already becoming stronger.

He reached awkwardly toward me, as if to give me a hug, but he patted me on the arm instead. Then he turned around and began to walk away. I followed behind him, sharp tears stinging my eyes. I don't know what I'd expected as a welcome, but surely more than this. In the past I'd believed Da never loved me, and I knew he was never one for showing his emotions, but still, I'd hoped for a change. I'd just come back from the dead, for God's sake, could he not have done more than just give me a pat on the arm? I fought back the tears and marched on. *America made you too soft, Nora*, I said to myself. *You're going to have to harden yourself up.*

We climbed up into the pony cart, and Da shook the reins. "Your ma is back at the house, so," he said. "She's cooking a big dinner for ye."

The old horse began to plod his way forward. It was evening time, and the February day was drawing in, but it was still light enough to see around me. Memories bubbled up of my young childhood, out playing with Delia on the hills behind the farm. Delia! We liked each other's company then, before Ma put the wedge between us.

A sudden, fierce wind came up, and with it sheets of driving rain. I shoved my hands into my sleeves to keep them warm and bowed my head to shelter my face against the storm. The sound of the wild fury of the Atlantic thrashing against the cliffs filled my ears. Donegal was giving me an angry welcome.

As we neared the cottage, I started to get nervous. What kind of a welcome would Ma give me? Would she be angry I'd stayed away so long or, worse, that I'd not stayed and tried to get Aidan O'Hanlon to marry me? Would she treat me like the prodigal daughter, or would she make me turn on my heels and go straight back to America?

I needn't have worried. She was waiting at the gate, a scarf around her head and her hands clutched to her chest. She looked smaller than I remembered. When she saw us, she ran through the gate, her arms outstretched, screeching like a madwoman.

"Ah, Nora. Is it really yourself, darlin'?"

She almost pulled me out of the cart and stood pawing me all over, as if making sure I was flesh and blood.

I laughed. "I'm not a ghost, Ma. 'Tis myself, large as life and twice as ugly!"

She began to cry. "Nora. My beautiful Nora. Ye've come back to us. Thanks be to God. My prayers have been answered." She turned to Da. "Don't just be standing there, Peadar, get her bag and bring it in."

She led me to the cottage, her arm tight around my waist, as if afraid I would disappear. She chattered on, half talking, half weeping. Suddenly, all I wanted to do was go to bed and sleep, but I knew there was no chance of it this night. When we came through the door, my old cat came hobbling up to me, mewing to beat the band. I picked her up and held her in my arms.

"Ah, hello, puss, sure I thought you'd have forgotten all about me," I whispered, stroking her soft fur.

"Sure none of us forgot you, daughter," said Ma. "Even after we thought you were dead."

She crumpled in a flood of tears. I put my free arm around her and pulled her in close. "Don't cry, Ma," I said, "I'm here now."

She dried her tears with her sleeve. "I'll go and heat the kettle."

I went back to stroking the cat. *'Tis going to be a long night*, I thought.

Ma had a thousand questions. They poured out of her so fast she gave me almost no time to answer them. The kitchen table was loaded down with bowls of stew, a big plate of soda bread, and my favorite apple pie was sizzling in an iron pan that Ma was after taking out of the turf fire. I was famished with the hunger and dived into food. There'd be plenty of time to answer Ma's questions later. Da sat in his chair by the fireplace, watching us but saying nothing.

"I didn't want to believe you were dead," Ma said. "I even wrote to that O'Hanlon feller to ask had you arrived. And I sent a photo of you. But he never wrote back." Ma's voice was bitter.

She straightened her shoulders and leaned into me. "We gave you a lovely wake, darlin'," she said, her tears flowing again, "didn't we, Peadar?"

Da nodded. "Aye."

"Everybody in Kilcross was here. Father McGinty himself came. We had your bed laid out in white lace with candles all around it. People said they'd never seen the likes of it."

As she described it, I remembered the visions I'd seen in my dreams back in New York. I saw again the weeping woman and the bed and the candles. A shiver went down my back.

"Of course, we could have no burial without your body," Ma said, "so we planted a wee bush up on the hill beyond in your memory. Father McGinty and a bagpiper came as witnesses. Ah, 'twas a sad thing all right."

Silence fell over the kitchen, broken only by the sound of the ticking clock and the wind rattling the windows. The old cat sat purring in my lap as I petted her.

"I'm dead tired, Ma," I said. "I've been traveling for days and I've hardly slept."

Ma nodded. "God bless you, daughter, sure ye must be worn out after such a long journey. Ah, but ye'll sleep well in your own wee bed tonight."

I set the cat down on the floor and stood up.

"Good night, Ma," I said. "Good night, Da."

My bedroom was much smaller than I remembered it. I looked around at the old familiar things: the dresser mirror with the crack in the corner where I'd flung a hairbrush at it; the shelf crowded with wee gifts from boys who said they were in love with me that I'd saved as trophies; the wardrobe stuffed with clothes I'd made Ma buy for me and then dropped like rags as soon as they went out of style. It was as if I was standing in a stranger's room. I didn't know the girl who'd lived here.

I crawled into bed between sheets that smelled of bleach and turned out the lamp. I lay there in the dark. I was home. For better or worse, I was home. I was too weary to think beyond this moment, not even to tomorrow, let alone to the weeks and months stretching ahead of me. All I wanted was to sleep.

The next morning, for the first time in my memory, Da stayed home. He'd been up early to feed the animals, but instead of spending the rest of the morning up the fields, he sat at the kitchen table sipping tea. Ma bustled around him, frying rashers and eggs for breakfast and tending the loaves of bread baking in skillets on the turf fire. The kitchen was so hot, and the smells so strong, I thought I might faint. I got up and opened the back door to let in some air.

Ma looked up at me. "Are ye all right, love?"

I nodded. "I'm just a bit warm, Ma."

"Ye're not taking sick, are ye?"

I shook my head. "Not at all, Ma. I'm grand."

"Sit down and eat your breakfast, so. You're skin and bone. Whatever happened to the fine, lovely girl we knew?"

I was sorry I'd opened the door. The last thing I wanted was Ma fussing over me even more. She was already starting to suffocate me. She stood now with a plate of sliced bread in her hand, as if deciding whether to say something. I knew it wasn't like her to be silent for long.

"What is it, Ma?"

"Well, young Dominic Donnelly was here for his sister Maeve's wake." She paused and blessed herself. "Poor child drowned, and they buried her somewhere out foreign." She paused. "Well, when he got back to New York he wrote to your da and me." She looked directly at me. "He said he'd run into Delia, and that she was alive and well."

I stopped eating and tried to take in what Ma had said. I was sorry to hear that young Maeve had drowned, but delighted that Dom was alive. I hadn't thought to look for either of their names on the list of the missing or the survivors. I'd only been interested in Delia's name. I supposed Dom had written to them to ease their minds that she was well.

"Aye," I said. "After I got me memory back, I looked on the list of survivors and found her name. But I couldn't go and find her because I didn't remember the name of the house she'd been sent to." My face flushed with embarrassment as I finished the last sentence.

Ma pursed her lips. "It would have made no difference. She never went to the house. Father McGinty got a letter from them. And he wasn't happy about it, I can tell you that."

I looked at Da, but he kept his head down.

"So where did she go?"

Ma shrugged. "Only God knows."

"Well, did Dom say where he met her?"

"Just that he'd seen her at a dance, and that she looked well. If he knew any more, he never said."

Ma sat down and began sipping her tea. "I can't understand why that ungrateful chit never wrote to tell us she was alive, not to mention telling us where she was." She looked at Da, who sat with his head down. "I can see rightly why she might not write to *me*, but you'd think she'd have dropped her da a line. Don't you think so, Peadar? Ye never heard a word from her, did ye?"

Da sighed. "I'm after telling ye a hundred times, Kate, no, I didn't."

I didn't know what to think. If Delia had sent a letter 'twould have been hard to get it past Ma. She would have grabbed it off the postman and Da wouldn't have got a look in. I shrugged. Anyway, it was Delia's business.

I knew Ma was setting me up for the raft of questions that were lined up in her mind now that I was here to answer them. It was the last thing I wanted to do at the minute. I knew I'd have to face her eventually, but right then, I needed to get away from her before she started. Da gave me the excuse I was looking for when he pushed back his chair from the table and stood up. He put on his cap and turned toward the door.

"I'll be away, so," he said.

I jumped up. "Wait, Da, I'll come with you. I'd love some fresh air."

He nodded and held the door open for me.

"But ye haven't finished your breakfast, love," said Ma. "And I have so many questions to ask ye."

I forced a smile. "Ah, sure, I'm only going for a bit of a walk, Ma. I'll be back before long."

She shrugged. "Suit yourself," she said.

I caught up with Da, relieved to get out of the cottage. How was I going to be able to stand this? I wondered. I used to welcome Ma's attention, but now it threatened to choke me.

"She'll not stop 'til she knows everything."

I looked at Da in surprise. I didn't think I'd ever heard him say a full sentence to me.

"Aye, I know," I said.

We walked on up the hill at the back of the cottage. Images of Delia sitting reading among the white stones came into my head. It had been another one of the visions I'd seen in New York. Again, a shiver crawled down my back.

"Aren't you curious too?" I said.

Da shook his head. "Only to know if yez were alive or dead. Now I know yez both are safe. What you did or didn't do in America is none of my business."

He walked on ahead of me, and I knew those were all the words I was going to get out of him. I let him go and sat down on a rock near Delia's stones. I thought about what might have happened to her, but Dom had written that she seemed well and happy. I shrugged. As Da had said, it was none of my business.

Last night's storm had passed, leaving the landscape clean and fresh, as if it had just been laundered. I sat on the rock for a long time, thinking over all the things that had happened in New York, from waking up in the hospital to being thrown out of Mrs. Shaw's house by Sinclair. I wondered how much of it I'd tell Ma and how much I'd hold back. Then I realized that she'd not stop until she'd pried it all out of me. Well, I wasn't having it, I told myself, no matter what she tried; they were *my* secrets and they'd stay that way.

The next few weeks were full of merciful distractions, so that Ma and myself were hardly ever alone. The villagers, hearing about my return from the dead, crowded the house day and night, one minute on their knees beating their breasts about the miracle that was in it, the next pressing me for every detail. Father McGinty was there every night leading the rosary, thanking God, Mary and all the saints for my safe return.

Many of my old school friends came as well, the girls more out of curiosity than relief that I had lived. I was never popular with them, and I sensed a not-so-hidden envy at all the attention I was getting. The boys, on the other hand, were openly in awe of what I'd lived through. They shoved one another out of the way so they could get close enough to talk to me.

"What's America like? Is it as grand as everybody says?"

"Will you soon be coming back to the dances, Nora? Sure, we used to have some great *craic*."

I smiled and nodded but said little. I suddenly felt the smallness of their world—my old world. Had I really raced out to every dance anxious to impress the boys and make the girls jealous? I sighed. How young and innocent I was then, although I'd never have believed that at the time. Now these fresh-faced, eager boys held no interest for me. I felt a hundred years older than them.

The distractions grew even greater after the local paper printed an article about me. *Local Girl Rises from the Dead*, the headline said. At first, I was embarrassed, but the more attention the article brought, the more I began to enjoy it. Reporters from other newspapers, even one from Dublin, showed up at the door, dying to interview me and take my photograph. For a while the old Nora crept back into me, and I posed and smiled and exaggerated all the details of my story, making myself out to be a selfless heroine. I said I'd tried to help passengers at every turn.

Da kept out of the way, but Ma was delighted with the attention, posing for photographs and telling the reporters all about the shock she'd had when she found out I was dead, and the even bigger shock when she was told I was alive.

"Sure it put me heart crosswise in my chest," she said. "Make sure you write that down, now."

I watched her with curiosity. I'd not realized until now how much Ma and the old Nora were two of a kind.

When all the fuss died down, and me and Ma were left facing each other, she finally started the inquisition. "What happened to ye after ye were rescued? Where were ye at all? Where were ye living all this time? Who looked after ye? Where did ye get the money to live? And who gave you that necklace you've been wearing since you came home?" And, finally, the question I wanted to avoid most of all: "Why did ye not go and find Aidan O'Hanlon?"

I started with the hospital. That was easy enough to explain. I said I didn't know how I got there—crew from the rescue ship must have brought me there. I explained I woke up with no memory of who I was.

Ma pursed her lips at that. "I never heard tell of the likes of that," she said. "If it was another girl that was in it, I'd have said she didn't want her ma and da to know she was alive. Maybe she'd have wanted to pass herself off as somebody else altogether."

"How can you say that, Ma?" I said, although I knew that she was partly right, I *had* pretended my memory hadn't come back because I wanted to stay with Mrs. Shaw. I hoped the guilt didn't show on my face.

I could have made up some wild story about where I was living, but Ma would never have believed it, so I'd no choice but to tell her about Mrs. Shaw. As I feared, Ma pounced on Mrs. Shaw like a cat on a mouse.

"What kind of a woman would take in a total stranger? Nobody takes in a strange girl for nothing. What kind of things did you have to do in exchange? Was it one of her customers gave you that locket?"

I knew what Ma was getting at and my anger flared.

"She wasn't running a brothel; she was a decent woman, and she expected nothing from me. And for your information, it was her gave me this locket as a keepsake."

"She must have been a spoiled one then, with a rich husband and too much time on her hands. Ye must have been amusement for her."

"You have her all wrong, Ma!" I shouted. "She was like a mother to me!"

The words were out before I could stop them. I braced myself, waiting for Ma's anger to explode. But instead of the tirade I expected, her face turned pale.

"I never thought my daughter would disown me," she said as she walked away with her back to me.

I could have run after her and said I didn't mean it the way she took it. But, again, there was some truth to her words. I *had* wished that Mrs. Shaw was my mother. I left the cottage without speaking to her and climbed up the hill to the circle of white stones. Delia's stones, I had taken to calling them. I began to understand why Delia had spent so much time up there. She'd wanted to escape Ma's constant harping, and now I wanted to escape from her too.

A soft rain began to fall as I sat looking out at the misty sea. I wanted to weep, but no tears would come. Since I came home, I'd been wrung dry as a dish towel. All the life seemed to have gone out of me. I began to wonder had I made a mistake by coming back.

In the days that followed, Ma hardly spoke to me. Instead, I was met with heavy sighs and martyred looks. Da took the chance to stay out of the house as long as possible, saying he had to make the most of the light to get jobs done before spring. Likewise, I spent as much time as I could up in my room. The walls started to close in on me, almost suffocating me. I felt like a prisoner as I looked out the tiny window over the green fields and hills.

I knew things couldn't go on the way they were. Either Ma or I would have to give in—and I knew rightly it wouldn't be Ma. One morning I went down to the kitchen and stood in front of her.

"I'm sorry, Ma, for what I said. Mrs. Shaw was a kind woman, but no one would ever take your place in my heart."

I thought I'd feel like a hypocrite saying those words, and that she'd know I was lying. But that wasn't the case. After all, she'd been a good mother to me up until I left for America. And now I'd come home and said a hurtful thing to her. She didn't deserve that.

It took her a couple more days to thaw out, but soon she was back to her old self, and the questions started up again. I told myself I should have let the standoff go on longer; at least it had given me a bit of peace.

Just when I thought I might go mad, one day in late spring, Dom Donnelly appeared at the cottage door. I nearly fainted at the sight of him.

"Do you not know me, Nora?" he said, his blue eyes twinkling.

"Ah, for God's sake, Dom, sure you nearly frightened the life out of me. I thought you were a ghost."

"No, 'tis me in the flesh."

I smiled, then. "'Tis grand to see you, Dom. You're a sight for sore eyes."

"So, are you inviting me in, or are we to talk on your doorstep?"

My hand flew to my mouth. "Ah, where's my manners at all?"

I was about to let him in when I had second thoughts.

"Why don't we take a stroll up the field, Dom?" I said. "That way we can talk without Ma sticking her nose in."

He grinned. "Ah, sure, I know the way of it."

We walked side by side up the hill toward the white rocks. I gave him a sideways glance. He'd filled out, more like a man now than a boy. And he was more handsome than I remembered. America had changed him too, just like myself. We sat down on the rocks and gazed in silence out at the ocean.

"It looks so peaceful, now," Dom said.

"Aye, you'd hardly believe how cruel it can be. It can destroy life in a minute." I looked over at him. "I'm sorry about Maeve."

He nodded. "Our Maeve was never fit for this world. She was like a delicate wee flower beaten and battered by the winds. I pray she's at peace now." He looked at me with sad eyes. "They buried her in Nova Scotia," he said, "but one day I'll bring her home where she belongs."

I made a silent sign of the cross.

"What are you doing back home?"

"My da died a fortnight ago. Ma needed me to sort out the farm. What about yourself?"

"I'm so sorry, Dom. God rest his soul." I shrugged. "'Tis a long story."

"Ma thinks I'm home to stay. I've no brothers, as you know, so she's expecting me to stay and run the farm. But 'tis not the life for me, Nora. You've been in America; you understand how it changes you."

"Aye, that I do."

I thought for a minute about how hard I'd tried to copy the toffs' table manners so as to impress everybody in New York, especially Sinclair. I'd even tried to get rid of my accent and speak more politely. And where had it got me? Landed back in Ireland! Well, at least here I didn't need to pretend I was somebody I wasn't.

"I'm looking for a man to manage things, then I'll be away back to New York. But I can't leave Ma until that's sorted out."

I smiled. "Is it a girl you've got there?"

He blushed, and I saw a glimpse of the Dom I'd known.

"Ma said you saw Delia in New York," I said.

We both knew I was fishing for information. Dom knew more than he'd told Ma, I was sure of that. He nodded but said nothing.

"Ma said you met her at a dance, and she looked well. But she wasn't working at the house she was sent to. The owners wrote to Father McGinty and said she never showed her face. Did she say where she'd gone?"

Dom shook his head. "No."

I knew he was hiding something, but I decided not to press him. I didn't want to spoil the moment by getting into an argument. It sounded like he'd be home for a while, so there'd be plenty of time for that conversation, if I ever decided I wanted to know. Besides, what Delia was up to mattered more to Ma than it did to me.

I saw Dom often after that, and even though I knew Ma didn't think he was good enough for me, she said nothing. Maybe she thought that being with Dom would stop me from going back to New York.

All through spring and well into the summer, we went for long walks, sometimes returning to the cottage by moonlight. I told him everything that had happened to me, except for the part about Sinclair. That was my secret, and it would stay that way. He laughed when I told him Ma thought Mrs. Shaw ran a brothel.

"Aye, sure, your ma would be suspicious of Jesus himself."

"She had my head astray with all her questions. I'm still waiting for her to bring up Aidan O'Hanlon. You know, the feller I was supposed to work for. Sure, I didn't even remember his name, let alone his address. She had it in her head that I was to marry him, and I know she's mad as a wet hen that it never happened."

Dom gave me a strange look, then said, "And what are your plans?"

I shrugged my shoulders. "I don't know rightly what I'm going to do, Dom. There's nothing for me in New York. But there's even less for me in Donegal."

Before he left to go back to New York, Dom took the notion in his head that I should learn how to swim.

"You're a fecking eejit, Dom Donnelly, if you think I'm going to set foot in water ever again after what happened."

"But what if you decide to go back to America? You'll have no choice but to face your fear of water again. Look what happened on the *Olympic*. There you were in first class and you locked yourself in your cabin out of fear. Think of all the *craic* you missed."

"Well, I'll not be going back there any time soon, if ever," I said stubbornly.

In the end, Dom won the argument. He took me to a nearby lake every day and, little by little, I began to get over my fear. If it had been anybody else trying to teach me, I'd have run a mile, but Dom was gentle and patient. I knew I could trust him with my life.

He left in late July. I'd cried when he told me—big, salty tears of despair. We'd become inseparable. What would I do without him now? We rode to Donegal Town together in the pony cart. On the station platform we stood without speaking. I tried to hold back my tears, but when I looked up at him, his own tears had already escaped. I threw my arms around him and held him tight. He tipped his face down to mine and kissed me gently on the lips.

"I'll miss you," I whispered.

"Come to New York, then."

"'Tis too soon."

"When you're ready, then."

I waved until he'd disappeared in the clouds of steam from the train's engine. Even after the train itself had disappeared, I stood there, unwilling to move. I thought what a lovely lad Dom was. He was worth a thousand Sinclair Shaws. Before New York I would never have given Dom the time of day, but now I saw clearly how wrong I had been.

As I shook the reins of the pony and pointed her toward the road back to Kilcross, I tried not to think beyond this minute. I couldn't begin to picture the future. It was as if time was standing still. As the cottage came into sight, the evening sun was slanting over the fields, turning them from green to purple to gold, and the beauty of it made me hold my breath. I'd been born in the most beautiful place in the world, but it was not enough to hold me. I realized then that I would soon have to leave again. America had changed me too much, and it was calling me back.

Dom had been in New York for over a month when I got a letter from him. "Two letters from America," the postman said, "and on the same day, so. I've never seen the likes of it." He held one out. "This one's for yourself, darlin'." I snatched it from him before Ma could get her clutches on it and ran up the back field to Delia's stones to read it. I tore open the envelope and pulled out the flimsy pages. Dom sounded in good form. The crossing had gone smoothly, and he was back at his old digs in New York. He had a job in the construction business and was learning everything he could. He'd told me his dream was to one day build tall buildings and own them. I smiled. He would do it too, I knew; he had a good head on his shoulders and the self-confidence to see it through.

"Come to New York soon" was how he ended the letter, "I miss you." And he'd signed it "Love, Dom."

My heart skipped a beat. I put the letter in my pocket and gazed out at the sea, picturing us together in New York. Dear, sweet Dom. I would feel safe with him. But a small voice whispered in my ear: *Is feeling safe all you really want, Nora?* I didn't know the answer.

I was in a dreamy state when I went back into the cottage, but as soon as I caught the look on Ma's face, I was jolted back to reality. She shoved an envelope into my hands and stood, arms folded,

Sighing, I sat down and studied the return address on the envelope. It was addressed to Da and it was from Delia! What on earth was she writing to Da about? Before I could open it, Ma pointed at it.

"'Twas sent in February," she said.

"And addressed to Da! Did he read it?"

"But it went astray in the post," she went on, ignoring my question, "and just arrived today.

"It says she was coming back home. But we've seen neither hide nor hair of her." Ma pursed her lips. "Another lie! But more important, she says she's been working for your man O'Hanlon." She paused, a look of triumph in her eyes. "And here's the best of it. The chit admits she pretended she was yourself—says she passed herself off as Nora! She even said she saw you drown. Well, what d'you think of all that?"

I put down the letter on the table and stood up. A strange feeling had come over me, and I shivered as if someone had just walked on my grave.

"Well, now we know what happened to her," I said.

Ma exploded. "Is that all you have to say?" she screeched. "That *slibhín* dared pass herself off as you and lied about it into the bargain. She's set her sights on O'Hanlon, mark my words."

"But if she had, why did she say she was coming back home?"

Ma was getting more impatient. "She says it's because O'Hanlon and the child are moving to Texas. Don't you see, she only said that to throw us off the scent. Pure malarkey! I'd wager we won't see hide nor hair of her in Donegal. I'd say she's angling to traipse after him to Texas. I'd put nothing past her. It won't be long before she lures him into marrying her! And after hearing all that, you don't turn a hair? What in the name of God's got into you?"

She finally paused for breath. I opened the back door and walked out. As the door banged shut, I could hear her crying after me like a banshee. I ran as fast as I could away from the cottage, past the stones and on up the hill until I could run no more. I sank down on the ground, my breath ragged, and lay staring up at the sky.

Ma's outburst shouldn't have surprised me. She'd always hated Delia, and now Delia had stolen the dream Ma had intended for me. She wanted me to be as angry as she was. She wanted to poison my mind the way she'd done my whole life, putting notions in my head that I thought she was doing out of love, but now I realized she wanted to live out her own dreams through me. Well, this time I wasn't going to take her bait.

When the sun finally set I got up and walked back to the cottage. A window was open, and I could hear Ma shouting at Da.

"She needs to go back to America this minute and find that sneak. She needs to step in and take her rightful place. I think she's in shock at the minute. You just wait, I'll convince her to go. She's always listened to me in the past."

"Why don't you just leave it alone, Kate?" sighed Da.

I pushed my way past them and went up to my room. Ma was right about one thing. I would have to go back to New York. I couldn't stay here a minute longer with her harping at me day and night.

That night I cried for the first time in a long time. They were tears of self-pity. Why had my whole world turned upside down? Why had Mrs. Shaw died? Why had Sinclair turned out to be a monster? Why was I left with nowhere else to go except back home? And now I was being forced out of here. What had I done to deserve all this? And why was I not even sure who I was anymore?

Now that I'd made up my mind to go back to New York, I was faced with the problem of how to get there. I had very little money left from what Ben had given me, certainly not enough for the boat passage—not even in steerage. I thought of writing to Dom to ask for money, but my pride wouldn't let me. Ma and Da hadn't that sort of money. I realized at last that my only choice was to sell Mrs. Shaw's beautiful locket.

My tears flowed as I pressed the locket against my throat. How was I ever to part with it? To do so would be like betraying the best friend I had ever known. That night I dreamed of Mrs. Shaw. In the dream, she gently unfastened the locket from around my throat and thrust it into my hand. "Take it, dear girl," she whispered. "This is a journey you must make. Take it with my blessing."

The next day I rode in the pony cart with Da into Donegal Town. He had business to attend to with some local farmers, he said, while I made up a story about wanting new boots. I left him at the corner of the main street, telling him I would be back in an hour. I went straight to the only pawn shop in town. I'd decided that instead of selling the locket outright, I would pawn it. The idea comforted me with the hope that one day I could buy it back. Still, I had a lump in my throat when I handed it over.

Ma was quick to notice the locket was gone. I had worn it every day since I'd been home, and my throat felt naked.

"Where is it?"

"I pawned it."

"Well, good riddance," said Ma.

The night before I was due to leave, I was in my room packing my few belongings when there was a knock at the door. I cursed under my breath. What did Ma want now? I opened the door roughly, but there stood Da. He shuffled his feet and nodded at me.

"Hello, daughter."

I didn't know what to do. Da had never visited my room before. I stood there like an eejit until I realized I should ask him in. He took off his cap and bowed his head as he stooped to fit through the door. I don't know which of us was the more nervous.

Without saying a word, he reached into his pocket and pulled out a small article wrapped in brown paper. He held it out to me, and I stared down at it.

"What is it, Da?"

"Open it, girl."

My fingers shook as I unwrapped it. There, in the palm of my hand, lay Mrs. Shaw's locket.

I gaped up at Da. "How did you know?"

"Your ma was after mentioning it last night and I guessed

that's what ye'd gone to Donegal to do. I went today and bought it back, so."

Tears filled my eyes. "But the money, Da; where . . . ?

"Sure your ma will hardly miss *one* cow," he said.

For a moment I thought I saw a twinkle in his eyes, but I told myself I was seeing things. Still, a warm feeling washed through me and I fought back tears. My da had done this for *me*, not for Delia. I had grown up believing Delia was his favorite and that I never counted at all with him. But now? Maybe I'd been wrong all along. Maybe he just thought I didn't need his attention as much as Delia did. The old Nora would have shaken off the thought as sentimental palaver, but Mrs. Shaw had taught me to recognize and accept love, in whatever form it took.

Da was about to turn away when I reached over and put my arms around him. I buried my head in his chest and let my tears fall. He patted me on the back as you would a child, but said nothing. After a while he gently eased me away from him and looked at me with his faded gray eyes. "I know, child, I know," he said, and then he was gone.

The next morning I fastened Mrs. Shaw's locket around my neck once more, picked up my bags and left the cottage for good.

Shotgun City

1913

Delia

❧✦❧

A week later, Mayflower rushed into the house, all business.

"Get Lily ready," she said. "We're going on a trip."

"Where to?" I said.

"It's a surprise. You'll find out soon enough."

"Oh, I love surprises, Aunt May!" said Lily as she raced upstairs to get dressed.

"What's this about, Mayflower?"

My first thought was that it had to do with Aidan. But I dismissed it. Surely Mayflower would not have arranged anything without talking it over with me first. No, she wouldn't have. *I've got to get this obsession with Aidan out of my mind*, I thought. *There are other things in the world besides him.*

"Like I said, darlin'—it's a big ole surprise."

A half hour later Lily and I were sitting in Mayflower's car, riding down Swiss Avenue in the direction of Dallas. Surely she wasn't just taking us to Neiman-Marcus, I thought; we could have ridden the trolley there. It had never occurred to me to ask Mayflower where she lived. I'd always assumed it was close by. Now, I thought perhaps it was outside the city, a ranch maybe, and she was taking us to visit. I was reluctant to inquire, because she had made it clear she wasn't going to spoil the "surprise."

It was a beautiful July morning. The sun was bright, but the temperature hadn't yet climbed to its usual sweltering level. I leaned back my head and closed my eyes, enjoying the sun on my face. I'd noticed lately when I looked in the mirror that my complexion was no longer as pale as it once was. I no longer looked like the ghost Ma used to call me. I smiled. This was one benefit of Texas I hadn't expected.

Lily chattered away, hardly taking a breath. She made dozens of guesses about where we were going, as if it was a game. Mayflower said "No" as every new question came up. Eventually, Lily realized she was not going to find out, so she turned her attention to the passing scenery.

We left Dallas behind us and rode out into the countryside. Manuel, Mayflower's driver, kept the car at a slow and steady pace. I sensed we were going south. Growing up in Donegal, I'd become quite good at guessing directions by the position of the sun. It was another skill of mine that convinced Ma I was a witch.

The landscape was different from what I had seen that first day I came to Dallas. Now, green grasses covered the land, there were more trees than I remembered and fields were filled with crops almost ready for harvesting. A field in the distance caught my eye. Small, white, fluffy clouds hovered in the air just above the ground.

"Please stop the car, Manuel," I said.

I got out and walked to the edge of the road, shading my eyes with my hand. I'd never seen the likes of it. Was it a mirage, I wondered, like the visions I'd read about that appeared in the desert?

"It's just a cotton field, darlin'." Mayflower's voice drifted over my shoulder. "As common in Texas as ticks on a coon dog. You should see them out west of here—fields and fields of them stretching on forever. They sure do make a lovely sight, don't they? If you were up close, you'd see those are white flowers on the plants. We call them bolls. In another day or two they'll turn pink, and the field will look as if it's lit by sunset."

Back in the car, Mayflower decided to give me an education on the vegetation I was seeing.

"Them tall, green stalks over there," she said, "they're maize. It's a kind of corn the Mexicans brought here. And them trees, they're pecan trees."

I looked over at rows and rows of leafy trees bending toward each other to make an arch.

"Too bad y'all got here too late in the year to see the blue-bonnets. It's like nature threw a blue carpet all over the state. The sight of them has made grown men cry. So beautiful. God surely has blessed Texas!"

Again, I heard the same pride in Mayflower's voice as I'd heard when she showed me around Dallas. This woman truly loved Texas.

I put down my head and closed my eyes. I was now well and truly in a strange and fascinating land. I'd never heard of cotton plants or maize stalks or pecan trees. And these were only the things I'd seen so far. What else was out there across the state of Texas—a state so vast that Ireland would fit into it eight times over?

My stomach tightened at the thought of Ireland. I'd been so busy exploring Texas that I'd hardly thought about Donegal. How different the two worlds were. I pictured Da carrying turf in a pail down the hill toward the cottage. No exotic plants grew on the rough, rocky land around Kilcross. It was hard enough to find places where sheep and cows could graze. Even in other parts of the county, between the wild gales that blew in from the Atlantic and the frequent rain—sometimes falling in buckets, sometimes fine as mist—crop farms were scarce.

I wondered then, as I hadn't done for a long time, what Nora would have thought of Texas. I smiled to myself. She'd have liked Dallas, with its fashionable shops and swanky houses, but she would hardly have been impressed with cotton fields or pecan trees, and she'd have been tortured by the heat. Nora would never have adjusted to Texas the way I was beginning to. Had fate intervened to correct the mistake Ma had surely made by choosing Nora to work for Aidan? A tiny twinge of guilt twisted my stomach. Would it ever leave me?

I was getting restless when Manuel suddenly took a left turn and began driving east. We left the main road behind and were riding on a rutted track more suited to horses than to cars. Eventually, we reached the outskirts of a town. Shabby tin shacks appeared, thrown up haphazardly on either side of the road. Small children and dogs raced across the road, narrowly avoiding the car, while tired-looking women hung washing on makeshift lines. I could take Mayflower's secrecy no more.

"Where on earth *are* we?"

"Look at the signpost over there, Miss Delia."

"Shotgun City, Population 400" was written on a white sign hanging on a pole. Someone had crossed out the "400" and written "4,800" in a crude hand. My mouth fell open.

"But we can't go to Shotgun City," I said. "Aidan has forbidden it."

Mayflower waved her hand at me. "Oh, pay him no mind." She grinned. "Besides, Hans told me he and Aidan would be down in Beaumont today, inspecting the eastern oil field."

Part of me was alarmed at defying Aidan's orders, but a bigger part of me was elated. I'd finally get to see this place I'd heard so much about. Manuel pulled over the car to the side of the road at the edge of town and parked. He pointed to a small café, with the sign "Taquería" above it, indicating he was going to have lunch. Mayflower, Lily and I got out. I clutched Lily's hand, and the three of us began to walk up the main street.

I couldn't take in the sights fast enough, jerking my head from left to right, anxious not to miss anything. Rickety, roughly constructed, one-story wooden buildings were crammed together on either side of the street. Signs on the buildings reflected the businesses within: saloons advertising card games and low-priced beer, banks that looked legitimate and loan shops that didn't, cafés with signs in Spanish and English. The only building made of brick was the Kearney Hotel and Saloon, which towered above the street.

A dizzying array of people rushed past us: men in crumpled, white linen suits with gold teeth and silver fobs, cowboys who doffed their hats to us, their horses tethered to railings, and women dressed in low-cut gowns as if on their way to a ball.

"Prostitutes," Mayflower announced. "They flock to every makeshift camp town like this one."

I noticed that among the well-dressed women and the men in linen suits were drably dressed men and women with weathered faces and stern expressions. Mayflower said they were farmers and ranchers.

"God-fearing people who disapprove of all these newcomers," she said, "exceptin' for the money they get for leasing out their land to wildcat drillers and oil companies."

As we walked, sweet and spicy aromas from the cafés wafted across the street, and I realized I was starving. Mayflower led us to one she said Hans had said was good and clean.

"Good and clean is important to Hans," Mayflower laughed. "He never lets me forget he's German."

"Can we sit outside?" I said, anxious not to miss a minute of the activity on the street.

We sat in the shade and ordered spicy, chicken-filled tacos with lemonade. I had come to enjoy these new foods, especially the jalapeño peppers, which sent hot waves of flavor up my nostrils and down my throat. I'd never tasted the like of them in New York, and certainly not in Donegal. As we sat, the sound of singing, shouting and laughter drifted out from the saloon next door, and the street was filled with accents of all kinds.

"That's where Daddy stays," said Lily, pointing up to the Kearney Hotel. Then her attention jumped back to the empty plate before her. "I'm thirsty," she announced. "Can I go in and get a soda?"

"I'll go with you," I said, standing up.

She put her hands on her hips and stuck out her bottom lip. "I can order it myself, Miss Delia," she said. "I'm a big girl now."

"Oh, what harm can it do?" said Mayflower, giving Lily a coin.

"But . . ." I began to protest, but the child had already run inside the café. I made to follow her, but Mayflower grabbed my arm. "Stay here, darlin'" she said. "I have to go see the dressmaker right quick." I sighed and sat down. I looked over at the Kearney Hotel and up to where Lily had pointed. I imagined Aidan looking out one of the windows, shirt unbuttoned and hair falling over his forehead. I imagined I came up beside him and he smiled and whispered sweet words in my ear.

"Should I check on Lily?" Mayflower's return called me back to reality. I shot to my feet.

"I'll go," I said. "She's been gone a while."

"Probably prattling to the owner," Mayflower said. "That child could talk the leg off a table."

A bad feeling settled in the pit of my stomach and I rushed into the café. There was no sign of Lily. In alarm, I asked the owner and customers if they'd seen a small blond girl drinking a soda. They shook their heads. Almost hysterical now, I ran outside to Mayflower.

"Did she come out?"

Mayflower shook her head.

My voice grew shrill. "Oh, Jesus, Mary and Joseph, she's gone!"

Mayflower stood up. "No need for panic just yet, Delia. Lily was always wandering off when she was a little 'un. Drove poor Mary crazy. I'll bet she went over to the hotel to see if she could find her pa."

Together, we rushed across the street and into the crowded ground floor of the hotel. A handsome, impeccably dressed man in his thirties, with silky, black hair and brown eyes, approached us. He took Mayflower's hands in his and kissed her on both cheeks.

"My dear Mrs. Humboldt," he said in a low drawl, "what a

sight for sore eyes you are. I see your fastidious husband far too often and you far too rarely. I tell him all the time to bring you— you are so much more fun than he is."

"This is Mr. Kearney, the owner," Mayflower began, but I was about to burst with impatience. I stepped between him and Mayflower and put my face close to his.

"Have you seen Lily?" I shouted. "Aidan O'Hanlon's daughter? She's lost. Did she come in here? Can you question your staff? Can you guess where she might be? Can you—"

Mr. Kearney's face creased in a smile. He put his hand on my arm. "Don't fret so, dear lady. I have an idea just where she might be. Wait here, please."

I made to follow him, but Mayflower restrained me. "Let it be, honey," she said. "You can trust Mr. Kearney. Come, sit down now."

I forced myself to sit still while we waited for news, but I couldn't keep my hands from fidgeting or my legs from trembling. I allowed myself a small sliver of hope that Mr. Kearney would find her. I had sensed immediately that he was a man who, despite his youth, wielded a great deal of power in town. I bowed my head and said a prayer.

"Delia? Mayflower? What are you doing here? Where's Lily?"

I shot to my feet as Aidan's voice called out from behind. Panic gripped me as I spun around to face him.

"S-she's lost," I blurted out. "Mr. Kearney's gone to try to find her."

Aidan's face turned pale. "What do you mean, 'lost'?"

Mayflower stood up. "I wouldn't jump to conclusions just yet, Aidan. I'm sure she's in the hotel somewhere."

Aidan gave us a wild look. His rage filled the space between us. Instinctively, I backed away. "For God's sake, she could be anywhere and yet you both sit here waiting for Kearney to find her? What is the matter with you?" He fixed his eyes on me. "And you—didn't I tell you not to bring Lily here? Didn't I insist on it? Didn't I—"

He was interrupted by Mr. Kearney approaching across the

hotel foyer holding Lily by the hand. "Here she is," he said, "safe and sound."

Aidan ran to the child and enveloped her in his arms. "Oh, Lily," he said, "thank God."

I wanted to seize Lily and hug her too, but I didn't dare go near Aidan. As I watched them, an elegantly dressed woman with red hair and too much rouge appeared and extended a gloved hand to me.

"You must be Lily's governess," she said in a smoky, foreign-accented voice. "I'm Francine. I manage the dance hall in the hotel."

I gaped at her, unable to utter a word.

"The darling girl came to the hotel looking for her daddy, and when she didn't find him, she came downstairs to find me. We've been best friends since she was a baby, haven't we, honey?" Francine beamed down at Lily, who looked up at her with a tearstained face.

"Why are you crying, Lily?" I said, ignoring Francine. "Everything is all right now."

"I didn't mean to . . . to get myself lost."

I looked at Aidan, then back to Lily. "It wasn't your fault, Lily, it was mine. I should not have let you out of my sight."

Lily let go of Aidan and threw her arms around my waist. I hugged her as I watched Francine slip her arm through Aidan's.

"Come on, let's go and have a drink to celebrate your daughter's safe return." She paused and looked at me. "I expect we can trust you and Mrs. Humboldt to escort Lily safely back home."

Mayflower looked from Francine to me, one eyebrow raised. I took Lily's hand and turned to go. But Aidan pushed Francine aside. "Another time, Francine. I will escort them to the car. I have something to say to Miss Sweeney."

Without waiting for an answer, he took Lily's hand in his and began to stride ahead of us back down the main street. Even though he must have been filled with relief that Lily had been found, I could see that he was still fuming, and that his anger was directed toward me. I was "Miss Sweeney" again and my heart sank. Mayflower tried to calm him.

"It was all my fault, Aidan. Delia had no idea where I was fixin' to take her when we set out. She knew nothing until we arrived in Shotgun City. Besides, Hans said you were going to be out of town. Blame me if you must."

"I had last-minute business here," Aidan said curtly without even looking at me. "Maybe I could forgive the disobedience, but I cannot forgive her carelessness." He spoke as if I was invisible. "Her only job is to look after my daughter and she cannot even do that. She is an irresponsible chit." He paused to draw a breath. "I knew it was a risk to bring her from New York after she deceived me, but I never expected this. I cannot imagine the awful things that might have happened to my daughter. It was an unforgivable lapse on Miss Sweeney's part, and she deserves the harshest punishment. I shall expect her to leave my employ at once and return to New York."

Aidan refused to look at me. He was right to be angry. Everything he said was justified. Mayflower put her arm around my shoulders, but I gently shook her off. I wanted to be alone in my misery.

When we reached the car, Manuel was waiting for us.

"Take them directly to Dallas, Manuel, and make sure they are safe inside the house before you leave."

"*Sí*, señor," said Manuel.

Aidan stood watching us as the car drew away, his lips tight in fury. I looked back at him for a moment, then I slid down in my seat and closed my eyes. For a while Lily sat sullenly beside me; then she moved closer and put her arms around me, resting her head on my shoulder. It was as if she knew as well as I did what would be the consequences of this day.

Mayflower tried to comfort me, assuring me that she was to blame.

"No, Aidan's right, Mayflower," I said in a low voice. "I should never have let her out of my sight. I should have gone into the café with her instead of sitting gazing up at the hotel, wondering which room was his. I was too busy with my fantasies to pay attention to the child."

After a while Mayflower spoke again.

"And what was this lie you told Aidan in New York?"

I wanted to tell her it was none of her business, but I was too weary to fight. Instead, I recounted the whole story. Mayflower let out a sigh.

We lapsed into silence for a time. Lily had fallen asleep, her soft breathing a comforting sound, like a purring cat. I was left with my own thoughts.

"He won't change his mind this time, Mayflower," I said at length, expressing my worst fears. "He'll send me back to New York. And I deserve it. Aidan is a good man, and he has principles that he will not betray. He expects everyone to live up to them."

It was late afternoon when we arrived in Dallas. Manuel carried a sleeping Lily into the house and gave her to Rosa. Mayflower embraced me, tears in her eyes. After she and Rosa had gone upstairs with Lily, I sank down into a chair. Ma had been right. I was a useless chit. I sat for a while, then dragged myself up to my room.

I pulled out my bag from under the bed and threw my belongings into it. It didn't take long. I had acquired little in the way of clothing or other possessions. As before, I cradled my books in my arms, my tears splashing on their tattered covers, before putting them in the old satchel I had brought from home and clasping it shut. I moved about in a trance, scouring the room to make sure there was no trace of me left.

When I was finished I sat down on the bed, breathing hard. Even though I was anxious to be gone before Aidan arrived home, I allowed myself some time to mourn. How could I have been so careless? Now, I had lost everything—my grand adventure, which had just begun in this strange and wonderful new place, my growing self-confidence and sense of freedom, my lovely wee Lily and, most of all, Aidan. Whatever feelings he may have had for me were surely gone, dissolved under the weight of his anger and disappointment. The future I had dreamed of for us was also gone. It struck me then that the loss of a fantasy is a greater loss than the loss of the thing itself.

When I had composed myself, I picked up my bags. I intended to take the trolley to Dallas and get on a train there. I didn't really care where it was going. I tried to ignore the voice whispering that I was running away. I had come so far, the voice said, from the shy, stuttering girl who had grown up believing no happiness would ever come to her, and now I was in danger of letting her inhabit me again. I set down my bags and a strange sensation overcame me. I realized it was anger. How dare Aidan O'Hanlon banish me to New York? It was none of his business where I went after I was no longer in his employ. Texas was where I wanted to be, and Texas was where I intended to stay. With that, I picked up my bags again and went down the stairs, my head held high.

Mayflower jumped up from her chair. "What's this, child? Surely Aidan didn't mean for you to leave tonight!"

"Maybe not, Mayflower, but the sooner I go the better. I don't want any more confrontations with him. And, besides, it would be better for Lily. Where is she, by the way?"

"Poor little thing was exhausted. Rosa and I put her to bed."

I nodded. I wanted to say goodbye to her, but maybe it was better this way.

Mayflower looked at me intently. "And where are you fixin' to go, missy, at this time of the evening?"

"I'll take the trolley to Dallas, and book into a hotel there. Not the Adolphus, of course; I don't have the money for that. After that I'll sort out what to do. One thing I know for sure, I'll be staying in Texas."

A huge grin crossed Mayflower's face. "Good for you, darlin'. You got more spine than I gave you credit for." She paused for a moment. "And I've got me an idea."

I was wary. Mayflower's last idea hadn't worked out so well.

"I'll take you out to my ranch. You can stay there as long as you like."

"Ranch?"

"My daddy's ranch over in Van Zandt County. I inherited it after he died. Hans and I go there to get some peace and quiet. It's between here and Shotgun City, so it's often easier for Hans to meet me there instead of our house in Dallas." She tilted her head and winked at me. "We're like two lovebirds when we're alone over there, lovin' on each other like we was still young'uns."

I blushed and Mayflower laughed.

She walked toward the door. "Well, come on now, before it gets dark."

Without waiting for an answer, she strode outside, pulling me with her to the car. It all happened so fast it was a blur. I couldn't think quickly enough to come up with a reason not to go with her. I got into the car and Manuel started the engine. I looked back at the house for the last time. A small figure stood at the window of the bedroom under the eaves, her arm arcing back and forth in a wave. I waved back.

"Goodbye, Lily," I murmured.

New York

1913

Nora

❦

I booked into the same hotel near the docks where I had stayed before I sailed for Donegal. I was grateful to be back on dry land. I wanted to go to see Dom right away, but I was exhausted from the journey, so I decided to wait until the next morning. I deliberately hadn't written to him that I was coming because I wanted it to be a surprise. I was dying to see the look on his face when I showed up at his door.

The next morning I set off for his lodgings, following the directions given me by the hotel clerk. The sun was shining and I was in better form than I'd been for weeks. Dom was renting a room in a boarding house in Hell's Kitchen, over in the west part of the city near the Hudson River.

Inside, the house was dark and dreary and smelled strongly of boiled cabbage. I knocked on his door and waited. He was taking his time opening it, I thought, but there again, he didn't know it was me. I was about to knock again when the door opened a slit and Dom peered out.

"Nora!" he cried. "What in God's name are ye doing here?"

"I wanted to surprise you," I said. "I'm just after arriving yesterday."

He stared at me, his eyes wide.

I'd expected he'd throw his arms around me the minute he saw me. But there again, maybe he was just in shock. I laughed. "Are you going to let me in, or am I to stand here all day?"

He bowed his head and opened the door wide. I stepped in and looked around. There was only a bed, a dresser and a couple of chairs. A faded curtain was drawn across an alcove. Probably a wardrobe, I thought. It was hardly posh, but enough for a lad on his own. He had photos of his ma and da, and another of his sister, Maeve, on the dresser, and on a small table by the bed was one of myself that I'd given him before he left Donegal. I smiled when I saw it.

A sudden rustle behind me made me swing around. A buxom, dark-haired girl wearing a bright-red, satin petticoat and matching lipstick stepped out from the alcove, a defiant look on her face. I turned to Dom in confusion.

"Em, Nora, this is a friend of mine, Kathleen. Kathleen, this is Nora."

He stood, his eyes lowered and his face flushed with color. He looked like a schoolboy who'd been caught doing mischief. The girl, Kathleen, showed no such shame. She glared at me, bold as brass, and stuck out her hand.

"Nice to meet you," she said in a thick, Irish brogue.

I ignored her hand and turned back to Dom. "Who is this?" I said.

"A friend," Dom said again.

Kathleen moved closer to Dom and put her hand on his arm. "Och, we're much more than that, aren't we love?" she said. "Tell her, Dom."

He pulled his arm away from her grasp. "This is my friend, Nora Sweeney. I know her from home."

Kathleen glanced at the dresser. "She's the one in the photograph?"

Dom nodded. "Nora and her sister, Delia, and me, we all went to school together. I expect she's come to New York to find her sister, Delia. Isn't that right, Nora?"

I didn't answer. I was so confused I didn't know what to think or say. I suddenly felt faint. The small, stuffy room began to close in on me. I slumped down on a nearby chair. Dom poured me a glass of water. He was about to speak when Kathleen broke in.

"Is your sister the one who worked for Aidan O'Hanlon?"

"What?"

She turned to Dom. "Am I right, Dom?"

Dom nodded.

"Did you know she passed herself off as you?"

I found my voice. "How did you know that?"

"Because I worked for O'Hanlon as well." She gave me a smirk. "Your sister was a liar and a schemer. She even tried to steal Dom away from me. Didn't she, Dom?" She didn't wait for him to answer. "She had her claws into O'Hanlon as well. Got him to agree to take her to Texas. But I tried to put a stop to that. A letter had come from your ma, telling him you were listed as missing but hoping against hope you had shown up there. She even sent a photograph of you. Well, I put two and two together and I gave it to himself, so he'd see what a liar she was."

"That's enough, Kathleen," shouted Dom.

"And do you know what that conniving wee bitch did then?" she said, ignoring Dom. "She sweet-talked the daughter into telling him she'd not go to Texas without your one."

"And have they left?" I said.

Kathleen shrugged. "How would *I* know? I was sacked not long after I gave him the letter. That's what I got for me trouble. But if they haven't, I'd say they'll be gone soon. He wanted to leave while his father-in-law, James Sullivan, was away in Ireland. You see, Sullivan would have stopped them. He wanted the child here."

"Was there anyone else working there? A housekeeper maybe?"

I could see Kathleen's patience was wearing thin, but I had to know more.

"You're a nosy one, aren't you? Aye, there was the housekeeper, Mrs. Donahue. She'd have been kept on until they left. After that," she paused and glared at me, "who knows? I'm not a bloody fortune-teller!"

I stood up. The room swirled around me and I took several deep breaths. I made my way unsteadily to the door and pushed through it, leaving it swinging open behind me. I hurried as fast as I could down the stairs, afraid I would die if I didn't get some air. Outside, I leaned against the wall of the building. Suddenly, Dom was beside me.

"It's not what it looks, Nora," he began.

But I turned away from him. "Don't bother, Dom. I know what I saw with my own eyes."

Somehow, I found the strength to walk away.

I wandered along the streets, not knowing or caring where I was going. I felt sick to my stomach. I could hardly take in what had happened, and just then I didn't want to. I tried not to think of anything at all.

The sound of church bells rang out, and I looked around me. I was passing a beautiful, stone building with stained-glass windows. I realized then that this must be St. Patrick's Cathedral. I'd heard about it all right, but I'd never seen it. On impulse, I climbed the steps and went in. The place was cool and dark, and filled with the scent of burning candles. It reminded me of our church in Kilcross, and a sudden homesickness came over me. I had never been religious, going to Mass only because it was expected, but now, in this cathedral, with the familiar comfort of burning candles and stained-glass windows, I fought back tears of loneliness.

When I got back to my room in the hotel, I turned off the lights, drew the curtains and climbed, fully clothed, into bed. I drew my knees up to my chest like a child. I freed the tears that had been welling up in me all day and began to sob—loud, convulsing sobs of despair.

It took me two days to get up the courage to leave the hotel and go outside. By that time I had no more tears left. I had wept for everything I had lost: Mrs. Shaw, my fantasies of a rich husband with Sinclair, the comfort of my old life in Donegal and now

Dom. I even questioned if I would have been better off if I had drowned. At least I would have avoided all this sorrow.

I realized that in all my life I'd never been alone. In Donegal I had Ma and Da and was surrounded by friends. Even on the ship, Delia had been there, even though I had ignored her most of the time. After that I'd had Mrs. Shaw to look out for me. And in coming back here, I'd expected I'd have Dom to rely on. Now, the fear of being alone gripped me and wouldn't let go. Eventually, I realized I couldn't hide from life forever. I told myself that I was not totally alone in the world. I still had a sister somewhere. I tried not to think what might happen if I found her and she wanted nothing to do with me, but she was all I had left. And so, the next morning, I set out to find her.

It was a beautiful, bright morning and I decided to walk. Ma had told me Aidan O'Hanlon's address and I had memorized it. I asked the hotel clerk for directions. I tried to push away my anxiety as I made my way up Fifth Avenue. I blessed myself as I passed St. Patrick's Cathedral, more out of habit than anything else. Everybody I knew in Donegal blessed themselves when passing a church. I thought maybe I should go in and say a wee prayer but decided against it. I couldn't stop now; I had to keep moving.

The O'Hanlon house wasn't anywhere near as grand as the other houses on the street. Some of them were even bigger than the Van Cline mansion, where I'd gone to the Christmas Eve party with Sinclair. I broke out in goose bumps at the memory. I shook off the feeling and went back to staring at the O'Hanlon house. It was white with black shutters, three stories tall, with windows that reached from the ceiling to the floor and a wrought-iron balcony on the second floor.

I straightened my shoulders and walked up the path to the front door. I let the brass knocker rise and fall with a thud. When nothing happened I knocked two more times. At last the door opened about six inches and a pair of eyes squinted out at me.

"What are ye after wanting? If you're selling something, ye may be on your way."

I pushed on the door to open it more. Standing in front of me was a sour-looking girl about my own age, dressed in a maid's uniform. I smiled at her, hoping to win her over.

"Oh, please forgive me, miss," I began. "My name is Miss Sweeney and I'm looking for my sister, Delia Sweeney, who works here as a governess. Is she about?"

The girl stared at me as if I was astray in the head. She gave a tired shrug, as if the effort of talking was too much for her.

"There's nobody by that name here."

"Delia. Delia Sweeney," I said again.

She tried to push the door closed in my face, but I put out my hand to stop her. I was desperate to get an answer. She must have seen she was not getting rid of me that easily. She heaved a lengthy sigh.

"There was a governess here," she said in a flat voice. "But her name was Nora Sweeney."

I realized my mistake. Of course. She had called herself Nora.

"You say was," I said. "She's gone away?"

"Aye, she and the child and himself. I never saw them. I was taken on after they left. But that's the story I heard."

"Do you know where they went?"

She shrugged. "How would I be knowing? I'm after telling you they're not here and they're not expected back. Now, if that's all, you nosy bitch, you may be on your way."

I wasn't giving up. "What about the housekeeper, a Mrs. Donahue?"

"She was sacked." She almost spat the words at me. "Now get away!"

Stunned, I stepped back, and she shut the door with a bang. I stood there for a moment, not knowing what to do. After a while I turned and went back out on to Fifth Avenue and walked in the direction I had come. I was filled with frustration and disappointment. What if I never found Delia?

I went back to the hotel to collect my thoughts. Delia had gone, that was certain. The maid, rude as she was, had no reason to lie. I believed too that she had no idea where they went. Was it to Texas, as the Kathleen one had said? I was determined to find out.

I reasoned that because O'Hanlon and Delia had left the house empty, someone else must now either own or be renting it. And surely that person would know where Aidan and Delia had gone. But how was I to meet him, short of standing outside the house day and night? I realized it would make more sense if I went in the evening. There would be a better chance that the new owner would be at home.

The next evening, I retraced my steps up Fifth Avenue and past St. Patrick's. I'd expected the streets would be quiet; it was teatime, and everybody would be at home. But I was wrong. This wasn't Kilcross, this was New York City, and people were out and about at all hours. I was excited at being part of the crowd, all of us rushing to one appointment or another. It made me feel alive.

When I reached the O'Hanlon house I knocked loudly on the door. The same sour-faced maid opened it a crack.

"You again," she said, scowling at me. "I told ye everything you wanted to know yesterday. What're you doing back here, annoying decent people? Go on about your business before I call the police."

I held my temper. "I'm here to see the owner of the house," I said. "Would you kindly let him know that Miss Sweeney is here to see him?"

"He's not here!"

She seemed to have gained more strength than the day before. *No matter*, I thought, *I'm not leaving until I'm sure the owner's not home.*

Just then, there was a shuffle in the hallway behind her.

"Who is it, Annie?" called a male voice. "For God's sake, don't keep them on the doorstep."

"Nobody! She was just leaving."

She was about to shut the door again when a man came up behind her and peered out at me.

"And who would you be?" he said in a heavy Irish brogue.

I extended my hand. "I am Miss Sweeney, Mr. . . . ?"

He looked at me suspiciously. "James Sullivan," he growled. "What business have you?"

He didn't move to invite me in, but I stepped into the hallway anyway. The sour Annie stood by with an angry look.

"I told her to leave, Mr. Sullivan," she said, "but she refused to budge."

Mr. Sullivan looked me up and down, then turned to Annie.

"Show her into the library, Annie, and bring us some whiskey."

Annie looked daggers through me, then pointed her finger toward a door. " 'Tis in there," she said and disappeared.

James Sullivan was a massively big man. He would have made two of my da. His hands were huge, his fingers like stuffed sausages. His face was red and veined, which I recognized meant a fondness for the whiskey, and he had hard blue eyes, which I sensed never missed a trick.

"Sit down," he said, pointing to an armchair beside the fireplace.

It was more of a command than an invitation.

"Thank you," I said and sat down, primly arranging my skirt. I smiled up at him. "It is so nice of you to see me at such short notice, Mr. Sullivan."

He stared at me in the way that toothless old men back at the pub in Kilcross used to do, their rheumy eyes traveling over me, saliva wetting their lips. But this feller was different. He had none of the hopelessness of those oul' men. Instead, power seemed to ooze out of him. This was a man who got what he wanted. It wouldn't be easy to charm him into telling me what I wanted to know. Inside, I was sickened with fear of what he might do to me, but I was determined not to let it show.

The silence was broken by Annie banging through the door with a pair of glasses and a bottle of whiskey on a tray. She set down the tray on a table and filled each glass to the rim. She set his down quietly beside him but slammed mine down so hard, some of the whiskey splattered out onto the table. Taking the tray, she left, almost taking the door off its hinges as she shut it behind her.

James Sullivan chuckled. "You mustn't mind Annie. She has the Irish temper. But she's a good worker and keeps me company."

He said this last bit with a sly smile. There was no mistaking what he meant. I pretended not to notice.

"Sláinte," he said as he raised his glass. "You're Irish too, aren't you, just like Annie. I like Irish girls."

I took a gulp of the whiskey, wondering how I was going to get through this without the oul' bastard pawing me with his big hands.

"My name is Nora Sweeney," I began. "I'm from Donegal. My sister, Delia Sweeney, worked here for the last owner, Mr. Aidan O'Hanlon."

Mr. Sullivan scowled but said nothing.

"I came to New York a few days ago, hoping to find her, but when I came yesterday, your maid said they'd all left, and she didn't know where they'd gone. I assumed, as the new owner of this house, you might know."

I let the words hang in the air while he studied me.

"Sweeney, is it?" he said finally, his Irish brogue growing more distinct as it seeped through the whiskey. "Yes, there was a girl named Sweeney here. But I thought her name was Nora as well. I didn't pay that much attention to her. She was skittish as a cat, afraid of her own shadow." He chuckled. "I think I frightened the daylights out of her."

I was right; he didn't miss a trick. He had summed up Delia well.

He drained his glass, got up and poured some more. "Now, let's see. She was working for the O'Hanlon boyo when I met her, but I'm not sure how long she was here."

He grinned, showing big, white teeth. "And just to set the record straight, Miss Sweeney, Aidan O'Hanlon never owned this house. It was my wedding present to my daughter, Mary, God rest her soul, and so she was the rightful owner. He was only squatting here after she died."

I sat up straight. So, this was the Sullivan Kathleen had said would have stopped O'Hanlon from leaving for Texas with his daughter. I became more wary.

It was clear from his tone that he had no time for Aidan O'Hanlon. "The bastard was my son-in-law. The only reason I let him stay here was for the sake of the child—Mary's daughter, Lily."

His face softened as he said Lily's name. "Loveliest wee girl you could ever meet. Just like her mother." He seemed to go away into himself, forgetting I was there. "I'm only here because my own house is being remodeled. But it's nice all the same, being around Mary's wee bits and pieces. It makes me feel closer to her."

I was impatient to ask where they had gone, but it didn't seem the right time. I'd have to be careful how I behaved in front of this man. I suspected he had a violent temper.

"I was on my annual holiday to Ireland in May when he took advantage of my absence and ran off like a thief in the night, taking my Lily with him," he said, looking directly at me now, "but I don't know if he took the one you call your sister. The other Nora Sweeney."

I cleared my throat and tried to look humble. "I understand that they, 'er Mr. O'Hanlon and Lily, went to Texas. Do you know if that's true?"

He threw back his big head and laughed. "Texas," he declared, "yes, they went to bloody Texas."

Without thinking, I blurted out, "But where in God's name *is* Texas?"

"The back of beyond," he said, "thousands of miles from here. I hear it's a desperate place, and the heat would kill you."

My mouth dropped open. "But—but, why? Why there?"

"Oil!" he said. "Oil! Ever since oil was discovered there back in '01, every class of blackguard's been running down there hoping to make his fortune. That son-in-law of mine dragged poor Mary there with him first time he went. It didn't suit her. Didn't suit her at all. She took the fever and he brought her back. But it was too late."

He was beginning to slur his words. Everything in me wanted to get up and leave, but I needed to find out about Delia. I pretended to sip more whiskey even though I never could stand the bloody stuff.

He began to study me again, his eyes roving all over my body. "You're hiding something from me, missy. There must be some reason that sister of yours would be calling herself Nora. I know you're wanting to know if she went with him and where in Texas they are, and I know you're plotting in your head how you'll get there."

He leaned forward. "I'll make a bargain with you. Come back here Friday night and I'll spell out for you where they are, but only after you tell me the real reason you're so anxious to find them."

He stood up and I got up as well, my legs weak and the sweat running off me. The last thing I wanted was to see this man again. But what choice did I have?

I nodded. "Very well, Mr. Sullivan."

He showed me to the door, but before I could leave, he rested his hand on my shoulder. "And once we have all that straightened out, I might have a proposition for you."

Alarm must have shown on my face for he laughed heartily. "Ah, don't worry, love, it's nothing like that. Although I'd wager such arrangements might not be new to you."

Without thinking, I raised my hand to slap him, but he caught it and held it. "You're a little spitfire, aren't you?" he said. "I like that in a woman. But you have it all wrong. The proposition I have in mind is something that will benefit us both, not only financially but by the revenge we'll get on those who've wronged us. This Delia has wronged you, hasn't she?"

It was too much for me to take in all at once. I slid out from under his grasp and fled down Fifth Avenue.

My visit with James Sullivan had scared the living daylights out of me. After I'd locked myself in my hotel room, I tossed and turned all night, wondering if finding Delia was worth the risk of taking up with him. He was a dangerous man. Who knew what this "proposition" was that he had in mind? And what else might he expect me to do? Was I to be his "companion," like that frightful Annie? What in God's name was I getting myself into? But the more I thought about it, the more my desire to find Delia grew. Fear was not going to stop me. I was reminded then that stubbornness had always been one of my strongest traits.

On Friday night James Sullivan himself opened the front door. He showed no reaction to my arrival, just stood to one side and waved me in. The old bugger was so sure of himself he knew I'd come, I thought, and for a moment I wished I hadn't, just to spite him. But it was too late; I was here now, and he knew he had the upper hand.

"Annie's laid up feeling poorly tonight," he said, "so I must fend for myself."

He left the room and returned with a bottle of whiskey and two glasses.

"Shall we have a toast to our success, Nora?" he said, raising his glass.

How dare he call me Nora? I thought. *It's another way he's showing me who's in charge. Well, I can give as good as I get.*

"You're putting the cart before the horse," I said. "I don't even know what your proposition is yet."

"Touché, Nora!"

I had no fecking notion what "touché" meant, but I could see he was impressed.

"I like feisty Irish women. I think you will be very suited to my plans."

He was like a cat toying with a mouse. I hadn't the patience for it.

"Get on with it, then; let's hear them."

He got up and poured another glass of whiskey, and I allowed him to fill mine. Maybe it was the whiskey that gave me the courage, but I meant to go toe to toe with him.

"Ah, you're forgetting our bargain, Nora. You tell me your whole story, so I can know what's driving you. In exchange, I will tell you where in Texas Aidan, Lily and your sister are. Oh yes, I knew from the previous servants that she'd gone with him, I just didn't want to tell you at the time."

I wanted to slap the smug look off his face. Instead, I took another sip of whiskey and told him my story, beginning with the letter from America and my near drowning on the *Titanic*.

"So you see, Delia thinks I'm dead. But now I need to find her. I want to be sure she's all right. And I hope she'll be able to help me get settled in America. I have no one else to turn to." I chased away a sudden image of Dom.

James threw back his big head and laughed. "Well said, Nora. You're a colleen after my own heart. I think you're still hiding a few cards from me. You'd make a good poker player, and I think you're just the girl I want for my plan."

I'd told him the truth, but if he wanted to believe I had some other fish to fry, I would let him. It could only stand to my benefit. Confident now that I thought I had control of the situation, I leaned forward.

"You haven't told me where in Texas they are, so I can still find them in case your plans don't suit me."

I had gone too far. He stood up and came close, his eyes narrowed and his face crimson. I shrank back, afraid he was going to lunge at me.

"You've a brass neck on you, girl. I have a good mind to throw you out on the street." He studied me for a long moment, then threw back his head and laughed. "But I like your spirit. You'll be perfect for what I need."

I wanted to protest that he wasn't holding up his part of the bargain, but I didn't dare.

He sat back down.

"My plan, pure and simple, is to ruin Mr. Aidan O'Hanlon. I want him made penniless, so he'll have to crawl back to me on his hands and knees. And as his thanks for me paying off his debts, he will bring Lily back here to me."

I gasped. This man had a taste for revenge that made Ma's demands look like child's play.

As if reading my mind, he said, "He deserves every bit of it and more. He killed my Mary."

He sipped more whiskey.

"Now, about my plan. To begin with, I knew you'd be going to Texas anyway, once I told you that was where they were. Because you were already going to be there, I thought we could join forces. You see," he went on, "I know something about the oil business. It's a dirty business. It's filled with thieves, spies and double-crossers. The way to make money is to drill a well that hits oil. But to drill a well, you must have a lease on the place where you want to drill. There's fierce competition over these leases."

I leaned forward in my chair, concentrating on his every word. I was a bit confused, but I was determined to understand. I didn't want him thinking I was an ignorant git.

"That's where you come in," he went on. "My spies tell me that O'Hanlon's leases run out soon. I want you to talk the landowners into renewing their leases with us instead of him. That way he'll be out of business and deep in debt. And don't worry, I have people down there who can show you the ropes."

"I won't need much help," I lied. "I'm a very quick learner."

He stood up, beaming. "Let's drink to our partnership."

We clinked our glasses together. The evening had gone better than I could ever have expected. Maybe the whiskey had given me Dutch courage, but no matter; I'd have my way to Texas paid for, a job, *and* my chance to find Delia. It couldn't have worked out better. And James Sullivan had been all business. He'd made no advances at all. All in all, I was very glad I had come. We agreed that I would come back the next night to go over the details, like what and how I'd be paid and where I'd live.

When I returned to the hotel I was hoping against hope there might be a message from Dom telling me I'd misunderstood about Kathleen and begging me to come back again. But there was nothing. I fought back tears.

You may put him out of your head for good, I told myself. *Stop the waterworks; there's no use crying over spilled milk. You've got James Sullivan now, and he'll get you to Delia, and in the meantime give you a chance to earn some money.*

But, in spite of all this, a thought nagged at me. I didn't like the idea of ruining Aidan O'Hanlon. What if it hurt Delia? I'd no notion whether she liked him or despised him. If she liked him and found out what I was doing, it would surely turn her against me. But what else was I going to do? Sullivan had thrown me a lifeline and I had no choice but to take it.

Humboldt Ranch

1913

Delia

Mayflower and I arrived at the ranch after dusk. I got out of the car and looked around, but everything had disappeared beneath dark shadows, except for the glow of lamps in the windows. I was reminded of lamps people set in windows of houses in Donegal to welcome pilgrims home. Mayflower led me up the steps to the front porch. I jumped at a squeaking sound, thinking maybe it was some animal.

Mayflower laughed. "Them's just our ole rockin' chairs," she said. "Many a night Hans and me just set here looking up at the stars."

She ushered me into a big, open living room. I was expecting it to look like Aidan's Swiss Avenue house, but I was wrong. This room had no polished floors or stained-glass lamps, and yet it was just as inviting. Everything in it was made for practical living, and by the looks of the furniture, it had seen a lot of living over the years. Brown, well-worn leather armchairs with silver studs along the seams stood on either side of a huge, stone fireplace. Strewn on the rough, wooden floor were rugs made of animal pelts. I stared at them, almost expecting them to rear up and growl at me. I looked away and up at the walls, where stuffed animal heads gazed down at me, and from the ceiling hung a chandelier made of antler horns.

"Them critters won't bite you." Mayflower laughed. "I'm guessing you never saw the likes of this back in Ireland."

I shook my head.

She took off her hat and threw it down on a chair. "I'll go and see if there's anything to eat in the kitchen. Maria, Manuel's wife, didn't know we were coming. She most likely went home to their cabin. She stays out there when Hans and I are away."

"Please, don't worry about me," I said. "I'm not hungry. I just need to go to bed."

The next morning, I woke up to the smell of bacon frying. For a minute I thought I was back home in the Donegal cottage, and Ma was cooking breakfast for Da. But when I threw back the red, white and blue quilt and slid my feet down onto a straw mat beside the four-poster bed, I remembered I was a long way from Donegal. Mayflower was waiting for me when I came into the kitchen. A brown-skinned woman with a smooth, broad face was setting a plate of food in front of her. Sitting across from Mayflower at a big, wooden table, its surface covered with scars and cigarette burns, were three men I supposed were ranch workers.

"Oh, there you are, honey. Come and set yourself down. This here is Maria, Manuel's wife, and these are our ranch hands."

The men nodded at me, their eyes cast down, the way the shy boys at our village dances always did. Maria smiled, exposing two gold teeth, and went to fetch another plate of food. I'd never seen so much food before. Apparently, a ranch breakfast consisted of bacon, eggs, potatoes, steak and grits. No matter, I cleaned the plate in no time, then looked around, embarrassed.

My hunger had made me forget my manners. But no one seemed to have noticed. The men rose, gave a little bow and shuffled away. Maria busied herself washing dishes. I picked up the mug of coffee she had set down. It was boiling, and I almost blistered my lips. It was so strong, I slammed the mug back down on the table. I had become accustomed to coffee instead of tea since arriving in America, but I had never tasted anything like this.

Mayflower laughed again. "Out here on the ranch we like our coffee strong and our men stronger, darlin'. You'll get used to it."

That wasn't likely, I thought. I picked up the mug and went outside, thinking I would dispose of the coffee under a bush. But I tried another sip and decided I could get used to it after all. I was in Texas now and needed to adapt to their ways.

I walked farther away from the house and stood leaning on a fence rail watching cattle grazing in a distant field. From my vantage point, they looked like the longhorns I had seen over in Fort Worth when I first arrived in Texas. How long ago that seemed. A stiff breeze came up and blew away the tears that were beginning to roll down my cheeks. I shook my head hard. There was no point crying over spilled milk. The damage was done, and now I had to face my future. I breathed in the fresh air. I had learned by now that early Texas summer mornings were the most pleasant time of the day. I inhaled the sweet smells of hay and dry grass, and again I thought of home. But instead of making me homesick, I found comfort in the smells. I watched the ranch hands mount their horses, their boots and spurs thrust into the stirrups, and their large hats, which I had learned were called "cowboy" hats, pulled down low, shading their faces.

When they rode out of sight, again I was aware of the wide-open space that was Texas, where the land stretched all the way to the horizon, as if it were the end of the earth. How different this place was from Ireland! Here there was room to breathe. The lives of people here were not confined by hundreds of years of tradition, by the fear of Hell instilled by powerful priests, by the ridicule of neighbors, nor by rigid rules of morality. This place was big enough to welcome risk-takers and rule breakers, dreamers and sinners and independent souls with their own moral code. Like the immigrants on the *Titanic*, people came to Texas looking for a better life—for freedom, adventure, wealth, peace and happiness—and unlike those wretched souls drowned on the *Titanic*, most appeared to have found it.

I sighed. I didn't know how long I would stay at the ranch. Mayflower had said I could live here for as long as I wished. But how could I? Aidan would not want me anywhere remotely close to Lily. I tried not to think too much about Aidan. I didn't even know if I would ever see him again. My heart sank at the thought.

I began to spend as much time outdoors as I could, sometimes walking, other times leaning on the fence, watching the ranch hands do their work, or "chores," as it was called here. I especially liked to watch them wash down the horses after a day's work. I'd always loved horses. Back in Donegal some of them ran wild, while others were kept on farms. There was a special, ancient bond between the Irish and their horses. I'd always been sad that the only horse we had on our farm was our sweet pony, whose job was to pull our old wooden cart. I would have loved to ride a horse the way many of the heroines of my books had done.

Mayflower came up behind me one day. "You sure seem fond of the horses, darlin'."

I smiled. "I am. And I've always wanted to learn to ride."

She said nothing at the time, but two days later, she presented me with a pair of trousers, boots, a blue cotton shirt and a cowboy hat.

"Got these from the dry goods store in Dallas. I figured if you were fixin' to learn to ride a horse, you'd better be dressed for it. The trousers are for boys, but I'm sure Maria will be able to fit them for you. She's handy with a needle."

I looked down at the clothes and began to laugh at the thought of Ma's face if she ever spied me in a pair of trousers.

"Now all we have to do is find someone to teach you!" said Mayflower.

A week later I was riding a small, solid, brown quarter horse around the paddock alongside a young man on what he called a "paint horse," so-called because of its coat of brown and white patches. I'd never seen a horse like it and was fascinated. The young man's name was Jeb, and he was the son of the ranch manager. He was very shy and blushed every time I spoke to him.

But he was a good teacher, and I was quickly getting the hang of western riding: leaning back in the saddle and holding the reins loosely in one hand. Every time I dismounted, I felt more and more like a real Texan.

During the days at the ranch I was able to keep thoughts of Lily at bay, deliberately concentrating on other things. But at night, with no other distractions, images of her filled my mind, and my regret at what I had done roared up as if to suffocate me. I also wondered how Aidan was. Did he think of me at all, and if he did, had his anger and disappointment with me softened?

Every day I peppered Mayflower with questions about Lily. Had she seen her? How was she doing? She answered that she hadn't seen her at all. She had heard that Aidan had brought her back to Dallas and was considering putting her in school in the fall. I winced. If she went to school, she would no longer need a governess. My final hope of one day going back to her would be shattered.

"I saw Aidan today," Mayflower announced one day. "He was looking darned puny. Worried sick about Lily; says she's not been eating, and she's stopped talking again." She paused and gave me a knowing look. "I know you've been wanting to ask about him as well as Lily, but you haven't had the gumption."

I said nothing.

"Anyway, you can see him for yourself," she continued. "He's coming here for our annual Fourth of July barbecue this Saturday. And he's bringing Lily."

Later, in my room, I lay down on the bed, not even bothering to undress. News that Aidan was coming to the ranch should have put me over the moon, but instead, I was miserable. How was I ever to face him? How was I going to look into his eyes and see the reproach there? I couldn't. I would have to find a way to avoid him, even if I had to leave the ranch.

But there was no time to come up with a plan before Saturday arrived. I wasn't ready to face Aidan, so I pretended I was sick.

Mayflower saw right through me and ordered me to get up. Reluctantly, I rose and dressed in my riding clothes; Mayflower had said we'd be riding over to the barbecue. When I came down to the parlor, Mayflower was wearing a long, silk dress with lace edging and a matching hat.

"B-but I thought we were riding," I said, looking down at myself.

Mayflower waved her hand. "Pay it no mind, Delia—some ranchers like to dress up for barbecues—it's often the only time we see one another during the year, and the young'uns like to impress one another. And it's expected that the hostess should gussy herself up as well." She smoothed out her dress. "I'd much rather be dressed like you are, but it wouldn't be considered proper, and I'd be gossiped about for a year."

"You look lovely, my dear," said Hans, and Mayflower beamed.

We set out on our horses, riding east from the ranch house. I thought Mayflower would ride sidesaddle, but to my amusement, she gathered up her dress, threw one leg over her horse's back and grinned at me. Hans, small, compact and smart in his shiny, black boots and white cowboy hat, rode straight-backed, leading the way. I was shocked that the barbecue was being held so far away.

"Gotta put some distance on it," Mayflower remarked, "else it might burn the house down."

I wondered how big this barbecue was going to be. I began to imagine a burning woodpile as high as the house itself. As we rode along the dirt road, several motorcars passed us, their drivers honking their horns and shouting greetings. Some of my anxiety receded as my anticipation grew. I'd gathered that a barbecue was like an elaborate picnic, but I knew it would not be like any picnic I'd ever witnessed, nor indeed read about.

After almost an hour of riding I couldn't believe we were still on the ranch. I hadn't realized just how vast it was. In the distance I saw plumes of smoke and knew we were drawing close. Soon after I heard the noise of a crowd as they came into sight.

My heart began to thud. I prayed Aidan had not yet arrived. We dismounted and tied our horses to a fence rail and walked toward the crowd.

People parted to let us through to a clearing where three wood fires burned, one in a large pit dug in the ground and two above-ground under tripods holding huge iron pots. An image of Ma on her knees tending iron pots that hung over the turf fire flashed in my mind. A stew of rice and beans in a tomato sauce bubbled in one of the pots, and the other contained strong black coffee. Round discs of crispy bread lay cooling on a table nearby. Slowly, I approached the pit where two men were basting what looked like an entire cow with sauces and molasses. The aroma was in-toxicating, and I swallowed the saliva that filled my mouth.

I melted back into the crowd, hoping to become invisible in case Aidan was there. Women, young and old, wore fine dresses and hats. Their fancy shoes were quite unsuitable for the prairie dust and gravel. I was curious why none of the women's faces were tanned. I concluded that they considered it unseemly, just like the Anglo-Irish aristocratic women did. I put my hand up to my face, which had been bronzed by the sun. I was aware of the women, particularly the younger ones, staring at my face and my trousers and whispering to one another. My fair hair, bleached the color of straw by the same Texas sun, fell in a braid down my back, unlike their elaborate styles tucked up under their hats. I turned to walk away and noticed that the women and men had split into two camps.

I didn't know which way to go, so I made my way to the out-skirts of the crowd, where musicians in tight black suits studded with silver buttons and huge, round straw hats were playing gui-tars. The music was enchanting. They sang in Spanish, their voices soft and melodious. They must be Mexicans, I thought.

Mayflower came up behind me. "Aren't they wonderful? They're called mariachis, and they're from Mexico. Where we're standing used to be part of Mexico. They've influenced many of our ways, including our music and our food."

"So, that's why there are so many of them around here," I said. "But I noticed that most are working as servants or ranch hands."

Mayflower pursed her lips and nodded. "Some things are slow to change, darlin'."

I began to feel sick to my stomach. The heat and the smells were closing in on me, and I was afraid I might faint and make a show of myself. I walked over to a nearby water barrel and ladled some water into my mouth. It was warm, but more refreshing than hot coffee would have been. I straightened up and turned around. Aidan O'Hanlon stood at the edge of the crowd, watching me. I took in a deep breath as panic gripped me. Francine, wearing a gaudy, low-cut dress and a feathered hat, hung onto Aidan's arm. Lily was beside them, crouched down with some other children examining what looked like a dead armadillo. My face flushed and sweat dripped down the back of my neck. I looked down at my riding clothes, feeling ugly and plain in comparison with Francine.

I was rescued by the unexpected appearance beside me of Mr. Kearney from the hotel. He was impeccably dressed in khaki trousers, a crisp white shirt and a white cowboy hat that he doffed to me. I turned away from Aidan's stare, which I felt burning through me.

I managed a smile. "Hello, Mr. Kearney."

He gave slight bow. "Good afternoon, Miss . . . er . . ."

"Sweeney," I said. "Delia Sweeney. We met before, at your hotel, the day Lily was lost." I reached out my hand to shake his.

Instead, he bent and kissed my hand, his fingers adorned with silver and gold rings. He asked me how I liked the ranch, and suddenly, words started flowing out of me unbidden

"I like the ranch well enough," I said, "but I can't live on Mayflower's kindness forever. It's time I found some way to make a living. . . ." I let the words trail off.

Mr. Kearney looked me up and down, as if mulling over something in his mind. "I know it's no place for a lady like yourself, but I may be able to find you a position at my hotel in Shotgun

City. Why don't you come and see me there? I'm sure I could find room for you as a clerk, or a saleswoman." He grinned suddenly. "Or you could be a dancer like Miss Francine over there."

I reddened.

"She's from Louisiana and her people were French. That's how come she has that accent that men just love. She's what we call Cajun." He paused and looked over at her. "And as long as we're speaking of Francine," he went on, his voice lowered, "I see she's draped over Aidan like an old coat. They go back a long time, even before he married his wife. I expect our Francine is planning to move into dear Mary's place. She's an ambitious hussy, bless her heart."

I could stand being there no longer. "I'm sorry; I have to leave now, Mr. Kearney. Thank you for your kind offer, but I do not plan to return to Shotgun City."

With that, I turned and ran away from the crowd, to where my horse was tethered. I fumbled with the reins and, when they were untangled, I mounted him and dug my heels into his flanks, as Jeb had taught me. Then I rode away without looking back.

I must have dug my heels in more forcefully than I intended because my horse took off at a gallop. At first I was glad—the faster and farther I got away from the barbecue the better. Eventually, though, I was ready to slow him down. I tugged on the reins, but he didn't respond. My anxiety began to mount. I had never ridden this fast before; the fastest I had ridden with Jeb was a slow canter. I tried yelling for the horse to stop, even though I knew it was useless. I dug my heels into his flanks again, but that only succeeded in making him run faster. I was in a full-blown panic now. All I could do was hang on as best I could and hope that I was riding in the direction of the ranch house.

A sudden wind came up and blew dirt and gravel like sharp needles into my face. Grit struck my eyes and I blinked them open and shut. I wore no bandanna, as the ranch hands did to cover their faces, and I didn't dare let loose the reins to wipe the gravel and dirt away. As I rode on, the sky turned dark, signaling a rainstorm. Lightning would no doubt come next, and then thunder. Terror replaced panic, and I began to pray aloud.

Thunder struck behind me, loud as galloping hooves. It was gaining on me, drawing closer. I prayed louder, shouting the words into the wind. I heard someone calling my name. *Maybe it's God*, I thought, *letting me know it's my time to die*. But it wasn't God. It was Aidan. He drew alongside me, shouting, but I couldn't make out his words. He rose up in the stirrups and leaned over to seize the reins from me. Just as he did, my horse jumped over a narrow creek, which had suddenly appeared in front of him. I screamed and let go of the reins. A sharp pain tore through me as I hit the ground. Then the world turned black.

I heard distant voices and I opened my eyes. Blurred faces hovered above me. Someone was wiping my forehead with a damp cloth. A vicious pain shot through my left leg and shoulder, and a sticky substance flowed down my cheek. I closed my eyes again.

A gentle voice at my side called my name.

"Delia? Oh, Delia, what on earth made you do this? You gave us all such a scare. Why did you run away from us—from me—that way?"

The voice sounded like Aidan's—not the recent, angry voice, but the gentle, loving voice I remembered from before. *I'm dreaming*, I thought. *They must have given me some medicine. It's made me hallucinate. I must sleep.*

"Nothing broken, the doc says." Mayflower sat beside my bed. "Do you realize what a lucky girl you are? I swear, if I didn't know better, I'd have said you were trying to kill yourself."

Maybe I was, I thought.

Hans stood behind his wife. "Leave the girl alone, May."

"I'm so sorry I scared you. I-I felt sick all of a sudden and needed to get away before I made a show of myself."

"You scared more than Hans and me," Mayflower said. "Jeb was scared to death. He shouted that you were riding too fast. He was fixin' to go after you, but Aidan beat him to it. He pushed that Francine out of the way and jumped on his horse to follow you. You were well out of sight by then. I'm amazed that he caught up with you. I would say he saved your life."

"That's enough, May," Hans said. He turned to me. "Rest now, fräulein."

When they had gone I lay staring at the ceiling. Suddenly, Father McGinty's face appeared. *'Tis lying again, you are!* he shouted, wagging his finger at me. *You weren't sick at all. 'Twas jealousy made you run. The Commandments say: "Thou shall not covet thy neighbor's wife . . . or husband." You wanted Aidan for yourself and that's the truth.*

He disappeared. He was right, of course. Even though Aidan wasn't Francine's husband, he was her companion, and I had let jealousy consume me. Why had I run? Why hadn't I stood my ground?

On doctor's orders I was confined to bed for the next week. I drifted in and out of sleep, dazed from the medicine he had given me. The pain eased when I lay still but came roaring back when I tried to move. Mayflower came to my room several times a day. She brought gossip about the barbecue and the women who'd been there.

"You should have seen 'em scatter when the rain came down," she laughed, "clucking away like angry hens. Some of them have been over here visiting since you've been laid up, pretending they're concerned about you when all they want is gossip. Clara Bines was here with her daughters—plain as pots, them two—seeing what she could find out, and that Bible-thumping ole heifer, Beula Hicks, showed up wanting to pray for your soul. I chased all of 'em out."

I couldn't stop myself from laughing, even though it made my shoulder pain worse. Mayflower had a grand way of telling stories. She'd have fitted in well in Donegal.

Her tone suddenly changed. "Aidan sat here through the night after he brought you back to the house, and he's been asking about you every day since." She paused. "I told Hans, for a man who ordered you out of his sight, Aidan sure is paying you a whole lot of attention."

I blushed. "I'm sure he would show the same concern for anyone."

Mayflower raised an eyebrow but said nothing.

Eventually, I was able to get up and move around. I spent most of the time rocking in a chair out on the veranda. In the evenings I watched the sun set in a blaze of red and gold. The sky looked as if it were on fire, and the sinking ball of sun looked close enough to touch. Of all the new sights I'd seen in Texas, the sunsets were the most beautiful.

Mayflower was spending a lot of time in Dallas, so it was Hans who kept me company when he was home. I liked the small, dignified man with his merry blue eyes. His self-containment gave him a calming presence. We talked about many things. He turned out to be well-read and well-traveled. He had studied engineering in Germany and worked for an oil company in Pennsylvania. He'd met Aidan in New York, he said, and was persuaded to travel with him to Texas.

I smiled. It seemed that Hans had the same yearning for adventure as I had—or used to have. What had happened to that yearning? Back in Donegal, I'd thought that adventure would save my life. Exploring new lands and meeting exotic new people would bring me all the happiness I needed. But now I realized adventure alone was not enough. I was still as alone and unloved as I had been in Donegal.

Shotgun City

1913

Nora

❦

The Adolphus Hotel in Dallas was the last word in luxury. I couldn't believe the size of the room, the fresh smelling cotton sheets, the wee bottles of every kind of creams and lotions and the lovely view over the main street. I felt like a queen.

The night I arrived, a knock came on my door. I opened it and peered around. There stood a good-looking boyo about thirty years old. He wore a white linen suit without the trace of a crease in it. He took off his big, white hat, revealing thick, glossy black hair.

"Miss Nora Sweeney?"

I nodded.

He took my hand and kissed it. "It's a pleasure to make your acquaintance."

His words came out in a low drawl. I stood there, fascinated.

"My name is Shane Kearney," he said, "and Mr. Sullivan wanted me to make sure you were settled in. Is everything to your liking?"

"Oh . . . er . . . yes," I said, realizing I'd been so busy looking at him I'd hardly heard what he said.

Mr. Kearney told me to take a couple of days to get settled, then he would be back to take me to Shotgun City. Apparently, he ran a hotel there. I wondered how he had time for that because he was working for James Sullivan as well, but there again, he never said exactly what he did for Sullivan. But, more important, he'd said I should go shopping for whatever clothes I needed and charge it to James Sullivan's account. He didn't have to tell me twice.

The hotel staff told me the best shop for women's clothes was Neiman-Marcus, so the next morning I landed there. I was over the moon when I walked in. I'd never been in a place like it. I'd loved style since I was very young, and I was like a child in a sweetshop.

The first floor smelled divine. All sorts of perfumes in wee colored bottles were on offer. The saleswoman was as attentive as the hotel staff. If all the Texans were like these ones, I'd be happy to stay. I bought a small bottle that had a beautiful scent, the sweetness of flowers with a hint of something more earthy. I told the saleswoman to hold it as I was going to look at dresses and hats. She scurried around from behind the counter and almost dragged me up the stairs to the second floor.

"This young lady wants to look at dresses and hats," she told another saleswoman, who dropped everything and ran over to me. I smiled to myself. She must have smelled a rich lover.

After my time studying the wealthy, first on the *Titanic*, then at Mrs. Shaw's, I'd have no trouble at all pretending to be a toff. I ignored the saleswoman and went over to the racks myself while she trailed along behind me. I couldn't believe the prices, but I passed no remarks. I let her carry my choices into the dressing room and fuss over me as I tried them on.

In the end it was worth her while. Besides the perfume, I walked out with six new dresses, two hats, two pairs of shoes and matching bags, as well as stockings, petticoats and drawers, which she called "undergarments." I announced that she should send everything, along with the bill, to the attention of Mr. James Sullivan at the Adolphus Hotel. Her eyebrows shot up when I said that, but I ignored her and sailed out of the shop as if I owned it. Ah, 'twas great *craic* altogether.

The next day, when I was expecting Mr. Kearney, I fussed over which dress and hat I would wear. I picked out a lovely pink one, which suited my complexion, and a matching hat and shoes. He'd told me to dress comfortably for the journey as the oil fields were very muddy and the town itself dusty, particularly when the wind was high. I ignored him. I was determined to make a good first impression on anyone I met. Ma had always told me how important this was. "Never set foot out the door unless ye are looking your best," she always said. "Ye never know who ye'll be after meeting."

When Mr. Kearney arrived he looked me up and down but said nothing. Anyway, who was he to judge me when himself was wearing a white linen suit and fancy leather boots with a raised heel? Comfortable clothes indeed.

As we rode in his car, he told me stories about the people who lived in the area. He was a grand storyteller and had me laughing 'til I cried. He was great *craic* altogether. I was almost sorry when we came to the outskirts of Shotgun City and he stopped talking. As he drove down the main street, I could hardly believe my eyes. The place was packed with every class of people you could imagine, from toffs to people wearing what I'd say were rags. Men in narrow trousers with some sort of leather coverings, boots like Mr. Kearney's except scuffed and dirty and big hats with wide brims, loitered beside tethered horses. They eyed me as we drove past, their eyes squinting against the sun.

Mr. Kearney stopped outside the biggest building in the town. A sign above it read "Kearney Hotel." I looked at him sharply. "You didn't say you owned this bloody place!"

He laughed. "You'll learn everything in good time, Miss Sweeney, including the fact that I know another Miss Sweeney who may come to work for me. Her name is Delia. Would you happen to know her?"

I sat bolt upright. I hadn't prepared myself for this question. Even though I had come all this way to find Delia, suddenly I wasn't quite ready to see her. I didn't want to know just yet whether she was involved with Aidan O'Hanlon. If she was, I'd have to forget about working for Sullivan. And I had to admit that

I was looking forward to the challenge of selling oil leases. In the back of my mind I also knew, but wouldn't admit, that I already liked being treated like a queen, and the lure of more money would be hard to resist. *What harm can it do to put our reunion off for a wee while?* I told myself. *After all, it's been well over a year since we've seen each other.*

"Sweeney's a common name," I said. "She *could* be my sister. I haven't laid eyes on her since the *Titanic* sank. But I heard a rumor she'd gone to Texas." I nodded to the hotel. "I can't believe she'd work in a place like this. She's very refined."

A smile stole across Kearney's face. "Don't worry your head none about that. She wouldn't be working in the dance hall. Would you like me to arrange a meeting?"

"I'd prefer to wait, if you don't mind. You see, my sister and I have never been very close. And I'm not sure she even knows I'm alive. I was listed as missing on the *Titanic*, you see. So, you can understand that I want to pick exactly the right moment to meet her—in case it *is* her, of course. And if you'd not say anything to her now, that would be better. 'Twould be an awful shock for her."

I'd rushed through my words, and I wasn't sure at all that Kearney believed me. I was nervous, and he could see it. He was the kind of a boyo who missed nothing.

"Shall we find a place for lunch?" he asked. "I was fixin' to take you into the hotel, but now that I know . . ."

He let the words trail off.

When we stopped at the first oil field, I held my breath. Huge wooden contraptions rose into the sky. Cables were tied to some class of a metal tool wrenching up and then dropping down into a big hole. What really fascinated me were the lines of rough-looking fellers walking back and forth on broad, wooden planks like they were on seesaws.

"Who are them boyos?" I said to Kearney.

"Ah, I thought you might find them interesting. They're what we call roughnecks, and they're every bit as violent as they look. A pretty young woman like you would want to stay well out of their way."

"Don't worry, Mr. Kearney. I can look after myself."

It had been raining and I was in mud up to my ankles, my lovely pink shoes sinking farther into the ground with every step.

Kearney looked down and smiled. "I think you would have been much better off in boots, Miss Sweeney."

I glared at him. I suppose he thought I was a useless woman. Well, I'd show him! I walked around the derricks, ignoring the whistles of the men on the planks, racking my brain to remember what I'd read in a big notebook Sullivan had given me to read on the train. I threw out as many questions as I could think of to show him I wasn't a fecking eejit altogether. They must have been good because Kearney lost the grin on his face and answered every one of them with respect.

Funnily enough, something about the place stirred my blood. For all the dirt and mud and the rough customers walking the planks, there was an air of excitement. Maybe it was the recklessness of it that drew me—that people would gamble all the money they had in the world in hopes that a shower of black oil would burst into the sky, and if it didn't, they'd have to crawl home penniless.

Now I really understood what James Sullivan was up to. Aidan O'Hanlon was one of these gamblers. If there was no oil in the wells he drilled, he'd be running short of money. Then he'd want more leases to try again. But if I was able to buy the leases out from under his nose, he'd be left penniless. I had to admit 'twas a brilliant scheme altogether.

After my first visit to the oil fields, I was anxious to get to work. I was glad he'd agreed that I could stay in Dallas. Shotgun City was dirty and noisy, and the Kearney Hotel looked shabby, not to mention the fact that I risked running into Delia. Besides, after a hard day touring the ranches and farms, I'd be dying to come back to the Adolphus and soak in a lovely, warm bath. I was getting used to luxury, no doubt about it.

Sullivan had hired a car and driver for me, but the following morning instead of going straight to Shotgun City, the driver took me to a building in Dallas. The sign on the door said "S&K Exploration." Two older men greeted me, and Kearney was there as well. That man seemed to be everywhere. He introduced the other two. One was a geologist name of Harris, a feller who studied the soil and guessed whether there was a good chance of oil underneath. Unless he was a magician, I thought, he'd be as much use as a hole in the wall. The other one was a slippery-looking boyo with a face like a rat who said he was a scout: Sullivan's eyes and ears on the ground. Scout, my arse, I thought; he was a spy if ever I saw one. His name was Grissom, and I made a point to remember it, even though I hoped I'd never run into him again. I still hadn't worked out what Kearney did. Did he know Sullivan's plan? I put the question out of my head. After all, I'd be getting paid a good wage and a bonus for every lease I arranged, and that's what counted.

Armed with a list of ranchers and farmers Sullivan had given me, I set out in high spirits. I wasn't disappointed. It turned out to be great *craic* sweet-talking these fellers into signing with S&K Exploration. Some were oul', whiskery *craturs* whose accents I could barely understand. I found if I kept smiling, maybe patted their hand a few times and insisted I was not from "back East," I had a good chance of convincing them to sign over their leases. I learned they didn't trust anybody from the East, so I made sure to tell them we were a Texas company. Often their wives hovered in the background looking daggers at me, but I soon found out the men paid no attention to them. This was "men's business," and that was grand with me.

The younger fellers were a different kettle of fish. They were suspicious of me and grilled me all about the oil business to make sure I knew what I was talking about. If I passed that test, they'd chance their arms by saying they'd agree if I did them a favor in return. When that happened I stood up and walked out. Some called me back and said they were sorry, and some didn't.

Sullivan's list included both Aidan O'Hanlon's leases as well as others. He'd said it would make it less obvious that it was only O'Hanlon's leases we were after. But I was getting bonuses for all the ones I signed, so I treated them all the same. The hardest nuts to crack, though, were with them that had leases with O'Hanlon. I was shocked at how loyal they were to him, even though I was offering them more money. Feminine persuasion only went so far in these cases, so I stuck to the money side of it. That often did the trick. If not, and the wife was hovering in the background, I would appeal to her. "I'm sure you could use the extra money, couldn't you?" The wives would give the husbands a pleading look, and often they'd give in.

I had to admit I was good, and I was enjoying myself so much that at times I even forgot why I was there. My memory was jogged one day when driving past one of the oil fields I saw Sullivan's spy, Grissom, standing talking to a handsome, dark-haired man who looked to be in his thirties. Curious, I told the driver to stop and made my way over to them. Grissom looked surprised and even a bit annoyed to see me.

"Hello there, Mr. Grissom," I said, ignoring his frowns. "I didn't expect to see you here."

He began to turn away from me, but I wasn't having it. "Aren't you going to introduce me?" I said.

Grissom looked even more annoyed. "Of course. Where are my manners? This is Mr. Aidan O'Hanlon. Aidan, this is Nora Sweeney, a friend of mine."

My God, so this was Aidan O'Hanlon. I'd expected a much older man, fat and homely. This feller was gorgeous. I extended my hand. "Lovely to meet you, Mr. O'Hanlon," I said, flashing my best smile.

He shook my hand and gave a slight bow. "Good afternoon, Miss Sweeney, a pleasure to meet you too." He scrutinized my face, and I had to look away from his deep blue eyes. "I have a friend named Delia Sweeney. I suppose it's too much of a coincidence to think you might know her. I understand she had a sister named Nora, but alas, she was drowned on the *Titanic*."

Jesus, I thought. First Kearney and now O'Hanlon.

I struggled not to give myself away. "No, I can't say I do."

He smiled. "No matter. I understand it's a common name in Ireland. Her family is from Donegal. You?"

I thought quickly. "No, I hail from Cork, Mr. O'Hanlon," I said.

Grissom cleared his throat. "I must be going, Miss Sweeney," he said.

I swung around. I'd almost forgotten he was there.

"And I must be going too," I said sweetly. "Goodbye, Mr. O'Hanlon."

Grissom escorted me back to the car.

"What was all that business about me being a friend? Why didn't you say we work together?"

"Don't be such a fool, Nora. He'll know soon enough what you are up to. I didn't want him to connect me with you."

"What *I* am up to? Don't you mean what *we* are up to?"

Grissom pushed me roughly into the car. "You need to mind your own business," he said.

As he turned to go, he paused and looked back at me. "And don't be getting ideas about O'Hanlon. He's spoken for with that Delia. And you have work to do. Mr. Sullivan wouldn't like to hear you're not following his orders."

I banged the door shut and shouted at the driver to go. I needed to get away from here, and fast. I closed my eyes and sighed. What had I got myself into? Grissom was a dangerous character, and so was Sullivan. I let my thoughts wander to Delia. Surely she must be in love with Aidan O'Hanlon. What girl wouldn't be? I hoped I was wrong. I hoped that O'Hanlon had a dark side and Delia wanted rid of him. I comforted myself with that thought because I really didn't want to hurt Delia. By the time I reached Dallas I realized that I felt well and truly trapped.

Delia

One early August evening Mayflower came rushing up the steps of the veranda, her face flushed. Hans and I gave each other a knowing look. What new gossip was she bringing from Dallas, we wondered.

Mayflower sank down into one of the rocking chairs, breathing hard and mopping her brow with a handkerchief. When I looked closely at her face sudden fear rose up in me. Something was terribly wrong.

"What is it, Mayflower?" I said.

"Oh, Lordy, Delia," she managed through ragged breaths, "you won't believe it, but lightning has struck twice."

"What are you talking about, Mayflower?" Hans stood up and reached for his wife's hand. "Take your time, my love."

"She's gone again."

"Who?"

"Lily. She's just up and disappeared faster than a prairie fire in a tailwind. One minute she was setting in the Kearney Hotel talking to Francine and the next she was gone. Miss Francine can't talk for crying. Folks' first thought was she'd gone back to the Dallas house, but they were wrong. Just grasping at straws, I guess. Poor Rosa's praying up a storm. Folks everywhere's out looking for her. And I can't imagine what poor Aidan is suffering. He's . . ."

I sprang up. "But why, Mayflower? Why would she do such a thing?"

Mayflower sighed. "I told y'all she'd stopped talking, but Rosa said she kept drawing pictures of a ranch, and then she drew you, Delia, and wrote your name beside it."

"What did she mean, Mayflower?" I said, my heart thumping. "What was she trying to say?"

Mayflower looked straight into my eyes. "I'd say after she saw you at the picnic, she was missing you and wanted to come to the ranch to find you. That little girl loves you, Delia."

"I didn't think she'd seen me at the ranch," I said. "She was busy playing with the other children."

"Most likely she saw you riding off and watched her daddy follow you."

"You don't think she just wandered off somewhere like you said she did when she was little, or when she wandered across to the hotel when we were in Shotgun City?" I looked up hopefully at Mayflower, but I could see by her face I was wrong.

"Not this time," she said. "There's been no sign of her all day."

The three of us were silent for a minute, letting the news sink in. Then Hans was suddenly all business.

"I will gather the ranch hands together and we will search every inch of this ranch. Mayflower and Delia, you stay here at the house in case she appears."

He made to leave, but I put up my hands to stop him.

"I can't stay here and do nothing," I cried. "I have to help search for her. Please!"

"It is best you stay, fraülein," he said gently. "I will be back as soon as I can with any news."

"He's right, Delia," said Mayflower. "There ain't much we can do right now."

Hans left, sprinting down the veranda steps two at a time. I sank down beside Mayflower, trying to hold back tears of despair. "It's my fault again, Mayflower," I whispered. "Lily ran away to try to find *me*. I am nothing but a curse."

Hans returned the next morning. He and his men had searched every square foot of the ranch, he said, and there was no sign of her. He had not really expected to find her, he said. After all, a child her age would have been unlikely to make it this far. But they had to be sure. He thought the best thing now was to concentrate the search in Shotgun City, where she had last been seen.

I jumped up at the news. "Take me with you to Shotgun City, Hans," I said. "I need to join the search."

Mayflower let out a small cry. "But your leg's not mended yet from the accident!"

But Hans nodded. "As you wish, fraülein."

I went upstairs and threw a few things into a bag. I was still limping, but I wasn't going to let that stop me. The night before I'd had a dream that Lily was hugging me, tears in her eyes. I believed with all my being it was a premonition, just like I'd had that the *Titanic* was going to sink. Lily was still alive somewhere.

Hans came in. "Time to go."

He picked up my bag and went out to the car. I hesitated for a moment, then went up to Mayflower and threw my arms around her. "Thank you for everything, Mayflower. You've been such a good friend. I don't know what I'd have done without you."

Her look softened. "Oh now, honey, don't be going on like you're never gonna see me again! You're going to find Lily in no time and then you'll be back."

Tears pricked at my eyes as I took Mayflower's hands in mine. The words that had been playing in my mind finally came out.

"Even after we find her, I won't be coming back. It's time I moved on. I'll stay in Shotgun City for a while and save some money. Then, who knows . . ." I let my words drift off.

Mayflower opened her mouth to protest but stopped. Instead, she nodded, as if she'd been anticipating what I was going to say.

"I know, darlin'. I was hoping you'd stay with us a spell longer, but you've got to find your own path."

She put her arms around me. "Don't you be a stranger, you hear."

"Never," I said as we both wiped away tears.

Nora

The night after I met Aidan O'Hanlon I tossed and turned, unable to sleep. I kept seeing Delia in my mind, sitting among the white stones, reading a book. How could I be sure she was in love with O'Hanlon? The Grissom feller had said they were a pair, but was he only having me on? I kept thinking until I was almost astray in the head. What if buying up his leases wasn't hurting O'Hanlon that much? What if he had more money behind him than Sullivan thought? After all, Kearney had said he had a partner. Yes, I'd pried a lot of his leases right out from under his nose, but maybe most of those would never pay off.

My thoughts turned to Mrs. Shaw. Some things about me hadn't changed under her influence. I still loved style and flirting and being admired. I still had a quick temper and was quick to put people in their place. And I wasn't shy about criticizing people when they deserved it. My tongue could be as salty as ever, and I knew a fraud when I met one. But some other things had changed a lot. Reluctant as I was to show it, I felt a kindness and concern for people in trouble that I had never had before. I would think twice now before I hurt somebody who had never done me harm. And right now that person was Delia. I wanted to curse Mrs. Shaw for making my life so complicated; instead, I cradled her locket in my fingers and drifted to sleep.

By the next morning I had made up my mind. Sullivan had paid me to the end of the week, so I would continue to work until then. I would visit all the remaining prospects on my list, but I wouldn't press them too much to sign with S&K. That should be enough to satisfy James Sullivan that I had done everything he wanted. After that, I would travel back to New York and hope that I hadn't hurt Aidan O'Hanlon too much. I buried the thought that by not seeing Delia before leaving, I was being a coward.

Relieved that I had a plan, I was about to step out of my room when a bellman appeared with a message. Instead of going straight to Shotgun City, I was to stop at S&K Exploration offices first. What now? I wondered. When I arrived there Shane Kearney, the geologist feller, Harris, and the rat-faced Grissom stood huddled together. They stopped talking when I came in. Grissom glared at me, and I glared back. If Kearney noticed—and I was sure he did—he passed no remarks. We all sat down. Kearney turned toward me.

"Listen carefully now, Miss Sweeney," he began. "We have some news that will affect your assignment, you hear?"

I wanted to give him a tongue-lashing for talking to me like I was a child, but I resisted the urge.

"Grissom here has it on good authority that well number eighty-eight—you recall I showed it to you, the one that's being drilled by O'Hanlon and his partner, Hans Humboldt—will be capped in the next few days. Harris, here, tells us they have drilled down three thousand feet and have only hit rock."

Harris nodded.

"Grissom tells us they're almost out of money, and their lease on that land expires the end of this week. Seems they're in a pile of trouble, bless their hearts." Kearney shook his head, as if in sympathy. "So, we need you, darlin', to approach the landowner in question and get the lease renewed to S&K."

"But why? If there's no oil, what good would the lease do us?"

Kearney grinned. "Well done, Miss Sweeney. Such a good question. The thing I haven't told you yet is that Harris is confident there is oil elsewhere on that land, in fact quite close to where number eighty-eight has been drilled."

"And you believe him?"

The words were out before I could stop them.

"Yes, of course," Kearney went on smoothly. "We don't just have Mr. Harris's say so, but several other geologists agree with him."

I pressed my luck. "But if that's the case, wouldn't O'Hanlon and his partner know that? Wouldn't he have dug other wells besides this one?"

Kearney gave me an exasperated look, as if I was a child with too many questions. "Of course they did, but their problem is they have no money to invest in more drilling. Must be real frustrating for them, real frustrating."

I took in all that Kearney had said. If I could get this lease signed over to S&K, it would surely put a nail in Aidan O'Hanlon's coffin. A sudden spasm of pain cut through my stomach.

"Mr. Sullivan is very anxious you get this done darlin'," Kearney continued. "There's a mighty fine bonus in it for you. After that, we won't need you any longer, and you'll be free to go back to New York, or wherever you wish."

I should have been relieved that after this last assignment I would be free of Sullivan, but instead I felt used. And I had another feeling too. I recognized it as shame.

Delia

❧

As we rode out to Shotgun City, some of the heaviness I had been carrying lifted from my shoulders. I was finding strength I didn't know I had—strength to forge my own destiny. And as for Aidan's anger toward me, this time I was not going to run away. Hans and I said little as we drove, and I was left to my thoughts.

As we neared Shotgun City, however, my anxiety began to build. Hans drove down the main street, and I saw posters with Lily's picture nailed to every building. My heart quickened. I prayed my premonition was true, and that she was alive and safe somewhere. When we passed the café where I had lost Lily the first time, I felt sick. *No matter*, I thought; *this time I have come to find her, and find her I will.*

Hans parked the car in front of the Kearney Hotel and jumped out. I followed him as he hurried in through the front door. As if expecting us, Kearney was there to greet us.

"Any news?" Hans and I said in unison.

Kearney shook his head. "Not yet. We have searched everywhere we can think of and there's still no sign of her. Francine is beside herself, and Aidan—well—poor Aidan is inconsolable."

I spoke up. "I'd like to take you up on your offer of a job, Mr. Kearney. I intend to stay here and help in the search for Lily, but I need to earn some money to pay my way."

Kearney raised an eyebrow. "Are you sure about this, Miss

Sweeney? Aidan O'Hanlon is staying here at the hotel and you would most likely cross paths. . . ."

He let the rest of his words drift off. I knew what he was getting at. He knew I had run away from Aidan once and thought I was likely to do so again. Well, he was wrong.

"It is of no matter to me that Aidan O'Hanlon is staying here," I said firmly. "My only concern is Lily."

Out of the corner of my eye, I saw Hans smiling.

Mr. Kearney bowed. "In that case I shall be delighted to take you on, Miss Sweeney. I have a room available at a reasonable rate. After you have settled in, we can discuss the terms of your employment. And by the way please call me Shane."

The room was belowstairs, small and sparsely furnished, with only a half window above the ground through which I could see the feet of passersby. I sighed. It was nothing like the lovely, airy rooms where I'd slept in the last couple of years. I was surprised how quickly I'd grown used to them. If I'd seen this room when I first came to America, I'd have been over the moon. It was a thousand times better than the cottage attic, and it was far away from Ma's sharp tongue.

I unpacked my belongings, smoothed down my dress and went back up to the ground floor. Mr. Kearney, as he always seemed to be, was engaged in an intense conversation with a tall, grizzled man with a face like a weasel and darting, nervous eyes. An unsavory customer if ever I saw one.

"Ah Miss Sweeney," Kearney said upon spotting me, "come, let me show you your office and introduce you to the staff. You will start tomorrow at nine."

I stared at him in surprise. "Tomorrow?" I asked.

"I see no point in waiting, Miss Sweeney," he said and left.

I hadn't expected to begin work right away. My priority was Lily. I hurried out onto the street. It was then I realized I had no plan for how I was going to search. I stood trying to conjure up the images of Lily I had been seeing in my mind. Perhaps some details would give me a clue. But nothing came. I went back into the hotel to find Kearney.

"What's being done in the search for Lily?" My tone betrayed my impatience.

He sighed. "We've done everything we can think of, Miss Sweeney. The hotel has been searched from top to bottom, room by room. I've sent men out to every establishment here in town, but no one remembers seeing her. It's as if she disappeared into thin air."

"But there must be something else we can do. Did you check out at the oil fields, or on the edge of town where I've seen children playing among the shacks?"

He stiffened. I had obviously pressed him too far. "I can assure you, Miss Sweeney, there is nowhere you can think of that we haven't already searched." He turned to go, then added, "Francine tells me the child was drawing pictures of a ranch with your name scrawled on them," he said. "Many of us believe she ran away to find you."

I struggled to hold my temper. He was as much as blaming me for Lily's disappearance. In the past I would have been filled with guilt, but I was not going to let it consume me this time.

"Hans and his men have searched every inch of the ranch," I said. "Thank you for your time, Mr. Kearney."

With that, I turned away and hurried down the street. Eventually, I slowed my pace and began to question various shopkeepers and passersby, and even some rough-looking men leaning against the wall of a saloon. No one had seen her. By the time I reached the end of the street, a gnawing feeling welled up in me. What if my intuition was wrong? What if we never found her?

Nora

I had no choice but to do what Kearney and Sullivan wanted. Up until now I would have been delighted at the challenge of stealing the biggest lease of all from under Aidan O'Hanlon's nose. But now that my conscience had caught up with me, the whole project had turned sour.

Kearney insisted on driving me out to where the landowner lived. It was clear he didn't trust me as far as he could throw me. And I felt the same about him. But I didn't argue. It was when he got out of the car along with me at the rancher's house that I drew the line.

"Where d'you think you're going?" I demanded.

"With you, of course, darlin'. This will be a tricky prospect, and I'd like to offer you the benefit of my experience."

Experience, my arse, I thought; *'tis to spy on me you want.*

Instead of showing my anger, I put on a false smile. "That's so nice of you, Mr. Kearney," I said, "but I really think it will be better if I go in alone." I winked at him as I adjusted my dress, pulling it down to show off more cleavage. "You'd only distract the man from what I'm offering."

Kearney's smile was more like a leer. "I get your meaning completely, darlin'. I'll wait for you here. If you need my help, just holler."

I turned my back on him and walked up to the house. The truth was, the last thing I wanted to do was sell this lease to Sullivan and his cronies. It would mean the end of Aidan O'Hanlon. I didn't want that on my conscience. But if I failed, the threat of Sullivan's revenge scared the wits out of me more than a guilty conscience.

My heart skipped when the door was opened by a wizened oul' feller old enough to be my granda. From my experience he'd be a much easier sell than a young feller with a jealous wife. But when he looked me up and down and spat tobacco at my feet, I suddenly wasn't so sure.

"Ain't no call here for what your selling, missy," he said and tried to close the door in my face. I felt Kearney's eyes burning through my back. I had to put on a show for him.

"Oh please, Mr. McCabe," I said, tugging the neck of my dress back up, "I'm no floozie from the town. I'm a respectable businesswoman, and I've come to talk to you about your oil lease." I pulled out a printed card. "I represent S&K Exploration Company."

I prayed that McCabe would let me in so I could close the door and get away from Kearney.

"If you'd let me in, I can tell you why I'm here. I know you'll find it worth your while. It just isn't polite to keep a lady standing on the doorstep."

McCabe turned his back and grunted as he walked down the hall, leaving me to follow him. I closed the front door and made my way into a big, open room where a fire blazed. *Jesus*, I thought, *and 'tis still hot as blazes outside.* Then I remembered that back in Donegal there was a fire in our cottage winter or summer. I shrugged. *No matter where you are, some things don't change.*

I started into my practiced speech, but McCabe put up his hand to stop me.

"I know why you're here. Plenty of folks 'round here have warned me about you. You're out to steal all of Aidan O'Hanlon's leases."

"Not just O'Hanlon's," I put in, "others as well. And we're not stealing them, just offering a choice."

He waved a bony hand at me. "As I was saying, I know what you're up to, and I won't be part of it."

I took a deep breath. "But Mr. McCabe, as you likely know, Mr. O'Hanlon will be capping well number eighty-eight in a day or two, and then he will be out of money and won't be able to afford to renew your lease. S&K has plenty of funding and is prepared to make you a good offer."

He shook his head and spat tobacco into the hearth. "Not sure if I want a new lease," he said. "Sick and tired of my land being dug up."

I sighed. I couldn't let this one slip away from me. Sullivan would crucify me.

"There's no guarantee S&K will drill on your land, and in the meantime you'll have money coming in from the lease. S&K will only drill if we are sure there is oil. We have a very good record of success, and you would benefit from that success. You really don't have much to lose, Mr. McCabe."

I sat back and waited. I'd done all I could.

McCabe muttered away to himself, then looked over at me. "Give over them papers," he said, "and show me where to sign."

I was delighted with myself as I stood and thanked McCabe. He refused to shake my hand, so I walked by myself to the door. I couldn't wait to show Kearney how well I'd done. But just as I was about to open the door, Mrs. Shaw's image floated in front of me. The thought of turning over the signed lease to Kearney suddenly sickened me. I folded it up and put it in my bag.

I opened the car door and got in.

"Well?" said Kearney.

"He wouldn't budge," I said.

Delia

❧✦❧

After I finished my first day at work in the hotel, I rushed outside. Lily still had not been found. She had been missing two days, and by now I was frantic. I raced down the street to the edge of town, where huts and lean-tos were crowded together. No one spoke English, but when I waved Lily's picture they understood. One person after another shook their heads. At last I gave up in despair and trudged back up the street.

When I reached the hotel I pulled open the front door and almost collided with Aidan. He stood back to let me in, but I couldn't move. I stared at him, hardly believing what I saw. His face was sallow and unshaven, and his clothes were crumpled, as if he'd slept in them. My heart filled with pity for him.

"Oh Aidan," I said, "I'm so sorry."

He nodded but said nothing.

We stood staring at each other for what seemed like an eternity. As I looked at him, I forgot about all the unpleasantness that had passed between us. None of it mattered now. I put my hand on his arm and led him into the lobby and over to a small sofa, where we sat down. He turned to me, tears welling in his eyes.

"What can I do, Delia? We've searched everywhere."

I nodded. "I know."

He stood up and extended his hand to me. "Will you come and keep me company, Delia? If I'm alone I'm afraid I might go mad."

"Of course," I whispered.

* * *

Besides the bed and dresser, a small table and velvet chairs stood under the window in his room. I sat down and watched him as he poured whiskey into two glasses. He took off his coat and unbuttoned part of his shirt. I had to pull my eyes away from the smooth black hairs on his upper chest. I took a gulp of whiskey.

"I've missed you, Delia."

"I've missed you too, Aidan."

"I'm sorry for everything. For sacking you that day Lily was lost. It was wrong of me. I was determined to punish you, but it was Lily I succeeded in punishing."

"But you more than made up for it the day you saved my life when my horse bolted. I'd say we're even."

He nodded.

"Oh, poor Lily," I blurted out. "Where on earth can she be?" I wanted to tell him about my premonition, but I didn't want to give him false hope.

"All I can think of is that bastard Sullivan. He never wanted me to bring her to Texas. And now if he finds out what's happened, he'll blame me for this too, as well as for Mary."

"Maybe," I murmured, "but he was away in Ireland when we left. He can't know for sure that we're here."

"He has spies everywhere." Aidan's tone was bitter.

I swallowed hard. "It's quite likely she ran away to find *me*," I said. "Mayflower said she'd been drawing pictures of me at the ranch. It's all my fault!"

Darkness had fallen, and the saloon across the street was lit up like a Christmas tree. Rowdy shouts and laughter drifted up from the street, the sounds occasionally muffled by the rhythmic beat of horse's hooves.

"No, Delia, it's not your fault she's missing. It's mine. I should never have left her alone." He turned to face me. "What if we never find her, Delia?"

I thought back to his words to me that night back in New York: *The ones you love will always leave you in the end one way or another.*

I could hold myself back no longer. I went over, sat on the arm of his chair and put my arm around his neck. He reached up and pulled my face close to his. Then he kissed me hard on the lips. I responded like a thirsty pilgrim drinking from a stream. I'd fantasized about this moment ever since our night on the train, but I never believed it would happen again. I moaned aloud. Still kissing me, he stood up and lifted me in his arms and carried me over to the bed. He put me down gently, lay down beside me and pulled me to him.

We turned to face each other in the shadows. His arms tightened around me as he pulled me close. He kissed me again and again, whispering my name at each pause. I reached over and unbuttoned his shirt all the way, so that I could run my fingers across his bare chest. He moaned as I let my lips trail across his chest and down his body.

Suddenly, he sprang up and, standing with his back to me, removed the rest of his clothing. I lay admiring his broad shoulders and slender hips silhouetted against the dim light. I let my eyes travel over his buttocks and down his strong legs.

When he turned to face me, my heart pounded. He was the most beautiful man I had ever seen. He sat down beside me and, quietly and gently, began removing my clothes. Impatience filled me, and I pulled the rest of them off myself. When I was naked his hands caressed me from shoulders to toes. His breathing was ragged. I could stand it no more and reached up and pulled him down on top of me. We moved together in a single rhythm, as if our bodies had long known each other. I called out his name as my passion mounted and I abandoned all reason and control. If this moment meant I was going to Hell, so be it. I didn't care. All I wanted was to cling to this man and never let go. When he entered me with a gentle thrust I felt a sharp, distant pain, but it melted away as soon as it came. His thrusts grew stronger, and I urged him on, faster and faster, raising my body to meet his. We reached the crescendo together, calling out each other's names aloud before collapsing, our breathing hard.

"Don't ever leave me, Delia," he whispered.

Nora

❧

Kearney brought me back to the hotel. He was spitting nails that I hadn't persuaded Mr. McCabe to sign over his lease.

"Mr. Sullivan's not going to be pleased," he said.

"Sure don't I know that."

When I was in the safety of my room I took out the lease McCabe had signed and threw it on a table as if afraid it might explode in flames. My heart was beating a mile a minute. What in the name of God had possessed me to lie to Kearney? I should have been over the moon at landing the biggest lease in the county. Sullivan would have been so pleased, he'd probably have given me a massive bonus. Now, he'd be more likely to thrash me within an inch of my life—or worse.

I began to pace the floor, gathering my thoughts. The sooner I legged it out of Dallas the better, that much was clear. But where would I go? I didn't know anywhere besides New York. If things had been different with Dom, I could have stayed with him, but as it was . . . I blinked away the image of Kathleen standing in her red petticoat, sneering at me. I could find Delia and tell her what I'd done. But my courage failed me. I still couldn't face her. Going back to Donegal was out of the question—I'd never go back there with my tail between my legs. I sighed. There was nothing for it but to go back to New York and hope Sullivan wouldn't find me. A small voice told me it was a foolish hope.

* * *

The next morning I asked the hotel porter for a train schedule to New York. There was a train leaving at two o'clock. I packed my suitcases and sat down to wait.

A knock came on the door. I was expecting breakfast. I'd ordered almost everything on the menu. *May as well,* I thought. *It'll be the last thing I'll be getting out of Sullivan.* I hurried to the door. My mouth fell open when I came face-to-face with Kearney.

"What now?" I said roughly.

He pushed the door wide open. It was then I saw a small girl standing in the hallway. Kearney grabbed her hand and pulled her into the room.

"Who's this?" I said.

"Never you mind," said Kearney. "You're to keep her here for the morning and then take her to the station in time for the two o'clock train to New York."

"I'm going on that train myself." I blurted out the words before I could stop them. My nerves were getting the better of me and I was acting like an eejit.

Kearney smirked. "So I understand from the porter downstairs. This will work out very well."

"And what am I to do with her when we get to New York?"

"Someone will meet you there, don't worry."

I looked from him to the child. "I'm not a bloody child minder," I said. "What do you take me for?"

"You forget, Mr. Sullivan has paid you until the end of the week."

"But you said you wouldn't need me any more after yesterday."

Kearney's tone was sarcastic. "That was only if you had a signed lease, Miss Sweeney. Unfortunately, you failed." He went to the door. "Two o'clock," he said, and then he was gone.

I wanted to yell after him, but what good would it have done? I looked down at the child. She was watching me with wide, blue eyes.

"So, what's your name?" I said.

I must have sounded impatient, for she didn't answer me. I tried again, more gently this time.

"There's no need to be afraid, love," I said. "I won't hurt you. My name is Nora. What's yours?"

I wasn't used to being around children, and I felt awkward talking to her like that. But she still didn't answer. I wondered if she was mute.

Another knock came. If it was that arsehole Kearney again, I was ready for him.

"What the hell d'you want now?" I shouted as I opened the door.

A young waiter dropped a tray on the floor and backed away. "Breakfast, ma'am," he murmured, then ran away down the hallway.

It was almost comical. I must have scared the daylights out of him. I picked up the tray, brought it in and set it on a table.

"Come on," I said to the child. "There's plenty for the two of us. I, for one, am famished with hunger."

She shook her head and sat down in an armchair. It was hard to eat with her staring at me. At last I had an idea. Didn't most children like to draw? I knew I did when I was young. I got up and fetched some paper and a pen from the desk and handed them to her. She took them without a word and went over to a wee table beside the window, sat down and began to draw.

My appetite disappeared. I pushed away the tray and sipped a cup of tea. The clock chimed ten. I sighed. What was I going to do with this child for another four hours?

I decided to take a long, sudsy bath. Who knew when I'd get the chance to have another one? I locked and bolted the door in case the child took the notion to escape. I didn't want to face Kearney if I lost her. I took my time in the bath. After I dried myself off I fixed my hair, put on some makeup and sprayed myself with the scent I'd bought at Neiman-Marcus. How long ago that seemed.

When I went back into the living room the wee one was still

drawing pictures. I crept over to look at them. When I picked one up my heart almost stopped. The picture was of a ranch, with the stick figure of a girl, and scrawled beside it was the name Delia.

"Holy Mother of God," I said aloud.

I looked at the child, remembering the posters I had seen in Shotgun City. "Is your name Lily O'Hanlon?"

She nodded at me without a word.

Delia

❧

I'd been sitting daydreaming about my night with Aidan when Mayflower showed up without warning, as was her habit, and announced she was taking me to lunch. She had something important to tell me, she said.

Once we were seated outside the café across the street—the one where I had lost Lily—she looked around to make sure no one was listening and started to talk.

"I heard tell there's some highfalutin' woman in town trying to buy leases for a company nobody 'round here ever heard of. From what I hear, she's good at seducing men into signing up with her. All silk and flounces and sweet talk. I'd say this isn't her first rodeo."

"Is she hurting Aidan and Hans's business?"

"She sure is," said Mayflower, "although she's going after other folks' leases as well."

My temper rose. How dare somebody set out to deliberately destroy Aidan?

"D'you know her name?"

"No, not yet," said Mayflower.

"Her name is Nora Sweeney," said a voice behind me.

I swung around. There stood Aidan.

"Sorry. I didn't mean to startle you," he said. "Shane Kearney told me you were both over here. I thought I'd join you."

I wanted to tell him it wasn't his sudden appearance that startled me; it was the mention of Nora's name. My heart had missed a beat, and a sick feeling had come over me. Had I heard him correctly?

"What did you say her name was?"

"Nora Sweeney."

"How do you know?"

"I met her out at the oil field. She was with an unsavory character named Grissom. He said they were friends, but I saw her arguing with him as they walked away."

I hardly heard what he was saying. My head spun so alarmingly, I thought I might faint. Surely this woman couldn't be my sister. Nora was dead. I had seen her drown. I heard Aidan and Mayflower's voices as if through a fog.

"Whoever she is, she's been trying to buy up our leases, particularly the ones that will expire at the end of the month." Aidan breathed a deep sigh. "If she succeeds, this could be the last straw. She could ruin us."

"We ain't gonna let that happen," said Mayflower. "We need to find out who she's working for. I'd wager Shane Kearney knows. He seems to know everything goes on in this town."

Ignoring the urgency in Aidan's voice, I went back to Nora Sweeney.

"What did she look like? Did she say where she was from?"

Aidan looked at me. "What?"

"Nora Sweeney. What did she look like?"

'Pretty, dark hair, slender, about your age. She had an Irish brogue and said she was from County Cork. I asked if she knew you; she said she didn't, and that Sweeney was a common name."

I tried to think. Nora was buxom, not slender. And this woman was from Cork. Besides, Nora would never traipse around muddy oil fields talking to poor farmers. And if she was really in Texas, she wouldn't be staying at Kearney's hotel. She'd be staying in Dallas at a fine hotel like the Adolphus. My panic began to ease. It had to be someone else entirely. But as I tried to convince myself, my own words came back to me. In New York hadn't I told the Boyles that Sweeney was a common name in order to throw them off the scent? Could that have been what this Nora Sweeney was doing as well? The thought lingered in my head.

I turned my attention to Mayflower and Aidan.

"We can't just sit here and allow this hussy to ruin us," Mayflower said.

Aidan put his head in his hands. "To tell you the truth, I don't much care anymore. It's Lily I'm worried about and the business be damned."

Eventually, he looked back up at us. "Anyway, it may be too late. Well number eighty-eight is our last, best chance. Our geologists tell us they are sure there is oil somewhere nearby on the same land, but if eighty-eight doesn't come through by the end of the week, we'll be left with hardly enough money to pay off the crew, let alone renew the lease." He looked at Mayflower. "I'm sorry, May, I thought Hans had told you."

Mayflower shrugged. "He never tells me bad news. He's got too much pride."

"Isn't there anything we can do, Aidan?" I said.

He shook his head. "No. We've tried raising more capital, but nobody will lend to us."

Mayflower and I exchanged glances. What else was there to do, except pray that a well somewhere would come in? Even if it was only a tiny drizzle of oil, it would be better than nothing.

After Mayflower left I walked back over to the hotel with Aidan. Shane Kearney, as always, was standing in the lobby watching us. My head was buzzing. Aidan's news about the business was bad, but that was dwarfed by the possibility that Nora might be alive. If the woman Aidan described *was* her, I should be over the moon. But if it was her, why was she trying to ruin Aidan's business? Eventually, it dawned on me that she must have found out I had passed myself off as her when I came to New York and was exacting her revenge. Nora had always had a vengeful streak. But who had told her? I reasoned it must have been Dom. He was the only one who knew.

I made up my mind then and there that I would find her and face her down. I wasn't going to let her get away with this.

Nora

❧

I gaped at the child, unable to take it all in. Standing in front of me was Aidan O'Hanlon's child—the child the whole town was searching for. How in God's name had she landed in my hotel room? Shane Kearney must have had her hidden in the hotel all this time. But why? There was no point in asking the child what had happened to her. She was either mute or afraid for her life to say a word.

I walked over to the window, trying to calm the thoughts that were tripping over one another in my head. Kearney had said I was to take her on the train to New York. He'd found a convenient chaperone in me. But he didn't say who was to meet her at the other end. What if I was delivering the child into some oul' divil's evil clutches? There was no telling what might happen to her. Well, I wasn't going to be part of it.

I began to pace the room, racking my brain. I was sure there was more to the story than Kearney was telling me. It was only when I stopped pacing that the penny dropped. Sullivan! That bastard Sullivan! That was who Kearney was sending her to. Why hadn't I realized it sooner? Hadn't he told me that night in New York that he was ruining O'Hanlon so he could get Lily back? Kearney must have told him I didn't get the biggest lease signed, so he decided to take the girl instead. And that black-guard, Kearney, had the girl already stowed away in case Sullivan asked for her. I felt sick to my stomach. How on earth could they treat a child like that?

It was clear to me now what I had to do. I had to take Lily back to her da, and the sooner the better. Who knew what else Kearney had up his sleeve? I went to the window and peered down to the street. By luck, the driver and car Sullivan had hired for me was still there. I took Lily by the hand and hurried her out of the room with me.

"Come on, Lily," I said. "I'm taking you to your da."

She didn't fight me. I decided to leave my luggage behind me. I wouldn't be taking the two o'clock train anyway—certainly not when I knew Sullivan would be waiting for me at the other end.

I told the driver to go as fast as he could to Shotgun City. When we arrived I told him to pull around the back of the hotel. I couldn't risk having Kearney see us. We were halfway around the hotel when Lily shot up and shouted, "Stop!" The car screeched to a halt. I nearly jumped out of my skin. The child had a voice after all, and a loud one at that.

"Delia," she cried. "Delia."

I looked to where she was pointing and there, behind a glass window on the ground floor, I saw Delia. I hardly recognized her at first. She had filled out, and her skin was bronzed. Her hair was bleached the color of straw and hung in a thick braid down her back. I took in a deep breath. Where had the faded, sickly looking girl gone—the one who was afraid of her own shadow? This girl was gorgeous. If it hadn't been for Lily, I might never have recognized her.

Lily bolted out of the car before I could stop her and was knocking so loudly on the window, I was afraid she'd shatter it. Delia sprang up, scattering papers in every direction, and raced out the door. When she reached Lily she sank down on her knees and threw her arms around her. The child hugged her back, and the two of them burst into tears. As I watched them, I felt a lump in my throat.

After a minute I knew I had to get them into the car in case Kearney showed up. I approached Delia slowly and tapped her on the shoulder.

"Delia?"

She looked as if she'd seen a ghost.

"Nora?"

I nodded. "Aye, Delia. It's me."

She stood up, rocking unsteadily on her feet. She looked as though she might faint. I took her by the arm.

"You and Lily need to get into the car now before Kearney sees you. He's the one stole Lily."

A steely glint appeared in Delia's eyes. I'd never seen such a look from her in my life. I backed away.

"Why should I believe you?" she cried. "You've been here trying to ruin Aidan's business just to get your revenge on me. How dare you, Nora? And if that wasn't enough, you stole Lily. You're still the selfish, greedy, malicious girl you always were."

She was screaming now, ignoring the stares of people on the street.

"Get out of my sight," she cried. "I wish you'd stayed dead!"

She put her arm around Lily and hurried away without looking back. There was no point calling out after her. I got in the car and told the driver to take me back to Dallas. Her words rang in my ears. She was right. I had persecuted her something awful when we were young, and I had tried to destroy her and Aidan. I deserved what I got from her.

"I'm sorry, Delia," I murmured as I let my tears fall. "I'm sorry for everything."

Delia

I clutched Lily's hand tight and ran with her back into the hotel. Shane Kearney tried to block our way, but I ducked around him and took the stairs up to Aidan's room two at a time, praying that Aidan would be there. Lily cried out to me to slow down, but I ignored her. I wouldn't stop until she was safely in Aidan's arms.

Aidan opened the door before I even knocked.

"Daddy!"

Lily ran to him and clutched him around the waist. He put his hand on her head and pulled her close. He stared at me and opened his mouth to speak, but no words came out. I was so out of breath I couldn't have answered him if they had. We stared at each other. I read gratitude in his eyes as his tears began to flow. I nodded.

"I know," I managed to say at last. "It's a miracle."

I followed him into the room. Lily still clung to him. He sat down, taking her on his lap.

"How? Who?"

"It was my sister brought her here," I began. "Nora Sweeney— the woman who's been stealing your leases—she's my sister, Aidan. I'm so sorry. . . ." My words trailed off as I began to sob.

"But I thought she drowned."

"S-so did I," I said miserably. "But she didn't. A-and she must have found out I passed myself off as her and came here to get back at me—at us—for what I did!"

Aidan stood up, gently easing Lily into the armchair. Then he came over and put his arms around me.

I sobbed into his shoulder. "I'm sorry," I whispered. "I'm so, so sorry."

He took me by the shoulders and forced me to look at him. "Listen to me, Delia. You have nothing to be sorry for. You are not responsible for your sister's actions. But . . . if she was really out for revenge, why did she bring Lily to you?"

"I don't know. But she was the one who stole her!"

"No, she wasn't."

Aidan and I turned to stare at Lily.

"It was Mr. Kearney stole me. He came up to me in the hotel and took me down to Miss Francine and said I was to stay with her. He said he would come back to take me to Daddy." She frowned and bit her lip. "I waited and waited with Miss Francine, but he didn't come back until this morning." She looked near to tears.

"It's all right, Lily," Aidan said, kneeling in front of where she sat. "Take your time. What happened then? Where did Mr. Kearney take you?"

"To a big hotel in Dallas. I thought he was taking me to see you, Daddy, but he wasn't." She heaved a sigh. "It was a lady named Nora. He told her to take me to New York on a train at two o'clock, and then he left." She gave Aidan a pleading look. "I don't want to go to New York, Daddy. I want to stay here with you and Delia."

Aidan wrapped her in his arms. "You're not going to New York, my pet, you're staying here with us."

"Forever?"

"Yes, forever."

When she settled down Lily told us that when Nora found out who she was, she brought her back to Shotgun City. She'd told her she was bringing her to her father, although Lily wasn't sure she believed her.

"But she did what she promised," said Aidan.

Lily nodded her head.

I slumped down onto a chair. Suddenly, I didn't know what to think. Had I blamed Nora too quickly? Was she innocent?

As if reading my mind, Lily came up to me. "Miss Nora didn't steal me, Miss Delia. She didn't even know who I was at first. Don't be angry with her."

Lily dozed off. Aidan lifted her on to the bed and covered her with a duvet. Then he poured two glasses of brandy, gave me one and sat down opposite me.

"Sullivan!" we both said in unison.

"I knew he was behind it," Aidan said. "He was the one bringing her to New York."

"Yes," I said. "And it seems Shane Kearney was helping him."

Aidan nodded. "Sullivan was behind the whole leasing scheme too. And no doubt Kearney was part of it."

"*And* Nora. She may have had no part in Lily's disappearance, but she definitely was helping Sullivan get your leases."

We fell silent, each lost in our own thoughts.

I remembered what I'd said to Nora. *I wish you'd stayed dead!* It was a terrible thing to say to anyone, let alone my own sister. I had no idea what she'd been through since that night on the *Titanic*. I had no idea why she was working for Sullivan. Maybe it had nothing to do with revenge. The one thing I did know was that she had done a kind and brave thing by bringing Lily back to us. She had risked Sullivan's temper—and I could vouch for the ferocity of it from my own experience—and she'd risked running afoul of Shane Kearney. Shane Kearney! I could hardly believe it. A wolf in sheep's clothing, Ma would have called him.

I drained my brandy, looked at the clock and stood up.

"There's somewhere I have to go, Aidan," I said. "I'll be back soon."

Nora

I cried all the way back to Dallas. By the time I reached my room at the Adolphus, I had no tears left to shed. I shouldn't have been surprised at Delia's reaction. I could understand why she'd jump to the conclusion that I'd taken Lily. And she knew I was the one buying out Aidan's leases. From her way of looking at it, I had hurt the two people she loved.

Delia's fierceness had stunned me, but what had sliced through me like a knife was when she'd said she wished I was still dead. I hadn't expected the likes of that—particularly from the Delia I remembered, who'd never say as much as boo to a goose. I'd almost doubled over from the pain of it, from the pain of knowing I'd lost my only sister once and for all.

The clock chimed one. There was still time to catch the two o'clock train to New York. I didn't care if Sullivan was waiting for me. He'd be raging that I hadn't brought Lily, but he couldn't hurt me more than Delia had. Nobody could.

There was a knock at the door and I jumped up to answer it. The driver was early. But it wasn't the driver; it was Delia. I stood, unable to move. I thought maybe I was seeing a ghost. But then she spoke. "Hello, Nora. Can I come in?"

I nodded and opened the door wide. She came in and looked around at my luggage.

"I thought you might be leaving town. I'm glad I caught you in time."

There was an awkward silence between us. I nodded to the sofa and she sat down.

"I'm sorry for what I said, Nora. It was unforgivable."

"You had every right," I said.

"No. I had the right to be angry with you for working for Sullivan, but I had no right to accuse you of stealing Lily when I didn't have all the facts." She paused, and I saw that she was fighting back tears. "And I had absolutely no right to say I wished you were dead."

I shrugged. "It hardly matters now. I'll be on my way to New York in an hour and I don't suppose we'll ever see each other again."

I was trying to put on a brave face, but my voice faltered. Delia began crying in earnest. She stood up and put her arms around me.

"Please forgive me, Nora. I never wanted it to be like this. You don't know how many times I wished you had survived, and we could be sisters again."

I looked at her. "I wanted that too, Delia. I came to Texas to find you, but then I got involved with Sullivan—ah, 'tis a long story."

Delia pulled me down on the sofa and sat beside me. "Tell me everything," she said.

I looked at the clock. "But there isn't time. . . ."

"You're not leaving until I hear it. I'm going down to send your driver away; then I'm coming back to make some tea and you're going to tell me everything."

I managed a weak smile. She sounded just like the bossy Delia I remembered from the *Titanic*. I waited until she returned and went about making the tea. Then she sat down.

"Go on now," she said.

Once I started talking it all rushed out of me like an overflowing river. I began with waking up in the hospital not knowing who or where I was. I smiled when I told her about Mrs. Shaw and how kind she'd been to me. I even told her about that lout, Sinclair. I was relieved to get that part off my chest, for I'd never told anyone about it before. I told her about going back to Donegal, and how Ma had me astray in the head after she found out she'd taken the job with Aidan O'Hanlon. And I told her about how Da had sold a cow to pay my passage back to New York.

"I think he loved me a little bit after all," I said.

Delia smiled. "He loved both of us, Nora."

I told her about the summer Dom and I had spent together and how I'd hoped to see him in New York, and maybe there would have been a future for us except for Kathleen.

"Kathleen?" Delia said. "The Kathleen used to work for Aidan?"

I nodded. "Would you be after knowing her?"

"Oh, yes. You see, Dom and I were friends in New York, and she accused me of stealing him from her. But Dom said he wouldn't give her the time of day. I'm certain she just wanted you to think they were going together. She's a spiteful girl."

I didn't know whether to believe her, but deep down I hoped she was right. I gulped down some tea. My throat was parched from talking.

"Dom gave me your address in New York and I went to the house to find you, and who was there but Sullivan."

"I've met him," Delia said. "He's an awful man."

My eyes grew wide. "Then you know how ignorant and dangerous he can be. He came up with this plan. I didn't like the sound of it, but 'twas the only way I could get to Texas to see you. But the more leases I signed, the more guilty I felt, and the more I was afraid to let you know I was here. It was only when Kearney brought Lily here . . ."

Delia took my hands in hers. "Oh, Nora, I'm so sorry for what you've been through. And I understand completely why you did what you did." She paused and frowned. "But there's something I don't understand. You're not the Nora I remember—there's something different about you."

I smiled for the first time. "Aye. You may blame Mrs. Shaw for that. She didn't take all the spit and fire out of me, but she taught me something about kindness—and about love." I fingered my locket as I spoke. "I think she saved my life, Delia."

The clock struck four. I was shocked. We'd been talking for almost three hours. And Delia hadn't even told me *her* story yet.

"Oh dear. I should be getting back," she said. "I told Aidan I wouldn't be long."

Just at that moment there was a loud knock on the door. I opened it just enough to see who was there, and a tall woman with black hair pushed past me.

"'Delia darlin'," she drawled, "I hear they found Lily! We gotta get ourselves to Shotgun City right this minute. Aidan just called me. Told me you'd likely be here."

The woman gave me a sharp look. "Who's this?" she said.

Delia smiled. "This is my sister, Nora Sweeney," she said. "She's the one who found Lily, and she's coming with us."

Before the woman or I could say a word, Delia rushed us out the door.

"I'll explain in the car," she said.

Delia

Mayflower was unusually quiet as I told her about Sullivan's revenge scheme and Shane Kearney's role in it. When I had finished she glared at Nora. She likely wouldn't forgive her as quickly as I had, but there again, she didn't know Nora's whole story. I knew she'd come around eventually. For now, Mayflower was satisfied with taking out her vengeance on Shane Kearney.

"I never thought Shane Kearney would turn out to be as crooked as a dog's hind leg," she said. "As for that floozie, Francine, I never did trust her. All gussied up and full of sweet talk, and all the while in cahoots with Kearney to kidnap Lily."

Nora tried to choke down a giggle. I was sure she'd never heard such colorful talk.

"Them two better high-tail it out of town before folks find out what they did. They'd be about as welcome here as a skunk at a picnic."

Having said her piece, Mayflower leaned back in her seat with an air of righteous disdain.

We rode on in silence until we reached the outskirts of Shotgun City. The area around the lean-to huts and shacks, usually buzzing with activity, seemed eerily quiet. No children played in the yards, and the tables outside the *taquería* were empty.

"Where is everyone, Manuel?" I asked the driver, expecting him to tell me today was a holiday.

Manuel shrugged his shoulders.

When we drove on to the main street that ran through town, Mayflower and I sat straight up. Ahead of us, a crowd was gathering. People were pouring out of the stores and cafés and saloons. Alarmed, I told Manuel to stop the car. He pulled over to the side of the road, and we all jumped out. Mayflower, Nora and I joined hands and followed the crowd. Everyone was running in one direction, their pace quickening.

My heart began to pound. Something had happened. When we reached the hotel I tried to run inside to make sure Aidan and Lily were safe, but I was met with a wall of people streaming out through the front door.

"What's going on?" I shouted to a young lad whose face was flushed with excitement.

"Heard it was a fight," he answered as he ran.

"Most likely an accident," exclaimed a dour-looking woman in an old-fashioned bonnet.

"Or a killin'," shouted the grizzled man beside her.

The crowd was moving so fast now I feared it would turn into a stampede. Mayflower, Nora and I clutched hands as we were carried along by the throng. Ranchers, preachers, dance hall girls, roughnecks and drunks swept past like a raging river. I spotted the town schoolmistress holding on to her bonnet, and the newspaper editor behind her. It seemed as if the whole of Shotgun City was on the move.

My breath came in short spurts and sweat ran down the back of my neck. A sharp pain radiated across my chest and I thought my heart might explode. I felt Nora's hand slip out of my grip. I tried to turn around to find her, but the pressure of the crowd made it impossible. I shouted her name, but my voice was lost in the uproar.

When we reached the end of Main Street, released from its confines, the crowd began to fan out. I was finally able to catch my breath. We were near an oil field—Aidan's oil field. I could see the outline of the derrick poking up toward the sky. As the crowd slowed, I pushed my way through them. I had to see what was going on. I had to make sure Aidan was safe.

I reached the edge of the field. The crowd, strangely silent now, pressed in behind me. From this distance everything looked normal. The roughnecks still walked the plank and the drill bit rose and fell into well number 88. Still, something seemed out of place. A man holding a bucket was pointing to its contents, gesturing wildly to Hans.

I scanned the field for a sight of Aidan. *Please let him be safe*, I prayed. Then I saw him, walking hand in hand with Lily around the well, in deep conversation with the site manager. I breathed a sigh of relief.

"Thank God," I uttered aloud.

The newspaper editor appeared beside me. He squinted toward Aidan and then back at me. "Looks like your boy might have found oil!"

I took in a sharp breath. "What?" I choked.

"May be just a rumor," he said. "They travel fast in these parts. From what I can see, they're inspecting the sample right now. That's surely a sign they've found something."

My heart began to thud. I could stand it no more. I broke away from the crowd and ran toward Aidan. He didn't see me until I was beside him.

"Delia?" he said. "What are you doing here?"

I pointed behind me. "The entire town is here. Is it true, Aidan? Did you find oil?"

He shook his head. "I don't know yet. I don't want to get my hopes up. Hans is looking at the samples now."

He pushed Lily toward me. "Here, take her. I couldn't leave her in the hotel alone, but it's not safe for her here. You either."

He glanced over at the crowds and groaned. "I hate to disappoint them all, Delia."

I had never seen Aidan like this. Usually so confident, he now had the air of a defeated man.

"You have to understand, Delia. An oil find in this area would change all their fortunes. If there's oil here, there's bound to be more nearby. And—"

He didn't finish his sentence. Hans came running toward us, waving his short arms. I had never seen the dignified man in such a state, and I started to laugh at how comical he looked. But I stopped.

"Aidan, fräulein, it is true. The samples prove it. *Gott im Himmel.* We have found oil."

Aidan paled and stiffened. I gasped aloud, and Lily let go of me and clapped her hands.

"We don't think it's a deep pool that could give us a gusher, but if it's wide enough, it could flow for years."

Suddenly, Hans stopped talking. He turned around and looked back at the well. A tremor had begun to shake the ground. I thought it might be an earthquake and I clung to Aidan's arm. Then a sound, like an animal's growl, rumbled near the well. It grew louder and louder until it was almost deafening. Aidan pushed me back roughly.

"Get away," he shouted.

I ran with Lily to the edge of the field, while Aidan and Hans raced toward the well. When I looked back the derrick had begun to shake violently, sending shards of metal everywhere. As it did so, the roughnecks leaped off the plank, and site workers started running in all directions. Hans and Aidan stood as if paralyzed. The onlookers watched and waited. Then, without warning, a widening column of black liquid thundered out of the well with an ear-splitting roar. As it rose into the sky, silhouetted against the setting sun, the crowd murmured in awe as if witnessing a miracle.

Mayhem erupted. People cheered and wept and applauded, children squealed, gunfire exploded and church bells began to ring. From somewhere in the distance came the sound of mariachi music. Townspeople ran toward the well and pranced around, wiping their oil-covered hands on their heads as if in baptism. I stood, not knowing what to do next. I was afraid to go back to the well when Aidan had ordered me to leave. Suddenly, I was grabbed from behind. I swung around, and there were Mayflower and Nora.

"C'mon," shouted Mayflower above the din, "don't stand here like dummies."

Nora's eyes were wide. "What in the name of God is happening?" she said, blessing herself.

"It's my daddy's well," shouted Lily. "There's oil in it." She grasped Nora's hand. "Come on, Miss Nora."

"But . . ." Nora hesitated, looking down at her shoes. "Ah, sure I'll never see the like of this again!" she said and, kicking them off, ran barefoot with Lily toward the well.

The oil was still pumping out, the plume well over one hundred feet high. Aidan and Hans were covered in the black, sticky liquid. Aidan looked stunned, while Hans was jumping up and down. He ran over to Mayflower, grabbed her around the waist and began dancing. Lily ran to Aidan, who picked her up and swung her around. He set her down and extended his hand to me. I walked into his embrace.

"There's money to drill a hundred new wells now," shouted Mayflower.

Aidan turned somber. "Unfortunately, Mr. McCabe told me he has signed his lease over to Sullivan. We can't drill any more wells on his property. But my father-in-law can and will get rich." He took a deep breath. "But we must thank God for what we have." He looked at me and Lily.

Nora looked from me to Aidan. Then she let go of Lily's hand and pulled a paper out of her bag. She held it out to Aidan.

"'Tis the lease Mr. McCabe signed," she said. "I never gave it to Sullivan or Kearney. I'm sure Mr. McCabe would be very glad to tear it up."

We stood in silence for a second before Hans and Mayflower let out loud whoops and Lily cheered. Aidan went toward Nora and took the lease from her.

"Thank you, Nora," he said. "I see now that you and Delia are true sisters."

I walked over to Nora and we hugged each other through tears.

Hans and Mayflower began to dance again, and Lily twirled Nora around. Aidan turned to me and bowed.

"May I have this dance, Miss Sweeney?"

"Why, of course, Mr. O'Hanlon."

As we danced, oil rained down on us, painting rainbows on the ground beneath our feet.

Delia

The day after the oil find, Nora and I stood facing each other on the train station platform. I reached out and took her hands in mine.

"Do you have to go so soon? We're only just getting to know each other again."

My words sounded shallow. They could never express the profound love I had for my sister at that moment. Nor could they adequately express my fear of losing her again.

Nora waved her hand at me dismissively.

"Ah, 'tis best I go now." She forced a smile, although her voice trembled a little. "I'd never survive in Texas. 'Tis hot as hell, and it's filled with dangerous men and dangerous animals. Could you picture me up to my knees in snakes and armadillos and every other class of vermin?"

I had a glimpse of the Nora I remembered—the one who valued her creature comforts. But I saw through her. She was covering up the girl she had become, the one who was a far cry from the selfish girl she had been.

I tightened my grip on her and moved closer. I looked into her brown eyes and saw they were moist from restrained tears.

"You're not fooling me, Nora. You've changed. You're not the girl you were."

"Ah, Delia. Sure you have every reason to hate me after the way I treated you back in Donegal. I know *I* would in your shoes.

But you were always the good one. I don't deserve your kindness."

"But you do," I said, "and it's more than kindness. That night when I believed I had seen you drown I felt a sense of overwhelming loss. I didn't know how I could survive without my sister. And now here you are, and I don't intend to lose you again."

Nora grinned. "Haven't *you* turned into the bossy one!"

"I mean it, Nora."

Her grin faded. "I felt the same way after my memory came back. You might as well have been dead because I was sure I would never find you again. And I believed you'd have no reason to look for me. I felt so alone in the world."

"Then why not stay here?"

She let go of my hands and stepped back and shook her head.

"It's hard to explain, Delia, but this is something I have to do. I need to prove to myself that there is more to me than an empty-headed girl who wants nothing more than to land a rich husband." She paused and moved closer. "I may not be as well educated as you, Delia, but I have a knack for business, especially selling. I could sell candles to a blind man." She smiled. "There's bound to be plenty of sales opportunities in New York. I think I'll try my luck there."

"But could you not go somewhere besides New York? I'm afraid Sullivan might find you and take it out on you for the way things turned out. He's not the man to be on the wrong side of."

Nora waved her hand. "That oul' bastard? I'm not afraid of *him* anymore. He'll be lucky if they don't send—what is the word?— a posse—up to New York to give him a taste of Texas justice."

"Would serve him right!"

We looked at each other in silence. Then I said, "Will you see Dom?"

Her face clouded. "Ah, sure at one time my pride would never have let me go near him again, but if what you say about the Kathleen one is true . . ."

"It is," I said, taking her hand. "Please promise me you'll give him another chance."

Nora smiled. "I suppose I'm saying I wanted adventure, just like you always wanted, but now I've seen you and Aidan together, I realize that all the adventure in the world is a bit empty without someone to love and who loves you back."

"If we're lucky, we can have both."

"Aye."

"We've come a long way, haven't we, Nora?"

"We have."

We hugged each other tightly, both of us in tears.

"Don't be a stranger, Nora," I said. "This is just the beginning of life for us together. I don't want us to be apart."

She shook her head. "We never will be, Delia. I'll always be thinking of you. Besides, New York is only a train journey away."

"And you'll come and visit Aidan and me, despite the heat and the armadillos?"

Nora laughed. "Ah sure I suppose I could get used to them."

As the train steamed out of the station, Nora opened the window of her compartment and leaned out, waving. I waved back until the steam from the engine enveloped her in a fog. I thought back to another time when we were at a train station, back in Donegal when we were setting out for America. Who could have known what awaited us? Disappointment and sorrow, and self-doubt that nearly destroyed us. But we also found the courage and strength to become who we were meant to be. And we finally found each other.

"Good luck, my sister," I whispered, "and Godspeed."

Acknowledgments

First, my thanks to my agent, Anne Marie O'Farrell, of Marcil-O'Farrell Literary Agency, for her constant support, encouragement, and friendship throughout my writing career. I also want to salute my editor, John Scognamiglio, at Kensington Publishing, for his concise and focused editing that never fails to improve the quality of my manuscripts. In addition, my thanks to the competent Kensington staff for their careful attention to all aspects of production of this book.

A special thanks goes to my dear friends, and "first" readers, David Hancock and Bernard Silverman, for their eagle-eyed comments and for giving so generously of their time. And an extra shout-out to David—a self-described *Titanic* maven—for keeping me straight on all things *Titanic*, right down to the menus.

And as always, a toast to all my friends and staff at the infamous "Lucky's Café" in Dallas, who have cheered me on throughout the writing of all four books to date. Likewise, warm thanks to my dear "Pawley's Sisters" and the "Wonderful Women of the Warrington Book Club" for their support. I am grateful to have all of you in my life.

And most of all, my enduring love and gratitude to my dear sister, Connie, to whom this book is dedicated.

THE TITANIC SISTERS

Patricia Falvey

ABOUT THIS GUIDE

These suggested questions are included to enhance your
group's reading of Patricia Falvey's *The Titanic Sisters*!

Suggested Questions for Discussion

1. Was it fair of Da to make Nora split fare for the *Titanic* passage with Delia?

2. Why do you think Ma continually manipulated Nora?

3. How was each sister's personality demonstrated by their behavior when the *Titanic* was sinking?

4. Do you think Nora's personality changed because of Mrs. Shaw's influence? Or was it because she had suffered a concussion and lost her memory?

5. Was it wrong of Delia to tell Aidan a lie about who she was, and to continue lying?

6. If Lily had been a badly behaved child do you think Delia would have stayed at the O'Hanlon house?

7. Do you think Aidan led Delia on by his inconsistent behavior?

8. Was Aidan justified in dismissing Delia when he discovered she had lied to him?

9. Would Nora have been justified in seeking revenge on Delia for taking her place?

10. Do you think Delia changed after moving to Texas, and if so, how?

11. Do you think Nora will contact Dom when she returns to New York?

Connect with Us

Visit us online at
KensingtonBooks.com
to read more from your favorite authors, see books
by series, view reading group guides, and more.

for sneak peeks, chances to win books and prize packs,
and to share your thoughts with other readers.

facebook.com/kensingtonpublishing
twitter.com/kensingtonbooks

Tell us what you think!

To share your thoughts, submit a review,
or sign up for our eNewsletters, please visit:
KensingtonBooks.com/TellUs.